PAS

"I have to go," tionally gruff.

Kate came up against him, her arms twining about his neck. Her movements were seductive yet her words were a desperate plea. "Don't go. Please, Brady. I need—" She wasn't sure what to say. She only knew that there was security in Brady Rogan's arms.

"What you need, I cannot give," he said gently. "What I offer would be of no service to you. I don't want to hurt you."

The tenderness of his claim touched her but she would not release him. "I am past feeling pain. Stay."

He hesitated and she was quick to take advantage. Her lips moved insistently over his until he could no longer resist. He seized her shoulders and urged her closer.

"Kate—" His voice was a ragged whisper that made her shiver.

"Shh," she whispered against his protesting lips. She wanted to hear no arguments, no cautioning words, not even ones of tenderness. She wanted only Brady and the delights with which he had tantalized and awakened her. She wanted his love . . .

THE BEST IN HISTORICAL ROMANCES

TIME-KEPT PROMISES   (2422, $3.95)
by Constance O'Day Flannery

Sean O'Mara froze when he saw his wife Christina standing before him. She had vanished and the news had been written about in all of the papers—he had even been charged with her murder! But now he had living proof of his innocence, and Sean was not about to let her get away. No matter that the woman was claiming to be someone named Kristine; she still caused his blood to boil.

PASSION'S PRISONER   (2573, $3.95)
by Casey Stewart

When Cassandra Lansing put on men's clothing and entered the Rawlings saloon she didn't expect to lose anything—in fact she was sure that she would win back her prized horse Rapscallion that her grandfather lost in a card game. She almost got a smug satisfaction at the thought of fooling the gamblers into believing that she was a man. But once she caught a glimpse of the virile Josh Rawlings, Cassandra wanted to be the woman in his embrace!

ANGEL HEART   (2426, $3.95)
by Victoria Thompson

Ever since Angelica's father died, Harlan Snyder had been angling to get his hands on her ranch, the Diamond R. And now, just when she had an important government contract to fulfill, she couldn't find a single cowhand to hire—all because of Snyder's threats. It was only a matter of time before the legendary gunfighter Kid Collins turned up on her doorstep, badly wounded. Angelica assessed his firmly muscled physique and stared into his startling blue eyes. Beneath all that blood and dirt he was the handsomest man she had ever seen, and the one person who could help beat Snyder at his own game.

LIAR'S PROMISE

DANA RANSOM

ZEBRA BOOKS
KENSINGTON PUBLISHING CORP.

ZEBRA BOOKS

are published by

Kensington Publishing Corp.
475 Park Avenue South
New York, NY 10016

First printing: January 1990

Printed in the United States of America

For Orysia, in lieu of the one promised.
Your perfect hero is still on my shelf.
Someday.
Thanks for being critiquer, cheerleader, and friend.

Chapter One

Conversation stopped. Silence rippled back through the room on a breeze of fresh, evening air. It stirred the stagnant haze of smoke and stilled the raucous laughter as, one by one, heads turned toward the door. A new murmur of sound rose like a wave gathering speed on its rush to shore. It was a quiet sound compared to the boisterous roar of seconds before, one of surprise and speculation as the single figure stepped in from the night.

With lamplight from the street creating an aura about the spill of golden hair, she might well have been an angel come down to fetch some mortal man home—and many a man in that crowded taproom would have considered surrendering eagerly into so comely, if final, an embrace. But as the heavy door closed, the dazzling illusion was gone and she became simply the most beautiful woman the rough sailors had ever seen.

It might have been the crude, dank setting that

made her sparkle so purely. It wasn't merely the fact that she was a woman, for there were others in the room. She was a lady and that set her apart from the coarse-featured barmaids with their roughened hands and even rougher speech. Her well-made gown was of homespun, not the lustrous silk of the prominent, yet her straight-as-a-mizzen carriage hinted at a dignity beyond social standing. In truth, barely any of the appraising eyes noted the poor fabric, only the way it draped about the tall figure, hugging the long, lissome torso and swell of promising bosom disappointingly covered by a modestly arranged kerchief.

That she was a rare beauty not even the tavern's oily lamplight could disguise. It was the fresh, sun-warmed loveliness of meadow and sky rather than parlor pallor. No, this was no demure miss raised on stuffy catechisms of etiquette. There was too much starch in her stance, too much stubbornness in the set of her finely made features. That such a creature would grace the briny docks held the onlookers curious, and their stares followed her to the planked bar in as much question as in appreciation of the sway of her skirts.

"I seek a man," she told the bartender in a low, crisp tone.

"I be man enough for ye, missy."

She spared no glance in recognition of the crude comment called out from a nearby table. Instead, she fixed a steady stare upon the man she addressed, and finished, "A Captain Rogan."

Ah, wouldn't you know it, the man behind the scarred bartop thought, but he said, respectfully, "If you be telling me where you're put up, I'll see he gets word to meet you when his business be finished."

"I have no time or patience to wait upon his pleasure. If he is here, be kind enough to point him out."

A heavy brow rose. The man had seen many a woman wait upon Brady Rogan's pleasure, but none had ever been so bold about it. Frowning slightly, he pointed. "That be him, the dark one at cards."

"That's his business?" she challenged with a scornful cut of green eyes that flashed along the path of his gesture. They leveled upon a set of broad shoulders, then, almost distractedly, she said, "Thank you."

Captain Brady Rogan was one of the few men in the small tavern who hadn't noticed the stir among its other patrons. Having just returned from five weeks asea, little could sway him from the mug at his elbow and the spread of cards in his hands. These he'd sought even before his room and a bath to rinse away the salt and weariness that clung to him, and he did not welcome interruption, even in such an unexpected form. At the quiet call of his name, he loosed a quick glance, then his gaze returned to linger overlong until the beauteous lady blushed, hot with annoyance, he noted, rather than in embarrassment.

"You are Captain Rogan?" she repeated a bit more tartly as his bold stare swept the length of her once more before returning to his cards.

"I am."

With that admission, he seemed to dismiss her

from mind as he made a careful play, for much was riding on the hand. Coin heaped high between the five men and sharpened their concentration. They held little tolerance when it came to distraction.

"Owner of the *Prosper*?"

"I am," he said again, favoring her with but slight attention.

"Then I would have a word with you, sir."

That command won a squaring of his broad shoulders, for he was not a man accustomed to receiving orders. Yet, still, he would not look away from his game. "I fear my time is already spoken for this evening."

"But I must talk to you."

"You may call upon me in the morning if you've something to discuss. Pray, not too early, though, for 'tis doubtful I shall retire anytime soon."

Had he glanced up then, he might have caught the brief tug of desperation that tightened her determined features. She drew a slow breath and tried again. "'Twill only take a moment. I have come a long way and . . ." The slight faltering that trembled in her voice was quickly mastered. "And I would like to be gone on the morrow."

"And I would like to be richer."

"Be ye in or out, Rogan?" one of the men at the table growled. Females and cards had naught to do with each other to his thinking. They were for a man to enjoy separately, in order of importance, and it seemed their companion was confusing his priorities. "If ye be meaning to lay the wench down, don't be expecting us to hold your chair open."

"The lady is leaving," he answered calmly. He took a long draw from his beer, very aware that she continued to stand at his shoulder apparently undiscouraged. He hated to behave rudely to a woman, even to one so plagued persistent as this, but it seemed he would have little choice if he were to stay in the play. In a measured tone, with the exasperation one would exhibit toward a pesty child, he said, "Please excuse yourself, madam. This is not the sort of place in which to entertain a lady."

"I do not ask to be entertained," she ground out, still hot over the previous insinuation. Lay her down, indeed. "All I seek is information."

"'Tis nothing so pressing that it cannot wait on the finish of this play," he said bluntly.

Brady Rogan liked dangerous things. He would have appreciated the flash of temper his callous remark brought to the young woman's green eyes. But he was not a foolish man, and had he seen the spiteful narrowing of that gaze, he would have known enough to be wary.

"Far be it for me to take you from your game, but a more prudent man would not risk so much on such a feeble hand."

The cards he held came together with a snap as a chuckle rode through the other players. Never had any of them caught the impassive Captain Rogan in a bluff and they were all the more appreciative considering the circumstance. But he was not amused.

Steely eyes rose slowly from the impotent hand of cards, and the young woman seemed to hesitate

11

before returning the piercing stare just as coolly.

"It seems you have managed my full attention," he purred in silken fury. "What is it that demands you take me to near ruin?"

For the first time, she seemed aware of the wealth of coin on the tabletop and his share of it that she'd lost for him. Though she felt no remorse, she did adopt a more subdued manner.

"Have you news of the *Prosper*, Captain?"

In no mood to be overly civil, he asked, "What is your interest in her?"

The direct gaze wavered, but only for an instant. "My father is aboard."

"And his name is . . . ?"

"Nathan Mallory."

"Mallory? I haven't the pleasure, to my recall."

"But he spoke of you—"

"By reputation, I suspect." Her flush brought a crook to one corner of his lips. So she did know of it. And still she'd come. "I was at sea when the *Prosper* sailed. He would have dealt with Abraham, my partner."

"Then 'tis he to whom I should speak."

His smile broadened. It wasn't a particularly amiable gesture. But then, he didn't feel particularly amiable. "You would have to have even greater patience, I fear. He mastered out on the *Jenny* bound for the Gold Coast last week. If you have a year to spare, I am sure he wouldn't mind if you had a mind to wait."

Her tender mouth compressed to hold in sentiments she would not speak in such a place, to such a man. Finally, in a voice surprisingly gruff, she said, "That gives me little comfort, sir. I can well see we waste each other's time."

Something in that brusque speech captured his notice—perhaps the quiet anguish that weighed each word—but it was too late, for she was gone, striding quickly between the clutter of tables and into the night. Brady Rogan stared thoughtfully after her for a long moment.

"Another hand, Brady? We could use some more of your commission gold."

He didn't respond right away, and when he turned back to his companions, it was with an air of preoccupation.

Kathryn Mallory leaned against a lightpost and closed her eyes to combat the rise of tears. It had taken every bit of her courage to step inside the dank male bastion. It seemed the effort had been for naught. Her breath quickened into deep irregular gulps as helplessness and upset moved to overcome her. What would she do now? Captain Rogan had been her only hope and he had told her nothing.

Thinking of him made Kate straighten. The burn of anguish in her eyes became a more vigorous simmering. That man. He'd sat there mocking her distress with his smug indifference. Fool, that she had expected different. Her father had told her all about Brady Rogan, the notorious Rogue—privateer, pirate, smuggler, slaver. That last made her lip curl in disgust. Why had her father trusted the likes of him, a man of no political allegiance and no moral dictates? How could one who made his living by illegal means be expected to have honor? What had possessed Nathan Mallory to deal with such scoundrels—and to leave her no choice but to do the same? And she would have to deal with him again. She had to have answers, and in this strange town, she knew nowhere else to seek them. With a determined sigh, she resigned herself to the unpleasant task of seeking out Captain Rogan in the morning, a task made more distasteful when she thought from whom she'd be obliged to beg help. Well, she would not do so in meek humility, not before some scurrilous buccaneer who would doubtlessly take amusement from the cost of her forced abasement! Upon imagining his taunting smile, she began to stride up the street, steps echoing her annoyance with their quick staccato beat.

No man had ever dared take liberties with his eyes the way Brady Rogan had. If any of the boys in Washington County stared at her as if trying to discern the color of her stocking garters, she'd have laid them out with the flat of her palm. Not only had he looked, but he'd done so as if expecting her to enjoy the bold sampling. As if she would! Her pace increased and in her agitation she failed to hear the approaching melee until it was almost upon her. By then it was too late to avoid being swallowed up by the surging mob.

Kate knew a moment of absolute panic. There must have been close to five hundred of them, mostly boys and Negroes, flooding the street like a swamping wave of humanity and carrying her away from the safety of the walk in that sudden swell. Shouting and brandishing torches, they surrounded what seemed to be a ship's small boat. They dragged it toward the center of town like a beached whale or a condemned criminal to the gallows. The intensity of their fervor was frightening to one not a part of it. No one paid heed to her struggles against the brush of linen and jab of careless elbows. The harder Kate tried to fight her way to be free of the crowd, the more she became embroiled, sucked into that whirlpool of dangerous emotion. She tried to cry out, even to scream, but the sound was a whisper against the enthused shouts. Her skirt was trod upon and for one terrifying moment it seemed she would fall and be trampled in the crush. Then a steady arm closed about her waist and a large form provided a buffer to the forward push that had swept her along helpless, like a bit of driftwood caught in a dangerous current. But this stabilizing pull was stronger, easing her out of the seething mass without so much as a bruise until she was restored to the thankfully empty walk. When she was able to draw a less excited breath, she looked to her rescuer. "You!"

"For one so anxious for a moment of my time, you sound none too pleased."

How tall he was came her first irrelevant thought, even before she realized the bend of his arm behind her back had her arched toward him in a most provocative curve. For a moment, her sensibilities failed her and he had a tantalizing view of features flushed rosy and breasts hurried into a tempting rhythm. Then she remembered herself, who he was and where they stood. Her hand clamped firmly over his and pulled to discourage the embrace that brought her not against him but all too close. "I do not mean to appear ungrateful, Captain Rogan. I am glad to be untangled from that madness."

He released her at once and his rueful gaze followed the noisy throng as it pressed onward with its unwieldy burden. "Not madness of our making, Miss Mallory. 'Tis their way of venting protest of the happenings these last weeks since Captain Antrobus hasn't seen fit to recognize the governor's objections."

"To what?"

He spoke with quiet passion so that the words were clear even above the loud cries of those who still rushed past them. "Piracy and slavery of a different kind. That boat be a tender for the H.M.S. *Maidstone*. She's been plaguing the harbor for the last four or five weeks with the hottest press I've ever heard of on this coast. Her officers have visited every vessel entering the harbor, down to the wood boats and the smallest coasters till the port is shunned and the Wood Wharf stands nearly empty. No man wants to be an unwilling guest in His Majesty's Navy."

"But that's kidnapping, isn't it?"

"Aye. 'Tis the way I see it, but our gracious king sees it as a means of keeping his ships stocked with able bodies, albeit reluctant ones. It seems the press is not the only thing that grows hot. Only last year a similar mob seized the battery to fire on two English ships who thought to capture a vessel smuggling sugar. The government did nothing to punish the

16

leaders, even though they knew well who they were. I suspect like treatment for tonight's heroes."

Kate gave him a wry look. "You seem an unlikely champion when the current stand gives you work aplenty."

His gaze left the mob to touch upon her scornful expression. His mouth made a slight bow. "And so it does, Miss Mallory. Having delivered my entire political rhetoric, might I see you safe to your lodgings? I would hear more of your reasons for seeking me out as we walk."

Kate was of a mind to refuse his charitable offer after such churlishness moments before. But logic prevailed. She did need to talk to him. And she feared the unknowns of Newport's suddenly crazed streets. She would feel safer in his company. But she didn't have to like it and would have him know it. "Very well, Captain Rogan," she agreed stiffly and surrendered the name of her accommodations. With the utmost chivalry, he tucked her hand into his elbow bend and escorted her up the street, past the pyre of the *Maidstone*'s tender boat and the gleefully howling arsonists.

"You said you'd come a long way," he began conversationally as a turn in the street carried them away from the flare of flame and temper. She hadn't thought he'd been listening or would remember her words.

"From Kingstown across the bay."

"Surely you do not travel alone?" It was not with censure that he spoke but with a concerned softness.

"I have a companion with me," she said, both to

17

assure him and to warn him off.

"And this companion let you venture out alone at night, to search taverns on unfamiliar streets?"

"Hardly, sir. I left her snoring quite contentedly."

His chuckle was warm, as warm as the fingers that pressed fleetingly over hers where they rested on his arm. It was a fond, familiar touch. Had the gesture lingered, she would have drawn away, but as it did not, so *she* did not.

"What is your father's business aboard the *Prosper*?"

That question effectively took her thoughts from the caress of strong fingers. "He took some of our horses to Barbados to sell. They need such hardy stock to power their sugar mills."

"Aye. 'Twould seem a good investment." He walked with her in silence for a time, then asked, "So what brings you from the farm to search for me in such a taking?" He made it sound so personal, those smugly spoken words, as if he were all-important. And she supposed he would see it so from his rather self-indulgent viewpoint, for he was very much his own follower, from the swagger in his step to the calm affectation of his speech.

"I needed information and yours was the only name I knew," she answered coolly.

His conceit apparently didn't suffer for her dismissal of his importance. Instead, his cocky posturing grew more pronounced. "'Tis well known in many circles. I consider it an honor to be recognized in yours."

He was teasing her and she responded with a crisp,

"What I know of you is nothing a decent man would brag upon, Captain."

He wasn't chastened by her bluntness. His smile streched wider. "Were I a decent man, you would have no reason to seek me out. It would seem being what I am has its benefits."

She glowered up at him, having no notion of how attractive that pouty displeasure appeared. "You flatter yourself unduly, sir. I've no interest in you, only in what you can tell me."

"I could tell you many things, pretty miss," he promised in satiny seduction.

Though she viewed him more with annoyance than as a possible threat, she nevertheless pulled away from him, her green eyes snapping in a furious challenge. "Then start by telling me what has become of the *Prosper*."

"Become of her?" He looked genuinely puzzled as he turned to face her at the door to her hostelry. "What do you mean?"

"It's weeks overdue," she cried, then bit her lip to keep the rest of her fears from tumbling forth. That wouldn't do.

He laughed again, and this time she took no pleasure in the rich sound. "Is that what has you in a bother?" At her tight-lipped glare, his amusement faded. Were those tears giving brilliance to her fierce stare, he wondered, as his tone became calming. "Miss Mallory, a week or so delay is common upon the seas. 'Tis nothing to fret over. Were the *Prosper* in any difficulty, I would soon know of it and I have heard nothing. Could be a lull that slows her. Could

19

be a difficulty in dispatching her cargo or in taking on new. Travel on the seas is not as predictable as a spin in a carriage. Trust me. You worry for naught."

"You think me foolish," she accused in a temper of distress and disbelief.

"No." A roughened thumb sketched lightly down her cheek. That contact took her by surprise. She took a quick breath, choking on words of censure that oddly would not come, and he went on easily to say, "The sea is a mystery to those who know only the surety of the land."

"The land is not so sure, Captain Rogan," she countered in her defense.

"Nothing is sure in these times, Miss Mallory, but I am as sure as I can be that your father has come to no harm." When her eyes dropped away in silent doubt, he chuckled and added with a wry deprecation, "I have an investment of funds in the *Prosper*, so believe in my greed if you think it of greater value than my word."

Color warmed the curve of her cheeks. Her gaze came up boldly to meet his. "I have little choice."

"Will you be staying then, until the *Prosper* puts in?" He didn't know why he asked. It wasn't as though he planned to keep company with such a prickly miss . . . was it? His gaze caressed her pleasing figure. Perhaps he could endure her waspish tongue, he thought, but her reply soon ended that bit of fancy.

"No. As I have said, we leave in the morning." Nothing could make her admit she could not afford another night's lodgings. They would have to go even though the thought of returning home without definite knowledge settled like a poor meal in her stomach. There was no help for it.

Some of that despondency must have registered in her manner, for the bold captain fit his palm beneath her chin, lifting it so he could study her features in the shadowy light.

"A smile upon so lovely a countenance must radiate like a sunrise. To savor such a sight, I will bring news of the *Prosper* to you as soon as I hear it." His voice was low, as caressing as his look had been moments before, and Kate knew a thrill of anticipation and anxiety.

"I could not ask you to forfeit your time . . ." she began. The girlish tremor in her words made her blush, though he chose to believe it due to his courtly sentiment.

"'Tis my time, Miss Mallory, to invest as I see fit. A smile from you would see me well repaid for the trouble. Methinks 'tis not a reward you give often or easily."

The sudden want to lay her cheek against the curving warmth of his fingers made her draw back in alarm. What was it about the thought of having him come to her that instilled such unwarranted panic? Mustering at least an outward control, she said, "Thank you, Captain, but it really isn't necessary. Most likely my father will be in port before I reach the farm if your assurances are to be believed."

Grinning, he bowed. "I shall bid you good evening then, Miss Mallory."

"Good-bye, Captain Rogan," she amended firmly,

but his confident smile refuted her parting words. And though she would have liked to linger to watch his retreat, she forced herself to turn her back on him and enter the dim hall. The low ripple of his knowing laughter was all the prompting she needed to send her stiff-backed up the stairs.

Soft snores emanated from the lower half of the trundle bed, assuring her that Mistress Fitch still slumbered. The dear woman had insisted upon chaperoning her and the trip had exhausted her failing strength. Dear Fitch had been nurse and nanny to each of the five Mallory girls and refused to realize that she now needed more care than her charges.

Fearing to light a lamp lest it intrude upon the rumbling slumber, Kate undressed in darkness and sought the cool sheets of her rented bed. Though she was as weary as her muttering companion, Kate tossed and twisted for long minutes until she resigned herself to the thoughts that plagued her. Shamefully, they were not of Nathan Mallory or the family's troubles but were filled instead with a certain unworthy soul who shouldn't have warranted the time or space. He stole her thoughts, just as he stole for a living and that fact made her rest no easier.

Of all the information her father had imparted about the infamous Rogue, he had failed in typically male fashion to mention how handsome he was. When Brady Rogan had looked up from his game of chance, all her images of a rough and scruffy pirate had died. In that moment, she could admit in the dark privacy of her heart that she welcomed the keen ardor of his gaze, for what woman wouldn't yearn to be held desirable by so beautiful a man.

And a splendid man he was, of well-favored face and well-formed frame. Sun and wind had burnished the taut stretch of his skin, working it into a rich copper. Contrasting the blackness of his rumpled hair, soaring brows, and frame of thick lashes were eyes of startling blue, as crisp and clear as sea or sky. And just as unpredictable. Full, generously curved lips could warm like a balmy day with charming smile or brew a storm just as quickly with the beginnings of a frown. Instead of the squinting, shifty gaze she had expected from one such as he, he had met her with a strong, commanding stare that reduced her to an odd breathlessness. Had she been prepared for such perfection, she might not have been so stunned by it. Much of her frustrated anger stemmed from that brief loss of control when heart overruled mind and sighed, Here is a man worth loving.

Ridiculous, of course, she told herself sensibly, shifting on the straw-filled mattress to further the denial. Handsome is as handsome does, her father was fond of saying, and there was no doubt that Brady Rogan knew well his own charm. He would expect a woman to pine for him after warming her well with that indecent stare. Well, not this woman, she told herself, punching down her pillow with enough vigor to spit feathers from its seams. What would an honest, God-fearing woman do with such a man? She quickly closed her eyes lest she be wicked enough to consider an answer. More so, what use would he have for a woman of honor? She couldn't place him in a respectable role, tending a family and a wife with loving attention. Unbidden, the recall of his strong fingers covering hers and cradling her cheek caused her seditious thoughts to place her at the hearth of his home.

Bah! What was she about? He had no home, would revere no wife, would foster no children of his name. He was as her father had described him—an adventurer, a cunning, reckless man of the sea who would either laugh or flee in horror if he could see her cozying him up into some domestic scene. And why would she even think these thoughts about him, this man she'd known but an hour and not at all, this man she would likely never see again.

A smile from you would see me well repaid . . .

Could Brady Rogan have made her smile? How right he was to guess it a nearly foreign expression to her face. There had been little in her life to inspire lightness or laughter over the last years. Perhaps if he were to come to the farm bearing glad news, and she knew, of course, he would not . . . perhaps then she would spare him a smile.

And not realizing it, as she drifted toward slumber, her lips curved ever so slightly upward.

Chapter Two

"Those ungrateful wretches! How could they do this?"

Kate stared in dismay at a larder stripped nearly bare of its provisions. Flour, meal, lard, salt—everything, nearly everything gone of the victuals she'd been rationing so stringently these last weeks. How could such a loss be replaced? Not with her means, she realized wearily.

"When did they go, Sarah?" she asked in defeat.

The pale scullery maid fidgeted uncomfortably. "Last night and the one afore it. Crept off like thieves, they did."

"Thieves, they are," Kate declared hotly. "Who is left?"

"Meself and Mr. Cosgrove. He'd never go off and leave his horses. Prides on them like they be his children, he does. And Timmy. He'd not run off after all you done for him."

Kate waited. When the girl didn't continue, she

prompted, "That's all? The three of you?"

The cap bobbed briefly.

A groom, a young stable boy, a spindly kitchen sweep, and an aged nanny—all that remained of their fine household. That they'd stolen from her was not nearly as keen a pain as the fact they'd deserted her without word, people who'd served her family for years and been well treated in return. A sense of failure overwhelmed her. Nathan Mallory had trusted his hearth and home to her care and, in his absence, she'd let it go to ruin. Their people had scattered, doubtlessly afraid they would never see the payment owed them and had taken what they could carry in recompense. How could she blame them for having no faith when she herself had run to Newport in a panic? Well, good riddance, she told herself with a squaring of her jaw. When her father returned, there would be a new staff, and members of the old who came slinking back would find no open door. Betrayal would find no reward beneath her roof. She would manage with her sad little group. Somehow, she would manage until her father returned.

She was drawn from the desecrated storeroom by the sound of a wagon and a chorus of excited voices. She arranged her features carefully to show none of her misgivings and went to welcome her sisters. For a moment, her troubles were pushed aside in a flood of love and laughter.

Nathan and Johanna Mallory's marriage had yielded seven children. The two sons, born first and fifth, had died in infancy. The daughters, however, had thrived and blossomed beautifully, all golden hair and great blue eyes like their mother, save Kathryn the oldest whose green eyes mirrored her father's in all but outlook. Their ages spanned more than a decade: Kate, eighteen; Anne, fifteen; Jeanne, twelve; Roberta, eight; and Bertrice, the baby, nearly seven. For the past six years, Kate had been mother as well, assuming the position capably and without complaint at the death of Johanna. For the first time, as her sisters crowded about her, clamoring for tales of Newport, she felt inadequate in that post. She never betrayed her feeling, though, hugging each in turn and promising to fulfill their excited queries in the morning after she'd had time to rest and refresh herself. She begged the chance to change her travel-stained gown and sink into a warm tub.

But neither of those wishes were met. No sooner had she thanked the Simpsons, their neighbors who had taken the girls in overnight and seen them on their way, than the shape of another wagon grew nearer on their little-traversed road. Kate shielded her eyes against the retiring sun and waited until the red hair of Rufus McLain was unmistakable. He owned the mercantile in Kingstown where they kept their family account. Fearing she knew what brought him such a distance, Kate forced herself to greet him graciously, wishing at the same time not to be so suspiciously mussed from travel.

"'Evening, Miss Kathryn. Heard you was home."

Kate's expression tightened. How swiftly word spread when it concerned intrigue or misfortune. She'd hoped her trip would go unnoted, but it was apparent from McLain's nervousness that the alarm had spread on vigilant lips.

"Good evening, Mr. McLain. Might I invite you in for some of Daddy's cordial?"

The man's face fused with ruddy color. "That's right kind of you, but the missus be holding supper."

She stood on the step, letting him fidget beneath her unwavering stare for a long minute before asking, "What can I do for you, Mr. McLain? You haven't come all this way just to tell me that hank of lace has arrived, have you?"

"No. That is, not yet, it hasn't. I . . . I was wondering on your father and when he might be back."

"Why, any day now," she said with a confidence that made him sag in relief. When he continued to linger, saying nothing, she prompted, "Is there some message you'd have me give him?"

A folded paper was quickly produced from his shiny waistcoat and passed gingerly to her. She didn't have to look at it to know what it was. She simply held to it while McLain shifted and blushed bright.

"Have your papa stop by the store when he gets back," he mumbled.

"I'm sure he plans to, Mr. McLain," Kate replied. The frosty bite of her civility was not missed.

"My best to the girls."

"And to your wife."

And so it went until darkness sealed the road and had Kate staring dazedly at the pile of notes before her. The parlor was lit by a single lamp and the house was quiet, her sisters and the tiny staff already abed.

28

But sleep was a far stranger to the young woman who sat stiffly, still in her travel clothes, her agile mind flying behind the fatigue-darkened eyes. A glass of blackberry cordial lifted to her lips without awareness and she sipped from it as she thought.

They had come, prompted by rumor and greedy panic, following Rufus McLain in a steady stream to her door with papers in hand: Moses from the blacksmith shop, Milton from the gristmill, Jacobs from the tavern, Todbury the tinsmith, even Dr. Parrish, who tended creatures of both two legs and four. Some were apologetic, some brusque, but all wanted to know when Nathan Mallory would return to make good on his debts. She'd received them each in turn with calm assurances she was not sure she believed now that the presence of Brady Rogan was so distant. And apparently, these, her good neighbors, weren't totally convinced, either. They were polite, even embarrassed, but their sentiments were all the same—no more credit until the balance was paid.

So much owed. Kate had no idea how deep the debts ran; however, the proof of their existence lay before her, all neatly listed and tallied into a staggering whole. She took another sip and pondered.

Of course, once her father returned, things would all be put to right. He stood to make an ample profit off his sturdy cargo and the fair captain's agreement made it so in her mind. But what to do until that time, with foodstuffs next to nonexistent and the generosity of the folks in Kingstown abruptly at an end? She thought of the four girls tucked in innocent slumber and of the four loyal servants who all depended upon her. She considered the workers who had fled and couldn't blame them. For a moment, she, too, wished she could escape the yoke of her father's trust. But knowing there was no other to shoulder it, she didn't dwell on that instant of cowardice. She would stand firm and bind the family together, as she always had. And when Nathan Mallory returned, he would pinch her chin and declare fondly, "I don't know how we'd manage without you, Katie. You're my strength, like your mother before you."

Hurry home, Daddy. With a heavy sigh, she gathered the evidence of debt and doom and secreted them between the pages of the weighty family Bible. She touched the tattered cover, giving a wry smile. What better place to keep them, for only providence and prayer would see them paid.

Despite her weariness, Kate spent a restless night upon the bed she shared with Anne. It wasn't the bold, roguish stare of a Newport smuggler that disturbed her. It was dreams of a wave, a great, engulfing wave, surging up to swallow land and family whole. She woke in a nightdress drenched cold with sweat.

With fresh clothes and a cup of precious tea to revive her, Kate faced the new day bravely. Time to stop moping and start planning, she prodded at her own dismal thoughts.

"How are we set with livestock, Cosgrove?" she asked the wiry little man who'd joined her at the kitchen table while the girls bustled about their chores.

"Missing a sow or two and some good layers, but the cows and horses be fine. Would have gone after the blighters with a musket had they touched one of your papa's best."

Kate smiled. She believed him. Since they'd hired him on, Cosgrove clucked over the pampered horses like a protective mother. He was a kind, mild-tempered man, but a threat to one of his prized brood had him in a fierce bristle. She suspected he would work without pay for the privilege of handling the stock. Ironic that she might be forced to ask him to.

"How long can we continue to grain the stock with what we have on hand?"

The faded blue eyes crinkled in careful deliberation. "Few weeks. Three if I measure lean."

"As lean as you can, Cosgrove," she instructed soberly.

"Pasturing's good this time of year. Could ration it out for a month, I guess." He observed the young woman's serious expression and asked, "As bad as that, Miss Kate? Was hoping them n'er-do-wells was whistling down the creek. Bad news from Newport?"

She shook her head. "No news. But we'll be fine. I hope for the best but better to be prepared."

The man gave a toothy smile. Yes, sir, the girl had a good head twixt her shoulders, not like her pa who never saw past the minute. If Miss Katie said not to worry, he wouldn't.

"Don't you fret none, Miss Kate. Timmy and me can handle the work just fine. And I'd best get to it

31

now," he announced, setting aside the thin porcelain cup that looked so helpless in his large, gnarled hands. She put hers over them impulsively and said simply, "Thank you. And thank Timmy, too." She didn't need to elaborate.

"This be our home, too, Miss Katie. Wouldn't have it any other way."

She watched him amble out, feeling better than she had since pulling up in the strangely quiet yard. Her supporters were few in number but they were strong in heart.

"Got a caller, Katie," freckle-faced Jeanne called in. The singsongy teasing of the girl's tone made her older sister frown.

"Who is it?"

"Mister Fancy Britches from Briar Haven."

Kate's frown deepened along with her displeasure. Of all her hounding creditors, only one had yet to visit. Ezra Blayne and his father's bank were one in the impossibly arrogant young man's mind. Hoping that it would be father, not son who awaited in the yard, Kate smoothed her simple linen dress and went to the front of the house. A shrill cry and accompanying curse settled her heart with dread as she stepped into the bright morning to the ridiculous spectacle of the powdered and primped Ezra Blayne pursuing his tricorne as the gusty winds sent it skating in giddy spirals about the dewy grass. By the time he'd captured the elusive bit of heavy braid, he was puffing against the corsetting fit of his waistcoat and not at all pleased to see Kathryn Mallory teary-eyed and biting her lips to withhold her laughter. Hat

32

firmly in hand, he advanced with unwieldy dignity to the small porch and the woman who looked down upon him with such unflattering mirth.

"Good morrow, Miss Kathryn. A fine day."

"Albeit a breezy one," she murmured with a painfully straight face.

"You are looking fine, as well." That pronouncement gave him the excuse to run his avid gaze over her admirable figure. Even the unadorned styling of her gown provoked lustful thoughts and made him wish she arranged her kerchief lower, the way the daring young women at the tavern did. He could well imagine what creamy bounty hid beneath that modest drape.

"To what do I owe this visit, Mr. Blayne?"

The sharpness of her tone warned that he had ogled overlong. He had no desire to incur the sting of her palm, which once felt had never been forgotten. He was quick to ply what he considered his masterful charm.

"As if I needed a reason, Kathryn. The pleasure of looking upon you would bring any man from miles away."

Kate didn't appear charmed. In fact, her foot began an impatient tapping beneath the sweep of her hem. "I am flattered, sir," she stated flatly.

Ezra squared his narrow shoulders and puffed out his chest with the self-importance of a barnyard banty. In truth, his sense of importance wasn't totally of his own making, for Ezra's father's bounty carried nearly all the county's farmers. The Blayne home rivaled any of those palatial manors beginning to dot

Newport's harbor. The family's clothing was imported at great expense, and even though Ezra's ungainly figure appeared as an overripe end-of-summer pear in his coat of rich brocade, it was not due to the fault of the exquisite golden fabric. Invitations to a soiree at Briar Haven went to the best families in the state and to influential summer visitors from down South and the Islands. The Blaynes were a force in Rhode Island commerce and politics, but to Kate Mallory, Ezra was an overblown braggart and bully whose pedigree meant little compared to his performance. Unfortunately, however, he viewed her in the reverse.

"I hear you've had visits from local merchants," he began in a reedy voice inconsistent with his bulk. "How thoughtless of your father to leave you to contend with such troubles."

"You are misinformed, sir. We have no troubles." She said that so matter-of-factly, Ezra had to smile in admiration.

"Now, Miss Kathryn, we both know better," he intimated smugly. "You must realize that my position has me privy to everyone's finances, and yours, shall we say, are in sorry need."

Kate's eyes glittered through narrow slits as fury smoldered in difficult check. "We will take care of our own, Mr. Blayne, as always. When my father returns, your kind charity will be repaid." As if it could be called charity at the interest rates they charged!

Ezra coddled up to that sentiment with a wetting of thick lips. "There are many ways to repay a debt,

Kathryn. I have offered my help on several occasions."

"And I have thanked you each time and declined." The last offer had earned him a black eye when he'd thought to accompany it with the free use of his hands.

His smile was odious in its confident power. He knew she couldn't afford to anger him when his father held her own by the financial throat. Still, he kept out of striking distance. "This time, I suggest a permanent solution. Things need not be so hard for you, my dear, or for your family. I can provide for them and you. I can make life a luxury instead of a trial. You must know how I feel about you."

Kate stood silent, rage quivering through her. Before, his sordid suggestions had been flowery and vague, hinting that favors given would go far toward diminishing debt. Now, apparently emboldened by her father's absence, he was voicing his vile proposition right on the front steps of her home. If he thought her position one of helpless vulnerability, she would put that misconception to a quick and painful end. He would learn that the owing were not always the weak, and it would be her pleasure to mete out that lesson dare he continue to insult her. But continue he did, and the offer he made was unexpected and left her stunned.

"I would take you for my wife, Kathryn." He waited for a reaction and when none came from the rigid figure, he gave a wheezy chuckle. "I see I have overwhelmed you. Surely you realized how attractive I find your courage and intelligence . . . and, of

35

course, your obvious female endowments." As the green eyes widened, he thought with an arrogant pleasure that he had dazzled the poor creature. She'd probably never dreamed he was obtainable. "I know you think yourself far from my equal and that you could never manage a satisfactory dower, but I am disposed to be forgiving of your circumstances. You are not to blame for your father's ill-advised foolishness and I am sure my family and circle of friends could be made to understand and accept you in time."

Still, she said naught and he felt sorry for this simple wench who obviously could not believe her own good fortune. And shocked by disbelief she was, shocked and outraged at his condescending slurs and pretentious assumptions. She struggled with the want to laugh out loud or to crown him with the most ready truncheon.

"You need only say yes and I will see you from this meager, misery. You need never worry or want again."

"Forgive me for falling speechless," she said finally. Her quiet tone gave no hint of the violence with which she clutched her skirts. "I am quite surprised. And honored," she added with difficulty. He assumed a haughty pose as if that was as it should be. The buffoon. "But I must decline."

Ezra's proud chest dropped into an ill-restrained paunch and he gaped at her. Was she mad? Could she be rejecting him? No, it was too absurd. But as she went on mildly, she made herself well understood.

"I could never accept any offer no matter how

attractive or beneficial without my father's knowledge and consent."

"But—"

"When he returns, you will have to speak your wish to him. Until then, it would be wrong and frivolous of me to give you any encouragement, and I am certain you are too much a gentleman to expect any different. So until then, Mr. Blayne, I wish you a good morning."

Ezra stared. He began to speak, then floundered helplessly. The clever wench had neatly tied his hands with his own exacting code of honorable pride. Then he smiled. What a pleasure it was going to be to own such a bright and pretty miss. He could wait. There were women aplenty to see to his purposes until the girl's father returned. And then he would have Kathryn Mallory. The wait could only make her appreciate the life of ease he offered all the more. Yes, he could wait. Time was to his advantage.

"I shall call again, Miss Kathryn," he assured, and she was forewarned.

Stoically, Kate remained on the step, refusing herself the freedom of thought until Ezra's fine stallion was but a spot in the distance and the anger he'd fired had spent itself to a faint flickering of resentment. Then she walked, slowly, pensively across the yard, through the fragrant meadow grasses to the stone wall that embraced their property. With her back to it, she could view the substance of her lifelong dream, the acres of fine ground, the scattering of horses that grazed upon it, the small but neat house whose two-storied face slanted back to a single-floor

37

addition. Home. Her home, the one she'd longed for, the only one she'd ever known.

For as long as she could remember, it had been rented rooms and trunks, packed and repacked. She didn't fault her father. Nathan Mallory was an idealist, always beset by a notion that would see them set in high style. He saw the way to wealth through the eyes of a romantic, coining some scheme or investing in an eccentric's plan, not through labor and perseverence. He was quick to risk savings and security in ill-conceived ventures and, losing all each time, would gather his family and move on in search of new opportunity. Because Johanna loved the impractical yet endearing man, she'd supported his flights of fancy and never complained over another in an endless series of disappointments. She never moaned over not having her own things about her, about never being in one place long enough to harvest seeds she optimistically planted.

Kate hadn't wanted to follow in that silent, suffering mold. At her mother's death, she had taken her father up with a firm rein. She had convinced him to invest in land, had encouraged him to raise livestock when efforts to make a profit off the harvests had failed. She had fueled his imaginings with her dreams and kept him bound to them with her own determination. More than anything, she wanted a home, a place where her sisters could live, confident that each day would find them safe and secure. And to think that a man like Ezra Blayne might hold that security for ransom made her ill with dread.

Marriage to Ezra. She shuddered at the thought. Whereas the image of holding the hearth for Brady Rogan had been an intriguing bit of indulgence, considering the same with the pallid, puffy Mr. Blayne was appalling. The touch of the captain's strong hands had stirred a frenzy of distress. The thought of Ezra's soft, pudgy palms created a distress of a different origin. Daydreams about things promised in sea-blue eyes became a nightmare of disgust if such liberties were contrived with the pompous landowner's son. Neither her home nor she herself would ever be subject to that humiliation, she vowed with passionate fervor.

Kate's apprehensions were forestalled by a rigorous routine of work as she threw herself into each task as if it would soon be denied her. After a stingy noontime meal, she sat at the cleared table to schedule a regimen for the household to follow, charting distribution of food for beast and family, delegating duties for their shrunken number and listing provisions they would have to have. One of the horses would have to be sold. There was no other way. She would put the choice to Cosgrove and trust in his judgment. Things would be tight but not uncomfortably so in the next three weeks or so. After ponderous hours, she felt well pleased with her arrangements. To toast her inventiveness and to ease the stiffness from her neck, she allowed herself a cup of Madeira. It was a tradition between a father and his eldest to raise a glass to boast of a success. Without Nathan Mallory to partake with her, it was a bittersweet celebration, and she hoisted her cup

39

toward the one that sat unused on the sideboard, promising herself the next time she would not have to lift a toast alone. She swallowed somberly and replaced the cup.

Kate's silent musings were distracted by the shush of bristles along the yellow floorboards in the hall. She glanced about to see Anne moving the broom with lethargic strokes that wouldn't have stirred a dust mote had there been any on the clean, painted floor. The girl was taken by a sigh of exaggerated proportion and her sister hid a smile.

"What has you moping about, miss? One would think you owed the dirt some special kindness with such delicate treatment as I have witnessed here."

Again, the labored sigh. "'Tis nothing I wish to bother you with" came the martyred reply.

"I see. Very well then." Kate began to walk past her.

"'Tis about Saturday next." The girl spoke up quickly and Kate halted to hear the rest. Anne cradled her broom in a dreamy embrace. "'Tis a party at Briar Haven."

"Oh, yes. What of it?"

"Jonah Edwards and Todd Wilkes will be there."

"Oh?"

"And Daddy promised I could have a new gown." She mumbled that, her eyes downcast and breath held fast. Finally, the bright blue eyes risked a hopeful peek at her sister's unpromising features.

"Anne, I am truly sorry. He could not have known what our circumstances would be when he gave that promise." The welling of disappointment in the young girl's gaze brought an empathetic pang to her breast. "Perhaps when he gets home."

"'Twill be too late by then. Mistress McLain was showing me the most beautiful red damask. She vowed it would make me look quite regal. And older."

Kate looked at the youthful face, so flushed with eager anticipation and desire. Undoubtedly, the new cloth would suit her fair coloring to perfection, but coin could not be spared for cloth when there was nary enough for food. She had to be made to understand that. As Kate explained as gently as she could, the girl's crestfallen features made it clear that she did not.

"What about your ivory brocade?" Kate suggested as a weak alternative. "You look so lovely in it."

A tender lip pouted outward. "'Tis my Sunday best and everyone's seen it at least a score of times. If I go wearing it, Sylvie Blayne will sneer at me and call me a pauper's daughter. I'd rather not go at all."

A rebellious anger fired Kate's thoughts. How dare the prim and prissy Sylvie Blayne belittle her sister and bring tears of humble shame to her proud gaze. Anne was far more comely than the bloated Miss Blayne. Even if she wasn't bedecked in the latest silk from England, her golden beauty would far outshine the other girls and bedazzle the simply county boys. But with the fragile confidence of the young, poor Anne could only see herself judged harsh because of her lack of finery, and that knowledge was crushing. She was a budding young woman full of promise and graceful poise. A shame to shadow her brilliance with a gloom of spiteful taunts. Kate remembered her own youth, when parties were missed because she had to tend a sick mare, when visits were avoided because she had no decent shoes or stockings. She'd convinced herself she had no need of such frivolous entertainments, that the giddy court of the local boys was of little consequence. Yet looking into her sister's shattered expression, how could she expect, or want her to feel the same?

"We'll alter the silver lutestring."

Anne's eyes grew round with a conflict of rapture and dismayed guilt. "But, Katie, that was Mama's. You were saving it to make your wedding gown."

Fine lips curled into a rueful smile. "'Tis needed now. Mama wouldn't have wanted it to molder away forgotten and unused."

With an ecstatic cry, Anne cast her arms about her older sister, not seeing the sadness on the other's face. But the warmth of the embrace was not lacking and the look was gone when Kate held her away.

"Go up and unpack it. 'Twill need to air before we can refit it. You are going to be so beautiful, Anne. Jonah and Todd won't be able to look away."

"You are sure?" A brief concern overshadowed the younger girl's elation. It was to have been for Kate's wedding, after all.

Kate nodded and shooed, "Off with you now."

In a swirl of untamed blond hair and calico, Anne was gone, racing up the stairs in breathless joy. How good it was to see the girl so animated, Kate consoled herself. After all, it wasn't as though she planned to put the dress to use. She could foresee no altar vows in

42

her near future. Better the gown be used by one still young and light of heart whose pretty fancies included romance and a slew of beaux named Jonah and Todd.

The excited call of her name intruded on her melancholy.

"Kate! Katie, a caller's coming."

Jeanne's frantic cry was a world apart from her announcement of Ezra Blayne. Curious as to who could stir the child into such an agitation, Kate went to join her at the door, following the goggle-eyed stare down the drive, where her own eyes were provoked to a similar widening. Surprise and an unexpected thrill of delight coaxed forth a sunrise. A dazzling, irrepressible smile spread uncontrolled, for there, looking as dashing on horseback as he undoubtedly did on the deck of his ship, was Brady Rogan, come to collect his willingly surrendered reward.

Chapter Three

The reason for her expectant smile faded away seconds after their greeting. There was nothing specific she could pin her finger upon, just a quivery feeling that began small and frightened in the corner of her belly when his eyes affixed hers and held for a long second. There was nothing in his manner to foster such growing apprehension, for he greeted her with an easy formality. When she would seize his arm to demand he tell her the worst, they were set upon by a gaggle of giggly, awestruck girls all clamoring at once to be introduced to this handsome stranger who apparently was not one to their sister.

Once she'd run down their names in chronological order, Kate gave a brief summation of her meeting with the captain in Newport and the receptive gazes grew moony with adolescent fancies. Anne, who was old enough to experience a palpitation within her budding breast, was the first to speak, in a tone so honeyed and adult that the younger girls stared at her in frank amazement.

"Why Captain Rogan, you simply must sup with us. Our father would expect us to show you every hospitality."

Questioning eyes went to Kate for her response.

"You'd be most welcome, Captain," she concluded quietly.

"Then I'll accept. I could not refuse. One seldom finds such beauty collected under one roof."

It was charmingly said and the younger girls giggled delightedly. Only Kate suspected the clever banter was for effect, for the words lacked the silky roguishness with which they'd sparred in Newport. What had he come to tell her that couldn't be imparted to all? Anxiety contained behind an impassive face that would have befit a high-stakes game, she led the way to dinner.

If their guest noted the scantiness of the meal, he was too much a gentleman to speak of it. Brady Rogan was captivating company, entrancing the sighing girls with bold, exciting, and most likely censored tales of the sea, the Gold Coast, and the Islands while Sarah awkwardly served up the food. His continuous narrative spurred on by "ooh's" and "ah's," and breathless questions filled in for the silence of their hostess who heard none of his witty stories. Instead, her thoughts flew in panicky circles, inventing dire tidings that would soon fall from those smiling lips. It had to be grim news, for glad circumstance he would have shared in the yard. She picked at her food in a fever of consternation and was generous with the Madeira in both his cup and her

46

own. Then there was the way his gaze slipped to her betwixt his glib phrases. There was no amusement in those looks. What then? Warning? Pity? Remorse? Her palms grew slick against the cool pewter, filled again and quickly drained.

Finally, the torturous event was over, yet still, Kate could not contrive a moment alone with Brady without the tag of her enamored sisters. With an eye to the darkening heavens, he turned to her with a serious mien that fueled her blaze of fears.

"Miss Mallory, I require a word with you but we've foul weather rolling in so I daren't stay longer. Is there an inn nearby where I might quarter my belongings?"

Distractedly, she mapped the way to the Kingston Inn. Her desperate gaze begged him to impart some knowledge before he left her to her worries.

Softly, for her ears alone, he said, "I should like to return this eve for that talk."

Kate nodded jerkily and, with reluctance, watched him say his courtly farewells to her sisters before his dark head canted toward her. Then he was gone. She was slow to respond to the squeeze of fingers upon her arm.

"Oh, Katie, he is divine!" Anne gushed in a rapturous daze. "I think my ivory brocade will do service for next Saturday. Methinks you'll be needing Mama's silk."

That won the elder's attention and a sharp, "You speak nonsense, Anne."

Lips pursed saucily, Anne regarded her sister. "Then you be a fool. Such a man does not happen

47

along by chance, I'm thinking."

Kate snorted. "Better a fool by my own making than another's." She spoke with wearied cynicism. "Captain Rogan may be a pretty man, but 'tis surface beauty alone. Who can say what lies beneath."

The young girl's eyes sparkled mischievously. "If you try to tell me you haven't given thought to it, I shall call you liar." With a gay and naughty laugh, she escaped the stern cuff from her sibling and over her shoulder called, "You best keep the silk for yourself, Kate."

As Brady had predicted, the storm broke loose before he'd made the circle back to the Mallorys' farm. Leaving his winded mount with a boy who hurried it to a well-maintained barn, he was met at the door by the shy girl who'd inexpertly tended the table. She took his sodden outerwear with an uncertain hesitation. He was puzzled. Everything he'd seen told of comfortable success, if not modest wealth, yet servants were strangely lacking and the meal he'd shared befit a pauper's table. He suspected there was much that lay untold behind Miss Mallory's forthright stare. It was a mystery he meant to uncover before returning to the road.

Brady followed the timid figure who trailed his coat to leave a path of dampness all the way to the parlor. Kate sat before a cold hearth, mindless of the chill that had settled with the darkness. Her gaze lifted slowly. The fire in her eyes was cold as well. They were dull and dark with desolation. Instinct urged him to cross the room and take her up in his arms, yet prudence warned against it, and he was, despite her claim in the tavern, a prudent man. He was a stranger to her and he sensed she was not one to readily receive comfort from any source save her own strength. She sat silent, plying him with that wounded stare until the maid retired. Then she spoke one sentence without expression.

"My father is dead."

That flat summation took him aback. "No," he told her quickly, then added with care, "That is, I've had no word of him."

Her expression was momentarily blanked. Then, with fingers pressed to her temples as though they pained her, Kate murmured, "Then why have you come if not to deliver such news?"

With a tug of conscience, he noted the pinch of anguish to her lovely features and a nearly empty decanter beside her—not the one they'd almost completed at dinner. Had the poor creature been drowning her sorrows before they'd been confirmed?

"Forgive me, Miss Mallory. I'd no idea you would assume the worst. It wasn't my intent to put you in a fright." He did move to her then, lifting her hand for a consoling pat. He frowned. "You're cold. This room is like a sepulcher. Is there no one about with enough sense to raise a fire?" She simply stared at him as if at a loss until he concluded, "I'll see to it."

She watched him stock the grate with logs and kindling, attention vague and thoughts sluggish. Not dead. Her father wasn't dead. If he hadn't come to tell her the worst, what then? He hadn't laughed when she'd voiced her deepest misery or reassured her with any pleasant truth, which left a truth not so pleasant that he had yet to speak. She closed her eyes to the sight of his bronze profile warmed to a molten glow by the sparks he nurtured with skilled hands. She needed to numb her heart to what she would hear.

Brady rose and hesitated at the sight of the worn and ravaged spirit before him. She looked so isolated, so alone. He glanced at the other seating, then chose the spot at her side rather than to shout at her from a proper distance on an opposite chair. Her eyes came open at the settling of his weight and regarded him with a wary misery that touched upon his more tender sympathies.

"If not dead, then where is he?" she demanded with no echo of her former tenacity.

"I came only to warn you to have patience. It may be some time before the *Prosper* puts in. A bit of a blow is moving up the seacoast. 'Tis the onset of her we're feeling now and she looks to be temperamental. Most likely, ships held in the Islands or if they had taken to water, sought a sheltered port to wait out the worst of the winds. Captain Prouty be a good man. He'd see the ship and her passengers safe."

She didn't welcome the news with relief or gratitude. Instead, she looked hard into the flames and asked, "How long?" with the same hollow dread.

"The delay? Could be a month or more if she be damaged. I'd say a good six to eight weeks."

"You speak of an eternity."

Brady waited, but she didn't follow that claim with

50

further words. Nor did she seem to remember his presence, so caught up was she in her own dismal thoughts. He should go, he knew. He was intruding upon her private musings and he rightly supposed she was not one to air her emotions. He'd delivered the message for which he'd come and there were no more assurances he could give. The fate of the *Prosper* was not in his hands nor the feelings of this woman his responsibility. He would have risen then but for a small sound that snagged in her throat, a sob that managed to escape in a moan of despair. Impelled to do something but uncertain as to what, he spoke her proper title, then, more softly, her given name. "Miss Mallory. Kate."

She looked up then but not at him, for her anguish clouded recognition. That, and the wine that wafted sweet upon her breath. Her eyes were huge and beseeching. He'd seen such brilliant color before— such rich, fluid texture where lush mountains bled into still cove waters in a shimmer of emerald—and for a moment, he was lost in them.

"What if he doesn't return?" she asked of herself rather than of her forgotten company, and that question wrought panic. "What if he perished in the storm?" Unsteady hands flew up to cover trembling lips as if by stilling the words, likewise the possibility. "What am I to do?" she mumbled. "I won't lose my home. I won't. What will I tell them when they come for payment? How will I see my family fed? How could he do this to me? How could he fail me just as he failed Mama so many times before? How could he let my dreams die with him? It's not fair. It's not. I've worked too hard. This is my home. I won't let it be taken, not even—not even if it means the likes of Ezra Blayne. I won't give up my home."

Those glimmering eyes spilled over on the rush of frantic words. Unthinkingly, his arm encircled the defeated slump of shoulders and she took to his chest like a child seeking comfort. It was the wine, he decided, for only an unhealthy dose of spirits could so undermine her strength and allow her to take solace from him. He surmised tears to be a greater rarity than smiles, and as they flooded to wet his shirt linen the way the storm had done his coat, his arms tightened protectively.

"You've given up nothing yet, Kate," he soothed against the crown of golden hair. "Just a bit of courage, which I suspect you'll find by morning."

Uttering a doubtful sound, her arms wound around his middle to secure her place against him. A damp cheek nudged and nestled innocently above the top button of his waistcoat. A contented murmur preceded a sudden stillness.

"Kate? Miss Mallory?" One dark brow rose in helpless question. No answer. With a sigh, he positioned his left arm to cradle her heavy head and shoulder and let the right settle cautiously upon the curve of fabric pulled snug against her ribs. He certainly hadn't come here to involve himself with this woman or her difficulties; nor had he planned to spend the evening supporting her in her drunken slumber. Well, he *had* considered spending a dry and pleasant night beneath this roof but certainly not under circumstances such as these. Surely, there were more pleasing rewards than a soggy shirtfront and a cramping leg where her elbow pressed to muscle. Thoughts of such rewards had plagued him as persistently as the young miss herself, and he'd found himself wondering after her since their less-than-friendly parting. She intrigued him, the first woman to do so since . . . for a very long time. She made him think of sweetbriar, with its delicate blooms and alluring fragrance making one risk the bristle of thorns for the sake of its wild beauty. She was a beauty, all right, and the prickliest wench he'd ever crossed. Something in her bold, green-eyed stare held a constant challenge, daring him to provoke their fire. My, what a spectacular burn they held, making him contemplate if temper could be bent to a passion that would flare just as hotly. And just as quickly he'd dismissed such thoughts. Yet, still, he'd come across the Bay to sample that dauntless spirit, only to find it sadly wilted and himself further ensnared in the wreath of thorns.

Tempted by the play of firelight upon Kate's silken tresses, Brady let his fingers thread idly through the tumbled strands. A wistful longing to spend more such tender moments with someone nudged within his chest . . . and even if she wasn't the one to give life to his fantasy, his mood was gentled just the same. Plying that luxurious gold, he smiled, imagining how she would react upon discovering she'd gotten herself sheets to the wind and made a bed for herself in his lap. His gaze skimmed along the figure curled against him, appreciating its womanly contours. Perhaps she would be disappointed if he didn't behave with the wickedness she attributed to his character. Would the dastardly pirate she most likely envisioned ravish such a comely miss under these opportune circumstances? It amused him for a moment to think of how he might taunt her into believing the worst she'd thought of him. Then, as he beheld the fatigued and trusting features of the beauty in his arms, he dismissed such a game as unworthy of her honor. No, he would make no jest of her moment of weakness nor would he shame her for it.

"Sleep well, my lovely," he whispered into the froth of gold as winds and rain raged without the peaceful warmth of the parlor. "The morrow waits with little sympathy."

And with little sympathy it greeted her. The echo of her heartbeats resounded between Kate's temples to scold her excessive drink. A flannel-lined tongue rubbed across dry lips. The sweetness of the wine had soured upon them overnight and her features puckered into a grimace.

"Good morning."

The rumble of a masculine voice shocked her into a moment of confusion and forced her eyes open to the thankfully overcast day. Good Lord, it was Brady Rogan bold as brass and in her parlor! Parlor? Bewildered eyes assessed her position in growing distress. She found herself tucked up on the sofa beneath the warm drape of his coat while he, in intimate shirt-sleeves, was pouring from her mother's tea service. Clutching the sides of her head in hopes of quieting its thunder, she sat up as cautiously as an old woman.

It was with great restraint that Brady held to his grin, but it finally escaped once he turned from her to pick up the fine porcelain cups. Balancing them carefully, he crossed to the sofa to present one to the haggard miss slumped there.

"This will open your eyes a bit."

Contrarily, they squinted at the dark brew. "I prefer tea."

"This will serve you better. Trust me."

Kate glowered up at that smug assurance and took the cup. "I require milk and sugar if I must swallow this noxious brew."

"Take it neat. 'Tis the price of overindulgence."

"I do not overindulge," she countered with a vehemence that had her cringing in distress.

"Of course not, Miss Mallory," he murmured agreeably, and diplomatically assumed a seat on one of the fiddle-back chairs set adjacent.

"What are you doing here?" she grumbled.

"You offered your home's hospitality, if you might recall."

"Not to take you on as a boarder, sir." Expression screwed in distaste, Kate sipped the coffee and eyed him. He was maddeningly unaffected by her glare and just as maddeningly attractive.

"Do you treat all your guests so uncharitably? 'Tis plain the morning hours do not favor your temperament."

"They are usually my own, Captain," she returned.

"A word of advice then. A man prefers to wake to a

sweet-mannered companion."

The smooth implication of that phrase made her stare. Her eyes widened by degrees, then abruptly narrowed. He could well feel himself wearing the coffee in the cup she now clutched between unsteady hands, but he was pleased to see she refrained from such a tempting display and instead, merely said frigidly, "Why are you here, Captain? The company obviously is not to your pleasure."

"Oh, but it is and I was about to make myself some breakfast since no one else appears to be about. Have you no servants at all or are they all just incorrigibly lazy? Besides that girl who wouldn't know a porringer from a chamber pot, I mean."

Kate's fury ebbed with a wash of humility. Her gaze lowered to her cup as she drew a steadying breath and searched for a means to explain her circumstance. She was startled by the press of his fingers upon her shoulder. It was a brief, heartening gesture and she stared up at him as he soared above upon standing.

"Go and refresh yourself. You'd best change before your curious sisters find you in my presence . . . and so charmingly rumpled. I'll see to the kitchen."

Without a yea or nay, he picked up his coat and strode from the room, leaving Kate to blink at his audacious assumption of authority. That he would dare take control of her household the way he would his own ship registered as a vague complaint and she should have been warned by her complaisance. Instead, she hurried to do as he suggested . . . but had it been suggestion or order? As it made sense to her, however, she didn't quibble with herself overlong.

Relieved to find Anne still asleep and startled that the hour had yet to claim five, Kate shed her crumpled gown and, after a cursory splash of water, opened her cupboard. She lingered over her neat row of practical gowns and wondered how the ladies who entertained Brady Rogan at such an early hour had been clad. Probably with a scantiness she would not dare emulate, she mused, then, irritated both by the thought and her curiosity over the man, she jerked a dress free at random, mildly pleased that it was the patterned India cotton. The bronze shades emphasized her coloring and made her think of Brady's amber-toned flesh.

Considering him so personally inspired further transgressing thoughts, ones of warmed and roughened hands with their gentle touch, of the unyielding firmness of his chest that contrarily supplied her with an agreeable rest, of arms strong enough to crush yet tender in their envelopment of her weary form. How marvelous it had been, nestled against his manly splendor in innocent and slightly incoherent abandon. Never would she have taken such liberties had she been herself, yet while her faculties were uncertain, she'd discovered an unthinkably sensual delight with not just any man, but *that* man, a man for whom she had no respect and little trust. Yet he hadn't taken advantage. He had been extremely pleasant, if not totally proper this morning. He'd made no ribald comments or hinted that he held her in any less regard. Why? she pondered, frowning as she puzzled over him. She almost wished he would

57

act abominably so to merit her righteous contempt. However, by behaving as he had, she'd no reason to despise him, only her own weakness. Why wouldn't he act predictably so she wouldn't feel so oddly as if she'd taken advantage of him.

With one last pin to secure her heavy hair into a provocative though severe style, Kate slipped from the upper floor of slumbering females down the stairs, whereon delicious scents rose to tantalize her. Then, anything would be more desirable than the questionable fare Sarah had dropped upon her plate the previous morning, too charred to be distinguishable. She found her stomach alerted and eager as she turned into the kitchen.

Brady Rogan appeared even larger and more masculine in the domestic confines of her kitchen, yet he seemed completely comfortable there as he motioned her into one of the two places he'd set at the small table and deftly split the contents of a skillet between their plates. She couldn't readily name the creation, but her stomach insisted it be sampled.

Seeing her wary approach with the fork, Brady grinned and confessed, "I will spare you the ingredients. I was always a fair hand in the galley. No one ever died from my cooking. Or complained. None I know of, that is."

Kate took a small taste, applying herself with gusto while the chef, looking well gratified, followed suit then efficiently cleared away the services and poured them both more coffee. This time, Kate didn't object, especially when he delivered the cream pot and sugar bowl.

As she doctored the hot liquid into a muted shade of beige, Kate surveyed her companion. He lounged easily in the rush-bottomed chair, idly blowing into his cup while attentive eyes watched her behind the fog of rising steam. Awkward beneath that steady stare, she let her gaze lower, only to find herself enthralled by the wide plane of his chest and her recall of its comforts. Color fused her cheeks and she applied her spoon more vigorously until the clamor of it against the delicate porcelain called her to stop lest she damage one of the few fine things the family owned.

"I would apologize for last eve, Captain," she began staunchly, feeling it necessary to vindicate herself before those probing eyes. "I am not foolish by nature nor an inebriate by design."

"You need not explain, Miss Mallory. I know well what you are."

She let that open statement go unchallenged, hearing no insult in its delivery or intent. Before she could continue, he leveled her a serious look and a rather startling observation.

"How desperate is your situation?"

Back starching, she replied, "I cannot imagine that to be your concern, sir."

"Let's say it was," he went on imperturably. "And for the sake of conversation, that you were sensible enough to ask my help."

"Why would you offer it?"

Her directness amused him. "Let's say I feel guilty for accepting my reward without earning it. You have every penny tied up with the *Prosper*,

59

haven't you?"

Kate studied him long and skeptically, then admitted what he obviously knew. "Yes."

"And owe besides?"

"Yes."

"And have creditors threatening you and your property?"

Again, the stoic "Yes."

"You're in for a long haul, Kate. Eight weeks on that pittance you served up last night for supper and you girls will be but bones."

"I am well aware of that, Captain Rogan."

"You need provisions and an extended line of credit."

"Again, you tell me nothing new."

"If you would stop being so damned stiff with pride, I might be able to help you."

Her stare flamed. "I appreciate neither your cursing nor your assistance."

"You'd best be accepting of both lest your father return to find Ezra Blayne in his stead."

He threw out the name because he'd remembered the loathing with which she'd spoken it, not because he knew anything of the circumstance or the man. The results were dramatic. Kate fell into a pallor.

It was unthinkable that Ezra would live in their house, but the use of his name returned her to her desperate thinking. She did need help—badly. But from this man? She assessed him narrowly and wondered aloud, "What is the cost of your help?"

"'Tis not cheap. I am a privateer, as you recall, not one to do things out of a goodness I do not claim but merely out of my own best interest."

"What payment do you request?" Her tone was as tight as her posture was rigid and she waited, expecting him to name something abhorrent and licentious.

"Your approval."

"Pardon? My what?"

"I would have you look upon me with favor. I am a vain and sensitive man and your cutting estimate of my better qualities has wounded me near to fatal. I would redeem myself in your eyes by offering my services without a fee save your gratitude."

He was teasing her, of course, but so sincerely, with such indulgent humility, that a smile rebelled against the severity of her expression. "Indeed, Captain," she drawled. "You'd have me elevate you to sainthood?"

"Oh, no. 'Twould be very lonely on that virtuous plane."

"Then what would you expect of me?"

"I would expect you to smile more often, to speak melodiously, to address me by my given name. Too much?"

"My pride might allow it," she conceded graciously.

"And—"

"And?"

"You must ask."

"Ask?"

"Me for my help."

Then, he feared he'd asked too much. Her expression closed and tightened as pride and need came into conflict. He could see the struggle in her resisting frown and in the urgency of her gaze, and he waited, afraid that with the slightest push, he might lose her. Why the respect of this woman, all jesting aside, would matter so was as curious to him as her want to trust him was to Kate. The silence in the kitchen gave audience to the crackling of the hearth and the creak of boards above as her sisters began to stir.

Kate gauged the man across from her, searching the calm blue eyes for a reason to spurn his offer. Would she be twice the fool, trusting the likes of him in her father's example? Had she any choice? He was making it easy for her, as easy as it could be. There was no mocking smugness, no glint of superiority in that expectant stare. She heard herself say the words softly.

"Would you help me, Brady?"

With the sharp points of her scissors, Kate clipped the long, running stitches and carefully unpicked the threads so as not to damage the lustrous spill of silver silk upon her lap. After the pleats were rearranged and the trimmings changed, her mother's lutestring would appear as new. The shimmering fabric had the same rich luster and crisp, elegant drape despite years of storage.

A hand upon the slippery skirt, Kate wondered if her mother would approve of its use. It was madness, of course, and the worst kind of deceit, yet Brady had convinced her, completely necessary were they to hold firm until her father returned. The girls and servants had been schooled as to their parts and took to the bit of playacting with unseemly enthusiasm. 'Twould appear she was the only one to suffer a pang of conscience. She wondered if that was due to the trickery involved or to the role she would play. Irrationally, she had to own it was more Brady Rogan than the lie itself.

How easily he had insinuated himself into her family and its troubles. They all, even herself she had to ruefully admit, had taken to his rascally charm. What an unlikely man to play the hero for five country girls and their desperate plight. Yet, she could scarcely afford to refuse. His plan, though plausible, was reckless, unscrupulous, and demeaning. Yet, she rationalized, what did another foot matter when the hole was already dug. Lest they be buried in it, they would have to take the gamble. Bending close, she plied her needle.

As the time grew near, she understood her father's penchant for taking a risk. It was exciting, that thread of danger coupled with the exhilaration of the unknown. It made her pulse race with anxiety and a delicious thrill of expectation. Or was that due to the man who had come to collect Anne and herself?

When she saw him, she felt a giddy lightening of her soul. It could work. It could.

With a wavering smile to ease the tension from her features, Kate placed her hand upon Brady's proffered arm and allowed him to draw her into the charade.

Chapter Four

Briar Haven stood in regal state behind fine brick walls. Wrought-iron gates were swung wide to receive an influx of guests on the windswept, misty eve, opening the way to the gable-on-hip roofed mansion in its majestic setting of rare trees and plants imported from France, the Indies, and England. Most of the district farmers had only managed a glimpse of the cupolas that crowned the high, isolating wall, and on this night, as uncharitable as the weather had become, a small group clustered by the gate to peer within in envious awe.

Kate sank back against the tufted squabs in an awkward embarrassment, not wanting to be classed with the occupants of the elegant equipages their own carriage followed by the excluded who knew her as one of their own. Anne knew no such restraint. She leaned forward in a flush of excitement, eager to be seen and too naive to prevent a look of like wonderment from rounding her bright eyes and parted lips. Only Brady seemed at ease, indifferent to the splendor without as he assessed the splendor within. A barely discernible smile softened his expression as he observed the two sisters, Kate pridefully trying to conceal her anticipation and young Anne nearly swooning with it. Never had he escorted two such lovely, though unlikely companions, and he was surprised to admit to himself that he, too, was looking forward to this evening. The idea of the masquerade amused him. The idea of Kate Mallory's gratitude was an anticipation unto itself.

Hooded blue eyes moved over the rigid figure sitting opposite. Lord, she was lovely, even with the pinch of discomfort tightening her features. Heavy golden hair was drawn up by simple combs and gleamed in the carriage's dim interior like a midsummer sun. Unbidden, the feel of it whispering between his fingers returned. He was glad she wore it unpowdered. It would be a crime to dull such brilliance by convention and it also encouraged the image of it spilling down as the combs were removed, rushing over his hands like lengths of raw silk. He rubbed his palms against the unsatisfying texture of the fine breeches that encased his thighs and let his gaze linger along the determinedly squared shoulders. Their formidable set was belied by pearlescent skin, a tender, tempting expanse of which was bared by the modestly low neckline. The momentum drew his stare to the shadowy contour that dipped with innocent provocation behind a tease of lace, inciting a continued image of what lay beneath the shimmery curve of silver silk. His smile grew thoughtful. How grateful would Miss Mallory be at evening's end? Grateful enough to lower the briars? If not, would their scratch be worth the price of plucking such a fragrant blossom?

As he studied the comely miss, Brady wondered why no man had claimed her for his wife. She was past the first bloom of womanhood that blushed so becomingly upon her sister, at an age where she should be bearing babes, not keeping house for her father. Most girls wedded at sixteen. If still at home two years later, the parents began to lose all hope. He couldn't picture Kate in the sad role of old maid, eking out her board by keeping a dame's school or fated to spend her days in the home of her father or married sisters. Surely she was not unattached for the lack of eager suitors. Was it then because Miss Mallory held herself unavailable? Or had she yet to meet the man determined enough to fight his way through the brambles about her heart?

Kate glanced up to catch Brady's pensive gaze. The wolfish grin that spread in some unspoken amusement set her back and hastened her to look away. Ahead, light spilled through the side glass at pedimented doorways and shone through dormered windows. Panic clutched in her chest. What was she doing? What had possessed her to come, to think this desperate game could gain her any time? How could she have allowed herself to trust this mocking stranger, to place herself and the hope of her family in the hands of a man she held beneath contempt? This was madness. *She* was mad. Her breath gathered in a constrictive bind. She had to turn them away from this course of folly before it was too late to save her self-respect.

Too late.

The carriage rocked to a halt and a liveried servant held open the door. Somehow, Anne retained the presence of mind to allow him to hand her down then stood in a quiver of excitement and impatience as Brady stepped out and reached up for her sister.

Kate regarded his hand for a long moment, her features frozen and eyes wide with distress. His dark brow rose. His hand stretched farther, offering, expectant, final. Her own shook as it settled reluctantly within his palm, and the curl of his fingers about it sealed her fate. He continued to hold it after he turned her easily to the ground, holding it firmly until she looked up at him to receive his bolstering smile. Then it was no longer the outcome of the charade but the pretense itself that caused the flutter within her breast. How could she have ever believed she could play the part with convincing aplomb?

She had no time to debate it further as the carriage drew away to make room for the next in line waiting to deposit its elegant occupants. Other than to bolt down the drive afoot, she had no choice but to take Brady's arm and advance into what she was sure would be the worst night of her life.

Briar Haven's spacious parlor was brimming with the county's elite, wealthy and powerful. They all came: the McLains, the Miltons, the Moses, the Jacobs, the Todburys, and Dr. Parrish in his antiquated finery. No gloomy drizzle or the threat of fouler weather to come could keep them inside when the stately doors of the Blaynes' home stood open to them. The men were resplendent in yards of silver and gold lace, powdered wigs and brocades, and the women adorned with necklaces of topaz, paste, French green-and-purple stones above squared necklines, bobbing plumes and heavy satins. All acted their proper best, gratified to be included. Knowing her invitation had come only upon Ezra's blustery proposal, Kate stood in the hall, her fingers tightening on Brady's arm as they waited to be introduced to the gaudy assembly.

The butler cleared his throat and announced grandly, "His Lordship, the Fifth Earl of Bradington, Misses Kathryn and Anne Mallory."

A hush fell upon the gathering. They stared. Oh, Lord, don't let them read of this deception upon my face, thought Kate as her posture straightened and she managed a stiff smile. But none looked to her to bear witness to her deceit. They were staring at the haughty aristocrat who stood at her elbow regarding them in turn with a superior disdain for Colonial gentry. Kate held her breath. Then it was over. Ned Blayne rushed to greet them, bowing to bring a creak of protest from his stays.

"My lord, an honor to have you here in my humble home," he gushed in fawning homage. Remarkably, Brady maintained a sober mien, accepting the display as though it was due him.

"Mr. Blayne, good of you to have me," he drawled with superb indifference.

"Are you an acquaintance of Nathan Mallory? I don't believe I have had the pleasure before." As shrewdly as if measuring him for a loan, a banker's eyes assessed his suit of French gray with buttonholes wrought in gold thread about gold basket buttons and the yards of heavy lace that adorned his waistcoat.

"Intimately, you might say. You may be the first to hear that Miss Mallory has consented to be my bride."

The avaricious gaze ceased its calculations of worth and darted between the two Mallory girls. Brady put an end to his question by fitting his palm snugly against Kate's small waist. That fond gesture was not missed by Ezra, as he had been staring at her over the head of the merchant who trapped him in conversation. Rudely, he broke away from the man and bustled to his father's side in a dazzle of chartreuse satin. His indignant glare fixed on the offending embrace.

"Good evening, Miss Kathryn," he nearly lisped in his outrage. "How good of you and your fair sister to attend this evening. And who is your guest?" That last was said with a distinct chill of displeasure.

Ezra's pompous display of possessiveness brought a wrathful enjoyment to Kate's sweet reply. "Charles," she cooed, touching the frothy waistcoat familiarly as she remembered to use the name Brady had elected for his part, "may I present Mr. Blayne's son to you. Ezra, the Earl of Bradington, my fiancé."

A vivid flush rose in the flabby cheeks, a glaring contrast to the color of his coat. Ezra sucked air like a gasping cod for several awkward moments then wheezed, "Why is it I have heard naught of this before? You said nothing the other day when—"

Kate cut him off quickly to avoid embarrassing them both with what she feared would be an impassioned outburst. "I only accepted a few days ago. I hope you will wish us well."

Ezra's bulging glower wished them obviously anything but; however, he bowed curtly and murmured it was so.

Anne's impatience saved them from further discomfort. She tugged on her sister's arm and pointed to a group of her friends, urging them forward. Kate was only too glad to beg their excuses and follow Anne's insistent lead. The plump, powdered Sylvie Blayne seized Anne up for an affected hug before drawing her into the circle of their peers. Her cherry-ripe lips offered a pretty smile and venomous words.

"Oh, Anne, how lovely you look. Only you could contrive to make the same old gown appear new each time you wear it."

Anne froze, mortified to the quick as attention was drawn to the ivory brocade. Tears started bright in her blue eyes, then Brady took up her hand to make the crooning declaration:

"When a flawless stone finds the perfect setting, 'tis a shame to separate them." He brought her fingers up to kiss them gallantly and a chorus of sighs went up from the bevy of young females. The nettled county bucks, including the gangly Todd Wilkes and tow-haired Jonah Edwards, were quick to crowd around to add their inexperienced compliments, not wanting to be outshone by some fancy-garbed outsider. Leaving a blissful Anne to their bumbling admiration, Kate and Brady slipped away.

"Thank you," Kate said softly as he dipped punch for her from the large china bowl. She did not mean for the beverage, and he met her uplifted eyes with a warm look in his own.

"My pleasure, Miss Mallory," he vowed and passed her the cup. His fingers brushed over hers in a not-unintentional caress. Kate nearly gulped the cooling liquid. He grinned at her nervousness. "Do I sense doubts? Can you deny that everything has gone splendidly?"

Her lips thinned contrarily. Unhappy eyes scanned the room. "These are good people. Why should you think I'd enjoy misleading them?"

Brady's smile didn't falter. "If they were such good people, the charade wouldn't be necessary, now would it, Kate?" he argued reasonably, and because it *was* reasonable, she was even angrier at herself and, irrationally, with him. He chuckled. "Besides, I do believe I detected a certain amount of malicious pleasure when you introduced me to our host's fat son. He looked as though he had some prior claim upon you. Could that be true?"

"No." She spat out the denial, then tempered it more calmly by saying, "Perhaps to his thinking but not to mine."

"You would not wish to marry into all of this?"

He was mocking her and she felt her temper rush up in waves of heat into her cheeks. "There are things I value more than pieces of Chippendale and imported shrubbery."

"Such as?"

She would not be provoked into revealing her wants or needs in a male companion, though she considered with satisfaction telling him at some later time how far he fell from her expectations. Instead, she smiled demurely and coaxed, "Come, beloved, I have kept you to myself for far too long. Let us mingle so I can introduce you to my good neighbors."

Brady followed, performing perfunctorily as she brought him up before couple after couple. His eyes never left her nor could he shake from his thoughts what she had called him. "Beloved," she had said. Of course it had been in jest and the irony of that desired title being tossed at him so lightly intensified the hollow ache about his heart. Having waited years to hear that endearment bestowed lovingly upon him, the cruelty of the circumstance now cut deep. Kate Mallory wasn't the one he'd longed to hear mouth that word, and the likelihood that he would never receive it from the chosen source was a bitter truth, indeed. Yet, what had he ever found affection to be but a game of pretense, of hiding the truth from others and from one's self, and what was this but another game.

Kate glanced up when Brady's fingers began a slow massage along the bare slope of her shoulder. It was such a personal gesture, speaking of intimacies shared and enjoyed, and she would have been annoyed if the touch hadn't sparked a more alarming response. How warm his hand was, how gentle, how firm. She was reminded of his compassionate embrace when her strength had faltered and of her own want to linger within it, safe and secure. It was a frightening feeling—one of vulnerability, of surrender and trust—yet how could she hold such emotions out to this stranger who by reputation scorned all signs of weakness or tender failings. He had come into her life offering help and salvation, naming no reason for his interest, no real price for his aid. How could she trust him? How could she trust her own willingness to let him take command of her fate? That was something she had never surrendered before, had never thought she would want to relinquish, but she was tired, so tired of being responsible, and Brady Rogan's broad shoulders seemed so capable and provident. Was she being a fool to give him even this brief concession of power over her? Would she regret it later when the threat of ruin was no longer more dangerous than the suddenly sultry gleam in his sea-blue eyes? Her shoulders squared. If she could not trust him, at least she could trust herself. The evening contained only a few more hours, then Brady Rogan would be gone and her father would return and the frantic pace Brady's touch inspired in her erstwhile sturdy heart would no longer keep her awake late into the night thinking foolish thoughts.

Kate smiled and shifted slightly to unsettle the errant hand, discouraging the familiar fondling with a piercing cut of green eyes. Warned but heedless, Brady tucked her hand in the bend of his elbow to escort her into dinner.

Even Kate could not conceal her awe upon

stepping into Briar Haven's dining room. It was set for thirty as easily as her own for six. The long mahogany table was aglitter with candlelight reflection flickering in real glass wine goblets and pieces of silver. Each place was dressed with porcelain, not the counterfeit Delft ware that she kept for Sundays and visitors. Sideboards of the same rare mahogany ran along each wall, soon to be heavily burdened with the removes of the meal. She couldn't help imaging how long her little family could feast on what would be carelessly tossed out after the extravagant dinner.

A dark-skinned servant held back a chair for her, but before she could assume the beautiful piece of Goddard's block-and-shell handiwork, the senior Mr. Blayne stepped in to personally take her arm and escort her to a seat farther up the table. Seeing herself seated above the cut-glass salt cellar that divided the guests into two distinct classes, Kate realized wryly how her charade had elevated her standing in the community. From across the table, Brady had noted her gaze and repressed a smug look of mirth that they could share together. Anne seemed not to care that she was situated below the salt, too ecstatic to be positioned between Misters Wilkes and Edwards to give a whit for her social ranking. Her blushing beauty inspired Kate with its sheer, unaffected enjoyment. And then Ezra Blayne settled in the seat beside her and the pleasure of the moment was gone.

Efficient servants supplied trenchers heaped with exquisitely prepared duck, hams, legs of pork, tripe, custards, fools, and floating islands, and an equal number circulated to keep the goblets brimming with beer, punch, or wine. Kate tried to ignore the amounts that disappeared from Ezra's plate just as she tried to avoid the gentleman himself—but he made both difficult. After moments of stony silence, he bothered her ceaselessly to pass any number of condiments, which she did with nary a glance in his direction. When his politeness failed to gain him notice, Ezra abandoned it entirely.

"You owe me an explanation, miss," he insisted in a squeaky undervoice.

Kate pretended not to understand. "I beg your pardon?"

"Your engagement is rather sudden, is it not? I thought we had an understanding."

The whining quality of his words made her grimace, but Kate kept her answer kind. "Please, sir. You cannot say I encouraged you, for I did not."

"No, you put me off with prim sentiments about wanting your father's approval. Shallow sentiments, it would seem, for they did not deter you from snapping up *his* offer."

That insulting slur was too much. Kate turned so she could pin his sullen countenance with a withering stare. "No such thing. The earl has been known to my family for years. I have known him since childhood. When we met again while I was in Newport, he pursued me home to speak of things that have been between us long before you made your interest known. I already know of my father's approval, but out of respect to him, will wait for his return before having the banns posted. I resent your insinuation that I played you false in any way."

Having delivered those rehearsed words, she sat back in her chair to attack her dessert, surprised that she should feel no remorse in spinning such a tale. She was acutely aware of Brady's amused scrutiny but feared to meet it lest she give herself away with a flush of guilty color.

Beside her, Ezra huffed and simpered, then allowed his imperturbable arrogance to control his thinking. He regained her attention with a grandly tendered, "I do beg your pardon, Miss Kathryn. I mistook the situation. You must own that the suddenness of this passion might be misconstrued."

Kate carefully set down her fork. Her expression was stiff when she regarded him. "How so, sir?"

"Given your debt and the man's obvious affluence . . ." he speculated, then was immediately moved to seize her hand between his own rather greasy ones to plead, "How can you consider him over me? I have offered to lift you from your plight to a pedestal. He cannot match what I have to give you, what I long to give you. He is not half the man I am."

"Please, sir," she managed in a strangled voice. The thought of him seriously comparing himself to the superb and vastly superior form of Brady Rogan had her dangerously close to giggling. It was hardly talk for the table and she feared they would be overheard.

"He is offering you riches. I offer you my devotion," Ezra's impassioned speech continued.

Kate choked and swallowed hard. "Mr. Blayne. Ezra, please. Again you mistake the situation. It is not for coin that I have agreed to his suit. It is because . . ." Suddenly, the words failed her and a tremendous heat rose to her face. She forced it, and her abrupt trembling, to subside. Why should this lie be more difficult than the others. Determinedly, she spoke it. "I love him."

Her gaze was pulled irresistibly up to be consumed by a bright blue fire. She was sure Brady hadn't heard her words so why was she so beset with feverish flashes of shame . . . and regret. Why did the mere invention of an intimate link to Brady Rogan provoke her into a clammy agitation? It wasn't as though she longed for the falsehoods to be truth.

Helplessly, she regarded him, the splendid figure he presented in his garb of make-believe affluence. He did look the fine, prosperous lord in his immaculately barbered wig. Its powdered starkness was an intriguing complement to his bronzed skin and slash of black brows. The elegant clothes, the cultivated manners, the suggestive caress of his fingertips had conspired to seduce her, making her want to believe the sham that he was what he appeared to be: a man she might love and belong to. It was such a surprise, this sudden recognition of the emptiness of her life. She had never missed having a man in her present or dreamed of one in her future . . . until now. Why would this inappropriate scoundrel create a need to know a fulfillment she'd never known was lacking?

Kate's gaze lowered to her plate, but the heat of confusion remained in bright betrayal. Thankfully, the host rose to signal the end of the meal and she was able to escape into the sitting room while the men gathered in the adjacent parlor to imbibe, smoke, and speak politics.

"Gracious, Katie, whatever is wrong?" Anne gasped in concern, clasping her sister's arm as if she saw the need to steady her. "You look as though you're about to swoon."

"Ridiculous," she argued faintly. "'Tis a bit too warm and the food too rich is all. I'll be glad when this evening is over." She lifted her handkerchief to blot away the dappling of moisture that felt cold upon her brow.

"How could you say so? 'Tis like a dream come true," she sighed.

No, Kate thought grimly, it was a nightmare. The lies, the guilt, the roil of silly emotions all wrought from the desperate need to survive. She had been so anxious to find a way to forestall disaster, she'd plunged blindly into another. Even now, Brady would be mingling with her debt-holders, convincing them to extend her credit against the promise of future wealth she would obtain upon her "marriage." It had seemed a harmless ploy when he'd proposed it. When she'd agreed, she had never imagined she could feel so horribly conscience-stricken. Brady made it seem so simple, but he was used to presenting false colors and she doubted he ever suffered from twinges of guilt. How could she face them, her friends, neighbors, and creditors, if the truth be known? Keeping her falseness a secret was proving torture enough without exposure of the crime. But then, she reminded herself, she had to survive. Her family came first, before all others and before her own condemning shame. If there had been another alternative, she would have seized upon it. It wasn't just because Brady Rogan happened to be the most handsome and exciting man she'd ever seen, she told herself. That had nothing to do with her willingness to engage in such a deplorable game. It was for her family.

Resolute in that, she did feel better and was able to smile and pat Anne's hand. She clung to that determination when they rejoined the men and Brady squired her about with a possessive strut to receive congratulations upon her choice match. She could well imagine the fires of hell when she smiled at the village pastor and thanked him for his well wishes. After that, there were only a few tepid selections played by Miss Blayne upon the virginal and the good-byes to endure.

Kate collapsed into the carriage, exhausted in body and spirit and certain she would be eternally damned for the conscious lies she had spread. She listened vaguely to Anne's enthused chatter as the glow of Briar Haven was enveloped by a heavy mist of rain. From his place opposite, Brady was regarding her through veiled eyes, a half smile touching his lips. All too aware of him and the way he delved into the role of her betrothed, Kate could not meet his stare. She still tingled from the caress of his words of endearment and brief but intimate gestures. She was finding it hard to stop the fantasy and return to the reality of him as nothing more than a business acquaintance. She refused to believe that it was this particular man who had her emotions so miserably knotted, shaken, only by the unexpected knowledge that she desired *any* man in her previously celibate life. Perversely, she'd enjoyed his attention and having others think a romance flourished between them. But it was a charade, she reminded herself, and she'd lied to enough people for one night without including herself among them. She would be glad when Brady returned to Newport.

The rains were torrential by the time Brady hurried them into the house. Still radiating a happy glow, Anne stood on tiptoes to embrace their escort and blushingly thanked him. Chancing a quick, conspiratorial wink at Kate, she pleaded fatigue and excused herself, rustling up the stairs in a swirl of petticoats while Kate was left uncomfortably alone in the hall with their guest. Angered by her sister's desertion, Kate looked up into the swarthy features, wary and warning him with that single look. But he seemed singularly immune to it.

"I think this evening's success calls for a toast. What say you, Miss Mallory?"

He waited, smiling expectantly. Amusement creased his eyes when he read of her reluctance.

"Or is that too much to ask before being banished into the cold, wet night?"

She sighed with helpless resignation and gestured to the parlor. A fire crackled invitingly in the grate, emitting a pleasing warmth. Brady let his outer coat drop carelessly over a chair. His wig fell atop it amid a sprinkle of loose powder. He gave his scalp a brisk scratching, leaving his hair in a disarming tousle.

"I loathe those things. Unnatural and unmanly."

He shuddered eloquently and took the proffered cup of port. He lifted it and said jauntily, "To credit restored."

"To the swift return of my father," Kate countered softly. Sobered, he gave a slight nod, and together they drank. After a moment, Brady returned his cup to the sideboard. Kate hadn't invited him to sit so he remained where he was, wondering over her sudden timidity.

"I trust our little playacting achieved the desired results," he said with a note of satisfaction. "Your accounts are reopened. I only hope you shan't be scarred by joining your name with mine, even for the most innocent of reasons."

She lifted a golden brow, choosing to react casually. "With the Fifth Earl of Bradington? If anything, my standing has soared." Then her forehead furrowed. "But what if one of them thinks to ask questions of that name?" She was referring to the spiteful Ezra. Why hadn't she considered it before?

Brady smiled, unconcerned. "You needn't worry. Consider it an evening of pure profit."

"For my family, yes, but what of you? What did you gain from helping us in this charade?" Her question was direct and unavoidable, so he would answer it the same way. He took the cup from her hand and smiled. A shiver began in the pit of her stomach and rose quickly to quiver through her. She had time to take a small step back but the move wasn't decisive enough.

"Oh, my motives weren't quite so pure," he

confessed with a silky rumble.

Kate stood transfixed, trembling like a defenseless creature mesmerized by the serpent intent upon devouring it. His hand rose slowly to shake free one of her combs. Brown fingers tangled in wisps of spun gold. Her eyes closed and that was all the invitation he needed to breech the space between them. A sound escaped in a tiny squeak before his mouth settled irrefutably over hers. She didn't breathe. She didn't move. Then he stepped back to regard her. She looked dazed.

"Kate?"

Slowly, the tip of her tongue traced her lower lip, tasting his kiss upon it. "That was nice," she said quietly, as if surprised.

"Nice," he repeated. Not exactly an overwhelming compliment, but he was encouraged. A smile made a sensual curve. "I am a nice man."

Kate smiled, too, ruefully unconvinced. "Oh, I don't think so. I think you are—" She didn't get to finish. He concluded for her, physically stating her sentiments more eloquently than she could have managed in words.

He kissed her again. His hand anchored in the heavy strands of hair to draw her against him, but it was not her want to struggle. Tentative fingertips touched at taut middle, unyielding chest, and wide shoulders. At her hesitant response, Brady's arm curled about her trim waist, tightening until her ripened contours submitted to his own muscular planes. The gentle insistence of his first parry grew more aggressive and her inexperienced lips opened to him, to the inquisitive, conquering probe that brought a restless fervor to life. She was innocent but eager. His own composure was rocked as her tongue explored his mouth and her fingertips, his face, then crumbled, when satisfied, she whispered in husky contentment, "Oh, Brady."

Desire flushed hot, filling his loins and prompting him with an unqualified urgency. His lips ravaged hers, thrilled and encouraged by the intoxicating flavor of her compliance. She more than complied; she demanded. The knowledge of her excitement rushed him to lay claim to more. Her head rolled to one side as his mouth scorched hot against her throat, exulting for a moment in the frantic pleasure he felt pulsing there before trailing down to the soft sweep of her shoulder. There was no rigid set to them now.

To complete his earlier fancies, Brady's hand slid purposefully up the snug fit of well-warmed silk to be filled with the heavy swell of one perfect breast. She trembled. She tensed. Before his mouth could return to quiet hers, she panted, "Captain, please." Palms pushed against his shoulders and he gave, albeit with great reluctance, until an impersonal distance opened between them. She looked so frightened. It was not a fear of him but of herself and her own actions. There was a passion there, wild and yearning, in her wide green eyes and he knew . . . and she knew that she would not resist him beyond that faint token of protest.

Then, he surprised her again. Gently, with a show of humbling respect, he lifted her unresponsive fingers to his lips. His breath brushed warm with promise upon them.

"Good night, Kate."

He had retrieved his coat and shrugged into it before she recovered herself to the point of speaking his name. He looked at her in question.

"Thank you." Her hushed words were all-inclusive.

For an instant, his gaze was intense, then it softened with his roguish smile. "'Twas my pleasure." That concluded all as well.

Anne didn't bother to pretend she wasn't waiting up for her sister. The younger girl studied Kate's face. Then she nodded to herself as if well satisfied and rolled away under the covers.

"Good night, Katie." It was a pleased, smug sentiment.

Chapter Five

"Damn!"

Brady crumpled the crudely penned note and discarded it in the remains of his beer.

"Sir?" The hefty barmaid looked at him, startled by his tone. "You be needing me to fill that up for you?" She began to reach for his mug, but he waved her hand away with a choppy gesture. She sniffed at his rudeness and was quick to turn to her regular customers.

He did need a drink, badly, but Brady knew he would have to call upon clear thinking to get him through the unpleasantness ahead. Why hadn't he sailed on the early tide? Then she would have heard the news from someone else and he would be uninvolved. But uninvolved was not what he was and that perplexing fact was what delayed him in the white-clapboard hostelry to brood over a mug of ale while the influx of tradesmen and travelers went on unnoticed about him.

He needed to be free of Kingstown and of Kate Mallory, and now there was no help but to remain. Damn, he thought again as he ran distracted fingers through his hair. He didn't need this. Not at all.

His unwise farewell to the delectable Miss Mallory had fired a passion that simmered unquenched for most of the long hours of the night in his tiny room beneath the gambrel roof above. He couldn't believe his own folly. He wasn't one to dally with virtuous women. An honest woman was too hard to dismiss casually. When plying coin, obligation was done when the service was rendered, and that suited him fine. He had no room in his thoughts—or in his heart—for the type of obligation Kate Mallory was becoming. He'd been a fool to let curiosity over the fiery Kate tempt him across the Bay and a bigger fool to be caught up in her troubles. And he was the grand fool for enjoying every moment of it, especially the feel of her in his arms, welcoming him with the press of her lush figure and the eager part of her soft lips. Thinking of it now wrought an uncomfortable fullness, and he scowled in recognition of his wayward desires. He'd wanted a distraction, not an obsession, and, by God, Kate Mallory had the makings of one.

She was a prickly spinster, a determined shrew, independent, unpredictable. She could freeze a man to the marrow with a glance or cut him to the bone with a word. She was maddening, she was intriguing. The contradiction thrilled him. Why couldn't she be homely? Why couldn't she be whiny and meek instead of so courageous it made him proud just to view her? Why hadn't she repulsed his advances in outrage instead of urging them on to a breathless anticipation. She made his blood boil with irritation, with explicit lusts. She was a lady and that was the worst of the lot. She had made him privy to her well-guarded vulnerability, and knowing that he was going to bring her pain was killing him.

Brady pushed out of his chair and strode from the taproom. "I need a horse," he called impatiently. The innkeeper stared at him as if he was crazy.

"You cannot mean to go out there. All hell's brewing."

His voice was a growl. "I know that, man. Just get me that horse."

Kate stood at the window, aimlessly watching the rain wash down the twelve-over-twelve sash. There was nothing to see beyond those steady rivulets. Darkness had settled early, along with a seeping chill. Even the well-stoked warmth of the parlor's fire couldn't prevent her from shivering as she remained, one arm hugging the other, staring sightlessly into the night. The harsh tone of the weather encouraged an early supper. While the younger girls retired above to do their nightly reading lessons out of the smaller Bible that had belonged to their mother's family, the elder sisters and Mistress Fitch shared the questionable comfort of the fire. Anne regaled them with dreamy tellings of Briar Haven while the nodding Fitch sewed industriously upon the torn hem of Bertrice's favorite calico. Later, after the old woman had gone to bed, Anne would rescue the garment by snipping the irregular stitches wrought of near blindness and arthritic hands and replace them with her own neat seam. Dear Fitch never knew of the innocent deception and it kept her feeling useful.

"I shall never see another night like it," Anne sighed dramatically, "nor sights quite its equal. Sylvie Blayne was wearing the most remarkable gown."

Fitch continued to nod, only half hearing. "Go on, dear."

"It was of salmon-colored tabby velvet with satin flowers and ruffles of Brussels lace. It must have cost all of twenty pounds. Her hair was all rolled and fastened with silver bodkins. Oh, Fitch, you should have seen how regal she looked. She has such poise. I felt quite the goose beside her."

"Poise," Kate scoffed unkindly, not bothering to turn away from the glass. "Her glorious coif was aided by a foot of horsehair and her enviable poise is from being bred to a backboard and stiffening coats. The poor creature probably cannot even straighten without their assistance. Better to be country born and hardy, Anne, than thin-chested and failing."

"Katie, how cruel of you to say such things," Anne chided, with ill-concealed delight. "Even if they are true. Jonah Edwards had the gall to ask me if I'd sneak out to meet up with him after Sunday service. Imagine!" Sounding more thrilled than scandalized, Anne went into enthused detail, not noticing how her sister leaned closer to the window then moved to the door.

The force of rain and wind nearly staggered her as Kate eased the door open only enough to allow the silhouetted figure to slip inside. It took both of them to close it as the elements battled to sweep within the hall. The heavy portal sealed out the howl of the gale and for a moment, all was silent. Kate's heart slammed hopefully against her ribs as she looked up at his features, finding them harshly handsome in the play of shadows.

"Captain Rogan, what brings you out on such a night?" She prayed he wouldn't notice how breathless she sounded. "I thought you'd be in Newport by now." *Yet here you are* came a whisper of anticipation.

Brady glanced about, seeing the two ladies in the parlor regarding him in question before he returned his attention to the woman before him. Never had he seen her look so magnificent. Golden hair spilled down her back as her head tilted up to offer green eyes wide with pleasure and a slight hint of bewilderment. It was a look that could bring a man home from the sea in a hurry, full of promising warmth and welcome. He would have given all he possessed to say nothing of what had brought him to her door in order to explore the potential of that look. But he could not. Carefully, he grasped her forearms, turning so the breadth of his frame shielded her from the curious gazes. He spoke her name. The sound was low and heavy with regret.

"Kate."

With the light behind him, she could see him

clearly, could read his face, and knew in an instant that he hadn't come to pursue what had sparked between them the night before. Dampness glistened upon his bared head and his cheeks were burned red from the sting of the wind. The lips that could cajole naughtily or tempt mightily with a smile were thinned with some displeasure. But it was his gaze that held her motionless and began a curl of suspecting dread. It was so expressive, letting her see into the misery of his soul. He tried to speak and found he could not. In the end, she didn't need his words to know the message he carried.

"Oh, no, Brady. Please." The words tore from her in an agony of disbelief. She tried to swallow, her shoulders jerking with the effort. With a wail, she thrust his hands away and fled blindly through the parlor.

Brady stood in the hall in his sodden coat, the weight of it slumping his shoulders with weariness and disgust at the senseless loss. Slowly, he followed her path into the kitchen. The sight of the hulking, dripping man stomping through their parlor brought Fitch to her feet to voice a protest. Anne was quick to catch her arm. She forced herself to speak cheerfully, though a great knot of fear had begun within her breast.

"Look how late it's gotten. Dear Fitch, why don't you go up to bed and I'll bring up a hot toddy to help you sleep."

In a fluster Fitch looked from her unconcerned visage to the kitchen. "Is Kathryn ill? That man—"

"The captain will see to what ails Kate. Come

along now. They don't need us."

Understanding dawned on the withered features. Ah, a lover's quarrel. Sweet, serious Kate finally had a beau. Fitch chuckled to herself and allowed Anne to draw her to the stairs. Yes, a toddy would be nice.

Kate sat before the fire, dwarfed on the long pine settle where she curled up like a child. The sound of her sobs, so hoarse and heavy with hurt, made Brady hesitate. She knew he was there. He could tell by her feeble attempt to gain control as she straightened and quieted her weeping into deep, seesawing breaths. The sight of her courage swelled his heart with odd emotions.

"Tell me," she said simply in a voice raw and wounded.

Brady's hands twitched at his sides. God, he felt helpless. "The *Prosper* set to before the storm. She never had a chance to seek a safe port. She's listed as lost at sea."

"Then you've lost a ship and I've lost a father."

That callous summation took Brady aback. He stared at her, a frown beginning to gather. Then she twisted to look up at him. Her features were stark with grief.

"Brady, please tell me to have hope." It was a poignant request.

"Have hope." His sincerity must have been at an ebb, for her tears began again, slipping down her pale cheeks in wretched trails. In two steps, he was across the room, settling beside her still in his wet clothing, arms bringing her to him. She clung. Her hair was sweet and soft, her tears warm upon his throat. She spoke out of panic and desperation, begging him to reassure her.

"Lost ships turn up, don't they? He might not have been aboard. This doesn't have to mean he's d-d-dead."

His embrace tightened convulsively. Trusting that she was too distraught to test the truth of his logic, Brady said firmly, "Lost doesn't mean sunk. It was a bad, bad blow. She could be off course. She could be beached on some isolated spot along the coast. We won't know for a while, and you're going to have to be brave for your sisters. There's no need to frighten them yet."

He could feel the effect of his words almost immediately. Her grief quieted into slow, hitching breaths. Lord, she was a strong woman. She could weather the storm better than the *Prosper*, he thought with welling pride. There were things he hadn't told her, like the slim chance of a lone ship surviving in a storm of such magnitude. Most likely, he had indeed lost a ship and she a father, and it was her loss he felt more acutely.

Kate rubbed her face upon his coat, then leaned back. Sorrow lent a bruised appearance to her eyes. "Thank you for bringing the news to me," she told him in a husky tone. He was reluctant to release her, sensing how fragile her courage was, but she stood away. Her hand touched to his lapel. "Take off this wet thing before you catch your . . . I'll put some water on for coffee."

94

"There's no need," he began, then he made no further protest, realizing she wanted to lose herself in busyness. She swung the pothook with its blackened kettle over the fire while he shed his soggy coat and folded it over the high back of the settle.

"What of the girls?" she was asking.

"Anne is seeing to them."

She nodded, but still didn't turn toward him. "You'll be staying, of course. I'll not send you back out into such a night as this."

Brady's gaze slid down the straight back to the inviting curve of her hips. His reply was unintentionally gruff. "No. I can't stay."

Kate pivoted, giving him the very look of authority she used to cow her sisters. A smile quivered upon his lips to think she would try to do the same with him. "Yes, you will. I'll hear of no arguments. You can use the downstairs room. I'm sure my f-father won't mind."

The starch went out of her in an instant. Brady was quick to catch hold of her as she swayed. Her fingers gripped his shirtfront, kneading the fabric in jerky spasms. He held her, letting her roll with the waves of pain until the rip and ebb grew too difficult to endure. Her damp face lifted at the persuasion of his hand and he kissed her.

Kate's lips were still as his brushed soft upon them. Then as the gesture, meant only to hearten her at first, began to deepen with insistent fervor, her lips parted to invite a more personal union. The caress of his mouth and the lingering stroke of his tongue calmed her restless hands. They clutched his shirt

95

linen, then moved up to clench in his hair. The kettle whistled impatiently. They were too caught up in what had begun to boil and bubble between them to pay it heed. Finally, Brady broke free, breathing hard and too close to losing all control to fall back into the simmering green seas of her half-shuttered eyes. Needing a safer distraction, he turned to move the kettle from the flames. Even distanced from the heat, the contents continued to roil.

"Brady." Her tone smoldered.

"I have to go."

Kate came up against him, her arms twining about his neck. Her movements were planned seduction, yet her words, a desperate plea. "Don't go. Please, Brady. I need . . ." Her petition broke off. She wasn't sure how to end it. She only knew that there was security in Brady Rogan's arms and if he was gone, she would be bereft of all comfort.

Gently, he took her forearms and tried to set her away. Her eyes searched his in confusion.

"What you need, I cannot give. What I can offer would be of no service to you. I don't want to hurt you."

The tenderness of his claim quickened a sheen in her eyes, but she would not release him. "I am past feeling pain. Stay."

He hesitated, and she was quick to take advantage. Towing him determinedly, she backed across the sweltering kitchen, her gaze never breaking from the intensity of his. He should have balked, he should have heeded his own sensibilities. Instead, he followed her into a dark room off the kitchen. It smelled of leather and tobacco, a man's room. The door closed off all warmth and light and, for a moment, he was the passive partner as her lips moved insistently over his. She was too persuasive, too luscious to resist. His hands dragged roughly up her arms to seize her shoulders, urging her closer still until the fullness of her breasts were crushed to his chest and there could be no mistaking what her invitation would mean.

Kate was too numbed for rational thought. Everything had a simple, basic meaning for her now, and she wanted Brady Rogan, wanted him to expand upon the delights he had tantalized her with. She didn't want to think, she wanted to be swept up in feelings far removed from loss and death and pain. The warmth of Brady's mouth spoke of living, the hard swell of him pressed against her belly, of life. She was aware of her fear, but it compared naught to the terror of emptiness the night would hold if she were to step from his embrace. Reality waited, stark and ugly, and for this moment, she needed the stuff of dreams to sustain her. And that, he was. She wouldn't think of what she was giving him, wouldn't think of what he was. It didn't matter now. Tomorrow, there would be the weight of grief and nothing would matter then.

"Kate . . ." His voice was a ragged whisper. The vital quality of it made her shiver.

"Shh," she whispered against his protesting lips. She wanted to hear no arguments, no cautioning words, not even ones of tenderness. She wanted to lose none of the momentum that was beginning to flare, hot and heady, urging her onward to spite her inexperience. She wouldn't have him guess that she knew more of horses than of men. Her apprenticeship had begun in his arms the night prior and she would learn all she could until the lesson's end.

He made it so easy. The demands of his lips called for instinct, not wisdom. She responded to him without reserve, letting her own desires guide her. The taste of his mouth was wildly, wonderfully exciting, so she delved into it to savor more. He made a noise then, a sort of rumble from way down deep in his throat, and it urged her to take more liberties. Her palm rubbed the smooth finish of his waistcoat, feeling the texture of muscle it covered. She needed to get closer. Fingers jerked the buttons free. The heat of his skin radiated through the linen of his shirt. She found she was trembling. What now? Did she continue to undress him? Should she herself begin to disrobe? Isn't that what couples did when kissing alone could no longer encompass the scope of one's passions? She was so painfully ignorant.

Then Brady took a step back. It wasn't a retreat, as she feared at first. Deft hands worked down the row of hooks and eyes then parted her bodice with an unhurried ease. That mannerly pace was at odds with the rush of his labored breathing. She guessed he didn't want to frighten her. And she wasn't frightened of him or of what he was doing but of her own lack of insight as to what to do next. How innocent she was, and how desperately she wanted to please him. The return of his lips to hers convinced her not to worry.

Her gown fell of its own accord, her petticoats, too. His palms were hot against her thin chemise. He left her standing for an instant in the pool of her clothing, shivering because the room was cold and she was uncertain. Then his arm was about her waist to steer her to the fine Flanders tick from which the counterpane had been stripped. The linens were chilled and uninviting but Brady's covering warmth more than compensated. The brush of furred calf against her stockinged leg made her realize the only body linen he now wore was his shirt. That knowledge was enticing and intimidating.

"Brady . . ." It escaped her like a whimper and now he was the one to say, "Shh."

His kiss restored her confidence and brought her emotions back to that dizzying pitch of no return. His hand cupped her breast, fondling it gently, teasing it into a wanton peak that betrayed her as unerringly as her quavering moan. The sensations had her restless and shifting. Hands that had been bold before now lay still on the mattress, afraid to touch him lest the spell be broken. Then his mouth lowered to take a tender nipple with a tug and tantalizing flicker and her arms flew up of their own accord to grasp him tight. Wet cloth created a wicked friction, but the touch of his lips upon sensitive flesh after her chemise was skimmed off her was beyond all description. She craved more than just the feel of his hands upon her and tugged at his shirt. It was rucked over his head and given an impatient toss.

Now her fingers were busy, intrigued by the wisps of curling hair that matted his chest and by the hard male nipples that rolled between them to incite another of his throaty rumbles. She longed for time to study him leisurely and thoroughly, for he was a fascinating piece of sinewy work, but the stroke of his hand up the length of her thigh brought her attention to a critical focus.

All along, Kate had responded to every touch, to every insinuation of his desire. If she was going to protest, Brady knew it would be now. As his fingers parted and probed her woman's flesh, he felt her stiffen as if in shock. She made no outcry so he continued the purposeful caress. When her breathing stopped, he feared he had somehow stunned her beyond response, but then her body was possessed so violently by her completing passion, that he himself was startled. The tremors ebbed and she lay panting, disbelieving.

"Oh, Brady," she gasped in awe. "What did you do?"

Her honest wonder ignited his spirit, stimulating his senses to near frenzy. "That's not the half of what I intend to do" was his low promise.

Hungry kisses took her lips, provoking their sated softness into like fervor. He initiated her intimately by touch, reaching the barrier of her virginity with remorse. He hated that he would have to hurt her when she'd come with him so trustingly on this her first journey into sensual pleasures. He let her know what to expect with several plunging motions and she reacted intuitively, clutching him, trying to drag him over her.

Positioned between the straddle of her legs, Brady

kissed her deeply and made one sure thrust. Kate jerked, a startled sound bursting against his lips. Her fingertips entrenched in the ridge of his shoulders. With each move, her tension eased, becoming an encouraging arch of slim hips. Her reception was so giving, so complete, Brady lost himself in a matter of minutes, spilling life rapturously within her.

Time passed dreamily. The absence of warmth woke Kate from her luxurious dozing. Fear that Brady was leaving ended with the sound of flint clicking on steel. She hugged herself and drew knees up, anticipating the heat the fire would soon issue. Slow, licking flames of memory encouraged an inward heat and she was anxious for Brady's return to bed. She lifted up on elbows so she could view him where he crouched all dark and exotically delineated by shadow and flickering light. It was a mistake, for with the advent of heat, there was also brightness.

The sound of her renewed weeping was a surprise. Slowly, Brady straightened up and approached the huddled figure upon the large bed. Remorseful sobs began a peal of regret within him. What had he done, taking her when she was crazy with grief, hurrying her into an action she would have recoiled from at any other time. Her tears were a sign that she already bemoaned what she'd surrendered in her weakness. How she would curse him, and deservedly so, after this night. The full weight of obligation settled uncomfortably in his belly. Why hadn't he heeded his own vow not to trifle with her? Damn his lusts and her unwise willingness.

Brady sat cautiously on the edge of the tester. He

couldn't just glibly say he was sorry and walk out, but what else could he do? Even if he were to do the honorable, what a greater cruelty that would be to her. A marriage to him would prove no salvation.

The fractured laments demanded he do *something*, so he said with unnatural dignity, "Kate, I cannot take back what I've done, but please believe it was not my intention to see you hurt. There is no excuse and I know you cannot forgive me for—"

Kate sniffed abruptly and rolled toward him. "What?" Her expression was perplexed and, for a moment, so was he. But he continued, doggedly. "I have shamed you."

"You've *what*? Brady, what are you talking about?" She sat up then and his breath staggered. Drenched in firelight, her skin held a glow like liquid silk, her hair like spun sunlight. His faculties faltered and he felt his desire rise hot and hard. Then he remembered himself and that she didn't want him for himself.

"The advantage I took was unforgivable," he mumbled, trying to drag his stare away from the glorious swell of her bosom and lissome curve of her legs.

"I don't understand—"

"You were crying—"

"And you thought—"

"Because of what we—"

"No."

Her denial gave him pause. "Then why?" he blurted out.

Shimmering eyes detailed the fringe of drapery

102

that hung about the tester bed, the empty chair of Russian red leather, the black walnut case of drawers. Her splendid breasts rose and fell. "My father's things," she said, and that told him all. He enfolded her easily within his embrace. Beneath the soft contour of her cheek, his heart hastened with relief.

"Then you've no regrets?"

Her gaze sought his. How intense he looked. Then she understood. Her palm fitted to his exquisite face, thumb tracing over the jut of his upper lip. "Regret what just happened? How could I? You have my gratitude, not my remorse." To convince him, she stretched to capture his mouth, relaying her thanks most eloquently.

He nuzzled her, murmuring huskily in her ear, "Does it bother you to remain here?"

Her cheek rubbed against his, her graceful thigh pressed close. "It would bother me more to leave now."

"Whatever you wish," he said agreeably. He lay down with her, bringing up the counterpane to cut the chill. Soon its extra heat was unnecessary and by morning, it was discarded on the floor in a tangle atop the indiscriminate mixing of waistcoat and stockings.

Chapter Six

The scent of bitterly brewed coffee teased Brady into the kitchen. He hadn't been surprised to find Kate gone when he awoke, though he had been disappointed. He'd expected to see her tending the cookfire and, hopefully, his breakfast. Instead, four pair of bright blue eyes regarded him in his stale clothing and dark stubble so calmly he might think it was a daily routine to greet a man emerging from one of their bedrooms. They were obviously aware he'd spent the night and he chafed, not knowing what Kate had told them to explain away his presence. Surely they didn't know he bedded their sister upon their father's covers. Their gazes accepted him without question. Anne's eyes fluttered down coyly and her smile hinted at secret knowledge, most likely some romantic fluff that would pale beside the truth. Incredibly, he felt the beginnings of a blush.

"Good morning, ladies."

The sound of his voice animated them and they all

talked at once. What a lovely din. He couldn't help smiling in response as they overwhelmed him with their greetings and cheerful chatter. A cup of the burnt-smelling brew was shyly offered by the freckled Jeanne, who told him Kate had said he liked it strong. Strong, yes, he mused, sniffing the wafting steam. Mention of Kate brought his gaze about the room to attest to her absence with a growing sense of curious longing. Had their actions so embarrassed her that she feared to face him this morning? The image of Kate cowed by shame and regret provoked a frown. That notion was abruptly quelled by the sound of her light step and low "Good morning."

A display of maudlin sighs or sullen tears wouldn't have surprised him. Those emotions he could expect from an honest woman whose respectability he had stripped from her. But somehow, the unflinching way she met his stare and her impersonal nod of acknowledgment was almost an insult to his male pride. He'd expected to have some effect upon her, to see some lingering trace that what they'd found together had changed her life ineffably. Irrationally, he wanted that to be true. But apparently it was not. He watched in surly humor as she exchanged words with her sisters, mostly to instruct them on their daily obligations. Then her gaze lifted to his and it was as if lightning from last eve's turbulent sky struck him square and forged him to the spot. It was a moment before he could breathe again, such was the consequence of that brief, complex glance. His mind scrambled to understand just what he had seen in those depthless green eyes, but it had been too fleeting, too intense for simple

106

description. She wasn't devastated or angry. Neither was she in raptures. A hard woman to figure, Kate Mallory.

Satisfied that all her duties to her family were performed, Kate regarded Brady a second time. It was an unfathomable stare. She needed to speak to him and such words were not suitable for kitchen or family. "Come walk with me, Captain," she said in her curt, commanding way and preceded him outside.

Despite the evening's violent weather, the day broke clear with its few spots of low-lying fog already beginning to burn off. The gentle northwest wind carrying the land's warmth to the edge of the sea would die down in several hours, and by noon the prevailing southwesterlies would kick up whitecaps in the shallow bay waters, returning the haze to obscure distant landmarks before dying with the sun. Brady tested the breeze, noting its difference. It smelled naught of crisp salt and sea but of balmy meadow, and the contrasts awoke his senses, just as the woman beside him did. From the fields, the scent of flowering buckwheat and mellifluous clover blended with perfumes from apple blossoms, cherry, plum, and pear. The faint fragrance of hidden arbutus and ambrosial azalea with its pungent honey-smell twined with the sweet, cool bite of the nearby pine woods. It was brisk, invigorating, stimulating with the suggestion of spring and life. And so was Kate Mallory.

She was garbed to suit the wild, fresh beauty of the land, simply yet with subtle sensuality. There was nothing provocative in the cut of her linen dress. It was the way it looked upon her. The bodice lacings pulled snug over her chemise, its frilled neckline curving softly against the swell of her breasts. The gentle wind set her skirt in motion, alternately belling about and molding to her long, graceful legs. There was nothing enticing about the plain styling of her hair, which was swept back and secured at the nape by a strand of black ribbon. Rather it was the inherent way the tresses gleamed all golden and warm that tempted a man's fingers to become lost in its glorious weight. Nothing in her proper carriage or sober expression was flirty or remotely promiscuous yet Brady found himself encouraged to the limit of his control. It would have taken little more than a welcoming glance for him to lay her down in the fragrant grass, for he knew what lurked beneath that prim exterior was a woman of fantastic responsive passion. The thought of the cool ground and her warm body stimulated his desires until subconsciously he began searching about for a likely spot upon which to live that fantasy. Then her direct gaze efficiently ended that delusion. He had received less sobering looks from his business partner.

They had reached a neglected grape arbor. Kate absently toyed with one of the corkscrewing vines, then confronted him like an opposing general.

"I cannot allow things to remain unchallenged," she began, and Brady was immediately alert. "I am not one to accept fate or to sit idle. What's happened I cannot change, but I need not be meek about it."

Brady's stomach tensed as if expecting a blow. How naive of him to believe her impassioned words holding him blameless. His warm, romantic thoughts

108

seized up into a defensive denial.

She continued. "I know what I'm to say will not please you and I don't want you to feel responsible. I've given the matter much thought. In fact, I was up most of the night."

His lips curled into a wry smile. Yes, she had been up most of the night but not, he guessed, to plot how she would trap him into marriage. What a remarkable woman she was to entertain such calculations while moaning into his kisses. Remarkable. His smile was a near grimace. Noting it, Kate took a deep breath and went on with determination.

"I just can't wait. Will you see me to Barbados?"

He stared. "What?"

Kate gave him a desperate look. "I need to know my father's fate. I have to make plans for my family."

Brady's lips twitched with helpless relief, and a shaky chuckle issued from them. Good God, the woman was proposing business, not matrimony.

"You needn't laugh, Captain. I assure you, I am quite serious in this." Her tone and expression were equally strict.

"Yes, I'm sure you are." He managed to get his astonishment under control and took a long drink from the mug he'd carried from the house. The coffee was even worse cold, but he needed time to redirect his thinking. "What exactly is it you want of me?"

"A ship."

"Ah." Of course. What else would she be thinking about after rolling in his arms half the night? A truly remarkable woman.

Kate began to pace. This wasn't going well. She faulted her own weaknesses, for it was hard to focus her thoughts when he was standing so near. The more she tried to concentrate on necessity, the more she was prone to fancy. The want to return to the strength of his arms, to the luxury of his lips, to the ecstasy she'd discovered a few short hours ago intruded upon more tangible needs. The mocking look he gave her helped fortify her position. Now was a time for the business at hand, not for tempting him back into a sinful bed.

"I need a ship and a capable man to pilot it. I wouldn't be able to pay for passage until the sale on the Islands, but I'm certain the profit will be adequate."

"Kate," he challenged quietly. "Even if you go to the Islands, there's no guarantee you'll learn the fate of the *Prosper*."

"Perhaps not, but it will guarantee our survival. I mean to take more horses to sell, that way we'll have the means to support ourselves until . . . until we know. I cannot afford to wait. By your own words, it could be months before we hear anything. I can't wait that long just to find out if he's dead or alive. If he's alive, we'll profit doubly. If he's . . . not, we won't sink with him."

He regarded her for a moment, amazed by her fortitude. "Such a risk need not be taken yet."

"No? Easy for you to denounce our risks. What have you to gain or lose? Do you know what happens when small farm families can no longer see to their debts? The children are indentured and the lands fall to waste. I will never, never allow that to happen here. There is no risk too great, no sacrifice I would not make. If you will not help me, I will find someone else—"

Fingertips touched to her mouth to halt the fervent words and the shimmery gathering of moisture in the proud green eyes.

"I never said I wouldn't help you."

Kate trembled. Tears threatened as she grasped his hand, holding it gratefully against her lips. The moment was fragile and quickly passed.

"How soon can we leave?" she wanted to know as she relinquished his hand and the tender sentiments that twisted tight within her breast. Her question was purposefully brusque.

"You haven't even asked if I have another ship."

"Do you?" Her impatience made him grin.

"Aye, a fine schooner, the *Elizabeth*. How many head did you think to take to the Islands?"

"Thirty." This was no time to be cautious.

He nodded and did some silent calculations. "I could fill out the bill in two days. Would that be soon enough to suit you?"

Relief weakened her reply. "Yes, that would be fine. I'll be ready."

A black brow arched. "You plan to go yourself? You could hire a factor to see to the sale. If you don't trust one, I could always—"

"'Tis not a matter of trust. 'Tis a matter of funds," she spelled out grimly. "I will go. I know what the stock is worth and I know how much I have to have."

The thought of several weeks aboard his ship with Kate Mallory in close quarters made him cease to argue. Prudently, he asked, "What of the girls?"

"They'll board with the Simpsons. Extra hands are always in demand during spring planting. They

111

won't mind working for their keep and the price will be right for the Simpsons. Cosgrove can see to the property until I return."

"You seem to have thought of everything. And all of this last night?" he mused with a teasing note she chose to ignore. "Have you no qualms about sailing with the notorious Rogue? You seemed to have little use for me when we met. Have you changed your opinion, then?"

"Not changed," she told him staunchly. "Altered. I do insist that you have naught to do with human cargo while I am aboard."

For a moment he was perplexed, then he realized she referred to slaving. So she really did believe the worst of him. Let her. He could always set her thinking right at a later time and enjoy her deserved embarrassment. "I see." His smile was provocative. "And have you no thought to your reputation?"

Her gaze narrowed. "My virtue is no longer a barrier." It was the closest she'd come to acknowledging their relationship and the fact that she sounded so prickly made him smile all the wider.

"I suppose not," he said agreeably. "Well, I should be off if we're to be in the water by midweek."

Kate accepted his cup with sudden reluctance. She didn't want him to go, not even for the few days they would be apart. That was ridiculous, of course. He had made love to her, not arranged to be her lover and she had no right to hold to him. She had put no conditions on her surrender. Nor would she press any obligations upon him now.

"Where will I meet you?" she asked evenly. Her tone betrayed none of her inner frailty.

"I need to stop in Providence. You can catch up to me there. You can find me on Benefit Street." He gave her the number, and suddenly he looked miles away. The wisful look was gone in an instant and he regarded her with a slight smile. "I've left my coat at the house."

She nodded, thoughts flying back to the way he'd held her in the kitchen. Her cheeks felt warm in the bright spring sunshine. Wordlessly, she started back.

"Are those the horses you mean to sell?"

The questioning tone made her follow his gaze and she laughed. "That is hardly draught stock, Captain. Stick to your ships. Those are Narragansett Pacers." The pride in her reply made him assess the small creatures with their broad backs and short legs. "They are bred to suit the likes of Mr. Blayne as luxury transportation. Riding upon them is likened to sitting in an extremely comfortable rocking chair. I convinced Father to invest in them."

"Seems profitable," he owned. "There's no shortage of wealthy gentry here." He regarded her with growing admiration. She was clever as well as beautiful. He wondered what Nathan Mallory was like.

Kate went to fetch his coat while the boy Timmy brought round his horse. Brady looked about the neat farm and was proud of Kate and her determined family. *A man could do worse* came an unbidden thought. Then she was before him and he pursued that image no farther.

"I'll see you in a few days," he said with a sudden constrictive quiet.

"Yes," she answered in an equal hush. Her lips

parted slightly and her breath drew in slow. Then Bertrice came scooting about the side of the house, wailing balefully with her newly mended calico pulled up to reveal torn stockings and bloodied knees. Kate knelt instinctively to offer a haven within her arms then, when the child quieted, saw to the scrapes and gashes. By the time she looked up, the yard was empty.

Kate hadn't lingered in Providence since the death of her mother. Though years had passed, the pain of loss remained to put her in a melancholy mood as they rumbled across the bridge on Weybosset Neck to the east bank where shops and warehouses of the shipping business stretched to the wharves. The ride in the ancient buggy with Timmy at the reins was far from comfortable. He was inexperienced with the leads but seemed to have no trouble in locating every bump and rut along the way. Behind them, Cosgrove tended the string of horses and the sight their caravan made had many a merchant and shopgirl pausing to admire the animals and the young woman.

Kate's restlessness had a definite focus, and much of her mood was due to her unwillingness to recognize that it was her eagerness to see Brady Rogan that made her so impatient. It had been two days ago that he rode from her yard, but she'd been able to think of nothing else save reuniting with him here. Arrangements for the girls, instructions to Fitch and Sarah, her hurried packing, and even the teary farewells had occupied only a small corner of her mind. The rest was full of the way Brady Rogan looked with his dark hair ruffled by the breeze. Silly, she knew, but her heart enjoyed the lightness of that folly. That and the wondering if he would have kissed her had Bertrice not interrupted. She wet her lips as if she could taste it even now.

They had no difficulty in locating the *Elizabeth*. She was a sleek vessel turned out in sienna and yellow-ochre with two masts to boast fore-and-aft sails. The sight of her nodding gently on the harbor current only increased Kate's unease. Rather curtly, she ordered Cosgrove to see the horses safely boarded and was secure that he would not leave until assured of their welfare during the journey down the coast. Then she sent Timmy on to Benefit Street.

Benefit was designed as a back street to relieve the congestion on Towne, the busiest street in Providence, where houses crowded together, hugging the curb on either side of the street. Businesses conducted from their ground floors prospered from the big merchant sailing ships anchored at piers beyond the west side of the street. In contrast, Benefit was newer, cleaner, and without the constant clamor. Orderly homes sprang from close to the street with gardens behind to terrace the hillside. She bade Timmy to let her off at the number she'd been given. The neat, shingle-clad house was not the sort of place in which she'd expect to find the likes of Brady Rogan. It looked comfortably domestic. With a squaring of her shoulders, she advanced to the door and let the knocker fall. When it opened, she stood for several long, awkward seconds staring impolitely.

"I'm sorry," Kate mumbled finally. "I must have the wrong number." She began to retreat a step when the lovely woman within spoke to stop her.

"Oh, no. That is if you are Miss Mallory. I'm Elizabeth. Please, won't you come in. Brady told me to expect you. He and Jamie should be back directly. Might I offer you some tea while we wait? I hope you won't take offense, but it is my favorite beverage and I dearly love a cup in the afternoons. Brady sees I have a supply and I don't question where he comes by it. Please have a seat."

Kate followed, listening to Elizabeth's cheerful ramblings and obediently settled into the puffy, feather-filled cushion of an engulfing Queen Anne easy chair. She was grateful for the seat, for her knees were most unsteady. Through round, dazed eyes, she watched Elizabeth pour from the service set upon a large covered tea board. Her thoughts were moving slowly, perhaps because she didn't wish to believe what they would tell her. This house, this lovely woman waiting for Brady to come home—to her hearth . . . The growing pain in her breast made breathing difficult. Why would Brady arrange to have her meet him in the home of his mistress? Or worse, a fiancée.

The beautiful Elizabeth looked to be no mistress, though Kate could hardly claim such knowledge of that group of women. She was petite and pretty, with fine chestnut-colored hair and warm hazel eyes. Her stylish taffeta gown was split in front and drawn up to form panniers on either side and to display an embroidered petticoat beneath. Kate's numbed mind took in the delicate stitches in appreciation. It was not the way a woman of easy morals went garbed. Nor were her polished manners suspect. She was obviously a lady, and Kate's mood sank deeper into gloom. She forced a stiff smile and accepted her tea. The fragile cup clattered briefly in its saucer before she set it on the small table beside her. A worse thought struck her. What had Brady told this woman of their relationship? Apparently nothing, for there was no hostility in the other's gaze. There was plenty mounting within Kate, however.

How dare he, Kate seethed. How dare he expect her to sit and make polite conversation with . . . this woman, for she knew not how else to describe her. Spite and jealousy rippled up her spine. It was a cold, unfamiliar feeling, one she had no true right to claim. Brady hadn't given her the right. He hadn't given her anything beyond that night of unforgettable passion and his word that he would help her. What did he give to this woman? Her stare narrowed viciously as numerous things occurred to her. What indeed besides contraband tea.

I will get through this, she told herself as she sipped the fragrant tea. Brady Rogan is a means to an end, not the end in itself. What would she want with a privateer, a restless rogue who would never be content with the existence she desired? She couldn't imagine him tied to a farm. Nor could she imagine him in this dainty parlor with its stenciled floor and patterned curtains. She blinked back the burn welling in her eyes. No, she couldn't see him here, either. This woman was a passing affection, a temporary port in Providence. What then did that make her? The sting intensified and she blinked more rapidly. I will get to Barbados, then I will tell the arrogant Captain Rogan exactly what I think of him, she decided. But no, she couldn't be that truthful with him. She would tell him only part of it—the bitter anger that made her lips clamp white and her insides tense . . . She was drawn from her bitter musings when she heard the front door to Benefit Street open.

"Mama, that damned *Gaspee* is back in the harbor on a new tour."

Elizabeth came up from her comfortable chair, pulling a stern expression. "Jamie, I'll not allow such language in this house. You are an eight-year-old boy, not one of those profane seamasters you're so fond of."

The boy tucked his head, but his lower lip showed a betraying pout, not at the censure but in having his tale interrupted. He stared at the visitor and his sullenness gave way to curiosity.

Kate returned the stare with a terrible sense of knowledge. She didn't have to look up to Brady when he walked into the room to see the boy was a smaller version of the man. The unruly black hair, the brilliant blue eyes, even the trace of a swagger in his pose. There could be no mistaking it. The comely Elizabeth was more than a casual harbor.

"Good morrow, Kate." The caressing voice drew her gaze to his face where it remained in miserable fascination. "Your horses are aboard and I'm sure you're anxious to be on your way." He turned to the petite woman, and Kate could not make herself look away. She didn't want to witness the sudden gentling of his darkly handsome features or the softening timbre in his tone. "Are you certain you have everything you need until I return? I should only be away a few weeks lest there be some unforeseen delay."

An unforeseen delay. Kate wondered in an agony of envy if that was how he termed his stay in Kingstown.

A small hand rested familiarly upon his shoulder. "Nay, I've everything I need." That truth cut straight to Kate's heart.

"I'll be going then." Reluctance was plain in his voice, and Kate felt she intruded but could see no way to tactfully retreat to leave them alone with their good-byes. Her hands clenched in her skirt as she waited for Brady to kiss her. He only touched a forefinger to her chin. The intimacy in that simple gesture was shattering. "I'll get my coat."

Kate managed to gain her feet as Brady strode into the hall with the boy on his heels. A red-haired maid bustled into the room to gather the teacups and tendered a dipping curtsy.

"Be there anything else, Mistress Rogan?"

Kate never heard Elizabeth's reply. Her mind swirled with a sickening clarity. My God, she was his wife.

Chapter Seven

Brady imagined many ways to embrace Kate on their journey to Barbados, some of them sheer inspiration but never, never had he dreamed the only way he'd get to hold her was over a bucket. In all his days at sea, he'd yet to see her equal. From the moment she'd come board, Kate proved to be a miserable sailor. He'd even given her his cabin in hopes that they'd be sharing it that first evening out, but she'd crawled into the bunk and there she'd remained. Never had he seen such all-consuming bouts of *mal de mer*. He himself had taken to the water as a bird to the air. Kate loathed it. Between her episodes of illness, she was in a panic, certain she was going to drown. He'd sat with her, comforted her, tried to convince her the fear was groundless. She would have none of it, nor of him. His presence seemed to increase her discomfort so he tactfully withdrew, sure her pride was sorely injured in having him see her in such a pathetic state.

He looked out over the glassy waters from the quarterdeck and drew a deep breath to let the tangy air revitalize him. He paid only scant heed to the crew bustling about him. He was confident in their knowledge of their duties. That was the benefit of sailing with a seasoned crew. He'd been proud of his partnership in the *Prosper* but he loved the *Elizabeth*. She was his first ship and he, her only master. One day he would own many such ships, perhaps even to rival those of the Browns of Providence and the Malbones of Newport. Then he could turn his back to the past and live for himself, alone.

He smiled grimly when he thought of Kate primly calling him a slaver. It wasn't true, at least not really. The first time he'd crewed out had been for Aaron Lopez, the forerunner of Newport's slave merchants. Never would he forget that first and only run to the Gold Coast of Africa to take on the precious native cargo. He'd earned twenty-five pounds for that seven-week voyage. It hadn't been enough to erase the shrieks and smells of captive suffering. No amount would be enough. There was fabulous profit to be made. Lopez, Champlin, and Potter had proven that. Even ships' captains made out handsomely with their coast commissions and extra remunerations. But the memory of the shackles, of the grates, of the nets thrown around the ship's sides to catch those who would throw themselves overboard ate through him like the dreaded teredo shipworm. He'd vowed upon collecting that first stained pay that never again would he be a part of that particular profit venture.

Smuggling, however, was a different matter. He viewed his successes with pride, even with a degree of patriotism. He'd learned well, from a master. Simeon Potter was marked for his rascality and bravado along with his brother-in-law, Mark Anthony DeWolf. They saw themselves as a business operation, not merely as romantic buccaneers. From them, he learned how to get around the constrictive Molasses Act, how to falsify customs' papers, how to bribe officials. The deceit was an accepted and integral part of doing business. He made a comfortable living from the triangular trade and like most New Englanders was too accustomed to illicit trafficking to be hindered by legal or moral considerations. He'd laughed when the Colonies were referred to by the British as a confederacy of smugglers and smirked at claims by other colonies that Rhode Island harbored a den of pirates who smuggled without excuse and interfered with fair trade. Only Kate's haughty censure of his actions made him question his trade. Question, not actively seek to change. She would understand. She knew about obligations.

Thinking of Kate made him impatient with his stay above deck. He had seen his steward emerge from below with her untouched tray. There had to be some way to make her more of an agreeable companion. He could sympathize with a weak stomach but he refused to let it get the best of his plans. And he had plans.

Kate acknowledged the tap upon the door with a

feeble moan. If it was that pop-eyed little man bearing another tray of indigestibles, she swore she would do him bodily harm—had she the strength, which she didn't. A masculine weight settled beside her on the bunk which could only mean one person.

"Go away," she protested.

Unmindful of the request, his hand stroked gently through the tangle of dull gold curls. "Is this my fearless Kate?" he chided kindly. "I thought it would take more than a drop of water to quell your spirit."

She wasn't so far gone that she didn't experience the desired spark of irritation. She pushed ineffectively at his hand. "I knew you to be a cruel man, Brady Rogan," she muttered. "Leave me be." She could imagine his smile. She could imagine how she looked to him and cringed beneath the covers.

"I've an idea of how to cure you," he began cheerfully, like an inquisitor who enjoyed his grisly duty. "You need a bit of air to bring back your color and your appetite."

The suggestion of food wrought a sound of misery. "Go away," she keened.

But he was tugging back the damp sheets in defiance of her weak clutching. "Come on now. Up with you."

"Brady, no. I can't move, let alone stand. Let me die in peace."

He chuckled at her dramatics and hoisted her up all limp and disheveled. Her expression puckered with objection but he wouldn't let her fall back upon the bed. A wetted towel pressed to her forehead and cheeks did revive her somewhat. She glowered at her liberator.

"You'll feel more the thing when you get off this bed of self-indulgence," he guaranteed with disgusting energy.

She glared then sighed, too weary to battle him if he wanted to drag her about on the pretext of restoring her health. She knew she was beyond the pale. "I look a sight," she grumbled.

He examined the truth of that. Yes, quite a sight. Clad in a wispy chemise and lightweight petticoat molded close with perspiration, it was a sight he thoroughly enjoyed. And hoped to enjoy even better. His desires gave a lusty rumbling. More determined than ever that she recover herself, and soon, Brady pulled her to her feet. She wobbled, willing to let him support her. "There now, don't you feel better?"

Her forehead dropped against his chest with a thump. She made a pitiful noise.

"A little fresh air, a few turns about the deck, and you'll be yourself again," he promised as he wrapped her cloak about her sagging shoulders.

"The deck?" Her head came up with a jerk. Her eyes were huge. "You're taking me on deck?"

Thinking she was taken with a fit of modesty, he smiled and assured her, "You look fine, Kate, better than most who've been laid under the weather."

She began to pull away. It wasn't the struggle of someone feeble or sick. She was strong, damned strong, and determined to escape his grasp. "No, I won't. I won't go up there."

"Kate—?"

Then he saw her fear. Her eyes were wild with it,

her chest heaving with the effort of it. He immediately gentled his tactics but he didn't loosen his anchoring grip on her arms.

"Kate, don't be afraid. I'll be with you. There's nothing to fear. Let me show you how safe it is. Once you see, you'll rest easier. Trust me."

Kate laughed at that, the sound trickling out a bit crazily. Trust him, indeed. She closed her eyes and tried to summon a grain of courage. She trembled as he drew the cloak about her. It fit like a shroud. But he was right. If she faced it square, perhaps she would feel better; not secure, just better. And the fetid air in the cabin only encouraged her queasiness.

"All right." It was said faintly, with no great conviction.

From the moment Kate stepped onto the windswept quarterdeck she was living a nightmare. The smell of the sea, the pull of the breeze at the edges of her cloak inspired a suffocating terror. She burrowed against Brady's chest, hands clutching.

"Brady, please." It was a moan of sheer anguish. "Please take me below."

He held to her quaking figure, alarmed by the fervor of her plea. How she could conceive any danger bewildered him completely. But the fear was real, at least to her. He could feel it shaking through her and so he wouldn't make light of it. His arms tightened, letting her know of his strength and his ability to see her from any harm.

"What a glorious day," he said with enthusiasm. "There's a sense of freedom to be found at sea. This is what it must feel like to fly." He drew a deep breath,

126

feeling her ride with it against his chest. It wasn't an unpleasant sensation. "I've been at sea for ten years and each day still breaks clean and new." She was listening. She had quieted in his arms, though still rigid with apprehension. Her fingers seemed fused to the front of his coat.

"I designed the *Elizabeth*. Did you know that? Every time I'm out on her, I feel like a proud parent." Kate stiffened and he went on, hoping to tease her interest away from her own crowding fears. "She's a fast little lady. I had her fitted with a fore-and-aft stern and bow sprit sails. She's more weatherly than the square-riggers, can come about without losing way and it takes fewer men to handle her sails." She could also outmaneuver and outrun any British customs ship, but he didn't mention that. He had designed her for illegal trading. "See how proudly she plumps her canvas."

Kate's head lifted slightly. She peered over the rolled lapel of his coat to follow his gaze upward. It was, indeed, a grand sight. Brady's arm slipped down from her shoulders to curl about her waist, holding her snug to him yet giving her space to test her independence.

"Would you like to tour her?" His pride was infectious, and though she didn't answer, neither did she protest when he began to walk. "Watch your step," he cautioned as they moved about the shipboard ropes that looked like a careless tangling of seaweed strewn upon the deck. He told her the name and use of each cordage—stays, shrouds, halliards, lifts, braces—and her gaze was guided about by his gestures as he explained the function of the riggings. The topic didn't fascinate her but the way he spoke it did, with so much passion, so much possessive pride. He kept her attention focused upward, away from the endless spread of water, and was rewarded by a loosening of her posture as her head craned back and her thoughts were lost in the flap of ropes and sails and followed the fearless scurrying of the crew along the weblike ratlines. Though the men wore no uniform, they were dressed similarly in wide-brimmed hats or knit caps from under which wrapped queues trailed, their black neckerchiefs tied about neck or forehead and flared trousers fluttering in the wind. A chanteyman among the forecastle hands set up a bold and somewhat bawdy work song to which the sailors joined in on the chorus. Brady grinned, realizing the tune was meant to impress the lady, not to aid in the rhythm of pulls, and she was intrigued by the colorful picture they presented.

"The canvas dress supplies our power," he told her easily, but his attention was centered not on the crack of sails but upon the more feminine swells and curves close to the spread of his hand. "We crowd as much into the sky as possible to gain the greatest speed. For an extra push, we run up special square sails along the bowsprit rigging and studding sails."

An unexpected pitch of the deck beneath them had Kate reattached to him with a cry of alarm. The accompanying mist of cool spray increased her fright to a runaway panic. Her voice was a low moaning.

"Brady, Brady, don't let me drown. Dear God,

don't let me be swept over."

Her terror acted strangely upon him. His embrace was fierce, his words almost angry. "I've got you, Kate. Hold to me. You're as safe here as you would be in church. I swear you've nothing to fear."

"I want to go below."

This time, he complied with her strangled request, and, only when the cabin door was closed behind them did her fitful trembling ease. She collapsed upon the cabin's chair and let its curving arms support her, then gratefully took the mug of punch Brady provided. The concoction of spices and hot water liberally laced with rum slid deceivingly down her throat to collide with her empty stomach. For a moment, she feared it would come up just as rapidly, and her lips pressed tight. Then it settled and soothed with its potent balm of spirits.

Brady was kneeling before her, his expression intense and worried. She looked away, chagrined.

"What a whimpling you must think me."

Her disparaging tone made him smile. Its brittle cut assured him that nothing was terribly wrong with her. She'd displayed fear before him and now was shamed by it. What pride she had. His palm fit gently to her pale cheek, turning her head forward to face him. His words were a caress, filled with the admiration he felt.

"You need not tote your courage before me, Kate. I've seen the stuff of which you're made and can find no fault with it. 'Tis this fear you hold I cannot understand. You are safe. I would not have taken you above, otherwise. We are in no peril. This is not the

129

Prosper. How can I prove that and set your mind at ease?"

Her head tipped, coming away from his hand. "You cannot, Captain. My fears are my own and they have naught to do with you or this ship. If you please, I would like to wash and dress. The air did make me stronger and I thank you for it." She waited in stony expectation for him to take his leave.

His gaze searched hers for another long moment, finding no clue there. Finally, he stood. "If you have need of me, call." That was hopefully offered.

Her nod was dismissing, giving him no alternative but to go.

Alone in the cabin, Kate rose to unsteady legs and stripped off her well-worn linens. Bathing as best she could from the small washstand, she wished for the luxury of soaping her hair. She had to settle for a vigorous brushing to restore its highlights then twined it into a heavy braid. With fresh under-pinnings against her skin and a simple gown of ginger-colored muslin to warm her wan complexion, she felt better, indeed, and was even anticipating the arrival of the steward and the tray he bore. Her smile of welcome caught up in a likening to a grimace when she saw who tendered her meal.

"Might I sup with you this eve?" Already he was arranging their plates upon the single table. Kate frowned. With her seasickness at an ebb, other miseries took precedence. Brady Rogan was the last person with whom she wanted to share a private meal.

"Is this a request or a command, Captain?"

His blue eyes came up, bemused, then he grinned. "Ah, you are feeling more yourself. A plate of lobscourse will serve you well."

"How astute of you to divine exactly what I need." The prickly jibe was softened by the grace with which she took the seat he proffered. He continued to smile behind her back as his gaze detailed the slender throat left bare by her braid. She twisted, scowling up at him. "What is it?"

He shook his head, smile never faltering, and took to the edge of the bunk to serve as a seat. Her glower did not move him as he readily applied himself to the meal. She examined it more cautiously.

"What is this?"

"Dried potato slices and salt beef hashed together with dried peas and beans and . . ." The tightening of her features encouraged him to break off the recitation of ingredients. "'Twill stick to you and doesn't taste half bad." He nudged her fork. "Try a bite."

Her stomach was rumbling with hunger instead of distress so she sampled a morsel and was reluctant to admit, "'Twill do. I suppose you prepared it."

The arch sentiment made him laugh. "No. My days in the galley are over." He poured them both a cup of grog and watched with pleasure as she cleaned her plate. The steward, Bishop, arrived to haul away the dishes but Brady remained, apparently content to observe her in her growing discomfort.

"Have you nothing to do on deck, Captain?"

"No," he replied without time for thought.

"Couldn't you find something?"

A sultry smile played about his lips. Kate was very aware of him now, of the sleek power of his long limbs, of the confidence in his lingering stare, of the way he affected her. He was dressed like a privateer in formally styled officers' wear, his dark-blue coat with turned-back cuffs and lapels of red heavy with gold braiding. His frilled shirt gleamed white against the open vee of tanned chest it exposed, offering a titillating glimpse of dark, curling hair. Breeches of dark blue encased the negligent spread of his thighs ending at white stockings and buckled shoes. He was oozing with male sensuality and, damn, it made her want him. Her body was alive with the feel of him, the desire for him, and she hated that weakness and cursed him for being such a temptation. Why, why did the one man who fired her blood with longing have to belong to another?

"You'd better go, Captain," she stated with more conviction than she felt. She knew her own tendency to yield to him and still smarted from the proof of his profligacy. It was not safe to be alone with him.

"This is my cabin," he announced calmly, challenging her to make the first move.

"If you will not go, I shall remove myself." She began to stand. His chuckle stiffened her spine into a rigid staff.

"To where, Miss Mallory?"

"I will gladly bed with the horses." *Before I would bed with you,* the flash of her eyes finished for her.

"As you wish." He retained his seat and she stared in dismay. Did he actually mean to see her sleeping in the hold? Becoming color rose hot to stain her cheeks.

Then he stood to exact a mocking bow and withdrew with his cocky swagger to leave her fuming.

Darkness was complete when Kate's eyes came open to groggily probe the night. She had fallen deeply and instantly asleep and now it clung to her like heavy drink, making it difficult to shake off its traces to discover what had awakened her. Then she heard it, the wind howling in the cordage, and a similar wail escaped her. She jerked upright and nearly spilled to the floor as the ship listed sharply.

"Dear God," she managed to moan as stark images shuddered through her mind. She clutched for anything solid in the suddenly pitching world and, miraculously, he was there. "Brady, hold me."

Brady sat on the edge of the bunk. All the carefully phrased reasons he'd planned to explain away his presence went untested. She didn't question it. She was too grateful for it. He'd watched the squall brew up, rolling in low and ugly to swallow the horizon. He'd been able to think of nothing but Kate alone and frightened and, instinctively, had gone below to see if he was needed. Upon finding her resting easy, he'd become intrigued with the study of her quiet features and had settled into his desk chair to wait out the worst of the storm and to plot how he would weather her outrage should she wake to find him keeping watch. And now she was pressed upon him, her heart like frantic thunder through the thin covering of her chemise beating a panicked tempo against his chest. With one hand he anchored her back. The other plied the loose spill of her hair.

"Rest easy, Kate. I'm here. It's just a bit of a blow, 'tis all. I've ridden out worse. I'll stay if you wish it."

Her fingers clenched in his dark hair and in the frill of his uncovered shirt. "Don't go." It was a whisper.

The movement of the ship made them sway together and Kate's agitation doubled. Knowing it would be less pronounced when reclined, Brady urged her back onto the covers, following her down when she refused to release him. After a moment of awkward shifting, they lay comfortably side by side, Kate nestled in the curl of his arms, her cheek upon the rise of his chest. The buffet of wind and surge of the waves resounded in the darkness. Her voice was so frail in comparison.

"Promise you'll stay until it's done."

"I will."

"Promise the sea won't take us."

"It won't."

She seemed to weigh the authority of his word and was apparently satisfied, for some of the stiffness left her. Her light, hurried breath was warm upon the opening his shirt bared.

"I can't let it take me, too." That was said more strongly, with a ring of defiance.

"You don't know that your father perished at sea." He had wanted to reassure her, but her next claim stunned him.

"But my mother did. I saw it take her."

The horror of those softly said words held him in a taut silence, then he prompted gently, "I don't understand. Your mother was lost at sea."

Her head moved jerkily. "No, it took her. It rose up and took her. A huge wall of it. It came up out of nowhere and carried her away." Her breath was coming quicker, like the gathering of that surge.

"My God, Kate, what are you saying?"

Slowly, haltingly, she replayed the torture of that instant when mother and daughter had rushed along the wharf, anxious to escape the torrential rain. The sound of it was like nothing Kate had heard before or since. She had turned and screamed. The force of the hurricane that swept up the seaboard from the Caribbean had swelled the tide and stirred the ocean into mountainous waves. One of those breakers crashed against the shore in an enormous wall of water, tearing sailing ships of all sizes from their moorings, driving them ashore and smashing them together. An entire waterfront block of houses was swept away. And with it went Johanna Mallory. She had been holding fast to Kate's hand. And then she was gone. Kate's skirts had entangled about a mooring post and for hours she clung with arms trembling with fatigue to keep from being pulled out to sea.

Brady lay silent, compassion crowding his throat with an aching tightness. What an ordeal she'd endured. How righteous were her fears. And yet she'd come aboard the *Elizabeth* knowing she'd be confronting the stuff of her nightmares. Still, she had come.

Her hand kneaded his shirt linen restlessly. Her voice was low, raw. "Tell me we shall make Barbados

135

and I will believe you."

The unqualified trust made his own words tremble. "I promise you upon my very life that no harm will come to you upon this ship."

Kate was thoughtful, then mused with an unexpected touch of cynicism, "A rogue's promise?" Her body settled against the long line of his and she sighed. "'Twill do."

The twists of her pliant form as she snuggled close into his side provoked Brady's into an unbidden response. The way this woman worked upon him was nothing short of mystifying, lulling him with her miseries, fortifying him with her strength, taunting him with the unconscious seduction of her every move. He had never been at such odds with himself, wanting both to cradle her to protect her from hurt and to ravage her again and again with unbridled passion. Desires warred with gallantry over the lush battlefield of Kate Mallory.

Comforted and consoled, Kate relaxed in Brady's arms, releasing her tensions to the gentle pull of exhaustion. The continuous stroke of his hand over the ripples of her hair was calming, quieting, coaxing her to let go. Her eyes closed as she felt his lips brush her crown, once, then again. Though her mind was too weary to react to that subtle suggestion, her body responded quite naturally, arching, rubbing against him. He felt so good, so solid, so strong, a bastion against all of her fears—save one. That apprehension rose with a guarded yearning as Brady's mouth showed a want to stray downward, toward her own.

Kate tucked her head into his shoulder, the gesture slight but effective, denying that she wished his offer of comfort to extend further. It wasn't what she wished at all, but she couldn't afford to weaken. He'd promised she'd come to no harm—a rogue's promise. Only she could protect her heart.

Sensing her rejection, Brady took a measured breath to expel the tension that had gathered in his loins. It was no easy feat. The woman in his arms was a mighty temptation. That quality of trust in her voice held him in check, that and her noble spirit. He would not injure either for the world. Resolved to a martyred night of unmet frustrations, he closed his eyes and prayed for a merciful sleep.

Chapter Eight

Though he'd been on deck for several hours to watch the mounting palette of the dawn's pastels, the sun didn't truly seem to rise for Brady until Kate appeared on the quarterdeck. In the ginger-colored gown, her hair caught back in a simple ribbon to tangle freely about her shoulders, she looked like something bright and precious, indeed. She paused at the doorway, measuring the distance between its safety and the open stretch of deck that led to where Brady stood near the rail.

His first impulse was to go to her immediately, but Brady forced himself to remain where he was to watch the daily battle of will Kate had struggled with each morning since waking in his arms. And on this morning, as on the others, her courage proved the stronger and she came to him, moving slowly, cautiously but without hesitation.

"Good morning, Captain," she called, her voice warm with self-congratulations.

"A fine one, Miss Mallory."

The formal style had Kate regarding him in question. He needed it to remind him of the distance she imposed between them. All overtures from him that verged on the personal, she'd countered with a cool rebuff. The contradiction had him chafing, for while her demeanor maintained a reserve, her body cried out for the chance to succumb. The slightest touch from him, intentioned or not, and she turned all liquid and eager. Instead of recognizing her desires, her resistance redoubled to the point of mere civility. Sleeping in the officers' quarters was not what he'd had in mind for this trip and knowing that she stretched out each night upon his bunk, that she would most likely give in with aggressive persuasion, kept him restless in his own frustrations. He'd never seen a woman run with such rips and ebbs. More disconcerting was the increase in his determination with every small defeat. He'd known only one failure in his dealings with the fair sex. That had been nearly crippling. This would be unacceptable. After all, by her own words, her virtue was no longer a barrier. What, then, had become one?

Brady gestured out over the water. "Barbados."

Kate squinted against the glare to get her first look at the distant pearl of the Lesser Antilles. A sense of excitement and dread rose a rash of gooseflesh along her arms.

"You've seen to your promise well, Captain."

She remained beside him on the elevated deck as the *Elizabeth* approached the coral-ringed island. Brady's arm became a casual bolster about her waist.

She didn't object. He could feel her trembling and knew it had naught to do with fear. It was the unknowns that lay ahead. The want to shield her, to surround her with his embrace, to drown her anxieties with the wealth of his passions—all were a threat to his composure. His arm tightened about her slender middle as his thoughts carried them below to the privacy of the cabin where he would make love to her until she cried out her pleasure. He imagined the spread of her golden hair, the part of her lips, the long, shapely legs opening for him.

Kate gave a gasp of alarm as the erstwhile support of his arm became a circle of iron, turning her flush against him. The direction of his thinking was vividly outlined between them, pressing bold against her uncorsetted belly. Her gaze flew up in startlement only to be consumed by the hot blue fire of his eyes. That stare was naked of pretense and blatantly hungry. A wayward thrill coursed through her, and her arms trembled in their desire to twine about his neck.

"Kate." His voice was thick with intention.

He read of her longing in the uplifted green eyes, felt her quiver with like passions. Then that molten willingness turned cold and hard. She stiffened against him. Palms levered to push him away.

"Captain, you forget yourself."

Disappointment and confusion made his reply harsh as he stepped back. "'Twould seem you forget many things, my conveniently coy miss."

That he would dare accuse her of any wrongdoing arrested her. She stared at him, astonished. Then a blaze kindled in her eyes. There could be no mistaking her fury.

Kate's anger nonplussed him. He could fathom a modest indignation or maidenly objection, but this outright rage had him baffled. What reason did she have for such a fiery bit of temper?

The pain of jealousy and sting of self-reproach made her behold him with loathing. How could he look so innocent, so puzzled by her refusal to indulge him in willing adultery? That she had been willing, even for an instant, intensified her bitter mood. She would be no frail pawn to his lusts.

"At least my lapse of memory does not include the existence of a wife," she spat at him. She'd wanted to strike him and now the change of his expression was as abrupt as if she had.

"A what?"

"You may be able to put the fair Elizabeth from mind, but I cannot overlook the fact that she shares your son and even now sails with us in name. You are despicable, the lowest of creatures, the . . ." Her tirade broke off to a whisper as a chill stole over his features the like of which seized her with misgivings. Had she been wrong?

Brady spoke slowly, each word bitten off with brittle clarity, the way one would impart a piece of unwelcome, unpleasant information. "Elizabeth's name is indeed Rogan but 'tis my brother who had the honor of bestowing both title and seed. The name of this vessel is my only claim to her. Please excuse me, Miss Mallory. I have things to attend."

Kate watched him stride away, his displeasure

142

evident in the absence of his usual strut. Her thoughts reeled. Not his wife. What then explained away the tender look he held for her? What was the meaning of his cold reaction? The moment of brief elation was gone. He might not be wed to her, but neither was he free. Brady was in love with Elizabeth Rogan, his brother's wife.

Barbados lacked any deep water ports. The *Elizabeth* put down anchor in the glassy waters. Small boats would ferry cargo and crew ashore. Bishop assured her that the transfer of the horses would be no problem as he came to escort Kate to her boat. He toted her baggage, chatting about arrangements to see her to the island's best hotel while the stock was penned on the wharf for inspection of hopeful buyers.

As she was handed into the tippy skiff, only her confusion over the captain of the *Elizabeth* kept her apprehension at bay. Watching him stride about calling orders held her fear of the rolling surf in poor comparison. He had spared her one brief glance, and its indifference was wounding. As the boat prepared to cast off, she caught Bishop's arm rather frantically.

"Will Captain Rogan be coming ashore?"

"When he be finished here, miss. He asked me to tell you he be meeting up with you at the hotel when he has news of the *Prosper* and that you're to await him there."

Await him there. The imperious command rankled only a vague irritation. She eyed him moodily, then the boat settled into the water and she lost him in her thoughts as she clung anxiously to its side. Soon the *Elizabeth* and her captain were left behind.

Never had Kate experienced such heat. It was like a physical force, weighing on each breath and creating a continual sheen of moisture to dampen her hair and clothing. A cooling rinse of water and a change into a lighter gown gave a brief respite. She thought to open the slatted shutters to encourage a breeze but the haze of heat that filtered in made her reverse the action. The shadowy stillness was more comfortable and better suited to her mood.

She sampled a bowl of island fruit to occupy her fidgety hands rather than from the demands of appetite. Fingers damp from pulp and peel, she wiped them nervously upon her skirt before responding to the knock on the door. She regarded Brady for a long second, trying to read his news in the set of his features. They were carefully impassive as he stood in the hall.

"Might I come in, Kate?"

She stepped back. Her mouth was dry. Her sticky palms grew wet as they twisted anxiously in the crisp linen of her gown. "Have you word of the *Prosper*?" The words echoed in her heart.

Brady moved past her. He still wore the braided coat and now carried a tricorn in his hands, the way it was worried between them the only sign of his unease. He faced her somberly but made no attempt to draw near. His blue eyes were guarded, impersonal.

144

"Parts of her washed up along the Virginias. There's no telling where she actually went down. No survivors have been found. I'm sorry."

Kate waited for the grief to come. There was only numbness. But then, she had known that was what he was going to tell her. She had known her father was dead. Her hands seemed frozen in the folds of her skirt. She drew a slow breath as if to test for evidence of pain within her breast. It rose and fell unrestricted. If only this disembodied calm would last.

"If there's anything I can do . . ." he was saying. The offer was very civil. Very uninvolved.

"Thank you, Captain, there is." Kate matched him for detachment. "My father is lost to me, but I have others to think of. How can I get in touch with prospective buyers?"

For a moment, Brady, too, was lost. It had been so hard to come to her when the air was still clouded betweeen them. He'd wanted the chance to apologize for his brusque actions, for blaming her for thinking the obvious then letting her feel the backlash of his frustrations. He'd hurt her then, and now he was going to deepen that pain. He had steeled himself to endure her sorrow but—but she was talking of horses and profit. She looked so composed, so emotionlessly resigned. He was off balance. Gruffly, he told her, "I can determine which of the planters are willing to pay the most. We can meet with them over dinner. I will come for you at four. The dinner hour is early in the Islands."

"I would be most grateful. Thank you for your trouble."

"No trouble," he answered automatically, but that wasn't true. Kate Mallory had become nothing but trouble and he knew not how to free himself of it. Nor was he sure he wanted to.

Kate let him out then stood at the closed door for several long minutes. Slowly, she sank to her knees and wept into hands that smelled pungently of citrus.

Three men met with them for dinner, accompanied by their wives. White women were a rarity in the Islands, Kate was to discover, and the ladies were hungry to hear of anything to do with civilization, even of her isolated country routine. They pried details from her while the men sat back over their rum drinks to talk shipping and sugar with Brady. It was all very comfortable and the company amiable, but Kate was anxious to get to business. She could feel Brady's gaze from across the table, studying, intense, questioning, and uneasily, she wondered why. The misunderstanding over Elizabeth had built a barrier between them. He was very close with his thoughts. She couldn't guess if he was still angry with her or merely annoyed by her spiteful outburst. Whichever, he had separated himself from her, withdrawing his compassion and even, it seemed, his friendship. It was one loss she didn't know she could shoulder along with the other. But she would manage.

Reading her impatience, Brady opened the topic of the Mallorys' work stock. "Have you gentlemen had a chance to view the animals and come to a decision of their worth?"

Squire Peabody, a squat, perspiring little man, looked to Kate through limpid eyes. "Very fine creatures. Every bit as hardy as the batch your father brought. I bought them from him, you know. Very sorry I was to hear of his untimely demise. I'd be pleased to make you the same offer I made him." He named the figure and Kate forced a thin smile.

"If my father accepted that sum, he is better off drowned." Her bluntness shocked them. The ladies gasped. Brady raised a dark brow and his respect increased mightily. The woman had incredible nerve. And very keen instincts.

Peabody flushed scarlet and blustered, "I refuse to speak so ill of the dead."

"Come, come, Rupert," laughed Antoine DuVane, his handsome competitor. "The lady knows her trade. Shame upon you for trying to take advantage. Tell me, Miss Mallory, what do you consider a fair price?"

They haggled for some time, ending with DuVane agreeing to meet her cost for the majority, providing he had first pick, and Peabody and the other man, Chambers, snapping up the rest at slightly less. Kate was well pleased. She had named a high figure, expecting to be argued down. Her father would have been proud. An unexpected misting of tears forced her to stare down at the table. She merely nodded as the couples said their good nights and Brady settled back into his seat.

"Shall we raise a toast, Miss Mallory?" he asked, his silky tone an odd mix of regret and admiration.

There was nothing more she needed of him. "You have your fine profit. You can go back to your farm and pay off your creditors. You'll have a nice legacy to go to the man you marry."

Her gaze came up, shimmering like liquid emeralds. "I have not done all this so some man can step in and congratulate himself for a fine catch. I did not save it to bait a husband. I saved it for me and for my family."

Brady calmly raised his glass, bringing Kate to a blush for all her arrogant words. Almost ashamed, she lifted her cup. He couldn't have known the significance of the gesture but to Kate it felt right to share the tradition with him. After all, he was part of her success.

"To Nathan Mallory's daughter," he proclaimed and drank deeply.

She couldn't meet his steady gaze, reading question and sympathy in its sea-blue depths. She wasn't strong enough to bear up under either. Not yet. She lifted her drink to match his salute but forced her eyes to avoid his.

As Kate sipped and wandered the room with her slightly wavery glance, her attention was intrigued by an arresting man who had entered the hotel to stride up to the bar. Something in the walk tempted her eyes to follow . . . and his features made them linger. It was a ruthlessly handsome face, with a thin white scar running from temple to chin to heighten the sinister cast. Eyes as hard as honed steel cut through the crowd gathered for their drinks and dinner. Then they settled on Kate. He knew she was staring. Slowly, he began to smile, with confidence, with supreme arrogance, and Kate drew a quick breath of recognition.

Brady gave her a curious look and turned to see what held her so rapt. The man at the bar blinked sharply and she could see Brady recoil in like startlement. Then they stared stonily at each other. The exchange between the two men made the fiercest storm temperate in comparison. Brady stood, braced as if readying for battle as the other approached with the rolling swagger of the sea. They came toe-to-toe, stares locked like two superb males of a species preparing to clash over territory.

"You look as though you'd seen a ghost," the scarred man drawled.

"I was hoping to find one" was the frigid reply. "I wished you dead."

"You tried your damndest to see it done." His lips curved upward, with no warmth or humor. The near sneer served to emphasize the flaw that marred him, flexing the pale line so it stood out stark against his browned cheek. "What shall I call you? Charles? Brady? The infamous Rogue? Brother?"

Brady's face darkened with the infusion of blood. Fearing the violence that escalated by the second, Kate came to Brady's side, tentatively taking his arm. For a moment, she thought he would shake her off like an annoyance, then he glanced at her ashen face and his lost that glaze of malevolence.

"And who is this? You always had an eye for the lovelies."

Kate glared up at Brady's brother. How could she

have thought they looked similar? The smirk on his face was as unpleasant as his insinuation.

"Kathryn Mallory, Benjamin Rogan."

At that stiff introduction, Benjamin lifted her hand for a mock salute. When she felt his tongue touch her knuckles, she resisted the urge to jerk away. Instead, she drew her hand back with an icy contempt. He laughed and regarded her more intently. She didn't flush beneath his bold stare or lower her eyes. When he couldn't provoke her with his insulting perusal, he turned back to Brady. "Pray, how is Elizabeth? I trust you have seen well to my wife?"

Brady struck him. The force of his fist knocked Benjamin backward. He stumbled against a nearby table, upsetting it as he rolled across its top to sprawl upon the floor. Brady didn't linger to appreciate his fall. He was striding for the door. Kate remained frozen with astonishment while Benjamin touched the back of his hand to the blood that trickled from his lip. The sound of his derisive laughter sent her hurrying after the retreating figure.

Kate approached Brady cautiously. He paced the small, secluded garden with a lethal grace. Hands clenched and loosened at his sides. If he heard her, he didn't acknowledge her, but instead, began to speak, the low, hissing words not intended for her, but too maddened to contain the coil of his emotions.

"I wish I had killed him. I'd like to kill him now. I've searched the oceans for him for eight years. I didn't want to find him alive." As if realizing how that must sound, he looked to Kate, then tried to garner some control. An unsteady hand streaked through his hair. "I don't expect you to understand."

"That you hate your brother because you're in love with his wife?"

He viewed her with amazement, then gave a tight laugh. "How simple that sounds, but it's close enough to the truth."

Kate swallowed her desolation, but it lodged painfully in her throat. She'd wanted him to deny it. She didn't want to hear him admit his love for another. "But it's not simple, is it?"

He shook his head. "No. I wish it was. It would have been if he were dead."

"Then you'd marry Elizabeth and become a father to her son."

"I love that boy, Kate. Benjamin's never seen him. He should have been mine." The heaviness, the bleakness of his tone made her want to weep for his pain, and for her own. She longed to go to him and hold him, but she had no place in his private misery. So she stood quietly and let him speak.

He spoke of a father who raised his sons to compete, against themselves, against others. He made them believe that one had always to be the best. Unfortunately, only one of them could be and each wanted to be that one. Everything was a contest to be won or lost and as they got older, Benjamin took them more seriously. It became conflict instead of rivalry. Because Brady was older, he had already won battles Benjamin could never compete in. He could never become his father's heir so he begrudged losing anything else to Brady.

"Elizabeth was our neighbor—so pretty, so sweet. I think I always loved her, even when I was a boy. I knew when the time came to assume my father's estates, Elizabeth would be by my side. When we were growing up, she was the prize in our games. That didn't change. I had spoken to her father, the papers had been drawn. And then she ran off with him. Benjamin had gotten her with child and they eloped." His look was eloquent and it tore at her heart. "I would have married her anyway," he confessed without shame.

"To make it simple, they had nothing. Her father cut her off. Benjamin went to London, thinking to make his way. Elizabeth returned alone, great with child. Benjamin had been impressed, she said. My father wouldn't take her in. She begged me to find her husband for her. I gave her that promise and I hoped I'd never have to keep it. After Jamie was born, she wanted to come to the Colonies, sure she would find him serving the Navy along the coast. I set her and the boy up in that house on Benefit and took to the sea in search of my brother."

"And in eight years you couldn't find him?"

He heard her disbelief and shrugged. "The British Navy doesn't keep tidy records. I'd get word of someone matching his description now and again, but after a while, I quit looking so hard."

Kate could imagine his turmoil, the bittersweet pleasure of having Elizabeth and her son dependent upon him, but yet not having them. "And now that you've found him?" she asked quietly, sure he was tormented by the same question.

He looked off into the night toward the sea, toward the distant little world he'd established to keep his love safe where he could revere her. And that world was about to crumble. "I don't know," he admitted.

"You have to talk to him."

"I want to choke the life out of him. How could a man abandon his wife and child, just pretend they don't exist? I am not such a liar that I could pretend I want to see them back together. She deserves so much more. He ruined her life once before. I cannot let him do it again. She's my responsibility."

"She's his wife."

Brady turned to her, his expression drawn with helplessness. He expelled a weary breath. "I know that. I've had to tell myself that every day for eight years. I just don't know if I can bear the evidence of it."

Kate crossed to him then and, not knowing what to say, she put her arms about him. He stood quietly in the embrace, his cheek resting atop her fragrant hair and his own arms draped loosely about her. The contact felt good, comforting him with its unspoken warmth and empathy, but to Kate it was a torture of bliss, holding to him, as a friend, nothing more. In that moment, she realized it wasn't merely lover she wanted to be to Brady Rogan, it was his beloved. Somehow, during all the sparring and spite and the sharing of grief, she had fallen in love with this very unlikely man, well knowing the folly of it but unable to help herself. The unfairness of it, of him showering his love upon one who could not return it when she was anxious to bestow all she held in her heart. But life had never been fair to her. She'd always had to struggle to get what she wanted. And with her arms about him, with his breath stirring her hair, with the heat of him burning through her to run hot in her veins, she wanted Brady Rogan and wondered if she was strong enough to win him.

Brady began to take an active part in their embrace. His hands spread wide to rove the curving contours of her back and shoulders. His face nuzzled against the crown of her hair. Helplessly, she lifted her mouth to his and it moved with deliberation, conquering her will and inciting a panic in her pulse. For a brief moment of rapture, she didn't care what his motive was for that kiss nor did she scold herself for succumbing to it. Then, as his breath quickened with purpose and he sought to part her lips for access to her soul, it began to matter. It mattered that though he might want her as a warm, available woman to fill his arms, his bed, and the ache in his heart, it would be but for a moment. Even though she loved him, she was unwilling to play the substitute for his untouchable Elizabeth and she knew that was where his thoughts lingered on this sultry eve. She wasn't angry with him. She was filled wtih compassion for his pain. She did want him, but only if he saw her through those urgent, brilliant blue eyes and not the shadow of another.

Gently, firmly, she evaded his seeking mouth and eluded the tempting heat of his body. He stared at her, expression one of desire and confusion, until he saw the pity in her gaze. Then he understood the reason for her withdrawal and despised himself for

154

attempting to use this rare, special beauty as a balm to his bruised heart.

"I'm sorry, Kate," he said softly.

She gave a faint smile to show she held no ill feelings and touched one large, impotent hand. His fingers curled briefly about hers . . . then he let her go.

"'Twould seem we've both suffered more than our share of sorrows, Captain."

He nodded ruefully. "'Tis so."

"We'll survive."

"That we will."

"Good night, Brady."

"You're a good woman, Kate." Was that tinged with regret? She couldn't afford to be encouraged so she chose not to believe it. She simply nodded and returned to the hotel where the table had been righted. Benjamin Rogan had tipped her world with his careless laughter and his brother with his moment's passion . . . and for this night, both were best forgotten. If only it was that simple.

Chapter Nine

A cooling breeze came with the onset of morning. After a mostly sleepless night, Kate was grateful for the refreshing flutter against her cheeks as she sipped her tea on the hotel's broad veranda. She didn't deceive herself with the notion that the sweltering heat alone had her restless in her bed. But this was a new day. It would bring payment for the horses and an independence for her family. She refused to think beyond that, to when the money was gone, or to consider how they would manage, five females alone. She kept her thoughts controlled, fitting them into a narrowed scope that didn't include the loss of her father or her feelings for Brady Rogan. Those thoughts were too overwhelming so she forced them from her mind. She wanted only to finish her tea, collect her money, and ready herself for the return home.

"Good morning, Miss Mallory. Might I join you?"

Her surprise, and most likely her displeasure, were

evident when she looked up at Benjamin Rogan. So much for her idyllic morning. He was dressed casually for the weather, much like the planters had been the night before, only his white linen shirt was open at the neck to expose an indecent amount of firm chest. Noting the direction of her gaze, he grinned in his predatory fashion, amused to have brought a blush to the thorny miss.

"The chairs belong to the hotel. Sit where you like," she said crisply, and turned back to her study of the local flora. There was a fierceness to her observation that made him chuckle as he seized the nearest chair and drew it uncomfortably close so their knees were nearly touching. Kate's lips thinned, but she made no comment.

"So, Miss Mallory, how is it that you are alone? Brady didn't specify your purpose, but I expected to find him at your heels. I would be t'were you with me."

"I am not *with* Captain Rogan. I came to the Islands aboard his ship to do business here." What was it about the man and his silky suggestions that made her bristle and bare her claws? She moved her leg aside and twitched her skirts so he wouldn't brush against them.

"I see," he drawled, and she saw he'd already painted his own nasty picture of her relationship with Brady. That she couldn't deny it completely made her all the more irate. "And what type of business do you engage in, Miss Mallory? Something in which I might wish to invest?"

She swiveled to stab him with a glance. "*My* business, Mr. Rogan," she bit out with cold clarity.

He smirked at her outrage and settled more comfortably in his seat to reassess the situation. She felt she was being measured as a likely conquest to pull out from under his brother and was about to set him straight when a hand settled on her shoulder. The unexpected pinch of fingers gave her a start, and the claiming gesture made her look up with a scowl. However, Brady wasn't looking at her. His eyes were on the other man and, seeing the warning challenge in them, Benjamin smiled, for this was not the business relationship Kate would have had him believe it to be.

"Good morning, Brother. Your lady and I were just discussing her business here in the Islands. Care to join us?"

Brady grasped a chair and dragged it up to wedge between Kate and Benjamin's. Kate would have laughed at the possessive show had she not resented its implications. She would not be drawn into the dangerous game the brothers played and, with a cutting glance, she let Brady know it. Then he astounded her into speechlessness.

"I missed you upon waking, Kate," he said with a husky intimacy. His lips brushed her cheek before he settled beside her, and his hand remained possessively over hers. When her shock abated, she was angry enough to want to snatch the hand away and demand he explain his deception. But she didn't. She remembered him standing at her side claiming to be her fiancé to save her from ruin. Whatever his purpose for asking her now to play the part of his lover, she could not refuse him. She forced a sweet, benign smile and gritted her teeth as Benjamin smugly came to his own conclusions.

"So, Brother, how long has it been?"

"You know damn well how long it's been," Brady growled.

Benjamin nodded that concession. "You look well."

"As if you cared, *dear* Brother."

The mockery was abruptly set aside in favor of curiosity. "You've been looking for me. Why? I thought we said everything upon our last parting."

"Between us, yes. 'Twas Elizabeth who asked me to find you."

Feeling uncomfortable with the turn of conversation, Kate made as if to rise only to have Brady's fingers clench about hers. As he brought them to his lips, his eyes conveyed a complex message. She didn't understand it beyond the fact that it was a request for her support. So she remained.

"And how is my wife?" The indifferent tone incurred a tense fury in his brother.

"Well when last I saw her."

"And the boy?"

"Jamie is fine. Why the interest?"

"Just making conversation." He flicked some imagined dust off his sleeve, dismissing his family just as casually.

"They're in Providence."

"I know."

Brady's features registered surprise, then were carefully masked to give his nemesis no advantage. That Benjamin was aware of Elizabeth's whereabouts

160

made him wary and defensive.

"So what was it Elizabeth wanted?" The boredom with which he awaited the answer was eased as he detailed Kate's bodice with his steely gaze. She fought the urge to cross her arms to block that heated stare and just as strongly to keep her hand from seeking his unscarred cheek.

"She wants a husband," Brady ground out. "She wants a man who'll be responsible for her and her son. She wants what any woman wants when she takes on a man's name, what any decent man would be willing to give."

"She has you for that Brady. Why would she need me?"

"Damn your eyes. Why did you marry her then? Why did you condemn her to such a hell if you didn't even want her?"

Benjamin's lips twitched as if with the ultimate joke. He replied simply, "Why, to keep you from having her, of course. How does it feel, Brother, to be denied the one thing you want most? As long as she has my name, I'll have my revenge."

"For what? Is the fault mine for being born before you?"

"Born first, always first." The mocking pose dropped for an instant to reveal the man. It was an ugly sight, one of twisted hatred and envy. Then he laughed and the smooth arrogance returned. "And so you became her protector in my stead. Have you found the job rewarding? Has sweet Elizabeth been as generous with her charms as she was with me? Or has your sense of honor made your life a misery these past years?" His smug malice said he hoped the latter was so.

Brady regarded him evenly, betraying none of what tore through him. "Elizabeth is family. I have seen to her as an obligation, as I would for any wife you discarded. I have my own life and it pleases me immensely." His gaze shifted to Kate, lingering pointedly until warm color rose in her face. Benjamin looked between them suspiciously. Then Kate understood. Brady was using her to draw his brother off. He was wagering that if he showed no interest in Elizabeth, Benjamin would leave her alone. She was the bait to lure him off the scent. Benjamin tested the air like a cautious predator, not quick to believe the truth of his brother's claim.

"So you've come to restore me to the bosom of my family?" he sneered.

"I'd rather see you in hell, but the choice isn't mine. Elizabeth made me promise to find you and so I have. I care not what you do now." He waited while Benjamin weighed his words. Kate could feel the tension in his hand, could feel it flowing through him, but he dared not give anything away—not his concern, not his anxiety.

"Keep your precious Elizabeth. I have no desire to be shackled by one woman and her whinings. You're so full of duty and honor, you see to her. I've no more interest in her insipid passions than I did when I stole her from you. I have what I want now."

"And what is that?"

"My freedom. I answer to no man, and no man bests me. I feel sorry for you, Brady, tied to the past

162

with your ridiculous propriety. Had I been you, I'd have made Elizabeth my whore out of spite. But not you. Oh, no, not my noble brother. You're a fool. To think I once envied you."

His scorn was a mixture of self-importance and insecure bluster and Brady let him rant. This was too serious to be played as a game of one-upmanship. He had to keep Benjamin away from Elizabeth. Maintaining composure was near impossible. Fury raged within him, helpless and unventable. The idea that the woman he cherished could be held in such disregard by the man who had her, made him seethe. However, the thought of Benjamin returning to Providence, returning to Elizabeth, held him silent. Even after all the years without word, without hope, Elizabeth would welcome him back. He knew it just as surely as he knew Benjamin would go to her if he thought it would cause him distress. So he had to pretend it didn't matter. It was the only chance he had that Benjamin would free her. Once free, he would see Benjamin never hurt her again. That was the promise he'd made to himself.

Benjamin's gaze returned to insultingly appraise Kate from squared neckline to the tempting roundness of her lap. "Perhaps I yet envy you some things." It was an obvious taunt, one Brady refused to recognize.

"Is there a message you'd have me give Elizabeth?" He couldn't keep the stiffness from his tone, and Benjamin smiled as he thought a moment.

"Give her . . . my love." That last was said with a roll of sarcasm too heavy to ignore. Benjamin reacted quickly, catching his brother's wrist to halt his

163

impulsive swing. His hand tightened until its fingers bled white, but Brady's fierce stare never wavered. "I've tasted your right once and, before that, the bite of your steel. Next time you'd best be armed and plan your shot well. I take threats from no man, not even you." They continued to test each other's strength, neither willing to give. Then, with a laugh, Benjamin pushed his arm away. He stood and executed a mocking bow to Kate.

"Miss Mallory, a pleasure." His drooping gaze promised it would have been. She met it evenly, without expression. He smirked and looked to his brother, smug stare cooling. "Should we not meet again . . ." His sentiment trailed off.

Brady stood. They regarded each other long, neither betraying their thoughts as the past played through them. Not all the memories were bad, not all twisted by their father's influence. The hate made it hard to remember when they'd been friends, even confidants but Brady recalled those times now. He felt an intangible longing for a return of those childhood days when the rivalry had been an exhilarating game to hone adolescent skills, when Benjamin's laughter was pure and his smile spoke of enjoyment.

Brady's unexpected embrace caught Benjamin by surprise. A cunningly delivered blow would have been better received, but he stood rigid, enduring it with a shock of unwelcome feeling. His hands rose awkwardly, settling upon his brother's shoulders, tightening there before pushing him away with a growl of distaste. Brady's expression was already stoic, any fondness for the past overshadowed by a bitter present. Benjamin backed away, wary, off balance. Then his mocking smile flexed the scar that marked the impossibility of renewed affection. "Fool," he uttered softly, but the claim lacked its earlier sting of contempt. "Always sailing against the wind, Brady." He turned sharply and strode the length of the porch to disappear around its side. Brady watched him go, and for a fleeting instant, his features bore the gamut of emotions that warred within. At the touch of Kate's hand, his concentration was called from his inner torment. He regarded her briefly, almost without recognition, then he, too, left the porch to walk in the other direction.

The languid heat of the tropics made the day wear slowly. DuVane and the others arrived promptly with their payment. Coin was a rare commodity in the Islands, but Kate had insisted on it, and now the molten fortune spread upon her counterpane to attest to the success. She weighed the individual pieces and gave a thoughtful sigh. It was the weight of freedom at the price of her father's life and it was not enough. She gathered the gold and funneled it back into its pouch, secreting it beneath her mattress. Then she smiled ruefully. It was the first place a thief would look. She glanced about in search of another hiding spot but could find no better. It would have to do.

The indigo night was deep and intoxicating with its damp, exotic scents, luring her from her thoughts of fortunes and feelings lost and found to the cool sea breezes of her private balcony. From it, she could view the straight forest of masts that crowded the sapphire waters off shore. She wondered which belonged to the *Elizabeth*. Elizabeth. *Elizabeth*. The two loves of Brady Rogan's life.

Kate reached out to pluck a purple bloom from the vine that twined about her balcony. Emotions tendrilled through her with the same clinging bind. She touched the dark, luxuriant petals to her cheek and stared into the night, letting its quiet absorb into her weary spirit.

"A most exceptional blossom."

The smoky voice brought her about. The bloom fell from numbed fingers. Pressed back against the rail, her pale night shift fluttering on the same teasing breeze that lifted strands of gold from her shoulders in an aura about her startled features, she did look akin to the sultry plumage of the isle. There was nothing fragile in her cold demand.

"What are you doing in here?"

Benjamin Rogan smiled, unconcerned. "I knocked. You must not have heard. I came to speak to Brady." It was an easily spoken lie. He'd seen his brother at the docks and had known she'd be alone. His eyes traveled leisurely over the lush form silhouetted within the thin linen. A brighter, more determined sheen came to his gaze. This would be no difficult chore. Desire and revenge created an incredible excitement when combined.

Kate stood frozen, her mind spinning for a way to elude the lusty confidence she could see mounting in

166

his stare. Only she knew Brady would not be coming to her room this night. Her posture grew bold and defiant. The thrust of her tempting breasts against pale fabric offset the effect she'd meant the gesture to carry.

"He's not here, but I expect him soon. I was looking for him just this instant, in fact." Her stronger will conquered her voice's want to quaver. It would not do for him to see she was afraid or in the least bit nervous.

"'Twere I in his place, I would not tarry elsewhere. Not when such a sight was here to greet me."

Ignoring the smooth innuendo, Kate said, "You can await him below."

"But then we wouldn't get the chance to know each other."

"I know you, sir, and I'm not interested in discovering more."

He grinned at that, encouraged rather than put off by her tart words. Gad, she had spirit. What a bedmate she must be, he thought to himself in lusty expectation. "Oh, I think you would be interested in deepening our acquaintance. No one's ever complained of finding me a shallow fellow."

Kate's face flamed hot. "'Tis clear this over-abundance of self-worth is a familial trait."

"Has Brady disappointed you? I assure you, I shall not."

He advanced a step, and Kate fought to keep herself from shrinking against the restraining rail. She made her tone cold and confident. "Brady will not like your persistence and neither, sir, do I. You'd best go.

He'll not take kindly to you being here with me."

"Oh, upon that, I'm counting."

He reached her with a sinewy stride and stood close, using his body to pin her back and an arm on either side to keep her prisoner. Green eyes measured him with loathing and indomitable will shone in her steady stance.

"Touch me and you'll pay dearly," she warned.

Benjamin laughed. "Brady's love for Elizabeth cost me my handsome face. Do you think he holds you in higher regard? Do you expect him to make me pay some greater price than he already has?"

"I will."

He hesitated. The two words held a deadly certainty.

A tap on the door and the call of her name distracted Benjamin long enough for Kate to slip under his arm and to rush to pull it open. She filled Brady's arms, capturing his mouth with impatient ardor. Kate felt his shock. And his response. His hands spanned her waist, his lips slanting upon hers in urgent question. Then his gaze happened over her shoulder to touch on the indolent figure who watched their embrace. He pried Kate away.

"What kept you, beloved," she asked, refusing to be set aside. Brady's astonishment flowed too rapidly into fury and she wanted to avoid a confrontation with its source.

"Your lady's been trying to keep me entertained while we waited for you."

Frigid blue eyes raked over Kate's attire. "I'm sure he found you most obliging." She winced at his crude summation and he wished the words unspoken. Thinking of them together, of Benjamin and Kate, of him trying to seduce her with his silky charms, provoked the careless accusation. Her stare was withering as she began to pull away. He wouldn't allow it, his arm curling about her middle to keep her fast against his side. She didn't struggle, but neither did her rigid posture ease.

"That I did," Benjamin drawled. His slow, knowing grin implied many things. Brady seethed.

"What was it you wished to say to me?" he clipped out in harsh tones. He tried not to believe what Benjamin hinted, yet Kate was in her night garb and his brother was nearly bursting with self-congratulation. He didn't want to think it of Kate, but then, others had given before Benjamin's caresses. Why didn't she deny it? Why didn't she offer an explanation or make some charge against him? Instead, she stood silent and stiff, refusing to meet his inquiring glances. Dammit, what was he doing in her room?

Benjamin appeared at a loss, then waved a negligent hand. "'Twas nothing of importance. 'Twill keep till another time." He smiled at Kate, that grin well pleased and taunting. "I can see I'm intruding so I'll wish you a good evening." He walked by them, chuckling with quiet amusement as he closed the door.

Kate jerked away from Brady and stormed across the room, angry with both men. She was furious with Benjamin's presumptions and cut by Brady's conclusions.

"Well?"

The imperious command set her teeth into a snarl. She turned on him. "Well what?"

"What was he doing here? What was the meaning of all those looks? Why did you have him in your room?"

His unreasonable demands woke an equally belligerent rebellion. Hands on hips, Kate confronted him, chin outthrust and words caustic.

"What right have you to ask?"

His narrowed stare took in her lips, full and pouted from the crush of his own. From Benjamin's, too? Her eyes were hot, with indignation or guilty pleasure? The diaphanous cling of her shift would stir the beast in any man and he knew what manner of one his brother was. Benjamin could not let such a sight go untested, such lips go untried. He had himself to fault for leading him to believe Kate was his lover, for goading him into desiring her for himself. Why was she so angry unless it had to do with a twinge of conscience? Rage and uncertainty swirled within his head, clouding his thoughts with a haze of remembered betrayal. He had to know.

Kate gasped at the fierceness with which he gripped her arms. It was a hurtful, possessing gesture and she was momentarily stunned. He drew her up until she could feel the impassioned rush of his breath upon her face.

"Tell me, Kate. What did he do? Did he kiss you? Did he touch you?"

Then, he was doing those things, angrily, desperately. Kate squirmed in his grasp, unable to escape the domination of his mouth, part of her wildly not wanting to. He kissed her breathless, nearly senseless, crushing her to him with the band of one arm while his hand roamed the sweetly shaped contours of back, hip, and buttock through the unresisting garment. All the while, he could hear the taunting voice in his head: *I made love to her. She wanted it. She wanted me, not you. Me. She liked it, Brady. She liked it so much, she begged for more.*

"No," he growled against Kate's bruised lips. "You're mine. He won't have you." Savagely, he swept her up in his arms and in two long strides, took her to the bed.

Chapter Ten

Kate knew she should struggle, knew she should resist with the same determination that he insisted. She found she could not. His kisses had her weak. The thought of his loving made her tremble. Never had she wanted anything so much, well knowing the reasons were wrong. Brady didn't want her. He wanted to best his brother, to this time win the one contest he'd before failed. And she was the prize. She should have minded. She should have felt angry, resentful, used. She did not. Not when her body cried out for his touch, her essence craved the knowledge of his desire.

Brady fell with her upon the bed, his weight coming down hard atop her to crush any objection she might try to make. Physical resistance wouldn't have deterred him, but the sound of her small cry of hurt and surprise against his conquering mouth made him hesitate. Knowledge of what he was doing eked back, flooding him with shame. God, what had he been thinking, what had he been about to do? Realizing that she twisted beneath him in protest, that her features were etched with discomfort brought him up off her. He backed into a kneeling position between the spread of legs tangled in her nightrail.

"Kate, I'm sorry," he moaned. "I don't know what madness possessed me." The insanity of the moment's hurt and jealous suspicion gave to a misery of regret. He awaited a lash of her fury, of her contempt.

Instead, Kate's eyes glowed up at him, kindled to brightness by the fires he'd started within her untrained passions. Her voice was husky with it. "The same, I fear, that possesses me."

He frowned. If she welcomed his ardor, why the struggle? Kate answered him by twisting about, reaching under the mattress to dislodge the pouch of coin that had bitten so cruelly into her spine when she fell upon it. She gave it a careless toss and the contents scattered across the floor with a clatter and glitter of gold.

"There," she said with a sigh, settling back to regard him through those simmering eyes. "That's better."

They exchanged cautious, heated looks for a long minute, each affected by the uneven breathing of the other and by their telling proximity.

"Kate . . ." Brady began finally. That single word told of his uncertainty.

"Don't explain," she said, her voice equally quiet. "He didn't touch me. Nothing happened. He only came to goad you."

Brady's tone was self-reproachful. "And how he succeeded. I was crazy. I had no right to think such things of you."

Kate nibbled her lip. Now, she was the one beset with knowing the truth, unpleasant as it might be. "And were you thinking of me?" That was said small, teetering upon a fleeting hope that all the jealous fury was due to her, not some memory of past emotion. When Brady was slow to answer, those hopes constricted painfully.

Then his large hands settled upon her straddled knees. His palms were deliciously warm against bare skin. "I have thought of little else of late, of you, of this." His hands began a slow, exaggerated massage down the length of her slender calves and up again to rest atop her raised knees. The languid touch incited a tingle of expectation that quivered up her limbs to throb with the anticipation of his continued caress. It was all she could do not to arch toward him in wanton encouragement. The smolder of his gaze was tempered with care. "I don't want to hurt you, Kate."

"I know." Saying even those two words took an effort. Her heart was beating with a wild impatience. Her gaze was riveted to his.

"I can give you no promises."

"I ask for none."

"But you deserve them, Kate."

"I want you. Promises, be damned." That low, roughly spoken certainty conquered the thread of his nobility.

Brady's stare devoured her in slow, torturously thorough degrees, bringing her to the point of writing in her urgency. The hot blue coals of his gaze traced flame along features held in exquisite tension, down the exposed column of white throat, to the thin gown that tried so futilely to conceal the rose-tipped bounty of her breasts from his seeking gaze. She squirmed restlessly, trying to coax his hands to follow the path his eyes had taken, but he would not be rushed. His scrutiny moved lower, crossing the rapid rise and fall of her midsection to the covered junction of her thighs.

Kate's breathing had come to a stop as she lay tense in anticipation. Still, when his palms began to glide along the silky interior of her thighs, a sound of incredulous delight escaped her. Her eyes closed to give sensation rule as his hands continued, rucking up her night garb with the progression of his forearms until his thumbs met to explore and probe and provoke within the folds of her female flesh. It was a tantalizing inquiry, one that had her panting to realize its conclusion. And too soon it was abandoned, wringing a moan of protest from her.

His hands slipped beneath her, cupping her bottom and urging her toward him so her thighs rode up over the tops of his. The intimate touch returned, but from a source so different and unexpected, her eyes flew open with shock . . . then drifted shut in ecstasy. Never had she been so shaken with pleasure, with feelings so intense they were akin to pain. The forbidden delights evoked a quickening of perceptions, a sensitivity so sharp she alternately arched away and pressed closer in a mindless quest for relief. A quivering ache swelled within her, expanding moltenlike blown glass only to suddenly shatter when strained to the limit. She cried out as tremors scalded down her legs and tightened through her middle. Then all was calm. She lay limp and wonderfully replete in her twist of damp nightdress, scarcely aware that Brady had stretched out beside her until his mouth possessed hers, lingering upon her lips, letting her taste herself upon them. That returned some of her awareness, the knowledge of how he had brought about her devastating release, and she blushed bright with a confusion of shame and lascivious satisfaction.

Brady's kisses traced the curve of her hot cheek to brush upon her ear, mingling with his throaty whisper. "How remarkable you are," he murmured with a velvety roughness. "How I love to bring you pleasure, Kate."

His crooning compliments were as sensual as his caress. Then he was sitting up. Only when her hand caught anxiously at his coat did she realize he was still dressed. That discovery increased the eroticism of what she'd experienced and, again, she felt ashamed that she'd enjoyed it so.

The fragile way she said his name won her a chuckle as warm as his appreciative look. "Don't fret. I've no plan to go." As if to reassure her, he bent to remove his shoes and stockings, then stood to shed his breeches. Resigned to accepting her wickedness, Kate watched him disrobe through curious eyes. There was such graceful power to his movements as he stripped off his coat. Linen rippled over muscle like the play of the wind in the sails. His shirt extended to midthigh, revealing long legs of sturdy shape, lightly furred with black hair. As it was shrugged from his shoulders, she followed its descent down the length of his sleek back over firm, flat buttocks. When he turned, her eyes flew up in sudden cowardice to seek his face. He was smiling, having felt her rapt scrutiny. Her betraying flush returned.

"I've shocked you, haven't I, my naive little miss," he purred as he sat beside her. Her gaze flashed up, prideful yet embarrassed, as if she would deny what he knew to be the truth. "Ah, Kate, there is much I could show you—much I will show you and I promise there is no disgrace in letting yourself like it and learn."

Her heated stare showed her want to be convinced. The challenge of proving his statement was one he savored. Purposefully, he filled his palm with one well-rounded breast, pushing it up so his thumb could dip within the neckline of her gown to bring its nipple to immediate attention. She gasped.

"'Tis a warm night and I'm confident 'twill grow hotter soon. You've no need of this." Deftly, he lifted her and peeled the ineffective covering from her, giving it a casual toss. Though his manner was playful and teasing, the banking fire in his gaze flared with a more serious intent. It stirred embers of passions she'd thought extinguished in the earlier blaze. He stroked the full breasts carefully, knowingly. His fingers circled lazily to tighten impertinent peaks into eager nubs. When Kate expelled a raspy moan, he lowered his face between the cushiony mounds, letting his tongue stroke along that salty valley before climbing to meet each crest. Her fingers meshed in his hair and her torso arched in offering. He feasted unhurriedly, well aware of how his languor excited her. Her fingers began to knead, then tug, pulling him up so the hair of his chest made an unbearable friction against the swollen tips. Her kiss was plundering, unrestrained. Her desperate ardor pushed him beyond the pretense of composure.

Brady groaned her name. It was a question. It was its own answer. Hastened by the burgeoning demands of his manhood, he shifted so her lush form carried his weight. Her knees rose to hug his hips, her own rising against him in urgent welcome.

Kate bit back a cry. It was a rapturous sound, one of renewed wonder at the fullness that spread so completely within her. "Brady, oh, Brady," she moaned, wishing she could add, *how I love you!* She accepted his demanding thrusts the way she longed to give her love, unconditionally, with uncontrolled abandon. Receiving, returning, reveling, each plunging stroke lured her closer to the brink of bliss. She pursued her pleasure then, stretching out with her heightened senses to encourage and embrace the flood of consummate joy he offered. She clutched it briefly, rocking with it, then reluctantly let it go as Brady came to a like conclusion above her. They lay silent for a time, fused intimately by the heat and sweat they'd generated between them. Their labored breathing rasped in the quiet, then it, too, calmed.

Kate returned the gentle pressure of Brady's kiss, then he rolled from her to seek a cooler spot on the wrinkled bedding. His fingertips brushed her in a brief caress, sliding along the sheen that slicked her skin before remaining still upon her midriff. She listened to his restless shiftings until, at last he found a comfortable position. Warmth radiated from the heavy weight of his hand. It was a wonderful, claiming heat.

Though her body was sated and slumberous, Kate's mind knew a strange keenness that defied rest or weariness. Brady had gifted her with a precious contentment. For the first time, she had the strength to face the future, to consider what she must do. A confident calm clarified her thinking and eased the emotional burdens that had tormented her since leaving Rhode Island. She recognized the full loss of her father and found it was a manageable pain. She could let go the rein on her grief and not be overwhelmed by it. She considered what his death would mean to her family, what she had to do to compensate. All the while she was aware of the man who lay beside her. Reflecting upon what he meant to her and how he fit into her future was too complex for the hour, an issue too emotional for her frayed senses to weigh dispassionately. She thus kept her thinking channeled away from the frailties of her heart and set about determining a more controllable idea.

"Brady?"

"Umm."

The unpromising sound prompted her to give him a slight shake. "Are you awake?"

"Uh huh."

Unsympathetically, she pinched his side. "Brady,

are you awake?"

He made a protesting noise as dark brows furrowed over his nose. He started to roll away, but Kate leaned on his arm to trap him on his back. "What?" he grumbled, still too groggy to open his eyes. When she said his name a third time, his lethargy permitted a faint stirring of awareness. "Kate?" His eyes came open then, dazed and slow to show recognition. They focused, becoming a bedazzling blue. "Kate," he said again, half in hope, half in disbelief. Then he was awake; all of him was awake.

Kate let him topple her back on the sheets and relented to the leisurely sampling of her lips. The luxurious persuasion found no resistance as his tongue sketched the ripe contours of her mouth and dipped within to briefly taste her submission. His lazy movements were sensual seduction.

"Woman, you are insatiable," he mumbled against the part of her lips. It didn't sound like a complaint. He would have been content to indolently pursue that fact.

"Brady, how much illegal cargo are you carrying back to Newport?"

That casually rendered question stilled his kisses upon her neck. For a moment, he didn't move. Then his head reared back so he could meet her level gaze. "What?" His voice was weak with incredulity.

Assuming he was surprised that she should guess at his illicit doings, she continued matter-of-factly, "With you being a smuggler, I naturally reasoned that you wouldn't pass up such an opportunity."

"Good God," he burst out. "Doesn't your mind

ever stop turning? What does a man have to do . . ." He abandoned the sentiment and the sensuous assault to drop upon his back. His features were drawn with displeasure. Kate was at a loss with his display of bruised pride. She laid a tentative hand to his chest. His scowling visage turned toward her. "If this is to be business, Miss Mallory, please conduct yourself accordingly." To be awakened to make love was one thing, but to be shaken from his slumber to discuss smuggling, quite another. To be discouraged from the former in preference of the latter was, well, deflating.

"Business, it is. For the moment," she added more softly, in hopes of easing his pique. Darkness had settled to conceal all but the clean line of his profile. Moonlight filtered in from the open gallery doors to shimmer with icy definition along the muscular swells of his body. She forced her gaze to remain upon his face.

"How much profit do you realize from untaxed goods?"

His reply was given begrudgingly. "Sometimes double."

"Double," she repeated in a thoughtful whisper. "And what do you carry?"

"Sugar and molasses up from the Islands."

"And in return?"

"It's circular trade," he explained brusquely. "Sugar and molasses fuel our distilleries, the rum is shipped to Africa; 'tis the commodity they desire most, though not the only one, along with horses, provisions, and spermaceti candles. They, in turn,

182

provide slaves for the Islands and our plantation colonies."

"Slaves." She said the word with loathing, and he could feel that censure taint her opinion of him.

"Kate," he said quietly, needing vindication. "I've never run slaves. I never will." She tested the truth of that for a long minute, silent, studying him. Then her fingers stroked over his. It was a light caress, one quickly withdrawn. Apologetic, he thought, and that made him smile.

"How dangerous is what you do?"

Brady would have liked to flatter himself that her concern was for his safety, but he knew better. She was weighing the risks, cautiously plotting within that clever mind of hers. He didn't know whether to admire her or throttle her. "It has its perils. I've yet to lose a shipment to customs officials, but I don't think myself charmed. 'Tis a fickle business, like a woman." Let her think on that.

And she *was* thinking, though he wouldn't like the turn of her thoughts. Absently, she plied his forearm, testing its muscled tone with a distracted appreciation. And as he considered plying the more yielding softness she offered, her annoying single-mindedness interfered.

"Would you invest my gold, less your fee, of course, into Island sugar?"

His teeth ground. God, she was a frustrating creature. He wanted to pounce upon her, to fill her with the strength of his passions, to drive all thoughts from her calculating, pretty head save her desire for him. But then, he thought wryly, he would

183

probably spend himself and she would regard him with those unblinking jade eyes and demand to know the going rate for molasses. The humiliation could not be borne.

"Kate, 'tis a hazardous cause, one you'd be wise to stay clear of. You'd best stick with what you have than to gamble all."

His condescending tone made her bristle. "Captain Rogan, 'tis mine to wager."

"Miss Mallory, you are not the only one dependent upon that coin."

His pointed remark, hinting that she'd selfishly put aside the needs of her family made her seethe. "My sisters trust my judgment. After all, the venture cannot be too costly as you are supporting your brother's wife and child."

The chill was immediate. She regretted venting her spite so pettishly, for he was obviously provoked beyond her intention.

"Their welfare does not hinge upon my trade. Should I sink tomorrow, they would still be well provided for. I see to my obligations. Those I love will never suffer from my impetuousness."

There was silence. Both smarted at the carelessly parried words. Then Kate spoke. Her tone was stiff but her sentiments sincere.

"Forgive me."

Brady was still, then offered with equal inflexibility, "Done."

"Will you invest the coin for me?"

"If you wish."

Tension was heavier than the humidity. Finally,

Brady sat up and reached for his shirt. Kate was treated to the smooth play of taut flesh across exquisite form. That sensuous ripple of motion fascinated her. The purpose of his action alarmed her.

"Where are you going?"

"If I'm to start you on your career of smuggling, I need make arrangements."

"Now?" Her stare roamed the broad plane of his back. It was too tempting. Her fingertips slid from waist to shoulder, stiffening his spine along the way as if she was applying an iron to starch cloth.

"Business is business."

Kate came up then to lean against him, letting the cushion of her breasts pillow upon the unyielding brace of his body. His breathing stopped. "But business isn't its own reward," she cooed as her palms rounded his rib cage to move coaxingly upon his tight middle. As they drifted lower, his breath resumed in a rather erratic hurry. It wasn't modesty that halted her wandering caress but the immodest attention it provoked. She was aware of it the moment her hand passed his furred navel only to meet the bold interest she'd kindled standing firm and duly encouraged. She gasped.

"Are you suggesting we tend the business at hand, Miss Mallory?"

His question was silky. Her reply was hoarse. "Come back to bed, Brady."

His shirt dropped, forgotten.

Later, much later, while Kate languished in a marvelous drowsiness, she felt the brush of his lips

185

against her ear. She was too exhausted to summon a response.

"I have to go, Kate," he whispered. He was already dressed. "Our business awaits. Be ready to sail by noontime." Then, more softly, he added, "You're remarkable."

Sun was streaming hot and brilliant through the open doors by the time Kate roused herself. Her hand slid over the vacant sheets and she called, "Brady?" before she remembered that he had gone. Smiling then, with infinite satisfaction, she lingered a bit longer to savor torrid memories of his presence. By noontime. She sat up with a start. What time was it? It seemed sinfully late for one who rose with the roosters. She consulted her watch, one of the few valuable pieces she owned. It was nary ten o'clock. Relieved, she was about to sink back into the well-used covers when her attention was caught by the wink of precious metal on the night table. Several gold coins were stacked there. Understanding won a tender smile. He hadn't wanted her to risk all. He was acting as her conscience, saving a nest egg should his skill fail them.

"I love you, Brady Rogan," she said aloud, and was a bit startled by how much she meant those words. A frown creased her features. Loving him was by far more dangerous than trusting him with her meager wealth. The coin was an investment, the return a good possibility. Her affections for the man seemed an improbable risk. He desired her, yes. She didn't question the intensity that flared between them. That was physical and not the only link she wished to have

186

to him. Could that single link forge a chain strong enough to hold him? Could she make him relinquish his ill-fated longing for Elizabeth and turn those tender feelings to her instead? What would it take for him to say the words she'd just spoken? She didn't know. Brady was as much a mystery as the sea, as much a threat to her well-being should she try to conquer the unpredictable depths that even a glassy surface hid. But then, as she'd told him, nothing was simple.

Chapter Eleven

Kate paused at the entrance to the dining room. It was not so crowded that she couldn't find an empty table nor could she avoid seeing a familiar face at one of them. She saw in that individual not a pleasant luncheon companion but a great fount of information. There were many questions she dared not ask of Brady, yet here she might find the answers. Purposefully, she chose to join Benjamin Rogan where he took his meal from a mug. He looked pleased yet cautious at her request for a chair and eyed her like an attractive puzzle he meant to solve.

"May I offer you a beveridge or perhaps something stronger?" Civility came stilted to lips twisted in a perpetual contempt of graciousness.

"Something stronger, I think. I am a dreadful sailor and the extra fortitude will serve me well." Now that she was seated, she doubted her wisdom. Whatever prompted her to seek conversation with such a man? Hadn't he already proved he had no conscience, no sense of decency? Yet she'd been drawn to him, this man who instilled a prickling of unease and well-deserved distrust.

"You sail today?"

"In less than an hour. I grew restless awaiting Brady. 'Twill be good to be home.'' She took the rum-laced concoction with a nod to its server and stirred it distractedly. She could feel Benjamin's gaze upon her, bright, intent, probing.

"And home is?"

"Kingstown. My family has a farm there."

The steely gaze sharpened. "Forgive me, but I assumed that you and my brother . . ." He let that dangle meaningfully.

"No." She softened the blunt monosyllable with a faint smile. "Brady is not one to make himself a home upon land."

"And if he did, do you think it would be with you?"

Kate bristled, searching for a slur in that silkily asked question. She heard only curiosity, albeit of a personal nature, and forced herself to back down her defenses. "Why not?"

Dark brows rose in a challenging arch. "Why not in a word. Need I speak it?"

"No."

Benjamin regarded her quizzically. She was one straightforward wench, he'd give her that. "He's set up house for one woman. Perhaps the wrong one, you think?"

Kate didn't respond to the obvious baiting. She took a long drink and let its searing burn battle the

190

distress that dammed up in her throat.

"Are you in love with my brother?" he asked with brutal candor.

"And if I am, I would say that, too, is my business."

He laughed at the cool retort, then his smile was gone. "If you are, be warned. He's only loved one woman and he's a persistent man. If you think he means to do more than toy with you, think again."

The words hurt. Their probable truth was crushing. Kate's chin firmed and no weakness betrayed her. "Why would you be so concerned for my folly?"

"Can't say I am. I'll admit he'd do better to pin his fancy on the likes of you, but there's naught I can do for it."

"You could claim your wife or let her go." Her own vehemence stunned her. She hadn't meant to let her frustrations wave so freely. Grimly, she finished her drink and cursed herself for falling prey to his taunts.

"I've no interest in doing either, Miss Mallory. I like things the way they are."

"And it bothers you not a whit that your twisted vengeance is ruining the lives of others."

Her attack was unexpected. She saw him wince, then a chill appeared to come over him. His resemblance to his brother was then striking and disturbing.

"Not a whit."

"Then 'tis you I feel sorry for, right along with the rest of us, for you're as caught in this misery as we are. Only yours is the sadder case. You can change things, yet you won't. You're a pitiful man,

Benjamin Rogan."

His hardy color faded until the scar was barely noticeable. Whatever he might have said in response died on his lips as Brady approached their table.

If he was vexed to find the two of them together, it never showed upon Brady's stony face. His fingertips lightly capped Kate's shoulder but he didn't glance down. His stare was locked with his brother's. "It's time to go, Kate," he said with a deadly calm.

Silently, she rose and his hand fell away. She looked askance but could find no answer in his closed expression. Finally, she nodded to Benjamin and preceded Brady to the broad porch. Her bags had already been taken by porters to be stowed aboard the *Elizabeth*. Without a parting word, Brady turned and followed, walking determinedly away from this painful chapter of his past. He didn't look back just as Benjamin hadn't looked back nine years before.

The day was bright and balmy with a slight breeze to stir the surface of the sea into a glittery pucker. Kate remained on deck, keeping out of the path of the busy crew and keeping an eye on its captain. Threads of anxiety curled about the pit of her belly when the schooner bobbed away from its anchoring, but she kept her gaze upon Brady, concentrating on him with a determination to hold her fears at bay. After the first few minutes, the crawling of terror lessened and she became lost in the activity about her.

The *Elizabeth* tacked daintily about on her course for New England. Her sails pivoted to catch the wind as the sailors hauled lines in on the lee side and released the sheet ropes on the windward. Canvas snapped and strained as if sharing Kate's eagerness to get under way, to begin the journey home. Lines from the running rigging were brought to deck and whipped in a quick figure eight to belay them at the pinrail. The *Elizabeth* was on her way.

"You needn't remain up top if it makes you uncomfortable."

Kate smiled up at Brady. His concern filled her heart the way a forceful wind puffed the sails. "I'm fine, Captain. 'Tis too beautiful a day to spend below deck." The lines of worry eased to admiration upon his face for an instant, then a guarded look came over him. Her hope that he would remain at her side was casually dashed.

"Stay clear of the lines then and don't forget the sun off the water will crisp your pretty little nose if you're not careful." He tapped a finger there and smiled. She fought the impulse to melt against his chest with a sigh. Something in her wayward mood must have betrayed itself upon her face, for he took a step away. With a quick nod, he strode along the deck, leaving her to follow him with bewildered eyes.

Kate had no chance to speak with him for the remainder of the day. The mounting heat and continued glare off the water encouraged a pounding in her head and she was glad to seek out the cooler comfort of the cabin to sample what Bishop brought her from the galley. She ate without considering what she chewed, her thoughts occupied with a certain smuggler who had succeeded in oversetting her logic with a disarming ease. And as the half hours were claimed in a succession of bells, Kate found herself lulled by the rocking of the sea as surely as if she'd been a babe in a cradle. An occasional shrill of the boatswain's pipe was the only intrusion. Shadows stretched and filled the cabin until, too weary to hold her eyes open, she resigned her vigil. Brady wasn't coming.

Slumped with disappointment as much as fatigue, Kate shrugged out of her gown and stockings to seek the relative comfort of the built-in bunk. She'd scarcely closed her eyes when sleep overwhelmed her. And so, Brady found her.

He stood for a long while observing the figure curled and childlike upon his covers. Bare feet peeped innocently from beneath the hem of her petticoat and wisps of gold spread upon his pillow. A disquieting ache tightened within his chest. It wasn't just her beauty that held him. It wasn't the fact that he'd found her to be an enthusiastic lover. If he knew what fascination she tangled about him, perhaps he could find an escape instead of becoming more helplessly enmeshed with each unplanned turn.

Her uniqueness troubled him, for it made her hard to dismiss. In truth, the more he knew of her, the more his interest piqued. She was an irritant, a stimulant, an enticement he couldn't resist. And knowing his life held no place for her displaced more tender feelings that had a want to grow. It wasn't fair to use her casually. A more honest and honorable woman he'd yet to meet. He could tell himself that she was strong, independent, that she'd come to him willingly, almost aggressively, yet it would be a lie. Beneath her thorny toughness lay a susceptible nature. He'd convinced her to trust him and now he took advantage of that trust. Women like Kate Mallory needed home and family, attachments he could not give. Dammit, he'd warned her he couldn't supply those things. And just as he'd warned himself not to get involved, the cautions went unheeded. She deserved love and, instead, he'd tempted her with lust.

Angrily, Brady turned from the angelic picture she presented. Even now, his desires had the best of him, gnawing hot and impatient, urging him to join her on that yielding bed. But he couldn't yield. He'd witnessed her tears and pain and he vowed not to be the cause of any further suffering. Restraint was nothing new to him. It seemed he was always holding himself back from what he most wanted. With a wry smile at the constant irony of his circumstance, he sat himself before his desk and went about the work he needed to do.

The soft intrusion of light played about the fringes of Kate's lids, teasing her eyes open. The sight that greeted her wrought an unintentional smile. For a moment she was content in her study of the bronzed features bent low in the dim light over a spreading of charts. He was so handsome, so intense. She must have inadvertently moved, for his attention shifted up from the papers. The meeting of their eyes carried a potent charge. Brady looked quickly away.

"Forgive me. 'Twas not my intention to wake

you." He made as if to extinguish the lantern that hung above his table, suspended from the smooth wood of the ship's exposed rib.

"Please," she called. "Go about your work. You won't disturb me. I'm weary enough to sleep through Judgment Day." As if to assure him that it was so, she rolled over and snuggled deeper into the covers.

Far from reconciled, Brady scowled. His gaze found the measure of her gentle curves more rewarding than the approximates of longitude before him. He charted the fan of her hair, the degrees her rib cage rose and fell, navigated the swell of her hip and thighs beneath the sheath of linen. Surprised by the cold sweat that dotted his brow and slicked his palms, he determinedly faced his almanacs, but after struggling with his quadrant as if it was some foreign device instead of a much-used tool of his trade, he surrendered to his distraction. Muttering a curse, he gathered his papers into a careless armload and stormed from the room and its sound of seductive breathing.

From the bed, Kate smiled and closed her eyes.

The day broke hot and clear. Kate awoke refreshed and amazingly free of any trace of seasickness. After testing her legs on the imperceptible sway of the floor, she hurriedly dressed in a simple muslin gown and worked her tresses into a heavy braid, anxious to go above. The tang of salt tingled in her nose as she drew a deep lungful of sea air from the sunwashed quarterdeck. A hand up to shade her eyes against the

196

dazzle of refracted light, she scanned the deck, then waved to draw Brady's notice. He seemed to hesitate but came to join her. The breeze bristled his black hair and teased about his coattails and never had she beheld such a stirring sight as Brady Rogan in his element.

"Good morning, Captain."

"Kate. You're looking well. No ill effects from the journey thus far?" He spoke easily, but his attention didn't linger on her. Instead, his eyes moved restlessly about the schooner, settling anyplace but upon the figure before him.

"Put away your sago, arrowroot, and tamarinds. I've no need of their restorative powers. I seem to have become a sailor in spite of myself." His vague smile was not encouraging. She recognized a want to escape when she saw it, but experienced no little hurt that he should be so uncomfortable in her company. "I had thought to explore your ship. Perhaps you could spare one of your crew, Bishop or some other, to show me about."

Brady grinned, a quick flash of white teeth. "Ah, anxious to see if your precious cargo be safely stored, are you? Never fear, Miss Mallory, your assets are being well tended."

The playful mockery of his words made her relax. This was the Brady she knew, not the stranger of a moment before. "Still, you cannot fault me for being overcautious."

"I cannot fault you for anything."

As if suddenly realizing the smoky innuendo of his claim, Brady returned his guard. "Tobias, my clerk,

197

would leap at the chance to play escort. Since he's not assigned to either larboard or starboard watch, he tends to grow too idle. 'Twill do him good to have to wait like the rest of us till the sun is over the foreyard before he dips into his nooner of grog." He turned and issued a call, then regarded her with a forced smile. "I would give you the tour, but I find myself otherwise engaged."

Kate's smile was stiff, her voice properly polite. "'Twas not my plan to be a burden to you, Captain."

Brady hesitated, feeling her anger and confusion and at a loss to dispel either. If it was distance he wanted, he was succeeding. Yet, the plain truth was, it wasn't a safe remoteness he desired, quite the contrary; it was closeness, intimate closeness. He couldn't stand so near her and not want to pull her into his arms for a sampling of those disapproving lips, to taste the passion that hid behind the prudery. Thus, he drew even further away.

"Of course you're not," he protested.

Of course you are, she read in his evasive eyes, and her expression grew even more pinched. 'Twas with relief that she was introduced to the gangly Tobias so she could allow Brady his graceful retreat.

Since it was the captain and not the ship itself that interested her, Kate moved through the tour of the *Elizabeth* with an ebb of enthusiasm. She dutifully followed Tobias below deck, down the ladder into the dark and dismal regions where fumes of pitch, bilge water, and other unnamed odors were nearly suffocating. After several minutes, her stomach began its familiar roll of warning. Lanterns spotted at intervals did their feeble best to penetrate the gloom.

Compared to the privacy of the captain's cabin, the crew quarters were cramped, with every fraction of space in use. Boards hinged to the vessel's sides served as tables, then were secured up when hammocks were slung, hitched on hooks in the overhead deck timbers with little more than a foot allowed for sleeping space. Passing through the galley, they came to the hold, a dank, dark hole below the gangways where ballast casks of water and grog were stored along with provisions, powder, and ball. Tobias gestured proudly to the false flooring beneath which much of the illegal cargo was carried. That, he explained, would be unloaded in secret. The rest would go into port under falsified customs documents. To Kate, all seemed safe enough, with every precaution taken to assure that at least part of the untaxed goods would arrive undetected.

Further aft in the steerage were the officers' quarters and separate accommodations for the specialized members of the crew: boatswain, gunnery, steward, and clerk. Cannons were a part of the decor in these rooms and compartmental bulkheads could be quickly removed to form a gun deck. Kate was reminded that this was not a pleasure voyage and that those weapons could well be called upon at any moment to change the placid schooner into a bristling warship. Those somber thoughts made her conscious of the illegal act she'd involved herself in. And to think not long ago she was prudishly condemning Brady for the very trade in which she

199

now was engaged. Irony had a way of striking at the haughty, her father had oft times told her. How true, she reflected, considering her circumstance.

Restored to the captain's cabin, Kate thanked her guide and went to brood at her solitary lunch over the complexity of Brady Rogan. And there she stayed, restless and puzzled, until the later hour brought Bishop with an evening meal of pork and peas. And service for two.

"Might I join you?"

Kate's calm glance in no way reflected the sudden mad careening of her heart. If he was determined to be aloof, so could two play at this bewildering game. "Please, Captain. I am reminded that this is, after all, your cabin."

Brady frowned slightly. How cool she was. It was the reception he'd hoped for and yet . . . Disappointment acute, he took a seat at the small table that put them at an intimate proximity both pretended to ignore. They ate mostly in silence, Kate responding in short sentences to his queries over her afternoon. Finally, he let an uncomfortable quiet settle between them.

Kate plied her fork mechanically. Her thoughts worked with like listlessness. She, alternately, didn't understand and then was afraid she did—all too clearly. Brady was anxious to cool the fires that sparked between them. Now that he was returning to Elizabeth and the threat of Benjamin was at an end, he had no more use for her. She'd been a trifle, a mere distraction, just as Benjamin had warned. And hadn't she known that would be the way of it? She knew his love lay elsewhere, just as he would prefer to lie elsewhere 'twould it be possible. She had slaked his lusts and now he was trying, albeit kindly, to discourage her from attaching a serious meaning to their dalliance. Well, he needn't be so apprehensive, she told herself to shore up her sagging defenses. It wasn't as though the likes of Brady Rogan held a place in her future. Imagine being tied to such a scurrilous rogue, a smuggler, a restless wanderer! He would never be at home, always about some chancy exploit. Her future would be no more secure with him at the pursestrings than had her father continued to maintain them. And then there was the shadow of Elizabeth. How could she compete with that specter of lost love? No, Brady was not what she wanted or needed in a man, especially in a husband. She determinedly blinked back the contrary dampness that had begun to mist her eyes.

Brady scowled down at his plate. He'd seen the suspicious sheen in her eyes and knew with a guilty certainty that he was the cause. He wished he could explain to her the impossibility of them being together. He wanted no more commitments, no further obligations. Kate Mallory deserved everything he'd once hoped to be blessed with in life and could no longer obtain. It wasn't fair that she be limited by the confines of his affections. Affections? That took him aback. What, indeed, did he feel for this comely, courageous miss? He didn't want to explore that question lest it prove to be too attractive. Just as he didn't want to explore the availability of her here in his quarters, so close to him, he could smell the fragrance she wore so sparingly. So close that if he were to lean forward, he could claim her lips with no difficulty at all. And then it was just a step to the bed.

"So, Kate, what are your plans when you return home?"

She gave a start at the unexpected brusqueness of his words. She looked up with a challenging glint in her stare. What right did he have to sound so surly? It wasn't as though she'd asked anything of him, or expected anything from him. His fears were the product of his conceited male perspective that every female needed a man to guide her. She dared him to think that of her.

"I have a farm to run and sisters to nurture. The profits from this venture should provide a good beginning."

"And when that's gone?" He hated the image that came to mind, of Kate and the girls in want, dependent upon the charity of their merciless neighbors.

"We'll make do, I assure you. I plan to market the pacers in Newport this next spring. Mr. Blayne has assured me by his own offers that they will bring a good price."

"And what of the time in between? New England winters can be notoriously cruel." Was he sounding too concerned? He hoped not. It was, after all, just a friendly regard for her well-being.

"I have a wealthy fiancé to assure me good credit."

Brady returned her smile. God, he loved her sense of humor, the bite of it like a snap of briny breeze.

"And how long do you plan to retain this paragon before you're expected to post the banns?"

Kate's expression reflected the irony of her good fortune. "I will be in mourning. No one can fault me for not rushing into wedlock. The earl will be most understanding and will most likely wait out the mourning period in England."

She'd thought of everything, a way to postpone her debts, a way to excuse him from continuing his pretense, and a means to keep the overzealous Ezra Blayne at bay. He admired the cold logic of her thinking though it disturbed him with its calculating absolutes. She was making it clear that she needed no one, especially not him. Wasn't that what he wanted to hear? Her self-sufficiency should have cheered him. Instead, he felt irrationally discarded. Instead of being grateful that she'd provided him with an escape, he offered an excuse for her to hold him.

"Should you need me, Kate, for anything, don't let pride stand in the way of your asking."

Her reply was sharp enough to slice the hard biscuits before them. "You've done too much already, Captain. I don't wish to be obliging."

Stiffly, he nodded to that wish. Her rudeness should have put him off. It should have made him glad she wanted to be shed of him. It didn't. Desire, warm and persistent, flowed like heady grog through his veins. How he wanted to possess her, to force her, to let him care for her. The thought of dominating such a fiery miss quickened a desperate passion. It was that same need to conquer the untamable that bound him to the sea. To win her would be an exciting challenge, the spice of confrontation lending more intrigue. It had been bred into him, that desire to compete and control and, when faced with such an indomitable will, that need was overwhelming. God, how he wanted her.

Feeling the sudden confines of the cabin and dangerous lure of the rumpled bunk, Brady stood. He had to flee the small quarters that brought her all too readily to hand, yet he didn't want to surrender her company so soon. It was a delight to him.

"Come up top with me, Kate. There's something I wish to show you." At her wary look, he smiled and thus increased her uncertainty. "Come." His hand extended confidently. Hers was engulfed within it.

The night was surprisingly cool. Above the flap of white sails, the heavens were an endless indigo canvas spreading from yesterday to tomorrow on the horizons. A cache of diamond stars sprinkled in careless abandon upon that rich backdrop, a display of fabulous fortune nearly close enough for the taking. Kate gasped as she beheld its breathtaking infinity.

"Oh, Brady, how beautiful it is. I can see forever."

She understood it then, his need to be on the sea. She could absorb the wild sense of freedom it offered and felt her spirit soar. A light touch upon her spine held her to earth and inspired a different kind of enchantment. Compared to the grandeur above and magic that dwelt within her, all else was insignificant. She turned to the man beside her, lifting her face to study the intense beauty of his. Her lips parted in awe. Her eyes betrayed her dazzlement. She swayed. His arms went about her in an impatient embrace. His mouth was hungry, claiming, binding her with a limitless wonder. And she soared.

Brady stepped back, releasing her so suddenly she nearly lost her footing. Kate looked to him in question. A cautious invitation shone in her eyes, offering the stuff of dreams. The rarity of the stars paled in comparison. He trembled.

"Good night, Kate." Emotion roughened his voice like the rasp of fine velvet.

Regret gave her eyes the brilliance of the heavens. "Good night, Brady." Purposefully, she turned away, affixing her stare and concentrating on each step that carried her from him lest she be impetuous enough to fly back into his arms. One rejection on this starry eve was all her fragile heart could handle. She continued to walk, little knowing that had she turned back to him, he would have welcomed her without reservation. But she didn't, and his resolve went untested . . . for this night, at least—and Newport was sunsets away.

Chapter Twelve

Something was wrong. Kate awoke to the early dawn with a premonition of peril. She sat up, clutching her covers, and tried to convince herself that the chill of sweat had to do with a dream. She'd begun to believe that fancy and was about to settle back into the bunk when the call for all hands sounded from above.

She knew nothing of sailing, but Kate recognized the urgency in the scurrying overhead that had awakened her. Quickly, she was out of bed and struggling in to her closest gown. Trembling fingers began to rush up the bodice fastenings when the door opened without preamble.

"Do you know how to prime and fire a pistol?"

That single, curt question confirmed all of Kate's fears. She nodded with a jerk. Round, anxious eyes followed Brady as he gathered his charts and navigating tools and quickly stowed them behind a hidden panel at the foot of his bed. He didn't look at her.

"In my trunk," he told her with that same deadly calm, sending a shiver of fright through her. But she would not disappoint him with the evidence of her fears. She drew a deep breath to give her voice courage. "What is it, Captain?"

"Coastal pirates. They are after our cargo."

"Is there danger then?" That didn't sound quite so brave and he glanced her way with a brusque annoyance.

"To our lives or to our profits?"

"Are both in jeopardy?" She was very pale but continued to stand tall. A betraying quiver overtook the hands that gripped her skirts. Brady came to her then. His palm was warm and reassuring upon her cold cheek and the blue of his eyes sparked with intensity.

"No harm will come to you, Kate. I promise you."

A watery smile shaped her lips. "Another promise?"

His fingertips caressed the line of her firm jaw. "Do you doubt its value, Miss Mallory?" was his gentle taunt.

"No." That was said with conviction, and he gave her chin a squeeze.

"I'll send Bishop to stand with you."

She wished she could show herself unafraid by refusing his offer. Instead, she nodded her gratitude, thankful she wouldn't be cowering alone in the isolation of the cabin to await news of the fate of the *Elizabeth*. Then Brady readied to leave and thoughts to her own safety fled.

"Brady," she cried quietly, her hand on his arm

stilling him. "I would beg another promise of you."

He looked upon her worried features with a wry smile and his misunderstanding bruised her. "Don't fret. I'll keep your investments whole." When she made no reply, he turned and quickly gained the deck. She stared after him in dismay, for it hadn't been anxiety over the loss of profits that tightened like a fist about her heart. It was a fear for the roguish captain. Her tender plea for him to keep himself from harm remained unspoken.

The shifting of the deck as the schooner came about shook Kate into action. She knelt beside Brady's sea chest to search for a means of protection. After flinging aside several large squares of cloth, she gave them a cursory notice. They were the flags of a half dozen nations. She smiled to think he'd retained these tools of his privateering days. Then her fingers closed over cold metal and she sobered. Powder and shot were measured efficiently into the flintlock's barrel by the time the conspicuously nervous Bishop joined her. Kate sat with pistol resting upon her knees while the steward paced. A taut silence stretched out.

The boom of the cannon and shudder of the ship's timbers brought Kate to near frenzy, though none of that terror showed upon her tightly composed features. The consequence of a battle at sea seeped into her fright-clogged thoughts. They were going to sink. The *Elizabeth* was going down beneath the return of hostile fire. Knowing pirates wouldn't purposefully scuttle their prey before relieving it of its treasures might have given her some respite, but

Bishop was too much a victim of his own terrors to reassure her. All she could imagine was the consuming cold of the water as it sucked her below in greedy triumph. The sea would have its long-awaited victory over her.

Just as she'd begun to drown in the swirl of her own panic, the memory of Brady's words provided the means to stay afloat. *I promise you,* he'd said. She'd believed him then and she believed him now. He had taken her safely to Barbados and he would see her safely home. She clung to his words the way she'd held to the mooring in Providence. And she would not sink. Then she began to think of Brady, exposed to the dangers above.

"Do you think we'll be boarded, Mr. Bishop?" How calm she sounded. It heartened her.

Bishop's colorless eyes cast a nervous glance about, but he spoke with some confidence. "Not if the captain has his way. The Rogue, he be wily in battle. We never lost no goods to the likes of that scum. Most likely he'll get close enough to rake her stern with the big guns, trying for her rudder, tiller, or block and tackle. That'll disable her and we'll put up all our canvas to make a run. Ain't nothing on the water that can catch the *Elizabeth* under full sail."

To Kate, that sounded most logical. She sat quietly and prayed for the captain's skill and luck.

A pitching movement brought Bishop to the glass that ran along the stern. After a moment of anxious craning, he crowed, "Ah, we be moving windward to cross the enemy's stern. The captain will luff the canvas with the helm alee and let go the guns. We should know in a minute if our aim be true."

The four-pounders let go their bar and chain shot with a deafening volley. Kate was nearly tossed to the flooring as the *Elizabeth* rocked beneath the force of the guns. The acrid bite of burnt powder reached them. Kate overcame her insecurities and joined Bishop on tiptoe at the vista of windows. A phosphorescent spray trailed in their wake as the schooner made for open sea. They were granted a brief glimpse of the attacking brig, now crippled and smoking as she listed in the water. Kate gave a joyous cry and hugged a startled Bishop who went mortally pale as his captain regarded him with a chilling scrutiny. He disentangled the lady's arms and murmured an inaudible apology before slinking quickly from the room.

Kate regarded Brady. "Is all well, Captain?"

He hadn't moved from the door. "I saw to my promise, Miss Mallory."

"As I knew you would," she responded softly. Her gaze devoured him. His eyes were still ablaze with the excitement of conflict, his black hair left unruly by the breeze. An aura of black powder and danger clung to him. The apprehension that had crushed her heart released it in a wild flutter of anticipation. Passion roiled through her, rocking her more mightily than the schooner's guns. She said his name, low, throbbingly, letting him know that here was his reward for valor and victory. And he didn't hesitate to claim it.

Their lips met in an exquisite volley of breath and tongues, a battle of desire with no quarter given. Kate let herself drown in sensation without a struggle, dependent upon his arms to buoy her. She floated on waves of bliss . . . and abruptly sank.

The brisk knock at his door brought Brady away from her. She hung in his embrace, gasping for the return of his kiss. "What is it?" he growled as his hot stare roved her features like a prize he longed to plunder.

"Captain, a word with you."

He hesitated, torn by the lure of her parted lips and by the call of duty. Finally, he touched his fingers to her moist mouth and whispered, "A moment."

In the lull of his absence, Kate dropped strengthlessly upon the edge of his bunk. The knowledge that he would soon join her there had her senses all atingle. The danger and now the delight wrought her nerves into a shivering crescendo that rippled through her expectantly. When Brady went to the door, she was glad she couldn't be viewed by whoever stood opposite, for she knew she must look the wanton with her bruised and wanting lips and dazed, dreamy stare.

The words spoken were too low for her to hear, but when Brady turned, his expression told of the message. It was grim. She didn't figure in that angry glare that swept the room impatiently. Before she could ask the cause of his consuming fury, there was a second knock and Tandy, Brady's sailingmaster, stepped within. The dapper navigator acknowledged her with a quick nod, then looked to his captain. "Are you sure?"

Tandy responded to the curt demand without

pause. "Aye. I saw him signaling. The brig was trailing us, using the sun's glare to keep us blind until that bastard—begging your pardon, miss—called them in."

Brady's swarthy features worked with displeasure. "The man has been with me for over a year. What would make him turn his loyalties?"

"This be a powerful cause." A heavy pouch was passed from man to man, its contents examined with a frown. "He didn't have it on Barbados. Poor as a mouse, he was. Said he couldn't afford to wager a six pence in our last game and now he looks to be a bloody Croesus. He didn't come by this honestly. 'Tis blood money and 'twas meant to be our blood."

Brady weighed the pouch and the words slowly, then said, "Bring him to me."

Kate knew better than to interfere. This was ship's business and none of hers, but the taut distress on its captain's face made her wish she could impart her sympathies to ease the bite of betrayal etching such harsh lines there. Then Tandy returned, towing with him a reluctant seaman that she recalled speaking with just the day prior. She remembered because he'd seemed so pleasant and interested in her well-being. He didn't look to be a traitor, but she wasn't the only one to be deceived.

"Rawlins," Brady began with a rumble of quiet violence, "how came you by this wealth of good fortune?" The coin struck the floor with an ominous thud, the sound of an executioner's blade.

"Won it I did, Captain, from a gent on the Island." The sailor's face was slick with sweat and he couldn't

213

meet the eyes of his accuser.

"What were the stakes? Our cargo? Our lives?" That last was said with a crack akin to a blow and Rawlins winced at the force of it. A look of desperate cunning stole over him. "Tell me, man, is this the price of the trust of your friends? Of your honor? Me thinks you were sorely cheated. I wouldn't believe a man's decency could sell so cheap."

"And what would you know of it, you who never had to lack for nothing," Rawlins growled in his defense. His manner had gone from meek to surly, as if he challenged their right to hold him to blame.

"Damnit, couldn't you have stolen from us yourself to slake your greed? Why toss the lives of men you've served with to the mercy of indifferent thieves?"

"No one was to be harmed," the man blurted, then realized he'd sealed his guilt with that admission. His lips clamped together, bleeding white with the pressure of panic. A shiny blankness came into his eyes with the knowledge that all was lost.

Brady seized the sailor up by the shirt, lifting him from his feet to exact to a wrenching shake. "And do you consider yourself better off now? I shall let the men you thought to betray decide your punishment, but first, I want to know who paid you to bait us? Who? What man on the Islands?"

The glassy terror in Rawlins's eyes became something altogether different, a sort of deadly sheen of madness. In one jerking move, he tore free from Brady and stumbled backward. Grasping hands caught the pistol Tandy carried in his trouser band.

The bore measured in unerring purpose on his captain's chest.

It happened so quickly, like some nightmare she couldn't wake from. Realizing Brady's danger snapped through Kate's stupor of disbelief. With a fierce, objecting cry, she snatched the flintlock from the bed beside her where she'd dropped in false confidence that all troubles were over. She leveled it with a cool accuracy taught her by her father and squeezed the trigger. The pan flash blinded her. The powder discharge seared her nostrils. But she hadn't flinched. And she hadn't missed.

The smoke clouding the close quarters was slow to clear. Wreaths of it cloaked the figure of Rawlins, sprawled upon the planking, a vital crimson spreading across his bosom. The roar of the shot echoed, inciting a riot of excitement in the crew above.

"Is he dead?" Kate's voice was hard and even. The pistol was steady in her hands as if she was readying for another attack.

A stunned Tandy knelt, not knowing where to direct his gaze—at the crewman on the floor or to the equally still figure behind the unwavering gun. He put a hand to Rawlins's throat. There was a pause. "Yes, ma'am. Sent him straight to hell, you did."

The pistol lowered as if the weight of it had become too much and she surrendered it to Brady. He was looking at her with a strange intentness—not with surprise, not with shock, but with an assessing candor as if he knew not what to think. She'd killed a man and her hands weren't even shaking. Distractedly, he turned to Tandy to order, "Take him out of here and quiet the men. All's over and done with. I want them back at their stations."

Kate's gaze followed the wake of the dead man's heels as Tandy dragged him from the room, then returned to the pool of blood upon the floor. The calm that had served her to this point was beginning to fragment. Chills of reality took hold now that the crisis was past. Her eyes lifted. They were pleading. "He would have killed you," she said lifelessly.

"I know," Brady answered. He was watching her closely. "You saved my life, Kate. I know not how to repay such a debt."

"Could you just hold me." It was an eloquent request, accompanied by a diamond wetness in her expectant eyes. She burrowed against his chest, letting tremors of shock overwhelm her. But along with that horror came a savage pride. She'd saved him with her quick, instinctive action. Her hands tested the firm swell of muscle beneath his shirt-sleeves. His heart beat strong and vital beneath her cheek. She had saved him and now he would be hers.

Kate's face lifted. Her cheeks still shone with a vulnerable dampness; however, her gaze was crystal clear. Hers was no fragile beauty, no shallow loveliness. Strength and determination honed the fine contours, shaping them into a compelling whole. Such striking comeliness would have given any man pause, but Brady Rogan was struck helpless with longing. When her ripe lips parted in invitation, his could do naught but claim those lips tasting of tears and temptation, whetting his appetite for more of her.

With strong, tanned fingers tangling in her spill of golden tresses, Brady ravaged the mouth that had tantalized him with simple speech, that had overcome him with the merest touch, that taunted with a prideful frown or teasing smile. He ground against that yielding softness, seeking to conquer yet content to commune. The provocative play of his tongue preceded a more intimate plunder. That sensual inquiry progressed into aggressive plunges, encouraging her thoughts to follow his beyond the bounds of their embrace and exchange of kisses.

Kate came away from the marauding union, flushed and breathless. Her fingertips stroked along his bronzed cheek, gentling him with her touch. His eyes glowed with a lambent flame, igniting a passionate response within her own. Desire that had simmered above a low, continuous fire took to blaze, confined only by the boundaries of the room and imagination. Kate took a step back and he followed, entranced by the promise in her bewitching stare.

She sat upon the edge of the bunk and he came down before her upon his knees, coaxing her arms about his shoulders and her lips to return to his. While they indulged in that slow, searing reunion, his hands bunched her skirts up to bare her straddled legs and the way to the beckoning core of her femininity. Before she could recover from his thrusting kisses, Brady buried his face between her parted thighs to repeat that provokingly personal assault upon her senses. Her climax was instantaneous, soul-shattering bliss.

Brady pulled her down to the mattress and impaled

217

her with his urgent hardness. The smooth, commanding movement of his body encouraged her to a quickening of renewed sensation. Kate moaned into his fierce kisses. Her hands clung and coerced. Her breathing raced with the tempo of his, and her heartbeats competed with like fervor. Their coupling held the fury of a summer squall, blowing up quick with swirling violence to consume for one brief instant, then retreat into a placid lull.

With the storm of passion between them appeased, Brady and Kate lay side by side in a tangle of petticoats and arms. Though desires were spent, emotions still ran rich and expressive. Murmuring soft endearments, Brady nibbled along her ear and stubborn jaw. The words came easily from an unguarded heart, attesting to her beauty, to her courage, to her sexuality. They were pretty sentiments and doubtlessly sincere, but there were others she would hear instead, ones that spoke of devotion and commitment, ones he would not have said in the aftermath of his other conquests. That, she determined, was her price for saving his life, and she would hear him make those avowals. It no longer mattered if Brady Rogan wasn't the man of her dreams; he was the embodiment of them.

Brady was aware of her unusual quiet. He could almost feel the turnings of complex thoughts she held to herself. What was she mulling over so pensively, he wondered. Was she thinking of the rapturous love they'd made together or, more likely and unflatteringly, of the cargo they had saved? She was such an enigma. Unlike most females, he could boast no understanding of her motives or methods. She was not a frivolous miss, yet she'd been so giving in his arms. She was not one to be extravagant with her emotions, yet she'd lavished them upon him. However, her thoughts she kept private. She made no claims, no demands, and, irrationally, he almost wished she would. He wanted to do for her, now, even more than ever. That puzzled him. Everything about his reactions to her were a riddle. He'd taken countless women to his bed for bouts of unimportant lusting. He hadn't cared for them nor them for him. Whether he paid in coin or flesh, when the matter was done, it was quickly forgotten. Kate wasn't unimportant. Nor could he force her from his mind. The physical and mental pleasures she brought him were unimaginable and undeserved. Her wit was a constant challenge, her body a constant enticement. She was the only woman he'd bedded who had touched his heart. Even Elizabeth could not claim that, for they had never been intimate beyond a few youthful kisses. She was a first, a unique experience that affected him most strangely. What did one do with such a woman? Take her as lover? He couldn't picture Kate in such a mold, though she would fill it to perfection. Only one answer came to mind and he rebelled against it in a panic. Kate Mallory was the type of woman one took for a wife.

"How long until we reach the Bay?" Kate's quiet inquiry brought him out of his well of anxiety.

"Several more days barring bad weather." He was amazed. They nestled in each other's arms still warm with the sweat of passion only to speak casually of the weather. Such odd turns of conversation he'd come to expect from the woman cuddled against him. She was probably thinking of how long it would take to convert her illicit goods into coin. But she surprised him . . .

"I would not be adverse to spending those days occupied thusly." Her voice was a rough purr, her fingers a silken caress beneath his chin. It took him a moment to assimilate the direction of her thinking and then to overcome his unbidden delight.

"'Twould make for a most rewarding journey," he concurred huskily. "You'll not find me complaining should you wish to share quarters."

"And much more," she cooed. Her fingers busied with the buttons of his shirt, freeing them to give access to the tantalizing plane of his chest. They twined in his hair, twisting and gently tweaking. Brady was amazed to find himself so easily aroused a second time, especially when the first still had him weak and listless. His breath sucked in to make his belly hard and smooth for the passage of her palm. She tugged leisurely at the fall of his trousers. Now there was no denying his interest.

"Several days. And they call what we just left paradise," she murmured dreamily.

Brady's thoughts came into sudden unwelcome focus. Whose wife? Imagining Kate tempting another with her throaty cajolery, teasing them the way her fingers did him, exciting some other man with the dusky invitation in her gaze . . . With a rumbling sound of animal need, he rolled atop her, forcing those thoughts from his mind with the intensity of others, forcing her with his aggression to be aware of only him. And for a while, no other thoughts pervaded until they collapsed in simultaneous satisfaction. Holding her close, Brady began again to frown.

The days passed quickly, the nights, too, despite their want for them to last forever. The low, easy shore of Connecticut along Long Island Sound gave way to the deep indentation of Narragansett Bay where its islands moored like ships in a vast harbor. Kate couldn't appreciate the beautiful sheet of water with its wooded shores and rocky hills or the quiet coves and deep, ferny ravines. All she could see was an end to something that had grown precious and all-consuming over the last few days. She stood stiffly upon the deck while the *Elizabeth* stole into one of those tranquil coves to unload the bulk of her untaxed cargo. Then it was on to Newport.

Scores of great full-rigged ships lay moored at its docks while others waited a chance to berth and unload their cargoes of silks and cotton, ivory and ebony, tea and spices, hemp and copra, sugar and palm oil. The waterfront shipyards rang with mauls and axes as industrious builders framed and planked the hulls of ships that would soon join the melee. All along the Long Wharf, ships from the West Indies docked to discharge molasses, sugar, and slaves while those from Great Britain brought in manufactured goods and bricks to construct more of the elaborate manor houses that crowded Washington Square.

Brigs laden with native stores of tar, lumber, wool, pork, beef, cheese, and butter angled out to begin their ten-day voyage to the Florida Keys. Whale oil arrived from Boston and New Bedford to fuel the spermaceti candle industry. And the *Elizabeth* sidled in between them to the greeting of customs officials bribed to collect one dollar per hogshead in lieu of the duty and grant false clearance papers.

It was so easy, so casual, this transfer of illegal goods. Kate let out her breath, unaware that she'd been holding it, just waiting for one of the customs men to uncover their deception. But none had. All went smoothly, just as Brady promised. And soon the gold of her profitable risk would cross her palm and Brady Rogan would disappear from her life. Somehow, her success seemed more failure than victory.

Chapter Thirteen

The carriage drew up before the tidy home on Benefit Street and Kate immediately realized her mistake. Brady had insisted upon seeing her as far as Providence. He'd cited the amount of coin she carried and she'd agreed to his escort, not for protection but because she couldn't bear to part from him so soon. Now she knew she'd been wrong. The few awkward hours they'd shared on the road in the rented buggy in no way compared to the anguish of seeing him to the door of the woman he loved.

Her hope that she could deposit him and be on her way was ended when Elizabeth Rogan appeared at the door and called to her in welcome. The woman's generosity couldn't be spited without seeming rude. Gritting her teeth, Kate allowed Brady to assist her down.

"Brady!"

There was a flurry of long legs as young Jamie hurled himself onto his uncle for a crushing hug of

223

greeting. Kate's throat constricted. It was hard to see them together and not think of them as father and son. It was an illusion Brady would see a reality if he could, and knowing that lodged bitter in her breast.

"Come in. Come in," Elizabeth urged, linking her arm familiarly through that of her brother-in-law's. "How dry and dusty you must be. When did you arrive? Was your venture a success? Jamie's talked of nothing else since you left. Did you catch the tail end of that storm? Dreadful business that was."

Kate followed behind, listening to the animated chatter while her gaze held the browned hand that fondly covered the small frail one upon his sleeve. Nothing she'd endured in the last twenty-one days was more harrowing than crossing the threshold of the house her lover provided for another. She watched the three of them walking side by side, very much the image of a perfect family. Knowing the truth wasn't a comfort. When they reached the airy parlor, Elizabeth remembered her and saw her into the same chair in which she'd found so little ease on her last visit. The serving girl appeared promptly with a cool libation and Kate was grateful for the distraction. How arduous to maintain a vapid smile and pretend her heart wasn't breaking at the sight of Brady Rogan being served his beverage by a solicitous Elizabeth while her son lounged happily on the arm of his chair. He seemed incredibly content with the situation, not the least uncomfortable with Kate's presence, and that was the deepest cut of all. He should have at least displayed some degree of discomposure.

FREE

BOOK CERTIFICATE

ZEBRA HOME SUBSCRIPTION SERVICE, INC.

YES! **Please start my subscription to Zebra Historical Romances and send me my free Zebra Novel along with my first month's Romances. I understand that I may preview these four new Zebra Historical Romances Free for 10 days. If I'm not satisfied with them I may return the four books within 10 days and owe nothing. Otherwise I will pay just $3.50 each; a total of $14.00 (a $15.80 value—I save $1.80). Then each month I will receive the 4 newest titles as soon as they come off the press for the same 10 day Free preview and low price. I may return any shipment and I may cancel this arrangement at any time. There is no minimum number of books to buy and there are no shipping, handling or postage charges. Regardless of what I do, the FREE book is mine to keep.**

Name _____

(Please Print)

Address _____ Apt. # _____

City _____ State _____ Zip _____

Telephone ( ) _____

Signature _____

(if under 18, parent or guardian must sign)

Terms and offer subject to change without notice.

1-90

MAIL IN THE COUPON BELOW TODAY

To get your Free ZEBRA HISTORICAL ROMANCE fill out the coupon below and send it in today. As soon as we receive the coupon, we'll send your first month's books to preview Free for 10 days along with your FREE NOVEL.

GET
FREE
GIFT

ACCEPT YOUR FREE GIFT
AND EXPERIENCE MORE OF
THE PASSION AND ADVENTURE
YOU LIKE IN A
HISTORICAL ROMANCE

Zebra Romances are the finest novels of their kind and are written with the adult woman in mind. All of our books are written
by authors who really know how to weave tales of romantic
adventure in the historical settings you love.

BIG SAVINGS
AND FREE HOME DELIVERY

Each month, the Zebra Home Subscription Service will send you the
four newest titles as they are published. (We ship these books to
our subscribers even before we send them to the stores.) You may preview
them *Free for 10 days.* If you like them as much as we think you will,
you'll pay just $3.50 each and *save $1.80 each month off the cover price.*
AND you'll also get FREE HOME DELIVERY. There is never a charge
for shipping, handling or postage and there is no minimum you must
buy. If you decide not to keep any shipment, simply return it within 10
days, no questions asked, and owe nothing.

Because our readers tell
us these books sell out
very fast in the stores,
Zebra has made arrange-
ments for you to receive
at home the four newest
titles published each
month. You'll never miss
a title and home delivery
is so convenient. With
your first shipment we'll
even send you a FREE
Zebra Historical
Romance as our gift just
for trying our home sub-
scription service. No
obligation.

"So, Miss Mallory, was your trip successful as well? Did you sell your horses? Did you find your father?" The well-meaning questions stirred a tempest of emotion and, for a moment, Kate couldn't speak.

"Elizabeth," Brady began quietly, his eyes upon Kate.

"He's dead."

The blunt reply took the fragile woman aback. Her hand rose to her ovaled lips and then, amazingly, tears welled in her mild gaze for a man she didn't know and for the pain of a near stranger. "Oh, how clumsy of me. I am so sorry. Please forgive my intrusion upon your grief." She looked so genuinely aghast at her behavior that Kate was rushed to mumble an acceptance. Cool, well-manicured fingers patted hers in sympathy and Kate wished she could scream at the woman. Instead, she sat docile and suffered her condolences.

"I understand what it's like to miss a loved one," Elizabeth told her. The ache of loss in her tone made Kate glance up at her serene features. She stole a quick glimpse in Brady's direction. He was sitting stiff and expressionless.

"Brady, did you bring me anything?" Jamie burst out, oblivious to the subtle eddies that swirled between the adults in the room.

"James Rogan, what a bit of impertinence you are," his mother scolded. "Off with you. Finish your chores before suppertime."

"But, Mama . . ."

"Brady will be here when your work is completed."

225

"And so will your gift," Brady added with a conspiratorial wink. He gave the boy a pat on the bottom to send him off. His eyes glowed with pride and affection as they followed the lad from the room and Kate's misery twisted tighter. How could she compete with such a look unless she were to provide him with a son. Brady's son. Their child. That thought sunk deep, inciting a quiver of contentment. What a perfect link that would prove. And what an unjust way to use an innocent to trap an unwilling man. No, though the possibility could well exist, that was not how she wanted to win Brady Rogan. Her sense of honor wouldn't allow it. Her sense of pride wouldn't accept a victory lest it be truly hers.

So, how to capture a prize like Captain Rogan? It was too difficult to think within the lair of another woman. She was an intruder in this gracious setting. It made her uncomfortable and held her to a disadvantage. With the comely Elizabeth hovering near and the precocious presence of the boy, Brady spared her little notice. She needed to wrest him away from the false security of his brother's hearth in order to entice him with the benefits of her own. And that wasn't going to happen. He was staying here and she, going. In all likelihood, she would never see him again.

While he paid polite court to Elizabeth, Brady's gaze lingered inconspicuously upon Kate. How unsettled she appeared. He chided himself for not cushioning the topic of her father's death. He could see how distraught it made her, how much more painful the reality was as she grew closer to home.

There was no way he could make her grief easier to bear. That was something she would have to manage, and he had every faith in her strength. Such a strong, courageous woman. She would be fine and she would see her family survived. He needn't worry over her. Yet he did.

They were so different, these two women who'd caught at his emotions. Kate was an unpredictable storm that ravaged his senses, Elizabeth a gentle breeze that quieted his soul. There could be no comparison. Elizabeth was his life's love. She held his hopes, his dreams, his future, unpromising though it might be. Looking at her sweet face wrought an incredible wistfulness, a longing for what might have been, what should have been. She inspired unshakable feelings of duty, of responsibility, of protection. Even without the hope that she would one day be his, there was a satisfaction in knowing that it was he who provided for her, that she was dependent upon his care. And that was something he had no wish to surrender.

Then Kate had blown into his life like a coastal fury, tearing at the foundations of his well-made plans. Part of him wanted to retreat, to protect the way things were. Part of him was lured into the whirlwind of desires. She was a tempting unknown, Elizabeth a comfortable habit. He could fathom no way his life could encompass both. Selfishly he searched for one but could find no medium.

With Jamie's absence, Elizabeth turned to Brady, her expression softened with hope and helpless expectation. It was the same question she asked each time Brady returned from the sea. "Any word?"

"No, nothing" was his regretful reply.

Even though she'd anticipated his answer, Elizabeth's features fell. Her eyes grew hazy with disappointment. Only the presence of her guest kept her tears in check. "You're sure no one's seen him?"

"I'm sorry, Elizabeth. I wish I could tell you what you want to hear, but I cannot."

The meaning of their exchange dawned upon Kate. She stared at Brady, stunned by the smooth lie he delivered without so much as a blink. How could he withhold such knowledge from the woman, well knowing how she longed to hear the truth he could tell? Brady caught her look of astonishment and he warned her to be silent with a single glance.

"It's time I was going," Kate announced brusquely, then stood. She feigned a smile at her hostess and thanked her for her hospitality. Inside, she was fuming. How could he so abuse this woman's trust?

"I'll see you out, Kate."

She would have refused, save his hand closed upon her arm to convince her otherwise. She said a pretty farewell to the yet-weepy-eyed Elizabeth Rogan and let Brady escort her to the front steps. There, when they were alone, she rounded on him fiercely. "How could you?"

"Kate . . ."

"How could you be so cruel?"

"This is none of your concern, Kate," he cautioned. A forbidding stiffness seemed to overtake his features. It was the hard, unyielding look he shared with his brother and Kate hated the similarity. It made her anger steep.

"You've no right. The man is her husband."

"The man is an insensitive dog who deserted her when she was with child."

"She has a right to know the truth. 'Tis you who is being insensitive."

"You'd have me tell her the man she adores could care less for her or their son? You think that knowledge would be less cruel?"

"I don't think it is for you to decide. She will survive it. Were I her, I would want to know."

"But you're not, Kate." He said that harshly, not intending the insult she perceived. He was too agitated, too set on establishing his right to judge, to see the hurt in her eyes. "I've no doubt that you would survive it, but Elizabeth would be ruined. I think only of protecting her."

"Of protecting her or your place as her protector?"

Her observation hit a mark so true he flinched, then immediately formed a defense to deflect that unwelcome insight. His expression was a cloud of displeasure just waiting to let loose its thudner. "'Tis none of your business. Your interference is not wanted. Leave it be."

Kate drew a stabilizing breath. Her stare was dark with disapproval and the sting of disgust. She spoke with severe calm. "Forgive the intrusion, Captain. 'Tis your life and no concern of mine, as you said."

This was not how he would have them part. He searched for a way to make amends, but she thrust aside his want to heal the sudden breech between them with her concluding words.

"Thank you for your assistance, Captain Rogan. I shall not forget all you have done. I must return home now and put my profits to good use. Thank your . . . hostess again for her kindness. Good-bye, Captain."

"Kate," he began, but she ignored the entreaty. She had to get away before the burn behind her eyes betrayed her. With an indifferent nod, she turned and strode quickly to the buggy, swinging up without aid and applying the reins with a snap. She didn't look again to the man who stood upon the porch on Benefit Street nor would she allow him into her thoughts. Those tormenting visions would come soon enough.

The leisurely trip from Providence to Kingstown gave Kate the necessary time to compose her thinking. There was little travel along the Lower Post Road, which was unusual for the time of day. She enjoyed the solitude of the ride and the clop of hoofs and natural music of the countryside that welcomed her home. After weeks of endless sea broken by a tropical idyll, the quiet left her strangely wistful. Small farms blanketed the land, dotting the length of long rough roads that wound toward belts of settlement. It was a serene life, bred of the seasons where stock multiplied freely as it would and corn knew an eight-fold yield. Holding title to vast acres made no man rich. Often the most fertile ground gave rise to only clumps of blueberry, shadbush, tartarian honeysuckle, and raspberry, the only creatures thriving upon it the robins, thrashers, catbirds, and orioles that competed for berries.

A great gulf widened between the depressed lot of the farmer and the wealthy who used their dubiously earned fortunes to erect lavish estates that rivaled those of the southern plantation with their droves of slaves and bound servants and idle lifestyle. Their stately homes dominated the tranquility of the landscape in glaring contrast to the small, humble dwellings of those who worked the land. At one time, Kate would have looked with longing toward those majestic bastions of success, but no longer. Her thoughts and soul were tied to three hundred acres of fertile soil embraced by a low stone wall and by the dreams of a young girl desperate for a place to call home. All she desired was contained within those walls, at least it had been before she'd tumbled into the mocking, blue-eyed stare of an unscrupulous smuggler in a Newport tavern. Now, she wasn't quite so sure.

Kingstown was a quiet old village with a wide main street. In the midst of rolling, wooded hills, it served as county seat and a rural business center with law offices and mercantiles to serve the widespread populace. And business was what she'd come to attend. After nodding to several acquaintances, she drew her liveried buggy up before McLain's Mercantile.

McLain's was a fine store, swept clean and kept orderly by the industrious Mistress McLain and well stocked by her redheaded husband. The front-room shelves were crowded with dry goods, crockery, pewter, tin, ironware, brass, medicines, inkwells, a few well-chosen books, writing paper, tea, which was becoming scarce, and its acceptable replacement of coffee. Barrels, kegs, hogsheads, bins, and crates divided the floor space and, from hooks above, trunks, bandboxes, traps, and warming pans dangled to threaten an extravagant hat or hairstyle. The counter hosted, besides Mr. McLain's elbows, tin egg baskets, cheese, butter, dyestuffs and other perishables. Tempting scents of spices, coffee beans, mint, liquors, and newly smoked fish was a pleasant relief from the smells of the street.

Kate's presence drew immediate attention. A silence was accompanied by awkward stares steeped in sympathy, and she knew news of the *Prosper* had reached Kingstown. With head held high, she advanced through the discreetly whispering townspeople to the counter.

"I've come to settle my account," she announced with a quiet purpose that carried through the room as if she'd shouted her intentions.

Rufus McLain looked uncomfortable and began to mutter, "Now, Miss Mallory, this don't seem to be the right time." A swift poke in the ribs from his wife ended his charity.

"This is a perfect time," Kate said to ease his expression of distress. "If you'll total the books, I've a few things I'll be needing."

Mistress McLain sailed around the counter, the soul of self-serving commiseration. Her arm went solicitously about the stiffened shoulders. "We were all so saddened to hear of Nathan's passing. What a tragedy to befall five young women with no other benefactor." She steered the young woman forcefully to the bolts of imported fabric. "You'll, of course, be needing a wardrobe for a year of deep mourning. We have some fine black serge and merino and crepe for cuffs, collars, and bonnets. This would make a most proper veil." She fingered a thick black netting of crepe. "I have a nice selection of gloves and scarves to give at the funeral and, of course, you'll be needing handkerchiefs."

Kate regarded the square of sheer white linen with its broad black border. Her face showed no emotion. Taking her silence for compliance, the overbearing woman hurried on in an ecstasy of calculated sales.

"Knowing how close you were to your father, you'll want a token to remember him by. See this beautiful piece. It can be easily filled with a likeness or inscribed in memoriam."

"No."

The flatly spoken negative deflated her hopes. Regretfully, she replaced the large gold locket, resigning herself to have pushed too far for the girl's means. "'Tis a pretty piece, but I'll agree, a bit extravagant. Shall I have the mister total the rest for you?"

"No."

Mistress McLain looked askance. "What then can we do for you?"

"Some lengths of plain black ribbon, if you please, and the same in thread."

"No mourning garments?" The woman looked stunned by the sacrilege and the loss of coin to her coffer.

"My father would want us to use our coin wisely, not to encourage the English tax on these fine goods. We needn't wear our mourning on display. He will surely know what resides in our hearts. Just the ribbon and the thread, please and . . ." she paused as her glance touched on the display of fabrics, "a dress length of that red brocade."

Her features wearing the pinch of scandal, Mistress McLain went about her measuring with quick disapproving snips of her shears. The scant bundle in her arms, she preceded Kate to the counter where her husband had her account book open.

"All figured up for you, Miss Kathryn, including the goods your man Cosgrove ordered."

Stoically, she dealt out the coinage and with parcel under her arm, bade a somber good day to all. She went direct to her buggy. The payment to the remaining creditors could wait for another day. She wanted to be with her family, to share in the grief they must be suffering, for surely they already knew they were orphaned. Looking neither to the right nor left to acknowledge the curious, she snapped the reins and headed for farm and family.

It was late. She knew by the relentless burn of strain in her eyes and shoulders. Kate sat back in her chair and let her tatting settle upon her knees. The house was silent about her. The tears and wails and condolences had ceased hours ago and all were asleep, the heavy slumber of exhausted sorrow.

Tirelessly, her fingers worked black threads into intricate bits of filet to modestly and respectfully adorn the cuffs and collars of the Mallory girls' everyday dresses. Tomorrow she would go through their old trunks in search of the carefully preserved ebony lace that had served them after their mother's death. And she would have to arrange for a memorial service as there was no body to place in an empty grave. She fought back a more determined ache behind her eyes and drew a deep breath. Tomorrow she would also move her belongings into the downstairs room.

Unable to concentrate any longer upon the tiny stitches, she put aside her handiwork to take up an old copy of *The Mercury* she'd picked up in McLain's and skimmed through the articles to distract her thoughts. There was news of Masonic lodge balls, the arrival of a man to teach French, classes in psalmody, a notice of playing cards for sale at the print shop, and dates for horse races held on Easton's Beach for purses of up to a hundred pounds. Absently, she entertained the idea of having the girls learn French but dismissed it with a sigh. They would be better served in the study of accounts and fancy sewing, for those were more practical accomplishments for females of their standing.

Kate folded the paper for later reading and carried a Betty into the room across the hall. A cozy warmth spread from the fire Sarah had kindled earlier, making the transition from clothing to covers a comfortable one. Oddly, the room provoked no anguish within the firm resolve of her soul. She'd grieved for her father once within its walls and had found exquisite solace. Now the great bed and familiar furnishings contained tender memories of both men she'd loved and she found it a source of contentment. Those cherished recollections could be pulled forth for her private indulgence each eve, for they were all she'd ever have of either man.

Dismissing thoughts of what she'd lost, Kate looked ahead to the uncertainty of their future. Alone, in the quiet house, she wasn't quite so confident. Her profits from the Indies would dwindle fast, and then how would she provide? She recalled her bold assurances in the face of Brady's concern with a bittersweet smile. There had to be some way to maintain their tentative hold on the property and on the independence of their future. She owed that to her sisters, to the memory of her father. She owed it to herself.

She'd begun to consider the profit in horse racing, for Rhode Island was more tolerant of this worldly pleasure than the more Presbyterian colonies which had banned it. Restlessly, she rolled onto her side, her hand gliding along the crisp sheet. A wave of powerless longing overtook her quite by surprise, for upon that yet-cool linen, she could vividly recall a more vital warmth. *Oh, Brady, would that you were here* came a keening cry within her heart. How she could have used his supportive strength, his uncluttered logic in the face of insurmountable worries. Then the unbidden truth assailed her and she was humbled by it. It wasn't his assistance she wanted, it was him. She desperately wanted him beside her, to be lost in his arms, to be transported by his kisses, to be devastated by the delights of his body until worldly worries ceased to matter. Just his presence could lend her the strength to see anything through, just the knowledge of his nearness fueled her with an assertive confidence. Without him, she was . . . alone.

Her hand leisurely stroked the vacant spot beside her. Never had she felt such a kinship to another. Always before, she had found her strength within herself and it had never failed her. She couldn't afford to let it fail. Yet with Brady near, she'd begun to think that perhaps it was all right to fail in some things, that it was allowable not to wish to shoulder the responsibilities of the world. She smiled to think of her first opinion of him, that he was insufferable, arrogant, a scoundrel. Well, true, he was all those things, but she had discovered a deeper truth, a truer character, one of unshakable honor, of unfailing compassion, of tenderness and human failings. To have the love of Brady Rogan would be the power to take on all things without doubt or fear. To have his arms to fall back into, the threat of failing would lose its grip on her. To claim his love and his loving every night would make all else inconsequential. But she had neither and she was afraid.

Curled tight in the blankets, Kate considered their lot. Could she provide for them? Could she see their home secure? Could she maintain the courage not to falter before intimidating odds? Yes. Yes, she could. And she would. She would start tomorrow. Alone.

Chapter Fourteen

A solemn-faced group sat at the table. The kitchen's yeasty smell of baking bread pervaded yet did little to comfort the gathering with warmth. The somber topic forbade it. The day was golden with promise yet failed to stir a sense of cheer in the attentive listeners. They were silent, some out of anxiousness, some in deep thought, but all aware of the gravity of their situation.

"So, there it be," Kate concluded. "Now you all know how things stand and it isn't a pretty portrait. I need to know now how you feel before I make choices that will affect us all. What say you?"

For a moment there was no response. They regarded her with uncertainty, with helplessness. Then the youngest spoke with the clearest insight of all. "Without Papa here, will we have to sell our farm?"

Kate smiled encouragingly at Bertrice. "That's what we're going to decide, sweet." How difficult it was not to let her own desires cloud their free choice. They were young and she could have easily managed without hearing their opinions, but their futures were held in the balance and she owed them the chance to express their wants and fears.

Anne cleared her throat uneasily and said, "I know I am always complaining about being hidden away in the wilds, but this is our home and I'd prefer no other to it. If there's a way it can be done, I say we stay."

Kate's speaking glance blessed her for those sentiments and the other girls were quick to agree. Heartened by their enthusiasm, she tempered it with caution. "'Twill not be easy. There will be sacrifices to make and all of us must be willing to make them without complaint." There was a firm consensus in the nodding blond heads. "This winter will be the worst. We've known hard times before, but these coming days could prove a trial to Job. We're women alone and there are those who will take advantage of that fact."

"Not alone, Miss Kate," Cosgrove said. "If you don't mind me speaking my piece." When she prompted him with a look, he put a gnarled hand on young Timmy's shoulder. "This be our home, too, and if it's to be work for board, then we've no objection till the times get better."

"That be my thinking, too, Miss Kate," Sarah added with a quiet conviction. "I ain't much good to you but nobody else would ever let me serve as maid in waiting when I've no talents above the scullery. I be grateful for the chance to improve myself, if you can suffer my clumsiness."

"'Tis I who am grateful, Sarah, and you improve daily." This won a timid smile, albeit a doubtful one. Then Kate added casually, "You'd best check on that bread before it goes to the scorch."

With a dismayed "Oh!" she flew to the baking oven and opened the door with her apron. Black smoke billowed out to confirm the worst was already done. Tears filling her eyes, Sarah turned back to them. "Oh, 'tis no use. I be costing you more in my blunders than you can afford."

"A few loaves of overdone bread will not break us," Kate assured the dejected girl. "If we're to be a family, we will help one another. Jeanne is a competent cook. She can aid you in the kitchen until you're more confident in your skills."

"I'll make you proud, Miss Kate. I swear it," she vowed in a wavery voice.

"You all make me proud and together we shall keep our home."

There was heavy sign from Mistress Fitch, whom they'd all assumed had been dozing throughout their discussion. The old woman's keen stare proved she was not only awake but aware of what had been said. Her frail voice held a strength of younger days. "Methinks 'tis time I went to stay with my niece in Boston. She has offered me the charity of her rooms should I ever have need of them."

"But, Fitch, you cannot mean to leave us," Roberta cried in childlike despair. Her thin arms encircled the loosely fleshed neck and hugged tight.

"There, there, child. I'm not so blind that I cannot

241

see you've no more use for me. I am a burden to you. With my failing eyes and crippled hands, I've no means to earn my keep. You've kept me on out of kindness, I know, but 'twould be cruel of me to impose when your circumstances can scarce afford to feed another mouth."

Kate had no answer that would refute the quiet dignity of her claim. She dearly loved Fitch; they all did, but what she said was true. She couldn't argue it without offending the proud old lady with what she'd know to be pity. As pride was all the woman had yet to own, Kate was loath to bruise it. She could see no way to convince the beloved nanny that she'd not outlived her purpose within their household.

Anne was her salvation. She laughed gaily and said, "Oh, Fitch, I'd not thought you one to prefer an idle life. I suppose you have earned the right to an easy chair before the fire, but 'tis unfair to place the blame upon us. Not need you? How could you say so? You've always been our trusted counsel. Wisdom isn't something that fails with age. We need your guidance now, more than ever. You'd leave us without the benefit of proper watch and ward? What would our neighbors say of such neglect of duty? Have we proved such a trial that you'd be glad to be shed of us?"

The old woman blinked rheumy eyes, then straightened her hunched shoulders to affect a disgruntled pose. "Now, missy, you mind your tongue. Never in my life have I shirked a charge and I'll not be starting now just because the five of you bedevil me beyond endurance. Shame on you for suggesting such nonsense. I can bear up with the best of you. Just see if I can't."

Looking properly chastened, Anne patted her shoulders to calm the ruffle of indignation. "Of course you can, Mistress Fitch."

"Then 'tis settled," Kate announced. "We shall brave what comes together. Be warned, there is nigh enough coin to see to what's owed and none to spare for luxuries." She knew a moment of guilt, thinking of the crimson damask that she'd folded away until six months of mourning would allow for the return to social gatherings. Then she considered the glow of expectant youth in Anne's lovely face and the extravagance paled.

"What of Captain Rogan?"

Kate felt her insides tense into a knot of unrealized distress, but her question was quietly directed to Roberta. "What of him?"

"Were you to marry him, we'd have no more troubles."

Her simple reasoning left the adults agog. Again, Anne provided rescue with a gently chiding, "Bobbie, a lady does not ask a man to wed to save her from circumstance."

"Why? Katie likes him much better than that toad, Ezra Blayne, so 'twould seem he would be the suitor to pick. And he's much handsomer, too."

"Captain Rogan is not my suitor," Kate corrected. Her dismay had been bested by resolve and the words were unyielding. "We can depend upon none but ourselves to see our troubles to an end. Now we've work to do. Let's see it done."

*　　　*　　　*

The arrival of a liveried carriage in the drive washed bright by the midday sun brought a quartet of curious Mallory girls to the steps. Their excited titters distracted Kate from the household books and she joined them just as a bewigged postboy lowered the steps for elder and younger Misters Blayne. Kate's manner cooled immediately and her words were spoken with a crisp authority.

"Go inside, girls. I'll not have you staring like simple tavern wenches bedazzled by gaudy trappings. You owe no man homage."

The low aside prompted quick response and Kate stood alone to greet her visitors. Her features adopted a serene smile.

"Good morrow, sirs. Please come inside and accept our hospitality." She turned with that and led the way into the parlor. Once her guests were seated and served a welcoming cordial, she regarded them with a pinning directness. "What brings you here, gentlemen?"

"To offer our condolences, of course, and to see if you want for anything."

The elder Blayne's words held the rumble of sincerity and Kate accepted them with a gracious nod. "Thank you, Master Blayne. Your kindness is much appreciated, but we are fine." She sipped her fruity beverage and waited for him to come to his purpose. She didn't look to his son. She didn't have to to know his leering gaze settled upon her bosom. Her breasts felt all but burned under the intensity of his stare. Icily, she turned her glare upon him in quelling censure until he had the decency to blush and look elsewhere. But only until her attention turned back to his father.

"I admire your determination, Miss Mallory, and your courage, but facts must be faced no matter how cruel," their mortgage holder began in his condescending business tone. With the royal edict against the Colonies coining their own currency, wealthy men like Blayne stepped in to serve in lieu of proper banks, but, unfortunately, theirs was an ungoverned institution of lending. "With the loss of your father, some changes will have to be made."

"Changes, sir? I don't understand." Her gaze never wavered. She refused to let him think she was some helpless female ready to be intimidated from her home.

"Your debts, for one matter," he broached tactfully.

Kate sent another warning glare to Ezra, then said calmly, "I have the means to see to them."

"And to your delinquent mortgage as well?"

That was a stunning blow of revelation and Kate fought not to sway under it. Her voice was small but not frail. "How long has it gone unpaid?"

"A quarter past due and another pending."

"I see." Her thoughts spun frantically behind the steady set of her eyes. "Is it your plan to see us evicted then?"

Blayne was at once consoling and affronted. "My dear, 'tis not my way to set needy families out upon the road." Kate knew different but was willing to cling to the vague promise of his charity. What other choice had she? "I came to discuss alternatives. I'm sure we can arrive at an arrangement that will prove

245

beneficial to us both."

"I am listening."

"Is your betrothed willing to assume your debt in full?"

"Upon our marriage, of course, but as I am in mourning, it would be most improper to take such a step now."

"Would he be willing to come to my home and sign papers of note against payment, and interest, of course." Clever greed shone bright in his smug expression. Kate was quick to thwart it.

"I am assured he would, save he's in England seeing to his family's affairs and not like to return before harvesttime."

Blayne's displeasure was evident only for an instant, then his crafty smile returned. Kate was alerted and wary. "I would be willing to accept your fine Pacers as collateral pending his return."

She was silent. She knew the Earl of Bradington would not be returning to see her from debt and that the horses would be forfeited along with her hopes were the agreement made. There seemed no way around the damnable arrangement without exposing her charade of impending wedlock. She had been clever but Blayne was adroitly shrewd. He'd trapped her, and his patronizing smile betrayed that he knew as much. "I understand business, Master Blayne, and do not expect you to carry us without cause. I am willing to allow you the use of four of my best geldings for the season."

The audacity of the girl was incredible, yet Blayne continued to smile. Had his own son half her brazen gift of bluff, he'd be assured his assets would be well tended. Her tenacity bade him hear her out. At his nod, she continued with her emboldened proposition. "We both know well the profits to be made from a swift second at Little Neck. Racing my stock could earn you more than the price of our mortgage debt in a single month on the track. In gratitude I'd be willing to allow you a percentage of any sale made to your fine Virginia gentlemen friends who seek a comfortable saddle and of any breeding arrangements that come of our successful racing season. That way, I'd be responsible for care, training, and loss, and you would only have to count your coin."

Blayne pursed his lips, then laughed a booming testament to his delight. "Be Gad, girl, you've got spunk. No businessman would accept such a willy-nilly deal, but a sporting man would and I've admired those Pacers for years. You are right in your estimate of their worth and you've my hand on our arrangement."

Kate took the warm, fleshy palm and gave it a firm shake. She hoped the dampness of her own wouldn't give witness to her inner tremors of relief. She could scarce believe she had bested him yet was too wise to boast of it prematurely. She'd no doubts her horses would fulfill the bargain. They were the finest in the state. What nagged her with apprehension was what would happen when her nuptials never came to pass. Then how could she discourage the presumptuous passion that even now glittered in Ezra's avaricious gaze. She would have no protection save her wit and, with the power of his family behind him, she wasn't sure that would be sufficient. A shiver of disgust overtook her and, as if he knew he figured in her thoughts, the younger Blayne came to bow in courtly fashion over her reluctantly offered hand.

"Should you find yourself in need in your fiancé's absence, Miss Kathryn, pray come to me. I am most eager to be of service, in any way."

She would have spat her loathing in his insinuating face had they been alone, but under her banker's thoughtful gaze, she merely smiled and swallowed her ire. She would rather seek out the devil for help.

One week passed, then two. Spring languished into a sultry summer as lazy as the nodding hollyhocks that grew beside the porch. Phlox, tiger lilies, candy tuft, snowballs, and lilacs outdid the previous season in the brilliance of their bloom. Scents combined in heady indolence: the aromatic, the fragrant, the ambrosial. July settled in like a fat, tired hound opposed to moving, but such rest was a luxury at the Mallory farm.

Nathan Mallory's memory had been put to a dignified rest, an empty coffin in the town's cemetery. His extravagances were duly erased from account as Kate went from business to business doling out coin until no more palms were outstretched and precious little remained in her own. The Pacers made Blayne a happy profit and he left Kate alone. Lecture days on Thursday and Sunday service were the only events to bring the Mallory girls into town in their somber procession of black ribbons and black lace cuffs. Kate wasn't so strict outside society's censure, and, late in the day, the yard often rang with girlish laughter as the younger sisters indulged in an energetic game of battledoors and shuttlecocks. At night, they read their lessons from the Bible and retired early. Kate, a slumbering Mistress Fitch, and Anne remained in the parlor in silent company, Kate over her accounts and Anne working on pairs of silk stockings with open designs and commissioned initials knitted on their insteps. Her handiwork provided a welcome cushion in their coffer. When the candles burned low and shadows grew long, they'd waken Fitch and withdraw to their rooms. In her solitary bed, Kate would lie awake into the quiet eve to postpone the dreams she knew would come with slumber, dreams she anticipated as much as dreaded, dreams of a blue-eyed smuggler who had inadvertently captured her heart.

Kate wasn't one to give way to foolish fancy, but on some of those long, somnolent summer nights when a taste of her father's cordial loosened the tight rein of her control, she would lie back upon her counterpane and imagine that Brady Rogan was coming to claim her. She replayed the memory of his regal looks on the eve of the Blaynes' ball and pretended her fancy was reality, that her handsome, wealthy lord would arrive in autumn to duly wed her and lift the yoke of her daily struggle, replacing it with the longed-for weight of his arms. Those dreams gave way to the sight of him on the quarterdeck, all virile and bronzed, more a pirate prince than a noble lord. That fantasy would lure him to the cabin below, to where she waited to surrender to his desires and to her own. Then a final image would overlap both those pleasant pictures—the sight of his weathered fingers encasing the frail hand of his would-be lover . . .

And on one listless afternoon while her thoughts wandered over a book of verse, her sister's gleeful cry made her think she yet dreamed.

"Katie, your Captain Rogan is here" came Roberta's triumphant shout. For a moment, Kate sat as if rooted to the rush bottom of her chair. Then a frantic trembling seized her. *Brady is here.* She came up and was running. Somehow, she regained possession of her careening thoughts long enough to slow her pace. She could hear him in the yard. The resonance of his voice set up a quivering in her belly that rose hot to pound inside her head. Blindly, she blundered into a figure hurrying opposite.

Sarah's work-roughened hands lent support as did her calming speech. "Here now, miss, if you be rushing out at your pretty man like he be the Second Coming, you'll be scaring him all the way to Halifax." She wet the corner of her apron in the water pitcher she'd been carrying and used it to blot the vivid color that heated Kate's cheeks.

With the cooling wash and sensible words to restore her lucidity, Kate felt a giddiness akin to too many tipped cups. Flutterings of excitement quickened to an unbearable flurry. How indeed would it look were she to fly off the porch into his arms in wild-eyed urgency? Drawing a deep breath, she gave Sarah a grateful glance while straightening the folds

250

of her gown. She couldn't let him know his return had pitched her lonely world awry.

"How do I look?" she asked with feigned restraint.

A shy smile touched Sarah's homely features. "Like you was in love, Miss Kate. But I guess that be the truth of it."

And Kate could not deny it.

As she stepped out onto the porch and Brady turned toward her, all Kate's hastily gained reserve faltered and grew dangerously close to collapse. How he looked standing there. Her senses were stunned. She was bedazzled not by fancy finery but by the sheer maleness of him in his simple brown coat with waistcoat unbuttoned over dark breeches and high English top boots. He looked more country squire than privateer and more handsome than her fragile heart could stand. Her eyes, long starved for this sight, made a quick, ravenous meal. And his did much the same.

"Good morrow, Kate."

"And to you, Captain."

They stood, staring, unmoving, until Sarah stepped out and caught Roberta by the arm giving her a propelling tug.

"Come, Miss Roberta. You're to help me pluck that bird for dinner." It took a second, near wrenching force to convince her to follow. In that time, Kate recovered some of her shattered composure.

"Forgive me. Please come inside and let me offer you something refreshing."

His smoky stare said that had already been accomplished. "No," he said aloud. "Let's walk. 'Tis a fine day and I rarely have time to enjoy the pleasures of the country." Again, his glance was speaking.

They walked. For Kate, it was a sensual journey. Never had she been so aware, so sensitive to the teasing shifts of the breeze that spun about the loose tendrils of her hair, of the heat of the sun warming her flesh until it seemed to beat golden in her veins, of the grasses that brushed her ankles with brief, tickling caresses. Though she didn't look Brady's way, she was conscious of the rhythm of his breathing and the sighing of the meadow weeds that bent before his long stride. The textures of wind and sun and nature tantalized, making her chafe to experience those of a more intimate source. With each forward step, it was a struggle not to turn to cast herself upon him. With each moment of silence, she longed to cry out the dissonance of suppressed desires. His presence beside her was a most miserable enchantment, for it brought into painful juxtaposition what was and what she would have be. Reminding herself of the bitter truth was a thankless task when all it took was the innocent brush of his sleeve against her arm to incite tremors of unreasonable need. The pitiful truth was that it mattered not why he had come, just that he was here. To savor a few minutes in his company was to overshadow all the empty nights alone and, for that, she could weather the knowledge that he had not come for her.

They had reached a small, untended orchard. It shielded the house and outbuildings from sight. It was as if they were in their own private Eden. The light touch of Brady's hand upon her spine stilled her and brought her about to look up into his intense eyes. She searched the complexity of expressions there, hoping to single out the one she sought but able to discern only compassion and regret.

"I pray you do not mind that I am here."

"No." Was he mad? How could she mind when she'd been able to think of naught else?

"I wasn't sure if you would. We parted so poorly. I am sorry for that."

"I, too."

"I had to see how you fared. I thought of you often, Kate, and my conscience would give me no rest."

His remorseful tone puzzled her. She could see no reason for his guilt. "Captain, you've no obligation for my welfare," she began, but he cut her off with a quick, "Yes, I have."

His fingers caught a strand of gold between them and twined the honied lock into gentle swirls. He stood close, so close she could feel the graze of his breath upon her cheek as whisper-light as the breeze.

"How are you, Kate?"

Self-consciously she glanced down at her faded gown with its mournful badges of black. She felt mussed, untidy, like a servant pretending to be a better. Her voice was soft with chagrin when she began, "I fear I must look a—"

"You look beautiful," he vowed, and his gaze said he meant it. It consumed her. His fingertips touched her cheek. "A bit pale, perhaps thinner. Are you sure you're all right?"

His focus lowered with unintentioned meaning

to her middle and then she understood. He'd come to see if she was with child. Disappointment engulfed her and resentment came in its stead. How provokingly shallow and typically male of him. He'd shown no concern in the careless scattering of his seed, yet now he appeared anxious to find what might have taken root. And would he be pleased or dismayed if he found the ground to be fertile?

Tightly, she told him, "I am fine and fit." He received that news with such obvious relief that she could have wailed in anguish.

"I know how you must miss him and how hard you must be working to take his place within your family."

His tender words gave her anger pause. What was he talking about? 'Twas no reference to what had or hadn't been sewn between them. He spoke of her father. Now it was imperative to know what had brought him to the Mallory farm. Before she could demand it of him, he continued in that roughly tender cadence that bespoke more than obligation. "I knew your strength would serve you well, but sometimes 'tis better to recognize your pain than to disavow it. I know you, Kate, and I know you'd not give yourself time to grieve or to heal in the process. I wanted to see that you took the time to tend your own hurts before taking on burdens you should never have to carry."

Was he making light of her? His tone confused her and his proximity aided in that tumult of emotion. She frowned. "I assure you, Captain, I am doing quite well on my own."

Brady smiled at her tartness. It meant she truly was well. Yet the strain of her circumstance was evident in the weary circles about her eyes and in the pinch of perennial fatigue to her lovely features, and the wish to see them eased worked soft upon his heart. If she wouldn't accept his sympathies, perhaps she would acknowledge his respect. He sunk a hand into one coat pocket and lifted hers with the other. Her fingers tensed within his grasp, then curled in curiosity about the object he placed in her palm.

"For you, Kate, because I knew you wouldn't spare the expense for yourself. You're deserving of something in which to keep your memories."

Kate looked down and opened her hand. Nestled within it was the very same gold locket she had admired at McLain's. The thickness of tears crowded her throat, making a decent breath impossible.

"Open it."

She sent him a brief, entreating gaze, as if she feared opening the cache of feelings such a gesture would release.

"Go on."

The lid came up easily. Words had been inscribed, but it took several determined blinks for her vision to clear enough to read them. *In Memory of Nathan Mallory: May His Dreams Know Fulfillment Within His Daughter's Heart.*

Brady watched her. Her head was bent so he couldn't see her expression. Slowly, she closed the locket and simply held it in her hand. She was so still. He couldn't resist the need to touch her, to experience the smooth curve of her cheek. He found it damp beneath the gentle trail of his fingers and that crystal wetness glimmered in her eyes as he tilted her head up with a forefinger under her chin. His chest knew an odd constriction as she looked up to him in poignant gratitude.

"Thank you, Brady." Her voice was as hoarse as the rasp of his breath. The sound of it rubbed raw upon his emotions. When her arms impulsively topped his shoulders and her moist cheek pressed to his, there was no checking his want to hold her close. The grateful embrace matured quite naturally into an expression of mutual need, a craving to feel and share and revel in the other.

Brady's hands rose to cup her face between them, holding her in that unsteady grasp so he could command her gaze and read the like urgency within its jewellike depths. His dark head bent, covering the sun's brilliance like a midday eclipse as it drew nearer her own. Sight was no longer important so Kate let her eyes drift shut. Lips parted, she stretched up to greet his long-awaited kiss.

Chapter Fifteen

It was wonderful. For the first few seconds, she held her breath to savor sensations that left her all aquiver. Kate had thought herself lonely in the weeks she'd been parted from her love, but the first touch of his mouth proved she might well have been dead. Life, with all its wondrous creations, burst forth within her, making her feel again the beauty, the power, the sweet ache of passion awakened only in his arms. The urgent inquiry of his lips was met and returned. When his tongue charted the luscious sweep of her upper lip, she was quick to entice more thorough exploration, tempting him with the mating flicker of her own before a flirtatious retreat coaxed his to follow. That deep, probing union provoking a growing dissatisfaction so that when he drew back to rumble, "I want you, Kate," she sighed joyously, "Oh, yes."

It wasn't the most comfortable or private place to seek such intimate delights, but their eagerness knew of no complaints nor would hear of any delay. Impatiently, they tumbled to the meadow grasses, kissing, touching, murmuring unintelligible sounds of encouragement. Clothing was loosened and bunched and pushed aside to permit their anxious joining. For a moment, the world stopped so they could realize the infinite perfection of it. Then Kate's soft gratified moan prompted their rush to find fulfilling ecstasy.

It wasn't a tender coupling, one of gentle give and take or patient consideration. It was a vigorous mating urged on by desperate tension and passionate greed. One's excitement inflamed the other's and, like all fires that burned the hottest, it burned quick, flaring to a spectacular conclusion, then flickering to a quiet relaxing warmth.

Brady was content to bask in that lethargic afterglow. With the compelling drive of his desire satisfactorily sated, he had no will or strength to move. The sun was warm upon his face, his limbs felt heavy and his soul, at peace. It was an effort for him to roll from back to side, but the reward was well worth it as his gaze lingered over the woman beside him. A faint smile softened her much-kissed lips. Her mussed hair radiated like sunbeams upon the crushed grass. Petticoats and linen still wound up about her hips. After a leisurely sampling of smooth, silken thigh, he tugged them down in case her modesty returned with awareness. She made a soft sound of drowsy pleasure and eyes weighted with hedonistic languor opened to regard him.

"That was a surprise," he confessed, giving her a

complacent smile and idly plucking shafts from her hair.

"Was it?"

"Truly, 'twas not the purpose of my coming." Abruptly, he teased her with his disarming grin. "Then, perhaps it was. 'Twas what I'd been wanting since we parted. I should be in Newport even now to ferret out investors for my next run to the Islands, but my horse turned west instead of east out of Providence. 'Twould be a lie if I didn't admit the possibility of you in my arms made me push my mount to its limits. I had nearly reached my own, you know."

Kate was silent. Her gaze had turned heavenward as if to study the wisps of paintbrush clouds. The scent of buckwheat and mellifluous clover mingled with that of man and passions spent. Never would she draw a deep breath in the fields without linking the two in her mind and heart. It would return her to this instant when her body's splendid repletion fell before the bitter gall of knowledge. She scrambled to her feet.

"Kate?"

She looked down and the sight of him tore her asunder. He was everything she'd warned herself to be wary of: too arrestingly handsome, too tempting, too dangerous, too beguiling. He stretched upon the ground, black head resting on an indolently flung arm, his clothing rumpled from her impatient demands, his light eyes still steeped in the pleasure he'd taken upon her. His gaze was questioning. Damn him, even now she wanted to join him upon that well-matted grass in spite of the truth she'd discovered. She wanted to hate him, but she could not. Half the fault was hers.

"We'd best be getting back."

Brady frowned at her gruff tone. Her expression gave nothing away, but he knew the woman who had rolled so deliriously in his embrace moments before was gone. And he wasn't sure why. He picked himself up and made an attempt to straighten his garb into a less obvious disarray while she did the same. She didn't look at him again, nor would she speak as they walked back toward the house. He puzzled over her distraction, but could name no reason for it. Perhaps he should apologize more seriously for the discharge of his passions. It truly had been concern that lured him from his duties in Newport, that and the want of her company. The more delicious aspects of that company had been but a hopeful fancy considering they had parted on less than intimate terms. Seeing her standing in the door, her lovely features spiced with anticipation and like need, he'd succumbed to his desire for her like a callow youth. He'd almost seized her up right there in the yard, but a wavering control came in check. Then when she'd turned to him in a moment of vulnerable offering, he'd given way to that rutting frenzy and now, it seemed, she was inclined not to forgive him for it. Nor could he forgive himself should that be the case.

Anne was lingering upon the porch, trying to appear nonchalant, as if she hadn't been scanning the fields to discern where they had gone. Her quick gaze took in their wrinkled state with satisfaction, yet her sister's tense expression gave her pause. She didn't seem at all pleased with the return of her love. However, Anne was determined to see the most was made of it and she launched into her plan.

"Good day, Captain Rogan. 'Tis a pleasure to have company to entertain again. We get so lonely out here and our mourning restricts the chance for much socializing. You will stay to sup with us, won't you? The girls would truly love to hear more of your stories." She blushed becomingly and added, "As would I."

Since Brady had no intention of departing until he'd learned the reason for Kate's abrupt shift of mood, he gratefully accepted the offer, aware as he did of Kate's stiffening at his side. Anne, ignoring her sister's stern scowl, went gleefully within to call for another place to be set.

In a jovial aside, Brady murmured, "Has your kitchen girl learned to cook yet?"

Instead of responding with like humor, Kate's reply was crisply disapproving. "If you care not for the hands that prepare the meal, you are free to seek better somewhere else."

"I never refuse to take a meal where the company is so delightful." Her cool glance was at a variance with that smooth claim, challenging him to find it so. When his hand rose to gently cup her elbow to assist her up the steps, she drew purposefully away, as if the touch she'd craved so transparently was now abhorrent to her. With a lift of one dark brow, he followed her silently into the house.

The meal Brady had been steeling his stomach to

261

accept proved not only tolerable but palatable. His compliments to the whey-faced serving girl brought a flood of pleased color to her cheeks and an increased clumsiness to her movements. Only his quick reflexes saved his lap from hosting the earthen butter boat and its contents of thick brown gravy. His winning smile made her more flustered as she stammered her apologies.

Kate watched the dinner proceed with mounting irritation. Captain Rogan had no difficulty in holding his awed audience spellbound. He manipulated them with practiced skill, just as he'd done with her, and her anger steamed as hot as the vegetables she chopped to pieces with her knife and fork. She received his seemingly guileless glances with a withering glare. How slanderous his bewilderment sat with her. How dare he pretend innocence while bewitching her family with his amiable tales and enchanting grin. How dare he pretend his purpose for sitting at their table had to do with concern or genuine enjoyment. The lying cad, the soulless deceiver. Well, she wouldn't be fooled again by that charming wit or those come-hither eyes. She knew exactly what Brady Rogan was about and she would see the insult was repaid doublefold.

While Brady retired to the parlor with his quartet of anxious hostesses and even a blushing Mistress Fitch, Kate stewed in the kitchen, insisting upon helping Sarah clear away the dishes and removes. As she simmered, a detached calm settled to protect her bruised heart and soul from all but thoughts of revenge. Yet when she entered the cheery front room, her emotions took a traitorous twist. Brady Rogan sat before the fire with an adoring Bertrice upon his knee. His clever words held the other girls rapt in their seats. He didn't seem the heartless villain she knew him to be. It galled her to think he would fit so neatly into the tight weave of her family's trust and affection. That made the burn of his falseness all the more painful to realize. It wasn't his intention to fill the place at their hearth. It wasn't his plan to mesh within their family unit. Those were her dreams and they had no place in his thinking.

Then his eyes lifted and the rack took another turn to increase her agony. Everything she could hope for was offered in that gaze: warmth, desire, admiration. She longed to believe what her eyes told her to be true but rebellious heart and mind cried, "Liar!" to crush that empty hope.

"Girls," she called so sharply they all jumped as one and turned to her in startlement. Seeing their surprise, Kate forced her agitation to bow before a calming smile, then continued. "Time to go to your studies." The expected moans of complaint were quelled by a single look and they rose to utter reluctant good nights to their guest before shuffling out of the room. Even Fitch struggled from her chair after her nearsighted eyes shuttled between them.

"I shall retire as well," she announced. "'Twould seem you have much to talk about. Perhaps the captain could advise you on our circumstance, dear."

Kate didn't hear her cheerful wish of a good evening. She was rigid with indignant outrage. Was that what they thought, that she was waiting to ply Brady Rogan for aid? Did they all think her incapable? Did they have so little faith in her judgment that they would turn to a near stranger just because he was a man and, therefore, more knowledgeable? As if a scurrilous pirate was versed in maintaining a farm. As if she would beg assistance of him. She'd as soon turn to the devil himself.

Brady stood as the room slowly emptied, leaving them alone. He was uncertain as how to approach the suddenly unapproachable Kate Mallory. He could tell she was embarrassed. He knew well the barriers created by her pride and how loath she was to humble herself. She would as soon suffer as to be beholden. She wouldn't ask so he would offer.

"Are things indeed so grim, Kate?"

"I can manage, Captain."

That gruff, courageous reply made him smile. A tender respect shone in his eyes and made his words a caress. "Let me help you, Kate. If your 'fiancé' were to pay your debts in full, surely none of your neighbors would be the wiser." He'd never been generous with his detested personal wealth before. He'd never tapped into it except to see Elizabeth and Jamie provided for in trust. Now, the thought of coming to the Mallorys' rescue overwhelmed his aversion to relinking with his past.

"So you'd have me in your debt instead." Her green eyes were positively glacial.

"You'd find me an easy lender and the terms would be very comfortable."

Kate stood in stony silence, her hands working

fiercely in the folds of her skirt. When finally she spoke, her cold tone effectively dashed the warm insinuation of his. Each word was punctuated with an icy pause.

"Get out of my house. Get out of my affairs. Get out of my life."

Brady blinked. He looked as though she'd struck him. How easily he adopted that wounded air, that boyish confusion meant to endear him to a fragile heart. Well, he'd find no foothold upon the craggy surface of her emotions, no vulnerable spot in which to cling. She stormed through the foyer and threw open the front door, turning to command, "Get out."

He strode up quickly but not across the threshold. Instead, he closed the door, capturing her between the straddle of his arms. His expression was so sincere.

"Forgive me, Kate. 'Twas not my intent to insult you. I would never impugn your ability to provide. I only want to ease your struggle, to make it better for you. Let me help you, Kate."

His dark head bent with purpose and Kate held her ground. Her will battled with her want to yield as his mouth settled warm and firm upon her own. He leaned until his long, hard body pinned her to the door. His lips parted, trying to inspire in her those prior passions. What a devil he was, so tantalizing, so tempting. How familiar she found his words. She'd heard them before, but not spoken from lips so sweet. Brady Rogan may have surpassed Ezra Blayne in the attractiveness of his approach but she found it no less reprehensible. She wrenched her head to one side and ducked beneath his arm, letting him collapse into empty space. From the impersonal distance of the hall, she regarded him scathingly as he turned. "Not so simple, sir. You'll find I'm no easy wench with passions bent by a charming smile and the jingle of coin."

He gaped at her. "What the hell are you talking about?"

"I am no whore to be used at your leisure."

"Kate, honest to God, I never thought that of you. I assumed—"

"Too much. How dare you think I'd willingly serve in Elizabeth's stead. When she refused to service your needs, did you think I'd jump to the task. Oh, I'll admit I was the perfect foil. I even tried to tell myself I didn't mind. But I do. I do mind and you'll take no comfort here again."

The apology and guilt that colored his expression faded before a flush of offense. The blue calm of his eyes had become a stormy sea in the wake of her bitter words. "Is that what you think?" Her chin tipped up in a sullen demand that he deny it. "You think I came here to slake my frustrated lusts?" His laugh was short and ugly. "You flatter yourself, madam, if you believe I'd have to ride this distance to find a willing partner for that purpose or that I'd have to use coin as an enticement. And as for comfort, you are no comfort to me. You are nothing short of a provocation. You do not compare to Elizabeth, for she is a lady of infinite breeding whose affection I cherish. You, Miss Mallory, are a brash, ill-tempered shrew who knows not how to accept an honest show of humanity. God forbid that I forget you are an island unto yourself and challenge your right to rule. It seems Mother England isn't the only tyrant who knows not how to be tolerant or forgiving. You've made it very clear what you think of me and I will not try to argue you from your beliefs. Think the worst, Kate, and enjoy your spiteful misery. I will not interfere with you again. Good evening."

She stood white-faced and stunned. Only the slam of the door with the force to threaten its hangings shook her from her shock. Distress buffeted her like an ill wind, making her body tremble, an aspen in a bitter gale. The full brunt of the horrible exchange assailed her and she gave before it with a small, defenseless cry of his name. By the time she'd pulled open the door, he was gone. She sagged against the wooden frame, staring sightlessly through the blur of her anguish until a soft voice behind called her to collect herself. Slowly, she drew a breath. Her shoulders squared determinedly, and an unsteady hand dashed across her eyes before she turned with a watery smile fixed upon her face.

"Go upstairs, Anne. The captain and I exchanged some unfortunate words, is all. As you see, I'm fine."

Anne did see, all too well for her young years, and she was shaken. Kate had always been so strong, so indomitable. She never faltered, she never wept, yet here she stood ready to crumble in obvious grief, and Anne knew not what to do. How did one shore up a pillar of fortitude? Slowly, she crossed the foyer, arms opening to receive her sister in a supportive embrace. They stood like that for a long moment with Anne shedding the tears that Kate refused to allow escape. No questions were asked, no explanations offered, yet the communion was forged of a love that required neither. Finally, Kate stepped back, her features pale but revealing none of the emotions that had twisted them so wretchedly in her moment of weakness. Now, there was no sign of that frailty and Anne would never remind her of it. Quietly, she said good night and climbed the stairs to her room.

Kate sought her own by rote. A thankful numbness held her feelings at bay while she undressed in the waning light. It served her well until her fingers touched upon the weighty piece of gold that rested between her breasts on its fine chain. Distractedly, she removed the locket and stared at it in her palm as if it held the answer to the pain rushing up to seize her heart. The tears came then, in a flood of fearful magnitude. She threw herself upon the bed and gave way to the tumult inside her. Never, even in her youngest years, had she been so beset with a tantrum of frustrated tears and angry sobs. She flailed at the pillows, tore down the covers, and would have rent them with a passion had her frugal instincts not taken subtle control of the impulse. Even in her frenzy of despair, she could not wastefully destroy.

Panting and weak with spent emotion, Kate lay back upon the mattress and tried to discipline her thoughts. Her chest still ached with the need to cry, but she'd indulge herself no further, not over a cause that was lost to her. But what a cause. How she'd wanted him. Brady Rogan was the man she wanted to wed and bed and bear child with, and he'd been interested in only one of those things. Now, she wouldn't even have that pleasure. Part of her wailed she should have kept silent and kept him as a lover, but her more rational side recognized the folly of it. She wanted much more from him than just the physical aspects between man and woman. Better to cut cleanly than to let the hurt fester and destroy all. And she did hurt, deeply, clear to the soul as if the part of her capable of joy and love and laughter had been sacrificed. She couldn't imagine sharing those things with another.

With a vanquished sigh, she lifted the locket and examined again its thoughtful inscription. It seemed an extravagant gesture from a man interested only in cultivating a mistress. Yet she knew Brady was inherently a decent man capable of great tenderness and compassion. Then why would he be so casual in his treatment of her? She frowned and turned the pretty piece over in her hand. Then paused. Kate brought the locket close, squinting in the dimness to read words etched upon the back. Three words, simple and to the point. *Kate, love Brady.* She read them over and over, reading into them things that made her heart stagger then wildly race. *Love Brady.*

Clutching the precious locket to her breast, Kate got from the bed, pacing to better her ability to think. She needed to think, clearly, without the clutter of emotion to discolor the process. Carefully, she reviewed the scene in the hall, then went further back to replay each of their meetings in search of subtle meaning. How could she have been so stupid, so blind, so intent on playing the victim and wallowing in her misery as not to see the possible truth. He'd said she didn't compare to Elizabeth. What if what he felt for Elizabeth was obligation? Then what he felt for her could well be love. Kate leaned against the window sash and nibbled thoughtfully upon her lower lip. Never had he said he still loved Elizabeth. He loved Jamie. He'd stated that most emphatically. However, when speaking of his brother's wife, he used terms like duty, responsibility, cherish—and obligation. Those were not ways one described one's passion for another. He'd been so candid, wouldn't he have spoken the truth plain? Yet he hadn't. And how had he depicted her? A pleasure, a delight, a provocation. Sensory words with a sensual undertone. *Love Brady*. Could he be so blinded by his honor that he couldn't see? Yes, he could.

For a moment, the knowledge that her goal could yet be obtainable had her dizzy with relief. Thoughts of Brady Rogan in her arms, sitting before her hearth, sharing his smoky stares and smug smiles were embraced with rapture. Then that bliss was tempered with reality and she looked at the locket with a pensive frown. Such a risk. Such a reward. She weighed them along with the gold oval in her palm.

If obligation could bind him for nine years, how could she wrest him from it? Desire had brought him to her and, for the moment, she didn't dwell upon the fact that she'd driven him away. How to hold a man like Captain Rogan. A mystery to be sure but a most enticing one. Benjamin had laughed at her chances. The challenge she'd felt then served her now as well. She could have him if she could hold him, but how to do that? Honor was what he valued above all, but she refused to play upon his sense of duty. She knew he already felt a sort of responsibility for her and her family and that passionless consideration was a far cry from what she wished to demand of him. She wouldn't risk losing him to his code of obligation and, hence, could not become one. She wanted to be a pleasure to him, not a burden. A pleasure, an equal, a partner.

Lips pursed pensively. She padded barefoot into the parlor and poured a glass of cordial. Sipping of the fruity balm, she formulated a plan. The risk was great, but the reward, oh, the reward. Her eyes closed and she allowed a small smile. *Love Brady*. Indeed she did.

Darkening heavens and an even darker mood prompted Brady to turn his horse into the yard of the Kingston Inn. The taproom was crowded and agreeably noisy to prohibit quiet thought, and that he wanted to avoid at all costs. He brooded over his mug of birch beer, oblivious to all about him. Damn her and her sharp tongue. Never had he met a less agreeable woman. The lovely sweetbriar that bloomed exquisitely within his arms had torn at him with vicious thorns, the barbs still nettling his flesh. Why couldn't she be some dainty hothouse blossom, smelling sweet and trained to a trellis instead of a wild, aggravating bramble that snagged and clung with prickly tenacity. The woman needed a severe pruning, a trimming that would cut her back and free him from the tangle of complication. A swift clip right at the root.

With a scowl, he traded the mild beer for the mixture of cider and rum the barmaid affectionately termed a stonewall. Aye, that was what he'd come up against and, for the moment, he wanted to sag in its shade and nurse his barbed wounds before tackling the climb once again. After a few more of the potent drinks, he lacked the ambition and the coordination to so much as climb out of his chair and thus ended the night in a fitful slumber upon the tabletop.

A sound like thunder woke him. Brady straightened with a groan and blearily looked about. Tavern employees were busy cleaning tables, and the noise he'd heard was the rattle of a paneled wall on hinges being lowered to close off the taproom so as not to offend guests with such worldliness on Sunday. As the wall settled in place, he failed to see a man upon the curved stair who'd been watching him with sudden interest. The gaudily garbed gentleman spoke quickly to the doxy on his arm, then waited while she went to question the woman who'd delivered Brady's drinks throughout the evening. The information the harlot brought him encouraged a slow, self-satisfied smile upon the face of Ezra Blayne.

272

Chapter Sixteen

A Negro servant dressed in far better splendor than she herself issued Kate into Briar Haven's spacious study. For a moment, her composure faltered. She'd asked to be shown to Mr. Blayne, expecting father not son. Too late, she realized the mistake.

Ezra rose from behind the massive mahogany desk. His lilac satins and powdered side curls contrasted unfavorably with the staid elegance of the room. A wall full of haughty portraits seemed to sneer down upon him in distaste and Kate was not one to disagree with a man's relatives. He was a mockery of good taste.

"Ah, Miss Mallory," he gushed in his reedy voice, sounding ever so much like wind whistling through marsh grasses. "What a pleasure to see you. I missed seeing you at the morning service. I trust you are not unwell."

"I am fine. I had matters to attend at home 'tis all."

"And what matter brings you here?" He drew back

273

a chair for her with a courtly flourish and creak of stays. She assumed it warily, settling upon the edge as if to ready for a quick escape.

"I've come to do some business with your father. If you'll be kind enough to tell him I am here."

Her dismissing tone had no effect upon his gloating smile. Calmly, he perched upon the desk with one fleshy flank and looked down from that elevated stance into the promising dip of her bodice. Noting his interest, Kate was quick to adjust her kerchief. Ezra bore his disappointment with surprising grace. He studied his polished nails and drawled, "Father is not at home. He's in Bristol and 'twill remain there until week's end." Seeing her brief dejection, he continued smoothly. "He left me in control of our assets, so you can tell me whatever it was you came to discuss with him."

"I'd rather not."

When she began to stand, he motioned her to resume her seat with a flutter of pudgy hands. "Please, Miss Kathryn. Haven't I always vowed to be your servant. You know I'll help you in any way I can."

Kate sank back into the comfortable folds of the chair and regarded the benevolent features. Something in the close set of his eyes made her envision a snake trying to charm its prey. Though she wasn't fooled by his offer of generosity, she couldn't afford to shun it. Perhaps she stood a better chance dealing with Ezra who could be led by his lusts the way his father was by coin. She adopted a businesslike attitude. "Very well then, I need to apply for a loan."

When she named the amount, his eyebrows rose so high they descended with a dusting of hair powder.

"Miss Mallory, I'm afraid your property is already mortgaged beyond its value. I could never consider such a proposal."

She took a deep, sighing breath and Ezra's attention was riveted to her bosom in a fluster of cross purposes. When he glanced up expecting to weather her glare, he found instead a small, serene smile. He swallowed hard.

"Could you consider a personal loan?" she purred with a subtle flutter of dark lashes. Ezra was overcome. Then he observed her with suspicion. Kate Mallory was no one's coquette. It didn't matter that she was playing him for a fool with her coy glances. The rules were to be his and she didn't even know she'd just handed him the means to victory.

His wet lips twisted into a triumphant smile. "For you, Kathryn, I'd consider it an honor, but I must insist upon knowing its use."

Annoyance played about her mouth but she resisted her want to frown. It wasn't, after all, an unreasonable request. "I am investing in a profit venture to the West Indies." There. That was the truth, yet vague enough to give no real clues. She didn't realize she'd told him all he needed to know. "You should be repaid in full by month's end. I will pay whatever interest you deem appropriate."

"Interest? Come now, Kate. This is a personal matter between friends. Why bring such unpleasantries into it. I trust you will repay me and in full. I've no doubt whatsoever."

That generosity was so unlike him that she was instantly suspicious. If he was so willing to trust, then she surely could not be. "Perhaps we should put terms in writing."

He adopted an injured moue but moved behind the desk to locate paper and dip pen in ink. "Shall we make full payment due at the same time as your mortgage? That way 'twill be one payment and easier to remember. I insist upon my offer of no interest. 'Twill be my pleasure."

Kate regarded him narrowly. As much as she hated to take his personal voucher, she needed the funds immediately. She nodded tersely and Ezra put pen to paper. After a brief scratching, he turned the page so she could read it and add her name below his. He was quick to shake powder over it and slip it within the desk before turning to her with a well-pleased smile.

"Shall we toast to our arrangement?" He splashed a quantity of port into two fine goblets and extended one to her. "To your venture and our mutual interests."

Kate was slow to lift her glass to that obscure claim, but finally drank dutifully under Ezra's gloating gaze. How he would enjoy having her in this house all dressed in lush satins that accentuated instead of concealed her woman's figure from him. She would be a proper wife of mild conduct and the perfect hostess before family and friends. When they were alone, and only then would he allow her fiery temperament to have full rein. Oh, what a glorious future he foresaw. Anxiously, he wet his lips.

And after Kate had left with the promised coin in

hand, Ezra pulled up before his father's desk and began to pen a letter that would ensure his plan's fruition.

The White Horse Tavern was quiet during the midmorning hours, serving a few stalwart souls at its bar and several determined gamesters at its tables. Brady Rogan and his sailingmaster occupied one of the corner tables. A spread of charts lay between them and their heads bent together in earnest discussion over the course Brady navigated with his forefinger. Kate stood in the shadows, content just to watch him. The somber concentration upon his features belied the flamboyance of his scarlet coat. Its rich gold embroidery and braid claimed his profession upon the sea as if he cared not who knew of his dealings—and it was most likely few in Newport didn't know of the man and ship and the illicit doings of both. The very fact that the tavern housing them had once been properly run by the notorious pirate, William Mayes, who secreted his booty within the heavily timbered rooms, said much of the citizens' indifference toward those who bent the law to their advantage. No wonder they would embrace the Rogue as one of their own and turn a blind eye to his trade.

Kate repressed a wry smile on remembering her first opinion of the nefarious smuggler. How self-righteous she had been, how morally indignant and reproving. She would have denied to her last breath the chance that she'd one day be involved with such a man, yet here she was, about to deal herself into his ill-gotten schemes. Much had changed since that first night, both opinion and heart. Looking upon him now, she felt no taint of loathing. She saw a man of dedication and honor. She saw the man she would marry if she could.

Blue eyes lifted in an aimless sweep, paused and widened. The vaguest beginnings of a smile started upon lips too quick to firm into an uncompromising line. Well, she'd known it wasn't going to be easy. He watched her approach with a look of caution rather than welcome.

"Captain, am I interrupting something?"

He returned her question with equal civility. "When are you not, Miss Mallory."

"I can return," she offered, but already he was gathering up the shuffle of maps to thrust at his uneasy subordinate.

"Nonsense. Make yourself comfortable. This is important only to myself and 'tis thieves' business, after all." That was archly said. He was angry. It vibrated between them like something taut and alive. Still, his eyes were cool so she felt relatively safe in assuming the seat that was quickly vacated by his man.

"'Tis business I'm about, Captain."

His smile was most unpleasant. "Isn't it always with you." That surliness won him a frosty stare and frigid silence. Finally, he sighed and reached for his drink. "I'm listening."

"I'd like to partner you in your next venture."

Her blunt statement took him aback. He gauged

her with unflattering directness then said, "You'd best explain exactly what you mean by partnering. I should not like to insult you with any crude assumptions."

"I speak of an investment of coin, Captain. I profited well before and should like to do so again." Did she imagine the flit of disappointment in his expression? If it was there at all, he masked it well with apathy.

"Why should I wish to aid you, Miss Mallory? 'Twas you who saw me most vigorous out of your affairs."

Kate's smile was spun sugar. "Have you never said something in the heat of temper that you regretted, Captain?"

Brady eyed her warily. Such sweetness was suspect with this tart piece. "And you are repentant?"

"Of that. And other things."

He pushed back in his chair and nursed his drink while thoughtful eyes assessed her. She could read none of what worked behind that stare but refused to be disheartened. She sat even straighter, returning his appraisal with like candor. Finally, he gave a soft laugh and shook his head.

"Blast it if I could ever understand you, Kate. How much did you plan to invest?" His relaxed attitude was short-lived as she doled out coin upon the tabletop. When she straightened the last stack, he was frowning almost fiercely. "Where did you come upon such a fortune as this?"

"Suffice it to say 'tis mine."

That tight response was no answer and his

displeasure deepened. "Kate, have you done something foolish?" he demanded with a chastising rumble that set her back like a pike staff.

"Not recently," she ground out. Their eyes held in a challenge of wills, but when it was clear she was not going to relent, he broke the exchange and tossed back the remains of his drink. The mug settled with a thump of finality.

"I'll not aid in your ruin."

She surprised him then by not arguing the point. Instead, she merely gathered her cache of coin with a resigned rise and fall of her shoulders. "I'll trouble you no further then, Captain," she said and started from the chair.

Strong fingers closed about her wrist. The contact was unexpected and did giddy things to her pulse. With a firm tug, he convinced her to sit.

"What are you about, Kate? I don't trust this sudden complaisance."

"I thought you'd appreciate a more agreeable side to my character," she countered mildly.

He made a disparaging sound and observed her smiling guilelessness with disbelief. "Nothing could be more out of character," he maintained. "You're asking me to believe you'll just forget the whole matter."

"I said I'd not be a bother to you. What more could you ask of me?"

He wasn't sure, but he knew there was more she wasn't telling him and that more had him uneasy. "Might I buy you a drink?"

"'Tis yet morning, Captain" was her gentle chiding.

"Something spiritless then."

"Never that."

The smile they shared was sudden and spontaneous. Kate's hopes soared. She might have hurt him, confused him, angered him, but she hadn't lost him. To test that confidence, she touched a casual hand to the snug stretch of his breeches just above the knee. The rigid muscle of his thigh gave a jerk and she could feel the tremors run the length of his leg. No, he was far from lost, merely misdirected. Her trip to Newport would be twofold, to guide him back to her and to see to her independence in a run to the Islands. Brady would help with both, though little did he know it.

"Will you lunch with me, Kate." His voice was strained in the effort to maintain his polite distance. "I'd not like to think I sent you away disappointed and hungry." As there was little chance of that, Kate graciously accepted.

As they dined on beef and cabbage, Brady puzzled over the paradox of Kate Mallory. He had praised himself for his understanding of women, yet she had him completely baffled. Her reactions were never as expected, her motives never clear. Women were supposed to be the frailer sex, pious, modest, and virtuous to a fault. 'Twas their duty to build the home into a haven of peace, gentleness, and love. Pity the man who thought to bend Kate into that meek mold and a sure fool he'd be to want to. Her home would never be one of tranquility in which she'd be content to take to a distaff with a self-sacrificing smile. For a moment he indulged himself with thoughts of what a home would be like if shared with

281

such a woman. He could visualize her embrace of welcome each eve, the arguments they'd have over the table, the sultry looks they'd exchange before the hearth while children played at their feet, the long-awaited hour when the house was silent and she'd come into bed with him to reward him for his labors of the day. Thoughts of that reward provoked an immediate response and frustration reigned when he realized none would be forthcoming. No, Kate would make no docile wife but neither would she be tiresome.

Instead of registering surprise at the turn of his thoughts, Brady's concentration shifted from matrimonial bliss to a more tangible delight. His gaze roamed over his companion, finding the journey one of incredible pleasure. She was a beautiful woman and his more intimate knowledge of her charms served as a greater torment to the distance he must now maintain. But he allowed himself the enjoyment of sight, and he vowed to make the most of it. She was wearing the silver lutestring, although it was nearly unrecognizable due to her cleverness with the needle. The lines had been altered to a softly hugging drape, sobered by a trim of black crochet work along the modest, rounded neckline. The only adornment was his gift.

"It pleases me to see you wear this," he remarked, and used the locket as an excuse to reach out and brush the back of his hand against the smooth heat of her skin as he lifted the pendant into his palm. Her chest rose abruptly as she drew a startled breath and the contact was repeated with like result. The need to know more of that tantalizing softness quickened.

"Why would you think I wouldn't. 'Tis perhaps the most valuable possession I have." The husky quality of her voice acted on him like a caress.

"The expense was not so great." He laid it back upon her bosom and let his fingers spread wide to momentarily sample the sleekness of her flesh. Oh, dare he sample more. He withdrew, expecting her to protest that brief liberty. She didn't.

"'Tis not the cost that gives it value." She picked it up to examine the fine etching. The metal was still warm from his hand and that warmth radiated outward.

Noting her wistful expression, Brady asked, "Tell me about your father? Was he a good man? Did he love you?"

A faraway look came into her eyes as she focused on the lustrous piece of gold. "He loved everything to do with life. He saw none of its harshness. I envied him that."

"Yet you didn't resent him depending upon you?"

She looked surprised, then nodded to his astuteness. "I tried not to. He was my father. I loved him." And it was that simple in the loyalty of her thinking. She seized on the opportunity to return, "And yours? Is he still living?"

"Still living and manipulating all who'll let him." Brady took a long drink while the bitterness of his words lingered.

Having only her own family to judge by, Kate said quietly, "I'm sorry you are not closer."

Choosing to misunderstand her, he growled, "'Tis glad I am for the distance." His look warned her further questions would not be welcomed and, for once, she didn't press. She sipped at her cider, then regarded him directly. Her eyes held the mystery of the sea: cool, green, depthless, and engulfing. He didn't note their shrewd purpose.

"How do you plan to utilize your profits from this trip?"

Ah, back to that subject, he observed with renewed suspicion. He'd not let her wriggle her way into posing her case again. A devious wench to be sure. He almost forgot himself in a smile before remembering the sting of their parting. He wasn't ready to be so forgiving.

"I'd thought to buy into a distillery in Providence. DeWolf turns out two hundred and fifty gallons of rum daily off his smuggled goods. That way, I could make profits at both ends. There be upward of thirty distill houses already. 'Tis the hinge upon which our trade turns. I should like to be a part of that."

Kate heard only one word from his speech: Providence. Surely no coincidence that he would choose to settle there. Did he plan to cozily set up house on Benefit Street in the guise of a respectable citizen? The thought lodged painfully in her throat, but she refused to let him see her distress. Calmly, she asked, "You plan to leave the sea, Captain? I cannot envision you as quite so civilized."

He grinned, flashing a broad white smile that did fluttery things to her insides. "No such thing, I assure you. One must plan for his dotage, though, and I, being a prudent man, realized that this situation cannot go on forever. Britain will eventually give in to our demands and reduce this ridiculous duty. Then where would that leave a poor pirate like myself?"

"There are always laws to be broken," she encouraged with a wry smile.

"Indeed. Let someone else break them. I am getting too old."

Green eyes assessed him quite thoroughly. "An absolute relic."

It was difficult to remain angry with Kate. Her conversation stimulated his mind and her loveliness, his body. Brady leaned back in his chair to regard her over the rim of his mug. Remarkable. Even with the ugliness that had passed between them, he felt at ease and content in her presence. How quickly she'd managed to dispel his resentment and mellow his temper. And excite him to thoughts he didn't think she'd appreciate.

"I'm surprised you haven't thought to invest in shipbuilding. The design of your schooner and its success on the seas must have won you quite a reputation. I would think other scurrilous rogues would be anxious to have such an advantage over the custom patrols."

Brady chuckled. Such a brain to accompany her beauty. What a partnership they could have between them in more than just business. His smile froze as that thought sank deep. Good God, what was he considering? His desire must have made him daft as well as desperate. He took a long swallow of his beer and nearly choked in his haste.

Kate seemed not to notice his sudden distraction, for her look was thoughtful as if counting future coin. "Perhaps I should invest in such a venture. What would you advise?"

"I'm sure there are plenty who would welcome your finances."

His terse reply and omission of himself as one of them was not missed. Kate frowned slightly but plunged on. "Then you would not mind directing me to one of those grateful souls."

"No. Why would I mind?" His fingers tapped restlessly against the side of his mug. Why, indeed.

Kate stood abruptly, jerking him from his brooding thoughts. She put out her hand to him. "Thank you for the meal, Captain."

He was quick to rise and enfold those small fingers with his own, just as he longed to enfold her delectable person. Her grip was firm, disconcerting for a female, impersonal for a lover. He carried her hand to his lips, rubbing her knuckles across them. Before she could withdraw, his tongue stroked boldly over the back of her hand. Brilliant blue eyes lifted to test her reaction.

Kate held her features immobile so he couldn't guess what an effort it was not to melt against his chest in that instant. Surrender, though infinitely rewarding, would not net her the desired results. Coolly, she pulled her hand away and reminded, "Business, Captain."

He bowed slightly. "Yes, of course. How could I forget."

"I wish you a good morning."

Brady caught her arm a second time to detain her, then tempered the urgency of his question by taking a deep breath. "Will you return to Kingstown today?"

She glanced down at his offending hand and refused to reply until he'd released her. "No. As I said, I have business to attend."

"But I've already said no."

"You are not the only smuggler in Rhode Island. I daresay if I return here tonight, the room will be teeming with them and I can have my pick."

"You will not."

His forbidding tone earned a haughty lift of brows. "I beg your pardon."

"I will not allow you to mill about with such riffraff. They be dangerous men, Kate, men without conscience or honor."

Her chilling gaze traveled the length of him with unspoken meaning. "I am familiar with the type, sir."

Brady flushed. He chose to believe it was out of annoyance rather than actual embarrassment. His reply was curt. "You'll find they're not as obliging as I have been."

It was her turn to be cutting. "I do not seek a lover among them, only a means to further my cause." She heard his draw of breath and knew she'd struck a telling blow. He closed the distance between them as if to intimidate her with his greater presence. Intimidation was not what she felt at all as they stood toe-to-toe, eyes locked in challenge.

"You are naive, Kate. To these men, they are one and the same."

"I may have failings but ignorance is no longer one of them. You've seen well to my education and I feel well prepared to deal with the likes of you. Now, if you please, remove yourself from my path so I might pass."

Kate could see his incredulous anger build. Color, dark and furious, seeped up behind his swarthy complexion until he was livid with it. His jaw clenched. His teeth ground as breath hissed between them, and his words escaped with the same virulent sizzle. "Shall we continue with this where we've more privacy." It was not a request. Her forearm was cuffed by stern fingers and she found herself towed through the maze of tables out into a side alleyway. In those seamy shadows, she was jerked about to face him and the continuation of his tirade. Her features were set in defiant lines, her green eyes fierce as she readied for verbal combat.

"Kate Mallory, you are an exasperating woman. I don't know whether to strangle you or to—" His huge hands imprisoned her face between them, lifting it so he might seek his punishment or pleasure. Kate braced for savagery, so when his mouth claimed hers with tenderness, she was undone. The gusts of willful command that drove her left her sails deflated in a sudden sigh. Taking advantage of her collapse, Brady escalated the temptation. His lips dragged across the curve of her cheek and down the offered arch of her throat to torment the tender flesh at its base. Her hands rose to his dark head so fingers could thread through his hair in mindless encouragement. He rushed each sensation, giving her no chance to recover from the sweet insistence of his onslaught. And such was his intent. This was one time he didn't wish to appreciate her for the quickness of her mind.

"Brady, please," she moaned as his hands filled themselves with the bounty of her breasts and gently kneaded. Protest or entreaty?

In an agony of impatience, lest he take her in the inappropriate surroundings, he urged with harsh breathlessness, "Where is your room?"

"No, Brady."

A tremulous sound of disbelief escaped him. "Surely you don't mean that." His want of her was excruciating. He knew he'd felt compliance in his arms. Yet now her palms pressed firmly against his chest, never minding the frantic tempo there.

"I do."

He was quick to try to sway her but she'd have none of the nibbled kisses he sought to plant along her neck. This time her push was more compelling and her voice, more sure.

"No more."

His groan was eloquent, conveying his misery as he let his head fall heavily upon her shoulder. His arms tightened. "Oh, Kate, you're killing me."

"I'm certain you shan't expire," she said most unkindly.

He gave another anguished sigh and argued, "You can't know that. You don't know how I feel right now." His body rubbed against hers in a suggestive example. "How can you be so cruel? Do you wish my suffering upon your conscience?"

Her fingertips touched to his nape, massaging lightly. "There are worse things to bear."

He ceased his dramatics and leaned back to examine her face. How melancholy she'd sounded. His brow furrowed and his lusts cooled. Intent eyes searched hers. "I've hurt you, haven't I? I never meant to, Kate. I want you so much and I know that's true of you, as well."

"It may be true but it changes nothing."

He frowned. Inquiring fingers stroked along her cheek and she leaned into that touch to prove his words and lessen hers. The caress grew more persuasive. "Kate, I desire you as I have no other woman. I cannot be near you and not want to take you into my arms. Should I apologize for that which I can't control?"

"I seek no apologies and I have no regrets." Her words were a maddening riddle. He could feel his frustrations and his passion swell.

"Then why say no?" he crooned. His head lowered and hers twisted to the side to evade the kiss that would ruin her.

"Before I asked no promises of you. Now I must demand them and I know you've none to give. Can you tell me that has changed?"

There was silence. His breath whispered warm upon her cheek. Then he drew her close against his chest, holding her tightly, almost painfully. His words broke her heart. "No, it hasn't."

It was a moment before she could speak, and when

she did, she spoke with gentle resolution. "Then let me go, Brady. We've nothing to give one another."

He shoved away angrily to pace and mutter, aroused, annoyed and panicked. Physical needs and mental cautions clashed but offered no solution. "Dammit, Kate, that isn't true."

"Not entirely." He turned at that softly tendered hope. "We could be friends."

He stared. Then he laughed. "Friends?" He accepted that with the same relish he would a drink of whale oil. "'Twould be poor lip service to what we feel for one another."

"'Tis all I can freely give."

With a rumble, he snatched her up bodily. "And how hard would you struggle if I forced myself upon you?"

She was smiling. "You wouldn't." Her confidence was galling. But well placed. He settled her carefully to her feet.

"Ah, Kate, what am I to do?"

"Wish me well?"

He sighed, then offered a faint smile. "That I do."

"I will be in Newport at least until tomorrow. I will see you again before I go."

"Your promise on that?"

"Indeed."

Brady touched fingertips to his forehead and made a respectful bow, but as she walked away from him, his features took on a speculative look that would have had her in raptures had she chanced to turn.

Chapter Seventeen

After all her bluster to Brady, it took long minutes of pacing on the corner of Marlborough and Farewell before Kate's courage built enough to carry her across the threshold of the White Horse that same evening. Smoke wreathed the chamfered summer beams and girts about the ceiling and settled like a fog around men at drink and cards. Despite the haze, her passage drew many unflattering eyes as she approached the taproom bar. Her spine grew rigid as the men gauged her like a horse they meant to try, assessing glances touching upon chest, girth, and hock. She was gratified when all those who dared meet her withering gaze had the decency to look away. All but Brady Rogan. She allowed but a glimpse in his direction, just long enough to satisfy herself that he was near should she have need of him and to assure her that he knew indeed that she had arrived. Though he turned leisurely back to his cards as if indifferent to her, it wasn't long before his disapproving glower edged over the hand he held to watch her.

The bartender was a fatherly looking gentleman who welcomed her courteously but with an expression that took her to task. She plied him with her most winning smile, and after a few minutes of amiable chatter, Florry—short for Florence, he confessed with a blush—was primed to aid her. He pointed out the various coastal captains loitering about the room and summarized their characters in humorous quips. A wry smile tugged at her lips when he labeled the Rogue as one she could trust with her coin but not her virtue. How astute of the man, she thought, and gave credence to his perceptions.

Kate had barely sipped from her mug of earthy sassafras beer when a barrel-chested man came to fill the space beside her. His fine dark coat was cut too scant to contain the bulk of his muscular frame. Mannering, Florry had named him, captain of the sloop, *Tidewater*. His pale eyes, though they were quite thorough in their study, didn't harbor the same leer as the other men's.

"Good eveningtide, my lady. Might I offer you my company for this night?"

Kate managed not to recoil as his meaning took her. Instead, she smiled, albeit thinly, and said, "Perhaps we can be of service to one another. I seek a bold captain who is not afraid to earn us both a tidy profit."

"Then I be your man," Mannering boasted with a grin.

"Then I shall consider myself most fortunate." Kate turned toward the bar and untied the ribbon to her fashionable red cloak. The blaze from the center fireplace teemed with the warmth of the night was making her most uncomfortable. She began to slip out of the wrap.

From across the room, Brady let his cards drop faceup upon the table as Kate's concealing cloak parted. Her gown was of mulberry satin with a tulle kerchief folded over the bosom to accentuate the incandescent pearl and blushing-rose tints of her complexion. There was no mourning trim upon it and little modesty to its drape. Between the generous slope of her breasts, the locket lay gleaming, a beacon leading to the shadowed treasures below. He came off his chair with a violence that nearly overset it.

Kate gasped as the front of her cloak was drawn firmly together. She looked up into fierce blue eyes.

"Might I have a word with you, Kate? Excuse us, Mannering, won't you?" Neither had a choice or a chance to reply as he urged her out of her companion's hearing. Then the veil of civility was gone. "What do you think you're doing?"

Kate straightened into a haughty pose. "As if it were any of your concern, I am seeking a means of investing my moneys."

"And that fine gentleman was doing the same."

She blushed at his bluntness, but would give no quarter. "We were about to do business."

"The oldest."

"How dare—"

His words and anger intruded. "What can you be

thinking to wear such a gown in here.''

Kate looked perplexed. Was he outraged because she was no longer in the vestiges of mourning? ''I just purchased it yesterday. It's been so long since I've had anything new or half so nice and—'' She broke off. Why did she need to explain herself to his satisfaction? ''Don't you like it?''

''I like it fine. They all like it just fine. Seeing you in it has my imagination provoked to the point of embarrassment. Lest you wish every man in this room to be in a like state, I suggest you keep your cape closed.''

He was jealous. And aroused. The combination was heady knowledge to Kate. It flushed her with a purely feminine sense of power and that was new to her.

''I thank you for your concern, Captain, and see the wisdom of it. Now, please return to your game so that I might return to my business.''

Brady stood for a moment as if in indecision. The urge to both throttle her and to bed her rose strong once again—only he couldn't name which held priority. Finally, he bowed to her wish and, with a meaningful glance to Mannering, strode back to his seat.

Her feeling of victory was not of long duration, however. When she returned to her now full mug, she discovered Mannering in a mood to be flirtatious and talkative, but evasive when she broached him about his next visit to the West Indies. By the time her beer was empty so were her expectations where the brawny captain was concerned. Politely, she excused

296

herself from his company and turned to the next suggested target.

Hours passed and Kate was in a fog of confusion. It was not due solely to the quantities she'd imbibed. She'd spoken with every coastal captain in the room. They'd bought her mugs of cheer, flattered her with their interest and offers, then, just as Mannering had done, avoided the issue foremost on her mind. She didn't understand, not at all, and said as much to Brady when he came to stand with her at the bar.

"What is wrong with these hearty souls? You'd think they had an aversion to turning a profit. Were I a man, they'd not be so quick to buy me a cup then spurn my coin."

"Were you a man, they'd not have bothered with the drink." She was so disheartened, he took pity and put an arm about her slumped shoulders. "Poor Kate. Don't give up so soon. Come sit with me while I finish my game, then I'll help you find some worthy soul willing to part your coin from you."

Her eyes lifted to his, great, shimmering emerald ponds of gratitude and his throat tightened with tenderness and guilt.

"Would you? Oh, thank you, Brady. I would like to sit for a moment. I am very weary."

Very tipsy would be the closer truth, but he didn't chide her with that knowledge. He shepherded her back to his table and eased her into a quickly drawn chair, where she dropped on near boneless legs in a pool of lustrous satin. Brady resumed his play, acknowledging his opponents' bemusement over the woman sprawled beside him with an admirable nonchalance.

Kate's world was in a pleasant reel. The home-brewed beer and potent New England rum created a numbing warmth within her and her troubles ebbed on that hazy lull. Brady would take care of things for her. She didn't have to worry. She had his promise, after all. Conversation droned on from the men at the table, mostly expressions of anti-British sentiment that fell frequently from the lips of Colonists who felt themselves oppressed. There was much malicious chuckling over the three effigies hung upon the gallows earlier that week and the man at her right claimed Dr. Moffit and Martin Howard deserved to join the stamp distributor as targets for their ire. Brady could not agree, arguing that the two men held no official position and therefore should not have been subject to the vicious attack upon their homes that followed. Kate's attention sharpened. She'd never heard the lawless smuggler speak out so strongly on a political subject. She was bemused at the contrast.

"They asked for it," the first man insisted, "what with their obnoxious writings on question of the tax and relations with England. They should join that coward Johnston out in the harbor where he waits to escape to his Mother Country. Good riddance to them all, I say."

There were some rumblings of assent, but Brady's quiet reply stilled them. "They had naught to do with England but with the right to speak free."

"And you agree with what they say?" Hostility

edged the words and Kate found herself leaning closer to Brady as if in a silent alliance.

"Of course not." That won him some nods of approval, but his next words prompted thought. "But I don't agree that a man should have his house burned over his head if he thinks different. There are less violent ways than the overturn of authority to rid ourselves of a tax."

Another man found humor in that. "Didn't know you was such a supporter, Rogan. Must have been some other villain I saw unloading his contraband goods in months past."

With a good-natured laugh, Brady put them all at ease. "I am opposed to violence, gentlemen, not good business. I believe 'tis my deal."

From that brief controversy, their conversation drifted back to ships and their trade, and Kate let her energies lapse into a pleasant void. Brady's shoulder had become a steady resting place. He smelled good, of fresh linens, of spiced rum, of man. She breathed deep and sighed, her eyes closing with that long expulsion. Voices became a soothing hum and the vibration of Brady's speech, a comfort. It was an effort to retain her seat when his lap was so inviting.

Brady's concentration was sorely tested. As if Kate's delightful pressure against his arm hadn't been trial enough, now she sank down to pillow head and shoulders upon his knees. When she shifted restlessly in her search for slumber, his cards trembled. A disturbing tension grew from beneath that slumberous weight to tighten impatiently where her head had chosen to fall. He fought to retain a serious face while the others sniggered and offered to let her aid in the playing of their hands if he grew tired of supporting her. None were intimidated by his dark scowl. All were envious of his obvious good fortune. And as the game progressed, his hand had a want to stray down to the golden head nestled so trustingly upon him and his odd contentment held him mystified.

Kate murmured softly as awareness prodded her awake. She rebelled against it. All was too perfect as it was. She was warm, she was happy, she was willing to linger in the heavy luxury of sleep. As she stirred languorously, her cheek was teased by a crisp furring. That springy texture oddly familiar, puzzled her and she rubbed against it in question. Her hand rose to join in the quest, trailing from the soft mat of hair to an intriguing corduroy plane where supple skin stretched taut over ribs. Umm . . . Brady. Her lips bowed upward in a pampered smile. How good it felt to wake next to the long, powerful frame, to caress the warmth of his flesh at her lazy leisure, to snuggle close and feel protected, sheltered, treasured in the curl of his strong arms. She rolled to her side to meld against him, letting her leg ride over his thigh just as her arm did his chest. The constriction of her petticoat proved a vague annoyance and its presence created enough of a confusion to prod her thoughts awake. Good Lord, she was in bed with Brady!

He knew the moment realization hit her, for she went from a near purring compliance to an apoplectic stiffening. She seemed to shrink until they ceased to come into contact, and that withdrawal deprived him of a great deal of satisfaction. She regarded him through eyes round with surprise, confusion, and dismay, a look that demanded explanation.

"Good morning," he drawled with the offering of a sensuous smile.

Speech deserted her for a moment, then she stammered, "How did I get here?" accompanied by a vivid blush.

"Here meaning Newport or here meaning in my bed?" His smile stretched wider as her flustered state increased.

"Here meaning where am I?"

"In my arms where you should be. I trust you slept well."

Rather than answer, she tried to sit up and immediately was beset by wooziness. She was grateful for the bolster of his embrace that eased her back onto the steady comfort of the mattress. Her head was reeling. "Why do I feel so strange?" she mumbled and pressed fingertips to her temples as if to stop the swaying of the room.

"I wish I could claim responsibility, but I fear the credit goes to the bartender at the White Horse."

Kate groaned. Memory began to return with mortifying results. Had she actually fallen asleep on his lap in the middle of a tavern? No more spirits, not ever, she swore to herself. That still didn't explain how she happened to conclude the evening under Brady's covers, and if she couldn't remember how that came about, what else was beyond her recall? He made matters worse by nibbling and nuzzling at her neck in a most suggestive manner.

"I have to think," she murmured weakly.

"No, don't do that," he argued as his lips moved progressively closer to her own. "For once, don't think."

She pushed at him and contrarily tried to focus her whirling thoughts. "Why am I here with you? Surely I didn't agree to come." She was terrified to think that might be true.

"Would you rather I had left you in the taproom? I'd no idea where else to take you. You never did tell me where you had a room so I brought you to mine, with quite honorable intentions, I assure you."

"Then why are you undressed?" she demanded to know.

"'Tis the way I always sleep. You'd not wish me to be uncomfortable after I was good enough to take you in, would you?" He grinned, and she scowled in return. "Next you'll be haranguing me because I was thoughtful and saw to your comfort as well."

She assessed her own attire in alarm to find she was clad, albeit scantily, in her chemise and single petticoat. She allowed a petulant frown. At least he'd salvaged a tad of her decency. "I suppose you are waiting to be thanked for your charitable actions."

Her surliness amused him. "But, of course. Shouldn't I be granted a reward, some recompense for my good deed?" He wet his lips as a smoky gaze settled upon her own.

"I will share half the night's lodging expense with you."

Brady crowed with delight. "By God, leave it to you to hit upon such a practical solution." Then the humor smoldered to a sultry gleam of warmth. "'Twas not what I had in mind." He angled up so that he loomed over her. His knee bumped hers and rubbed presumptuously.

"I'm sure it was not" came her tart reply. She ignored him for a moment, which was difficult as he had no intention of being dismissed, and tried to decide what to do. That she hadn't leaped immediately from the bed was a telling fact she hadn't considered. Brady had, though, and his conclusions made him confident. She belonged where she was and she was content to remain there curled at his side, absorbing his warmth while they parried with words in lieu of what each would prefer to be doing with the other. It was a temporary stalemate. He would give her no reason for an indignant retreat and, as long as he behaved, Kate was disinclined to move. Both were enjoying the physical proximity too much to seek an escape from it unless their pride was provoked.

Brady's arm assumed a casual drape about Kate's middle and his head, a resting place between the curve of her neck and shoulder. From habit born of exquisite nights upon the sea, Kate's hand rose to ply his dark hair. She dealt only peripherally with the pleasure she took from his closeness. Her mind was busy, plotting, planning, and as her thoughts grew focused, she began to frown.

"Brady?"

"Umm?" It was a husky sound that blew warm upon her throat and incited all sorts of traitorous shivers from a body more receptive to sensual delights than logic.

"I don't understand why none would take my offer of coin. If you're to serve as an example, they be greedy profiteers anxious for such a plump investment." His chuckle provided a delicious tickling upon bare skin and her fingers meshed tighter in the black silk of his hair. "Why would they object to such a profitable venture?"

"Perhaps their greed was checked by higher priorities."

"Such as?"

"Life and limb."

"Brady?" A warning edged her pronouncement of his name. He could well imagine her pensive frown. The thought of her ire, rather than quelling him, provoked a stirring of excitement and an increase in the evidence of his desire. She couldn't help note that impressive expansion as it grew along the length of her thigh. Nor could she prevent a similar stirring within herself though she fought it the way she would a most persuasive argument. Succumbing to him now would destroy all she tried to accomplish. How could she alter his casual attitude when she gave with the slightest provocation? Though she had to admit this provocation was far from slight. What a struggle it was to remain still, to keep the husky sound of passion from intruding upon her question. "Brady, explain what you meant by that."

His voice was a low, seductive rumble. "I should think that would be obvious." His hips moved subtly. Not so subtle was the insinuating brush of his engorgement, all hot and temptingly firm against her more yielding flesh.

It was desperation rather than determination that strengthened her demand. "Answer me."

Brady's head lifted. He was smiling. He looked incredibly pleased with himself. "'Tis quite simple. I merely exchanged a few words with the gentlemen before you arrived."

"You bribed them?" She was aghast at his treachery.

"No. I but promised to scuttle them the next time we met on open seas if they so much as touched one piece of your gold."

Kate was too amazed to feel anger. At first. She gaped up at him. "You threatened to sink their ships."

An arrogant brow cocked into a dark arch. "No, of course not." More silkily he added, "I don't make idle threats." He came up further on his elbows, straddling her with a forearm resting beside either rigid shoulder. Her magnificent breasts grazed his chest with each turbulent breath. She stared at him, wetness gathering in her frustrated gaze. Her voice was small, defeated. "How could you? You've no idea what you've done." Her emotions seesawed wildly from despair to helpless fury. She was perilously close to weeping and that would be disastrous. There had to be some way to recover from his thoughtless game.

Gentle thumbs rubbed across her cheeks. His words were a caress. "On the contrary. I know exactly what I'm doing." His mouth settled warm upon hers, cushioning her anguish with a leisurely sample of his passion, tantalizing her with the tease of his tongue. She trembled beneath him, in anger, in surrender, in distress. Her hands were drawn to the hard swell of his shoulders, stroking, mesmerized by their implicit strength. Her will to fight was spent and her careful strategies crumbled. Perhaps a moment of his masterful loving would be worth the loss of all else. But even that victory was denied her when he lifted up to end their tender reunion. Her eyes were dazed, desolate as they searched his. Brady's glowed. "I'll invest your coin for you, Kate."

Instead of showing gratitude, her features congealed with vexation. "If you had intention of doing so, why this elaborate game? Brady Rogan, you are a hateful man and I would not accept your help were you the only pirate on the seas."

His knowing grin taunted her. "Yes you will, and I hadn't decided to help you until—"

Kate was frowning but well primed to insist, "Until what?"

He pressed a quick kiss to her pouting lips and warned, "Don't be questioning your good fortune, wench, lest I be tempted to scuttle you as well." A thrust of his hips conveyed his meaning; however, before she could protest or permit, he was up and off her. That unexpected departure left her wanting. Her voice was weak with it when she called his name in question.

"I've business to attend this morning," he told her over his shoulder as he stepped into his breeches. Her gaze followed the advance of fabric up his long, leanly muscled legs until it encased his firm buttocks with an enticing snugness. The journey had her restless. "I shan't be gone long. Will you await me here?" He turned then and commanded her gaze with the importance of that request. She was lost.

"Yes."

Brady hesitated. There was no gloating in his conquest, for, in truth, he was more than a little frightened by what that victory might mean. Finally, he said, "Good" with a firm conviction. He finished dressing while she lay docile on his covers, watching him through pensive eyes. He wasn't ready to probe that quiet look or, indeed, his own motives. He only knew it was very important that she remain. He came to sit beside her, suddenly awkward and reluctant to go. There was so much potential in the soft, uplifted gaze. "I'll have water sent up so you can bathe, then when I return, we can breakfast together. Is that agreeable to you?"

Her silent nod heightened his anxiety. His hand was unsteady when it touched to her cheek. "Kate—"

The lift of her brows encouraged him to finish. When he found he could not, he kissed her instead, letting that slow, expressive gesture relay the gentle confusion of his heart. She accepted his sentiments with an equal quiet and made no move to restrain him when he straightened. His breathing was much too labored for the simple kiss to explain away. Then he stood, prying himself from her with a mighty effort, and closed the door in his wake.

Kate sank back upon the downy pillows and let sensation and tendrils of emotion blow through her on the hurried pulse of her life's blood. She'd no doubt that when he returned, breakfast would be forgotten and neither would miss it. That she should have no remorse was troubling. The moment she gave herself into his embrace any hope she had of holding back for a commitment was gone. The terms of their relationship would be his and she found she didn't care. At least not now when the scent of him clung to the bedding and the taste of him lingered on her lips. She wasn't strong enough to deny she wanted him with an equal passion. She hadn't the courage to reject his offer of sensual pleasures when the chance it stemmed from true affection existed in her mind. And she held to that hope with a desperation. She had to believe he would want her enough to offer the security of his name. She knew well his uncontrolled passion and possessiveness and his want to be a factor and an influence in her life . . . but to what extent? To the extent of forsaking all others? To the extent of relinquishing his ties to his lost love? She wished she could be sure. She wished she dared to make that demand, but she had no faith in the strength or endurance of his feelings. She had nothing to lose by coming to him and everything to gain. Everything to gain.

She continued her moody reflections while a basin and urns of steaming water were toted in. At last she was able to sink into the soothing tub and escape from her plaguing thoughts in a leisurely soak. She scrubbed off all her exhaustion and the effects of her overindulgence until her skin tingled and glowed pink. Then she was content to slip down in the heated luxury of the bath with eyes closed and worries at an ebb.

Long, languid minutes had passed when she heard a tap at the door. When it opened, she smiled lazily to herself and remained where she was. On the other side of the screen she could hear Brady moving about the room. Thinking of him bearing her all wet and flushed from the tub to the sheets gave her the courage to call out in throaty invitation. "I find I am quite hungry now. Could you bring me a towel?"

There was a moment's silence, then the footsteps resumed, coming around the screen to pause at the far end of the tub.

"With pleasure."

The caressing words brought her gaze up with a snap to behold the grinning features of Benjamin Rogan. Casually, he extended a small square face cloth.

Chapter Eighteen

Water splashed out of the basin as Kate's knees hugged tighter to her chest. For a moment, she was too stunned to speak. Then shock gave way to fury as she demanded, "What are you doing here?"

Benjamin took his time in answering. In that lengthy pause, he studied the beauty whose efforts to conceal herself were all the more revealing. She had the most flawless skin he'd ever seen, and with the glaze of wetness upon it, it shone like alabaster. Her flashing green eyes held more anger than embarrassment, which made him savor the moment all the more. She was a rare woman indeed, and his want to possess her for herself was nearly as great as the attraction of stealing away his brother's whore.

"I came looking for Brady. How can you fault me for answering such a genuine call of distress."

"You know well I thought you were he."

"Ah, would that I were. I would be tempted to join you. I don't suppose you'd allow me to—" Her stabbing gaze silenced him and he gave an exaggerated sigh. "A shame. I would have enjoyed soaping your back for you. Another time perhaps."

"Not likely." Kate's gaze slipped beyond him to where the towel was draped over the screen. Between her and that offer of cover was the predatory stare of Benjamin Rogan. "Would you mind? The water grows cool and I should like to get out."

He shrugged eloquently, "I don't mind," and would not remove himself.

"Please hand me that towel." She fought to keep her voice level, but his calm perusal was fast provoking her temper to a dangerous degree.

He looked over his shoulder, then back with a helpless mien. "Oh, dear. I'm afraid 'tis out of my reach. You shall have to retrieve it yourself."

Kate glared. He smiled back mildly, unmoved by her plight. "Brady will be here at any moment," she warned, then regretted the words, for his playful game became a more devious scheming.

"And what a sight would greet him, of you and I having a polite discussion over your bath."

No, that would not do, she realized with a helpless determination. She would never be able to explain away that damning picture. He gave her little choice but to act. She came up out of the water like a Venus to stand proud, defiant. The square of cloth fell from his hand to float forgotten in the tub. Wide eyes skimmed down the exquisite form, then up again, but Kate had no intention of remaining still for his benefit. With an issuing spray of wetness, she stepped down, meaning to snatch for the towel, but she underestimated his quickness and the slippery condition of the floor.

As her bare foot slid on the wood planking, Benjamin's hand seized her forearms, at first to steady her, then to pull her close. With her sleek nakedness pressed to him, he was fairly seething with desire. His voice was thick with it. "Can you name a reason why I should not take you here and now upon my brother's bed?"

Kate's eyes never flickered. Her features never betrayed the sudden terror she experienced. She didn't know this man. She had no reason to think he had a scrap of honor or charity to him, nor that he would bestow any upon her now. Hysterics would not serve her, so she returned his hungry gaze with every bit of contempt she could muster. "I cannot stop you. I can only endure. But after your moment's pleasure, I suggest you slay me or I shall surely put a swift end to you whenere I get the chance."

He paused, then roared with delight. "By God, it might be worth the risk. And you might find it to your liking."

Before she could retort, his mouth silenced hers. It was such a surprise that she didn't object, not because he dared seize her, but because of the gentleness of his assault. He didn't hurt her. Indeed, she found his kiss a pleasant physical exercise; however, in no way did it threaten her heart. It wasn't due to his lack of skill that she stood cold at his touch, for he was quite masterful in technique. His only fault was that he was not Brady. And when his eyes slit open to discover hers intent upon him, such was his astonishment that he let her go. "Is he that special?" he then wanted to know.

Her reply was simple. "Yes."

"Damn."

He stood aside and let her pass, sighing as the towel whipped about the luscious figure to deny him the sight of its charms. Anxious to escape his leering, she struggled into her satin gown before adequately dry, tugging and twisting until his hands interceded, smoothing the pull of fabric at her back and side into a snug fit. His palms continued to rest on her trim waist for a long second, then, before she could protest, he let them drop away and regarded her with regret. "'Tis sorry I am that Brady bested me on the water. I would have loved to have stolen you from him and broken you of his spell at my leisure."

Awareness came to her with all its awful connotations. Kate stared. "It was you? You were the one who attacked our ship?" He did not deny it. "But why? Is your hatred so great that you would see your brother dead?"

Benjamin was taken aback by her suggestion and was quick to say, "Nay, not at all. I would have slain any man who did him harm and told my crew as much. 'Twas not injury I meant him, just a bit of crippling in his pride. I'd forgotten what a sailor he was. He could always best me on the water. Always." For a moment, a fondness twisted his lips into the likening of a smile, then it was gone.

"And you expect me to believe that folly? That you would attack another ship with guns in some foolish game and mean no harm?"

314

"Brady understands that. 'Tis the same sort of game we've always played, only now the stakes are much more interesting. I should have liked to take his cargo and his . . . lady of the moment." His finger brushed along the side of Kate's jaw. He could feel her anger working there. "Which do you think he would have missed the most?" He laughed cruelly at her look of haughty certainty. "You think he would have come after you?"

Kate gave careful thought to that answer. Benjamin Rogan was a devious man. She didn't want to give him any reason to think she was an important prize in the game between them. "No," she replied softly. "He wouldn't come for me."

He twined a lock of damp golden hair about his finger, twisting to the point of pulling but not pain. His eyes roved her splendid figure and comely face. "Oh, I think he would. He'd be a fool not to. Do you think it would be for you or because 'twas I who had you? Hmm?"

Kate said nothing. She had no answer. She didn't know.

Benjamin was gauging her response, his piercing gaze missing none of the turmoil she tried to hide. "Come with me now," he tempted. "Have your answer."

"I do not play games, sir, and surely not with those I love."

That had escaped her by mistake, but he was quick to pounce upon it. "Love? But, of course. Why else would you be here. Why else would you be pursuing a man obsessed with another woman. My dear Kate, you would do better with me. At least I am honest with myself as I would be with you. I would not encourage you to think you had a future in my arms. 'Twould be for the pleasure of the moment . . . and what a moment we could make it between us."

That was too much. His presence, his lusting stare, his obnoxious suggestions pushed too far. She would take such slurs from no man. In a cold, clipped tone, she told him, "I am not the type of simple wench who could take pleasure from such baseness. Furthermore, I find you contemptible, and the thought of enduring you in no way likens to pleasure. If you are here to taunt your brother, await him below. I am bored with your childish ploys."

The blue eyes narrowed in a chilling study of her arrogance. Then he, too, spoke with a frigid clarity. "'Tis a sharp tongue you have, missy. And you be protesting too much, I think. Were you of such sterling character, you would not be bathing in my brother's room. Or did I misinterpret that invitation when I walked in? Surely you're not claiming 'tis still business that holds you here."

Kate was very white. The ugliness of his words sank deep, and the truth of them was all the more vile. He was right. She had no cause to act as if she was other than Brady's pretentious trull. She came easily beneath his sheets with no thoughts to virtue. She had made herself available to him without reservation, and though she might term herself with less degrading words, like "lover," she was no more than Brady Rogan's whore in Benjamin's eyes, and now her own.

316

The door opened and both combatants turned to face a very surprised Brady. His gaze flew between them, seeking answers to the incriminating facts of his brother's self-serving smile and wet coat front, of Kate's alarming pallor and her want to escape his stare. He'd been mistaken in his conclusions before so he proceeded with care.

"What goes on here?" he asked with what he hoped to be an impartial calm. "Kate?"

She made no move to come to him nor would she reply, and those two facts were damning. Still, he held to his resolve of fairness. Though he was less likely to gain an honest answer there, he looked to Benjamin. "To what do I owe this unexpected visit? Or wasn't I the one you came to see?"

Benjamin's features took on the familiar sneer of smugness. "Though there is other company I prefer, 'twas you I sought. We need to speak, dear brother, but perhaps 'tis not the proper time. You seem otherwise engaged this morning. Shall we arrange a more convenient meeting?"

Brady hesitated. His instincts were all aquiver with a wariness that had served him well in countless battles. Benjamin's presence boded ill, but he couldn't afford to dismiss him without knowing his purpose. "At the King and Country. We'll sup there and you can tell me your mind. As I must eat, 'twill not be a waste of my time."

Benjamin made a mocking bow to Kate and nodded curtly to his brother before taking his leave of the room. When the door closed behind him, Brady turned to the withdrawn woman. Her stare was

317

concentrated upon the floor as if she found the pegging of some strange fascination. She twitched away from the light touch of his hand.

"Kate, what is it?"

She drew a funny little breath that was too shallow to serve any purpose and claimed, "'Tis nothing. I'll be going to my room now. I need fresh clothing and—"

He caught her by the forearms, forcing her to come about to face him. She shrank from the contact and he frowned his puzzlement. Her agitation stirred his own. "Kate, tell me. What has he said to upset you so?"

"Nothing." The way in which she moaned the word did naught to encourage his belief. She tried again. "He said nothing but the truth. 'Tis my want to disprove it that has me upset, but I know he does not lie."

"About what?"

She couldn't face him with that. Her head turned to one side as she blinked hard and struggled for composure. When he prompted her again, she said, "About what I am."

Brady wanted to shake her. 'Twas no answer at all, not one that made sense to him. His inability to comfort her was frustrating, and helplessness bred irritation. His demand was sharp with it. "Explain yourself, woman. I cannot read your thoughts and I would know what passed between you."

Her gaze came up then, her eyes glittering with withheld emotion. "He called me your whore. And I could not deny that 'tis what I've become."

318

Silence. Brady was slow to react with words. Her misery was evident, shame and pride ravaging her honorable spirit, yet desire refused to relinquish its hold. She was inexorably caught in passion's lure and he could not, nay would not, release her. Strong fingertips brushed her cheek, forswearing her negating shake by perseverance.

"I'll let no man cast such shame upon you" was his impotent vow, for there was but one thing he could do to validate that claim and he would not.

"The shame is rightfully mine. What else would one call a woman who hungers for a man the way I do you without benefit of priest or pulpit? I have flaunted myself upon your arm and in your bed and cannot confess regret. I have no right to demand respect of anyone, least of all you." With the utterance of those words, her wretchedness knew no bounds. His response held the power to crush her once-proud bearing if he mocked her misery. He embraced her. That gesture conveyed none of the sentiments she needed to hear to put her mind at ease. It was a physical reaction to a physical relationship and imparted no clue as to his thoughts. How he must despise her for this show of sniveling weakness, she decided in her anguish. Most likely he was holding his breath in the terror that she would now make demands upon his freedom. This was not how she had wanted things to go between them. She never meant to ply his guilt with pitiful mewlings about her lost, and cheerfully ignored, virtue. How amusing he must find this long-delayed mourning for her chastity.

However, Brady was not amused. He was panicked. Her candid admission of her desire for him had shaken him to the core with pleasure and dismay. The knowledge that he'd snared her tight wrought both rapture and remorse. Realizing the depth of her disgrace only sank his sense of blame further and, more unforgivably, into the well of selfish need. He'd known it would come to this when he chose to tempt her. He'd known she could not bear up under the strain of their transgressions, yet he'd done nothing to forestall it. He couldn't claim innocence or ignorance. He'd known from the first time he'd kissed her that she could be bruised and betrayed. Yet he hadn't the strength of character to deny his own wants in favor of her needs. Any more than he did now.

Kate didn't resist the roughened palm that tilted her head up, exposing her tremulous lips to the possession of his. She didn't object as his mouth tested and tasted and teased the response of her own. It was inevitable that his hands should seek the full offering of her breasts, that their clothing would prove an encumbrance not long to be endured, that the bed would yield to their joined weight. She gave herself up to the yearning for fulfillment, to the paroxysms of bliss wrought of their act of passion and, replete, wept quietly in the circle of his arms. Nothing had been answered, nothing changed. Finally, she dried her eyes on the warm flesh of his shoulder and took a steadying breath.

"Are you all right?"

She nodded and let herself enjoy the enveloping

heat of his body. There was no other comfort like it. Her infirm emotions had run their course and she was ashamed to have given them rein. She wasn't the type to bemoan that which she couldn't change or control. She made do. And that would be her course now. She had no regrets. She had no complaints. She had Brady Rogan. Though it was not the way she would wish to hold him, she vowed to wail no more over the portion of himself he would allow her. She would make do. But she would know exactly where she stood.

"Brady?"

He smiled slightly, wondering what she meant to spring on him as she had in the past whenever she used that voice. He never would have guessed the turn of her thoughts or he would have been better prepared.

"Have you many other lovers?"

The topic had him cautious. It was not the sort of thing one discussed while the woman who'd brought such complete ecstasy still remained nestled close. It was the type of question asked at swordpoint.

"I've had my share of women, if that's what you mean."

He felt her frown against his shoulder. Thank God there was no pistol in ready reach.

"I realize you have not gone wrapped in vestments these many years. I speak of now. Will you leave my arms to tumble with another?"

"This minute? You overestimate my strength." He caught her up to his chest as she began to roll away, angered that he would make light of her inquiry. His arms tightened until the struggle if not the willfulness was crushed out of her. "No," he said.

"No?" She would not take her understanding for granted.

"No. I shall seek out no others nor have I since . . ." He broke off and was silent for so long she feared he was searching for a palatable lie. Yet when he concluded, it was surprise that tinged his words. "Since I met you." He seemed stunned by that revelation. She was inordinately pleased. It gave her the courage to continue.

"And when you decide to . . . to seek other company, will you be honest with me and let me know of it?"

Brady pushed away from her looking very cross. "Kate, for God's sake, what are you prattling about?"

"Will you tell me when you tire of me so I might not make a fool of myself?"

He blinked.

Kate rushed on, trying to be as accommodating as possible. This had to be the most awkward bargain she'd ever struck, but she was determined that each point be made clear. Becoming a man's mistress was not something she took lightly.

"Forgive me for being blunt. I know of no delicate way to go about this business and I feel it best that we both know what to expect of the other."

His lips twitched suddenly. Very soberly, he replied, "Indeed."

"There are certain things I must know. May I ask you now?"

"By all means," he drawled, looking perplexed

and amused and intrigued. She was so beautiful when her features took on that serious mien, as if the world depended upon her ability for clear thought.

"Do you wish me to remain here or shall I return to my home?" When his dark brows lowered, she hurriedly said, "Please do not think I am making demands for money. I will not take as much as a coin from you. I want that understood. I am no harlot. If I am to return home, I shall have to make arrangements to protect my family from . . . from certain knowledge they wouldn't comprehend."

"Such as?"

Even that coolly phrased question didn't deter her. "Such as our sleeping arrangements. I would not have them thinking badly of you."

Of *him*. He was astounded. She was thinking to protect *his* reputation. An incredible tenderness overwhelmed him and he laughed with sheer amazement.

"I would have you mark me seriously, Captain," Kate was quick to scold. She missed the softening of his expression in her concentration upon the details she discussed. "I find no humor in this situation."

"Forgive me," he choked. "Pray continue."

"I shall ask nothing of you but a bit of consideration and, of course, you may expect the same. We must be completely honest with one another. There is to be no obligation should one of us decide the arrangement is no longer suitable."

"Meaning?" His tone was very serious then.

Kate plunged on bravely, trusting her own fragile feelings would not betray her. "Meaning that should one of us be dissatisfied, there will be no ugly display. We will both go our own way. As I've said, if you grow restless with my attention, I would as soon know of it as have you sneak about behind my back. I'll not share you while I have you. I will be completely faithful as well."

"Until . . . ?" That was asked low, with a dangerous rumble.

Kate blushed and looked uncomfortable. "There is still a chance I might make a good marriage. Then, of course, I would have to consider my family's best interest and accept."

Dryly, he remarked, "Of course. And if I should begin to bore you?"

She looked at him as though he were mad. "How could that ever happen?" she whispered, disbelieving. Then, she returned to the matter at hand. "Are these things agreeable to you? Have I omitted anything of importance?"

"You've covered things most thoroughly," he praised, that hint of a smile teasing about his lips once more.

"Oh, and if there is a child, I will not hold you to any responsibility. That is my risk and I cannot demand you asssume it. I will raise the child as my own. It need never know of its father."

Brady stared at her. An emotion she could only term as fury mounted in the blue of his eyes. His words were bitten out as if they had an unsavory taste. "How damned decent of you." She was silent, not knowing how to react to his anger. Then he gave a grim smile. "As usual, you have thought of everything. A most practical woman."

In a small voice, she asked, "Is all satisfactory then?"

"No."

"But I . . ." Her words faltered. Tears quavered in them. She forced herself to speak the rest. "But I thought you wanted me. Was I mistaken?" Humiliation flushed crimson through her cheeks, hot beneath the press of his palms.

"No," he reassured softly. "You weren't mistaken." Relief made her response to his kiss sweetly poignant. For a moment, he held her close then he rolled from the bed to reach for his shirt.

"Brady?" Kate sat up in alarm, clutching the wrinkled sheet to her breast in an ineffectual covering. He meant to spare her only a quick look, but his eyes were bewitched by her loveliness. He fought the fascination. He had to escape the room, to indulge in strong drink and sober thought. If he remained, there was no confidence that his control would serve him well and in his favor. Kate was too damned distracting.

"We will discuss the terms when I return from the Islands." When she looked disappointed and afraid, he leaned over to kiss her gently. "Until then, bring your belongings here. I won't be leaving until tomorrow and the room is paid for. You needn't waste your coin on quarters you won't be using. We'll talk more tonight." The sultry heat in his gaze promised more than just talk and she felt a tremor of anticipation. It overshadowed the fact that he would be gone for a month and she would be left with no answers.

The King and Country was a better class of tavern with an excellent bill of fare, a parlor used for women travelers, and a large taproom with a great fireplace and bare, sanded floors. A sign over the bar read, "My liquor's good, my measure just; but honest Sirs, I will not trust."

Benjamin Rogan was leaning against the mantel-piece, casually lighting his pipe from the smoking tongs left to coal for that convenience. Through the wreath of blue smoke, he watched his brother's approach between the ample crowding of seats and chairs. He replaced the tongs on the nail alongside the tobacco drawer and gestured with a deftly blown ring to the table at his right. Brady assumed a seat and a defensive posture.

Benjamin grinned. "Good evening, Charles. I took the liberty of ordering dinner and rum. I believe I know your tastes quite well."

"What do you want?" The question was blunt.

"Do I need an excuse to come visit you, my only relation on this side of the ocean?"

"You've never looked for an excuse to do anything. I assume you've put in for repairs."

Benjamin laughed. "Limped in 'twould be more accurate. Had to use double sail canvas lashed under the keel to plug your shot holes, but it kept us tolerably watertight. How did you know?"

"I could tell by the cut of her jib that she was your ship."

"And did you fare well?"

"Except for the loss of the man you paid to betray me."

A dark brow rose in dispute. He wouldn't believe it of Brady, yet he asked, "You slew the man for wanting more coin?"

"Kate shot him as he was about to do the same to me."

Benjamin looked entertained by that picture; then his gaze assessed the other. "You were not hurt?"

"Concern? Please," Brady drawled. "You would not suffer the news of my death as much as your failure to be the cause of it. Now, enough of this. Why are you here? Surely not to gloat, for you have no cause. For repentance then? I think not? To win Kate away? You know the futility of that. That leaves only to bedevil me with your presence."

Benjamin cut through to the quick of their banter with his single statement.

"I've come for the boy."

Chapter Nineteen

"No!"

"The boy is mine," Benjamin reminded with a narrow smile. "'Tis my seed which gave him life, not yours. Or am I mistaken in that? No? I thought not. Had that been the case you would have killed me that night instead of merely paring my looks."

Brady had recovered himself somewhat and his mind was churning ahead to forestall the logic of his brother's argument. He needed time to think. "Why? Why after all these years?"

"Curiosity."

"'Tis not what makes a father want to see his child. You've no right to intrude in his life. You're dead to him."

The cynical smile was gone, replaced by something not nearly as pleasant. "Is that what you told him?"

"'Tis what Elizabeth told him when he asked of you. She said you were lost at sea."

Benjamin laughed at that. "Ironic, the truth in that lie."

"What do you want of him? He's only a boy. He's no part of what's between us."

"He's what's between Elizabeth and me, and that's what has you so distressed. Did you think to take my place as his father? I'm sure you think you're better suited for the post."

The jibe worked on all Brady's painful wounds of the past and he responded to them as Benjamin knew he would, emotionally, without forethought. "At least I've been around while he was growing up. Where were you? Where the hell were you if you were so interested in being a father to him?"

"Here or there makes no difference. Blood is blood and the boy is mine to claim and keep if I choose. You have no say. Had I the desire, I could move right in under the sheets with my dear wife and we'd be one happy family. And where would that leave you?"

Brady was still. A hatred fierce enough to will his brother's death surged through him. He'd felt that helpless fury once before when Benjamin had mocked him, had delighted in telling him that Elizabeth was now his bride. That hot insanity had swirled up to cloud all reason. Jealousy had ruled and with sword in hand, he had sought his brother's life. How he had wanted to cut the heart from the one who had caused his to break. The vileness of their envy and spite needed to be severed, but when the chance was his, he could not take it. Something caused his aim to err on that stroke meant to dole out death. Perhaps the love that had somehow survived all the distortions of their upbringing had checked his swing. Whatever, it brought back this plague into his life to threaten it anew and, older now and more in control, he didn't reach for a weapon to slay him though it would be his wish.

"What use have you for an eight-year-old child?" he asked, seeking to touch on some sense of reason.

"None whatsoever."

That cruel sentiment sent a chill through Brady's heart. "He is better off not knowing you."

"Are you implying that my family would not welcome me to their bosom? That the boy, or Elizabeth, would choose you had they the choice?" He let that sink deep then prodded, "No, Brother. They are mine to take whenever I like."

Made nearly frantic by the thought of Benjamin insinuating himself into the house on Benefit Street, Brady snarled, "What do you want? What will it take for you to go back to whatever hell has housed you these past years?"

Benjamin lifted his rum in a leisurely toast and drank his fill before answering. His gaze was cold with satisfaction. "You have nothing I want, Brady. Nothing at all." His eyes grew heavy and thoughtful. "Except that spirited bit of petticoat I helped bathe this morning. Now, she's something that might distract me." Brady surprised him by laughing easily.

"Kate Mallory is not something I could give or trade even if I cared to. She belongs only to herself and, I hazard to say, is not very fond of you. If you wish to tangle with her, do so at your own risk. She is beyond your corruption."

"But not yours, eh?"

Brady tensed, remembering Kate's stricken look. That memory ate through to his soul. He made his voice purposefully cool. "She amuses me for the time being. A warm bed is better than a lonely one. She can go whenever she chooses. With whomever she chooses. I've no need for a woman complicating my life."

"Not when you have mine," Benjamin supplied silkily. He didn't believe Brady's claim of disinterest for a minute, but he let it alone. He had his brother on edge and anxious, and that pleased him enough to be generous. He gestured for another rum and regarded Brady with interest. "What does she see in you that I don't possess?"

Not knowing if he meant Kate or Elizabeth, Brady answered wryly, "Perhaps a heart or a soul. I've never known you to have an abundance of either."

Benjamin chuckled. "I'd forgotten how much I enjoyed your company. Life can be damned dull sometimes."

"Is that why you stir up your own excitement?"

"Exactly."

It was as much the want to know as the need to preoccupy that made Brady ask, "And where have you been these years? In search of that excitement?"

Benjamin kicked back on two legs of his chair and sucked on his pipe to create pensive rings of smoke.

"I was a guest of the Royal Navy for a time then, worse, got myself crimped and pressed into service on a Guineaman for three years. Managed to avoid the flux long enough to buy my way free and into a brigantine that made seven trips for black ivory out of Anamabo. When my new brig gets seaworthy, I'll be back to that trade. 'Tis where the money is, Brady. I'm surprised you haven't discovered that for yourself."

"Trading men like riding cattle is not a business I choose to be in." It didn't surprise him that Benjamin had chosen such an easy, disreputable course, but it did sicken him to know the depths to which he'd lowered himself. And apparently without conscience.

"Still a man of honor, eh, Brady? 'Tis why you'll never best me. You still have some scruples. I discarded mine years ago. Were that sword in my hand, I would have killed you. There's the difference between us."

Looking into the glittering blue eyes, Brady said, "And glad I am to claim it. Better honor than disgrace."

"But not half as amusing."

Their meal arrived and both took to it to ease the mounting tension that flared so quickly to a blaze. They sensed the need to back away, to reassess, to look for weakness like enemies of old anticipating battle. It was not an amiable feast. However, their personal animosity was drawn off by the increasingly loud talk from the next table, where a group of British sailors indulged themselves in drink. They were young and in need of the spirits to give them foolish courage.

"Would you look there, Talbott," slurred one of the young men. "Bold as you please, like he was as good as us."

Talbott, who appeared the soberest of the lot, fastened a surly gaze on Brady and sneered to his companions, "Here in the Colonies they treat thieves like heroes. In England, we have trees sporting his kind."

"Friends of yours?" Benjamin asked as he reached for another piece of bread.

"Professional acquaintances, I would guess." He lifted his mug in indifference to the glowering seamen.

That they would be treated as mild annoyances heated the resentment amongst the group of sailors. They grumbled and cursed and drank, then one grew emboldened enough to mumble, "Damned coward. Won't stand for a fight. Knows he doesn't have a chance against real, experienced guns."

"Should I tell the young pup why my ship is in port full of holes?" Benjamin offered, willing to forgo his bitterness in favor of boasting his brother's skill. "Doubtless they'd never attribute their inability to catch you with their own poor seamanship." His chuckle grated raw upon the pride of the young men.

"Cowards and traitors all," growled Talbott, warming to the subject. "Showing their disloyalty and ingratitude for all we've done to improve their lot."

"Ah, yes," Brady drawled, still aiming his conversation at Benjamin rather than acknowledging the brash youths. "Lowering the duty on molasses from six pence to three out of the goodness of their greedy hearts, well knowing that any would be prohibitive to our merchants. Then housing their troops under the pretense of our defense when we all know 'tis for riding rod and check over us. Such charity. Mother England fails to see her oppression for what it is."

The two negligently lounging gentlemen paid no attention to the fury they incensed as they shared a private toast. Their own ambivalence was set aside in response to the outside challenge almost as if they were comrades instead of sworn combatants. The sailors seethed and their attitudes grew openly hostile. One of them spat contemptuously upon the floor at Brady's feet, before speaking his piece. "'Tis always the excuse these whining Colonists give when asked to do their fair share. The truth be, they enjoy stealing from their countrymen as much as from us. They call themselves privateers, patriots. 'Tis pirates they be and they deserve to be treated as such. When our Lieutenant Duddington gets through, the waters will be safe for honest trade."

"The watchhounds from the *Gaspee*," Brady said. His tone was thick with loathing. "Doing their duty by choking off trade between our ports and harassing other shipping between our colony harbors. An intelligent group to be sure."

"Gleaned from the dregs of society," Benjamin offered with a mock salute.

"'Tis no wonder they be too stupid to know they cut their own throats."

With a roar, Talbott swung his mug. The crockery shattered against the side of Brady's head, the force of it pitching him from his chair. There was a rumble as the bartender pulled down the portcullis grate to protect his wares at the bar from the violence he'd seen pending.

Benjamin caught his brother before he'd gained the floor, then eased him the rest of the way. From temple to chin ran a river of blood and memories of another time when positions were reversed held him powerless for a heartbeat. Then he cried Brady's name, the sound torn with a desperate disbelief. He couldn't be dead. Movement from the other table sparked reflexes and his pistol was drawn and aimed before any of them could pull a startled breath.

"Get out," he snarled. "Get back to your ship, you pack of yapping dogs. If you've done my brother harm, by God I'll find you each one and make you beg to die." The steely glitter in his uplifted eyes encouraged belief, and the group of them backed away, realizing they'd tangled with more than they could handle.

With the threat at bay, Benjamin turned his attention back to the figure on the floor. The hand he put to Brady's throat was far from steady. Reassured, he sought to stem the vital flood with his kerchief. Pressure on the jagged wound wrought a groan of protest and a flicker of dazed blue eyes.

"Ben?" It was a soft inquiry.

"Right here."

A lopsided grin creased the pale face with its vivid slash of crimson a stark contrast. "Told you I could take that fence."

Benjamin looked blank for a moment, then memory prevailed to provoke a grin. He'd knelt beside a twelve-year-old Charles Rogan weeping with fright and a fearsome pride as he had cradled him, all battered and broken. On a suicidal dare, he'd rushed a green colt over an impossible hedge. The barrier had been cleared but Brady thrown as the horse landed poorly. That he'd survived it was a wonder. It had taken Benjamin a split lip and broken nose to collect that debt owed his brother when their summer guests refused to pay, and it humbled him to present the coin like a trophy to the bandaged boy in his sickroom. Brady had gestured him to come close with a feeble curl of fingers and had whispered, for he couldn't speak loudly with all the tape about his ribs, "Told you I could take that fence." How awed he'd been by that show of reckless courage. How he'd loved his older brother. His only want was to emulate him.

"That you did, Brady. That you did," Benjamin replied with misty sentiment. "And damned if I've ever seen the like of it again." Then the unfocused eyes began to roll up white and he was forced to put the past behind them. "Come on, Brady, wake up. Let's get you out of here."

A commotion hurried Kate into her dressing gown and brought her outside her door in time to receive a tottering Brady on his brother's arm. At first she thought with disgust that both men were reeling drunk, but then she saw the dark stains upon Brady's coat and snowy stock.

"Dear God. Bring him over here."

Benjamin followed her to the bed, steering his uncooperative burden. Brady sagged to the mattress with a moan. Kate was immediately beside him on bended knee, her worried eyes seeking the source of his injury. After studying the clotting gash, she stood and turned on Benjamin in a fury. "What did you do to him?" She was magnificent in her rage, like a sleek golden lioness posed for the kill.

"Brady, you'd best explain before your lady dispatches me."

Weak fingers caught her wrist to vie for her attention. "The fault wasn't Ben's. 'Twas my own arrogance that brought me down," he admitted with a mumbled slur. When he began to sway, Kate dismissed Benjamin from mind to concentrate on bolstering him with the support of her shoulder and an arm about his middle. "Get me a damp cloth," she snapped with a crack of authority. She took it with a murmur of thanks and gently sponged away the fluid from the wound. Benjamin watched her tender ministrations in silence, then after several minutes passed, said, "I'll be going. You seem to have all in hand."

Brady pushed aside the blotting cloth to focus on his brother. "Ben? We haven't finished our talk."

"I think we have." That was said quietly, almost with regret. To Kate, he added, "Take care of him.

338

He's blessed with a hard head."

"You're leaving then?" she asked, not knowing whether to feel gladness or a strange remorse.

"Yes. When my business here is finished." At Brady's abrupt frown, he concluded, "I have a ship full of holes, if you'll recall. And you?"

Brady's somber expression didn't lessen. "I sail in the morning."

"Then 'tis not likely we shall meet."

"Not ever?"

Benjamin responded with a small smile to his brother's soft question. They hadn't been so close in years, even before their dreadful parting, but he knew the cautious affection would not be of long life. Too much lay between them. Jauntily, he said, "Oh, in the next ten years or so I'm sure our paths will cross again."

Brady's eyes closed wearily in deference to the pain. "I shall be ready for it."

"Not with chain shot, I trust." With that, Benjamin grinned and nodded to Kate before starting to the door.

"Ben?"

He turned, brow arched in question.

"I wish things had been different. Smooth seas to you until then."

"And to you, Brady."

When the door closed, Brady surrendered all alertness. The sudden ebb of strength had Kate alarmed and she eased him down upon his back and applied the cloth once again to the jagged cut.

"'Tis a wonder you didn't lose your eye," she

scolded, anxiety giving her words a cutting edge. "Men are such fools with their brawling and their bluster and we women have to pick up the pieces. 'Tis a wonder what few brains you have weren't addled beyond repair." He groaned and twitched away from the hurt the cleansing caused, then moaned as movement brought even greater agony. Kate held his shoulders down and fell into contrition. "No, don't move. Be still, beloved, lest you do yourself more harm." When he quieted, she completed her task by binding a strip of cloth about his head to hold a wadding in place over the nasty wound. She sat beside him then, worry gnawing through her at his pallor and strange lethargy. He drifted in and out of awareness, and in one of his lucid moments, she suggested bringing a physician to tend him. His negating shake made him grimace and respond with an emphatic "No. I'll have no filthy leech cutting me over his bleeding cups. You've done fine for me. I need rest if I'm to take the *Elizabeth* out on the morrow."

"But you're in no condition for that." The grip of his fingers about her hand was very weak. His brilliant blue eyes had dulled to near opaqueness. She couldn't believe he'd be up to such a test of strength.

"Ah, but we've a fortune to make and we cannot afford to lose a day. I'll be fit by morning. You'll see." With that certainty, his eyes closed and consciousness was dismissed. Kate had no chance to vent her doubts, so after watching over him for long hours, she surrendered to her own exhaustion by removing

340

her gown and curling close to his body's heat to fall instantly to sleep.

It was not movement but the lack of it that woke her some time later. Her hand sought the empty sheets. *He's gone*, flashed through her thinking with quicksilver dismay. Then the interruption of soft moonlight spilling over the bed led her anguished gaze to the window where Brady stood looking out over the harbor. The white wrapping gleamed against his black hair. Silently, she slipped across the floor to join him in his motionless watch. Though he didn't seem to notice her, his arm curved about her waist to draw her tight against him, where she stayed listening to the rapid pulse of his heart beneath her head. His restlessness had naught to do with discomfort of the body and gently she asked its cause. "Brady, what is it?"

For a moment, he didn't answer and when she'd begun to feel he wouldn't, he said, "Benjamin's come for Jamie."

She understood his mood then and knew the demons that troubled his heart and mind. "Surely he won't take the boy."

"I don't know that, Kate." His cheek burrowed into the softness of her hair in search of solace. The breath that stirred it came quick and panicked. "I keep thinking I'll return to find them gone. How can I endure the journey not knowing what awaits me here?" The torment in his words was more than she could bear. Quietly, she said, "Don't go."

Brady said nothing for a long moment. She could feel him mulling over those two words and their

341

ramifications as his face nuzzled the rich gold of her tresses. Her eyes were squeezed shut and a single thought possessed her. *Go, Brady, go, and let him take them away.* How that would uncomplicate things. With Elizabeth and her child gone, there would be nothing to distract him. Brady would be hers, alone.

"If I remain to watch over Benjamin, there will be no one to make your investment for you. I've given you my word that I would see to it for you."

He paused and Kate knew he was waiting for her to make her wishes known. What could she say? She had to have the money the Island venture would bring. Her family's existence hinged upon it. How could she selflessly make such a sacrifice so he could give protection to the woman who was her rival? Yet, could she bear the guilt of his despair should she hold him to his promise and his loved ones escape him? His happiness at the cost of her own? She couldn't choose between them and so, ungenerously, she stayed silent.

Brady's arm tightened and she enjoyed the sensation of being mashed to his chest. His voice created a husky vibration beneath the pillow of her cheek. As if he'd read her uncharitable thoughts, he murmured, "'Tis unfair of me to expect you to answer. Never fear, Kate. I will see to my obligations."

Which? she wondered in a quickening of doubt and dread. Then he put her mind to rest with his unshakable sense of honor. "When I return, you will be a rich woman, Kate. It pleases me to know you'll want for nothing."

She held herself immobile while her thoughts spun. He'd chosen her. She nearly wept with relief, then sobered, thinking of his miseries. Was she being the unfair one to expect so much from him when she knew well the importance he placed upon his attachments in Providence? Could there be a way to salvage both their wants? And miraculously, it came.

"Brady, I could take your brother to Providence and see to your interests there. Perhaps 'twould be better for all that you not be involved. Benjamin might be more compassionate without the threat you pose to his sense of importance. I truly cannot believe he means to assume a life he's shunned for so long unless you provoke him to it."

Her head was tipped up in the cradling vee of his hands. His gaze was intense as it delved into hers. "You'd do that for me?" he asked with a penetrating quiet.

"Yes." *Fool,* she thought to herself, *doesn't he know I'd do anything?*

He continued to hold her chin between his palms, but his stare went beyond her as he considered the option before him. He mused aloud, "Yes, it makes sense. Ben and I tend to antagonize one another whenere we're together. Could be if I were not on hand to bait him, he would be content to leave things as they stand. And you would be there to see he does?" The compelling gaze returned, brilliant, desperately seeking.

"I will do all I can short of violence. However, knowing your brother, it may come to that with

343

little provocation."

Brady laughed. The sound trembled with relief. Then his attention was fully upon her and that anxious look had mellowed to a smoky appreciation. "You're remarkable, Kate. You've proven yourself invaluable time and again. Would that I deserved you."

Before she could argue on his behalf, he was kissing her, gently, firmly, with a thoroughness that had her breathless. As she clung to him for balance, his fingers stroked down her flushed throat to push aside the straps of her chemise. As his lips lowered to taste the sweet slope of her shoulders, she caught at his hair in helpless pleasure and, abruptly, he winced away to favor the split at his temple. Her apology and look of concern were quickly discarded as his palms tested the swell of her breasts.

While she could yet think with any coherency, Kate mumbled, "Brady, are you well enough for this sort of thing? Your head . . . you should be resting . . . you need . . ."

Brady pulled her close against the strength of his body and its telling contours. "That should answer the first, and this, the second." His kiss was devouring. "I need only to know that you'll be waiting for my return," he rasped against her parted lips.

"I will," she breathed.

"Then what I need this night is the memory of you to carry on all those lonely nights asea. I can nurse my head tomorrow and enjoy my misery, but the

torture I'm in this minute must have its release now."
And she could do naught but heal him.

And as he lay entwined with her in a heavy, sated
sleep, Kate absently rubbed the beautifully fashioned
line of his shoulders and questioned the wisdom of
what she'd done.

Chapter Twenty

The leisurely sail up to Providence was one Kate found anything but relaxing. Her confidence upon the water failed her in the small, unsteady craft and Benjamin's want to close his eyes against the morning's glare in his drink-ravaged condition did little to hearten her. She said few words. The knowledge that Brady had sailed that morning in the opposite direction held her melancholy and the chore pending weighed upon her spirit. She did little more than cling to her precarious seating and pray that Brady's image would carry her safely in his absence.

The harbor in Providence was less frenzied than that of Newport. It serviced the heart of Rhode Island more than the bustling external trade and wealthy vacationers. The waters of the Moshassuck and Woonasquatucket Rivers were harnessed to run great mills, and the town abounded with the small businesses of distilleries, tanneries, and cooperages.

Kate was tormented with the vision of Brady tied to such practical work while Elizabeth awaited him in their tidy home. The picture lodged painfully in her throat and again she wondered if what she was doing was aiding in that realization. She wanted no part of bringing Brady and his lost love together, yet she'd given her word and would keep it with the same nobility that he had displayed. After all, what could she do if Benjamin decided to claim his lawful wife? If put to the test, how hard would she strive to keep them apart? Perhaps she wasn't being noble at all but self-serving in her offer. Oh, why had he left her with the memory of his exquisite lovemaking but no permanent solutions to the dilemma?

With the boat secured, Benjamin seemed in little hurry to seek out his estranged family. Instead, he suggested that they partake in a meal and Kate, not anxious to return to Benefit Street, was quick to agree. It wasn't difficult to find a cozy inn with an ordinary established in its parlor, and after ordering the table be set with mutton, veal, garden produce aplenty, as well as cider and brandy—all for three pence sterling—Benjamin's attention seemed to sharpen as he assessed his companion. With his first piercing comment, she found herself wishing for the return of his silent stupor.

"So, Brady trusts you to bring the wolf into his lair. Am I the only one who sees the irony in his choice?"

"I am passing through on my way home and do this as a favor, nothing more."

He grinned at her tart defense. "Really? Passing

through Providence on your way to Kingstown? I would think the direct route across the Bay would have better served you."

His astuteness gave no recourse so Kate busied herself with cutting her meat. Benjamin toyed with his fork and continued his disconcerting study. "He sends you to see to his lover and yet you still maintain that he cares for you," he marveled.

"I don't believe I've confided such knowledge to you. I am not your concern, sir."

Still Benjamin persisted with his intimate appraisal and his uncomfortable turn of conversation. "Brady tells me you killed a man to save him."

Kate went very pale and her fork settled beside her trencher. "'Twas not my intent to take another's life, but I had little choice."

"Well done, I would say. Not many females have that kind of pluck."

"If not for my true aim, you would not have a brother to taunt with your presence here. The fault be yours more likely than mine for that poor man's demise." Saying it didn't make it so in a heart that still ached from the fatal consequence of her act. Benjamin Rogan may have set the stage but he hadn't pulled the trigger.

"I am in your debt."

She viewed him through a jaundiced eye, for such sincerity could not be genuine. "Why pretend that you care for Brady when you seek to destroy him?"

"I love my brother" was his incredible reply. His stare was unwavering in the face of Kate's contemptuous disbelief.

"How could you say so? If that were true, then why are you here?"

He rolled his mug between restless hands and stared hard into the amber liquid it held. His hesitancy gave her pause and, for a brief moment, she thought she saw to the heart of the man.

"Think what you will. I am not here to thwart Brady, at least not entirely."

"The boy?"

His lips pursed in rueful thought, then he said, "I've never seen him. Have you?" At her nod, he prompted, "What's he like?"

"He looks a great deal like . . . you." She caught herself before making the comparison to Brady. "He seems to be a spirited child, well mannered yet unbridled. I think you'll be pleased."

"And no doubt he dotes on Brady." There was such resignation in the way that was said. She couldn't make herself say yea or nay. "Of course he does. What lad wouldn't want to look up to such a figure of a man. I did when I was young." With that admission, he sat quiet as if expecting Kate to latch onto those words with a vengeance. She didn't.

"Do you plan to take the boy with you?" she asked with unexpected gentleness.

His laugh was harsh. "With me? What have I to offer a boy? Did you think I'd take him with me and have him learn to be a flesh merchant in my wake? 'Tis not what I had in mind for a son of mine. He'd do better thinking I was dead and follow in Brady's shadow."

His futile sadness filled Kate with sympathy. To

think of a man depriving himself of the joy of his only son was a suffering she could not imagine. She couldn't fathom giving a child of her body into someone else's care. "How unfair of you to withhold your love from a child. He deserves to know his father, not a substitute you think better suited."

Benjamin smiled wryly. "Do you honestly think he would welcome me into his life, choose me over Brady in his affections? I think not, nor would I want to force the choice. Brady and I lost our best years together struggling for attention and living in uncertainty. I'd not wish that on the boy. He's secure where he is. I mean to let him be."

"Then why did you come?"

"To see him. Almost nine and I've never had the pleasure."

"And your wife?" Kate posed that carefully, trying to be neutral. This pensive side of Brady's cynical brother confused her feelings toward him, making it hard to view him as an enemy who threatened her well-being. Though she warned herself to go cautiously, she was wont to extend him her compassion.

"Elizabeth is better off thinking me lost at sea. We could never have a life together."

That rankled Kate. Did men never consider a woman's wants when they singularly decided a future for both of them? Or was this a trait of the arrogant Rogan clan who thought they knew what was best for all concerned when in truth they knew nothing at all.

Benjamin observed her frowning countenance

then urged, "Go ahead. Speak your mind. I've grown used to your opinions."

"'Tis my opinion that you and your brother do Elizabeth a grave disservice. She should have a say in what affects her life and the life of her son. Did you ever consider that she might not care what kind of life you lead? Did you ever think she might love you enough to adjust her wants to suit yours? You have very little trust in those dependent upon you."

"And you depend too much on those you should not trust. Admit it, Kate, we're unlucky souls, you and I. Perhaps together we could give each other comfort." His forefinger slid sensually over the back of her hand. Instead of jerking away, she twisted to catch his hand in hers and held it firm. Benjamin Rogan was no longer a threat. He was all bluff.

"We make our luck, Ben. More's the pity you don't believe that."

"You've faith enough for us both." He lifted his mug in toast and she drank without reservation, aching for the unhappiness of the man opposite. What a tangle of torment they'd caught themselves in.

"If you won't see Elizabeth, how do you plan to see your son?" His stealthy smile gave her warning.

"Why, you did say you'd help, didn't you?"

Elizabeth Rogan greeted Kate with surprise and genuine welcome. She accepted without question Kate's story that she'd stopped on her way back to her farm to convey Brady's farewell wishes. A few inquiries were posed on the nature of his venture, then Elizabeth sank back in her chair with a heavy sigh. "Jamie will be so disappointed. Brady's been teaching him to sail, you see, and he was so hoping they'd have time to spend together before his next trip. Well, he shall just have to understand, but it's hard, you know, for a boy his age to weather the disappointment. He's been under foot all day, moping and crying of boredom."

"Perhaps he and I could be of service to each other. I need to make some purchases and could use a knowledgeable guide and it sounds as though he needs a bit of distraction."

Kate writhed with guilt at Elizabeth's enthused reception and profuse thanks. She was quick to summon her son, who sulkily agreed to escort the pretty Miss Mallory about, and the two of them embarked on their walk toward the dockside shops. Jamie was a handsome boy and Kate couldn't help wondering as she beheld him if a child shared by Brady and herself would own looks as pleasing as his. And thinking of Brady and her reason for this deception made her spirits sag.

"Good day, Miss Mallory. And who is your young friend?"

Pretending a spontaneous delight, Kate introduced father and son, repressing her puzzlement when the older man gave his name as Mr. Benjamin. Jamie solemnly shook the extended hand and she could see his reluctance to release it from his larger one. Though she didn't understand his want to pretend to be a stranger, Kate didn't challenge

Benjamin on it.

"And what are you about this fine day?" the scarred man asked with a nonchalant air.

"I need to do some shopping and Master James was kind enough to serve as my guide."

"Shopping? Sounds like tame work for a man. Why, I was just making my way down to my boat to rethread the rigging. Could sure use an extra set of willing hands." He dangled that bait casually and Jamie all but snapped his fingers off. His eyes grew large and round with longing, but duty made him scuff his toes and pretend disinterest. Then the bait was made more tempting. "I taught your uncle how to run lines."

Jamie glowed. "You know my uncle Brady?"

Benjamin's smile was bittersweet. "That I do. Sailed with him many times when we were younger. I could tell you a story or two . . . but no, I'd best be letting you get on with your business."

Jamie's manners were sorely strained. Still, he hesitated and glanced hopefully at Kate. He nearly wept his gratitude when she sighed and said, "Oh, go on with you. I can find my way from door to door and you'd be no use to me pining for stories that are most likely more fiction than fact."

She stood on the walk watching them stride down toward the dock engaged in easy camaraderie and felt a tightness in her breast. They looked so natural together, yet it wasn't her place to interfere. At least she could give Benjamin this precious time to know his son even if Jamie came away from it with only the pleasing memory of a friend of his uncle. She lingered through the ground-floor shops run by those who lived above and purchased small trinkets for her sisters to keep the pretext of her visit. An hour stretched into three before the twosome returned as familiar with one another as old friends—or as father and son. Jamie was immediately apologetic for keeping her waiting so long; then, upon her assurance that she hadn't minded, he launched into a detailed description of what he and his new friend had accomplished on the boat.

"A natural sailor," Benjamin boasted, placing a fond hand on the dark head. Jamie beamed up at him.

"Wait till I show Brady what you've taught me. He'll be so surprised."

"That he will," Benjamin mused. "You think a great deal of your uncle, don't you, boy?"

"The world," he claimed with childish over-statement.

"As you should." Benjamin rumpled the black hair and let his hand drop away. "Why don't you run ahead, Jamie lad, and let Miss Mallory and me speak some business." His brooding look followed the boy as he rushed along, clattering a stick between fence rungs.

"I needn't ask if you liked him."

Benjamin shook his head. "A damned fine boy."

"Are you sure—"

"Things are better this way," he stated firmly, though his softened gaze was less sure. "I make for an entertaining friend, but I'd be a disappointing father. Brady's better suited for the role. I'd rather he grew up in his mold than mine." When Kate had no reply, he gave her a crooked smile. "Now don't go shedding any tears for me and the choices I've made. I stand by them even now. But I would ask two more favors of you, if I might."

"Go on."

"Give this to Brady." The pouch weighed heavy in her hand. "'Tis for Elizabeth and the boy. I'd rather they think it came from him. And this," he gave her a sealed document, "should take care of past debts." He grinned at her curiosity and taunted, "Satisfy yourself before you pass it on. 'Twas time I did something. Tell Brady . . . tell him good-bye for me. And you, Kate, I wish you well." He leaned forward and she accepted his kiss without protest. That seemed to restore his mocking confidence. "There's still time. Come with me."

Smiling, she shook her head and he gave an eloquent shrug. With both legacies from Benjamin Rogan mingled with her parcels, Kate turned and hurried after Jamie.

Kate hadn't anticipated Jamie Rogan's propensity for chatter. The moment they gained the door, he rushed to find his mother to regale her with the details of his outing with his uncle's friend. Elizabeth stood patiently, listening to the boy's excited talk with a serene smile until he mentioned the scar that marked his new acquaintance's face. Abruptly, the color left her own and unsteady hands sought the back of a parlor chair for support.

Seeing her waver, Kate interrupted the boy's tale to say, "Jamie, why don't you see if one of the kitchen girls would put on a kettle. Your mother and I would so like a nice cup of tea." When he went to see about it, Kate quickly grasped the pallid woman's arm and steered her into a chair. She sank into it on jellied legs. "Mistress Rogan, are you all right?"

A tremulous hand pressed to an overtaxed heart. Damp eyes rose apologetically. "Oh, dear, what must you think of me. I am really not such a vaporish creature." She drew several long breaths and gratefully accepted Kate's handkerchief. "That man Jamie was with, do you know him?"

Steeling herself to betray none of her guilty knowledge, Kate said, "Not really. Brady engaged him to see me here from Newport." The lie sat poorly with her, intensified by the woman's apparent distress. "Is something wrong?"

"'Tis just when Jamie was describing the man, it made me think of . . . of another. But that could not be. Not if Brady sent him." She seemed more composed now and Kate floundered miserably in the deception she reluctantly shared with Brady and his brother to fool this unfortunate woman. She compassionately placed a hand over the frail one clutching at the chair arm and was regarded with a misty stare that tore her asunder with sorrow.

"I regret if my allowance of your son to spend time with the seaman caused you any despair. 'Twas not my intention." Her tone was thick with the truth of that statement and Elizabeth was gracious enough to ease her dismay.

357

"Please, Miss Mallory, none of the fault is yours. I am grateful Jamie was able to enjoy himself. He is so hungry for a man's attention what with Brady away so much of the time."

Kate forced a narrow smile. She was thankful when the arrival of the tea service forestalled her need to reply. As her hostess was still pale and shaken, she offered to pour and found herself calmed by that simple domestic task. With delicate saucers balanced in hand, the two women regarded each other with cautious interest. Politely, Elizabeth coaxed Kate to speak of herself, of her family and farm. Strangely, Kate found herself revealing more than she'd planned at the other woman's gentle promptings and, more curious still, was her want to do so. She hadn't realized before how rare it was for her to converse with someone outside the realm of her family. It felt good to confide her troubles and concerns to a sympathetic ear, and Elizabeth Rogan was a most attentive audience. Before she knew of it, hours had passed in the quiet parlor, and when she rose to beg her leave lest she be caught by darkness upon the road, Elizabeth stood also, stilling her with a sincere plea.

"Won't you remain to sup with us, Miss Mallory? You've journeyed long already and your kindness to my son has delayed you. You would be most welcome to stay the night and start fresh in the morning."

Kate began to protest. The last thing she desired was a night under this roof sharing familiar conversation with a woman she should by all rights despise. Yet, seeing she was about to decline,

Elizabeth touched her arm and renewed her efforts. "Please. I would so enjoy the company. Time passes so slowly when one's alone."

How true, Kate thought ruefully, and she nodded her assent.

The meal was quite a contrast from the ones taken in her own noisy, crowded kitchen. Dishes were served by a silent, efficient staff who appeared with the slightest jingle from the table bell. Young James ate with a proper stillness befitting his age, yet Kate found him more than once studying her with interest as if he harbored questions that burst to know answers. Table talk was refined to topics of local discussion and she had no trouble partaking in the shallow volley. While she spoke, her eyes took all in and she couldn't suppress her innate resentment. How well Brady saw to his brother's wife, keeping her in modest luxury with servants at hand so hers would never know toil. What a pretty social puppet Elizabeth Rogan was, conversing on noncontroversial subjects. Like all well-bred women, she was a charming hostess, avoiding converse on whist, quadrilles, or operas, instead speaking freely about geography and biographical readings. What an agreeable hearth she would hold with her virtues of moderation, temperance, and genteel behavior. Kate could only wonder how such a meek and pristine creature held two such vital, volatile men—and could only fall short in comparing herself to the mild, lovely woman. If Brady could find contentment to bind him for nine years in this placid setting, what could she offer to entice him away, she with her fiery temper and brusque, domineering ways? Elizabeth Rogan was the type men married. And what did that make her?

With the table cleared and Jamie dismissed to his studies, the two women returned to the elegant parlor where their talk turned to things not suitable for his ears. As they sipped the precious teas, Elizabeth began to speak of her failed marriage and the quixotic man who yet held her heart enthralled. Kate struggled to envision the heroic, gentle man she revered as the sardonic, often cruel Benjamin Rogan she knew. As Elizabeth spoke of him, a wistful softening enhanced her features to ethereal beauty. Love was embodied in her every word as if it was only the day prior that he had vanished from her life. She spoke of loneliness and dreams that went unfulfilled and she could have been expressing what lay in Kate's heart, so keenly did she feel those same sentiments. Finally, the words fell silent and the tea grew cold as both reflected upon the men who'd left them behind. Elizabeth's sudden, cheerful intrusion shook Kate from her gloom. "Here now, before we both start weeping upon each other's shoulders over what we cannot control. I should be showing you to your room. 'Tis late and I'm certain you'll want to make an early start. I can see you miss your family."

Kate couldn't argue that, and she wanted to linger over the melancholy turn of conversation no longer. Her heart was heavy enough without the burdens of another's. She followed her hostess up a flight of stairs into an airy room with a tester bed. All was tidy and clean and spoke not at all of a masculine influence. She could only see two other doors. If this was not the room Brady used, she could only conclude that he shared one with Elizabeth. Her chest constricted painfully, demanding she discover the truth.

"Does Brady take all his belongings with him each time he sails?"

Elizabeth looked at her in unabashed puzzlement.

"This *is* the room he uses, is it not?"

The laugh she earned was hardly what she'd expected. "Oh, gracious no. Brady never stays here. A woman alone with a boy and no husband; he would never allow for suspect talk to slander me."

Kate was unconvinced of the innocence she painted, for she herself knew well what could be accomplished without others being the wiser. Testily, she said, "I but assumed. Forgive me."

"Did you? Oh, I am so sorry." Elizabeth took up her hand and it required an effort not to jerk away and let her temper fly. How dare the woman be condescending. "You care for him, don't you?" And to taunt her atop it all. Kate was seething and perilously close to angry tears. But the next softly spoken words calmed her. "Brady and I are not, and never have been, lovers. I hope I don't offend you with my blunt speech but I cannot let you think wrongly of our relationship. Though he has been long absent, I love my husband and have been faithful to him. There can never be another for me as long as I have hope that he still lives."

It was Kate's turn to blush and show remorse for her pettish attack but Elizabeth would hear of no apology.

"What else could you think, my poor dear. I live in this house that he provides and on a livelihood that he supplies me. How hard it must be for you to understand. But you are brave and strong and clever and capable of making your own way whereas I am none of those things. Without Brady, I don't know what would have become of James and me. I have no skills and no husband I can claim. Brady has given me a home and seen to our wants and I confess I am not courageous enough to turn away his charity. Never have I met a more noble and generous man than Brady Rogan. All this he does out of the misguided notion that it was his argument with Benjamin that drove him from our lives. I know that is not true yet I prey upon that belief. I know in my heart that I am to blame for his desertion. Were I more like you, I could have held him. So you see, I have no choice but to live off of an honorable man's guilt. 'Tis nothing I am proud to do, but I've a son to think of as well as my own survival. Please do not hate us for what we do."

With a soft cry, Kate embraced the conscience-stricken woman and said, "We do what we must, Elizabeth. There is no shame in wanting the best for those we love and for ourselves. Brady sees to you because he wants to, not because he feels he must. He loves you and Jamie." She clamped her lips together lest she be moved to say more.

Elizabeth was heartened by those brief sentiments. She stepped away with a humbling embarrassment. "I should have married Brady, then this would be all truth instead of empty lie but I couldn't help myself. Benjamin made me feel so alive. I knew what he was but it didn't matter. Does that sound foolish?"

Kate shook her head. "No. I understand all too well."

Elizabeth offered a shy smile and said, "I'm glad we had this chance to visit. Will you come again?"

"I'd like that." And surprisingly, she meant it. She didn't say it would all depend upon Brady. Elizabeth Rogan carried enough qualms of conscience without adding the weight of her distant dreams. "Good night," she said quietly and let her resentments leave with her.

And as she folded back the superfine blankets from her borrowed bed, Kate felt a kindred sadness for the tragic figure of Elizabeth who held the love of one man only to long for another. As she put aside her gown, she felt again the weight of coin and drew out the two parcels given her by Benjamin Rogan. The coin, all in British sterling, was ample to see to Elizabeth's independence. She viewed it with a mounting sense of elation. With it, Brady would be freed of obligation. She closed her eyes and blessed her unlikely savior. Curiosity tempered her relief and she sat upon the bed to study the second missive. Compunctions soothed by Benjamin's permission, she loosened the seal and opened the document for a quick reading. The heavy parchment trembled in her hands. The words blurred before her eyes, words that sealed her hopes with the bitter stamp of failure.

It was proof of divorcement.

Chapter Twenty-One

September lingered into a blue haze of Indian summer. That warming spell followed the first frost of Squaw Winter to lend the last gentle smile of the declining year. Though a time of quiet beauty, few were at liberty to enjoy its slumberous hours in their rush to prepare for the coming winter. Cosgrove and Timmy spent their free time in the woods providing game for the larder and the women stocked the basement rooms in the hollowed-out portion of the chimney with canned and pickled goods where they would stay cool and preserved beneath the insulating ground. The wearying chore of candle-making involved the lugging of immense kettles and constant feeding of the fireplace and the entire house smelled of tallow, deer suet, bear grease, and stale pot-liquor. The younger girls partook in quilting bees, spinning bees, knitting bees, sewing bees, and paring bees to lighten the drudgery of the shortening days with a practical outcome to balance the enjoyment they took in the neighborly functions. Wheat, oats, and corn were threshed and made into flour and meal and bundled for feed, for the warm indolence fooled no one into thinking the harsh snap of winter would not be long in coming.

Kate busied herself with the seasonal tasks, falling exhausted into bed each night to spare her from the pain of thought. Try as she would, she couldn't ignore the fact that with the close of late summer, her reprieve with the Blaynes would also end. The date their mortgage was due ran a breathless race with the expected return of the *Elizabeth* and as that time was pared away, so, too, were her nerves. Her temper grew short and snappish until even the mild Mistress Fitch began to avoid drawing her into her evening ramblings and left her to herself to brood.

Compounded with her worries, Kate harbored a secret stashed beneath her Flanders tick. Knowing it was there, she could find little rest, yet she denied its consequence the way she did her longing for Brady Rogan. And each day, those hidden complications wore away the threads of her composure.

The autumnal equinox heralded an annual harvest ball at Briar Haven, and the inclusion of the names Kathryn and Anne Mallory on this year's guest list had the younger girl in raptures. She could speak of nothing else beyond her appearance in the grand foyer garbed radiantly in the crimson damask. Kate had to shake her from her dreamy listlessness on more than one occasion to remind her that her chores would not wait until the ball had passed. After a conscientious spurt of energy, she would lapse again into daydreams and Kate could only sigh over her inattentiveness.

For herself, Kate looked to the approaching ball with dread. It meant confronting Ned and Ezra Blayne without the certainty of her independence from debt. Daily, she went into Kingstown hoping to glean news of the *Elizabeth* from Newport merchants who traversed the Bay. Each day, she returned home disheartened and a little more frantic at the delay. She couldn't prevent the same aching fears that accompanied her wait for her father from haunting her waking hours. Then the nights gave host to tormented dreams of Elizabeth Rogan and the papers she concealed from her. The lies, the deceit and the desperation were a heavy yoke and even her strong shoulders sagged beneath it.

Her mood was not unnoticed by the others, though their efforts to lift it were to no avail. Finally, in the days before the ball, Anne called her into the parlor where the other girls waited, wreathed in expectant smiles. When Kate crossly questioned their delighted looks, Fitch doddered in from the kitchen bearing, with Sarah's aid, a pliant parcel wrapped in tissue. They gathered near to watch a bemused Kate tear free the paper and grinned at her gasp of amazement. Carefully, she lifted the gown of sapphire blue and held it up against her. The shimmery silk with its satin stripe was made to fit close to the body to the center of the back where it met to form graceful pleats. The sack and petticoat were trimmed with broad black lace, flounces of crepe, and blue ribbon. Along its flowing edge worked in black floss was an intricate design of embroidery detailed as exquisitely as lace. There was no mistaking the tiny, perfect stitches, and Kate looked up through glistening eyes.

"Oh, Anne, 'tis beautiful. When did you find the time? How could you afford such fabric as this?"

"'Tis Sylvie Blayne's doing. In her vanity, she insisted upon ten pairs of monogrammed stockings and it cost her dearly, indeed." Her smug smile told of her successful dickering upon the price of her handiwork. Her arms spanned the shoulders of her other sisters. "We all helped—the younger girls by aiding me in my chores and Jeanne and Mistress Fitch and even Sarah with the needle. Are you truly pleased, Katie? You've toiled so hard of late. We wanted to do something special for you."

Kate couldn't meet their happy gazes. Her own was too full of swimming tears. "'Tis truly special and I shall treasure your thoughtfulness long after the gown has been packed away with the memories of my youth."

"Try it on, Katie," Roberta urged excitedly.

"Yes, do" came a chorus of encouragement.

"But do be careful," Anne warned. "'Tis stitched together with basting seams. We'd not time to sew it properly so take care not to move too freely."

Kate carried the gown into her room, her steps lighter than they had been in weeks, and her heart lifted with like buoyancy. She shrugged out of her comfortable calico and eased the silk over her underpinnings. The fabric sighed lusciously as it conformed to her figure. Impatiently, she moved to the small mirror near her case of drawers to view the outcome of her sisters' love. She stared long at her reflection, at the gown that was the exact shade of Brady Rogan's eyes, and she didn't believe she'd ever been so moved by any gesture save the presentation of the locket she wore about her neck. It was just the token she needed to refresh her spirits and inspire her hopes that all would be well. She put aside all the despondency that had dragged her down into despair and assumed a confident pose. Yes, all would be well.

Thusly convinced, Kate swept into the parlor in a swish of silk to parade her new finery.

Briar Haven was aglitter. Its rooms were filled with a rich, glaring splendor of silks, satins, velvets, and brocades sported by the Colony's elect. Wealthy merchants, leisured dilettantes, and the last of the summer visitors enjoyed the profusion of spirits and sociability they would be denied during the long frigid winter months. An ensemble in small clothes played sedate renditions to accompany the hum of conversation and would later perform music to inspire dancing. Kate and Anne were issued in with little pomp but were immediately set upon by one who'd waited exclusively for their arrival.

Ezra Blayne was a frothy spectacle in ivory satin and endless yards of lace. With his thin hair powdered to an extreme, the effect paled his skin and gave him the appearance of a whipped syllabub. Only his eyes showed any color and they were feverish when detailing Kate's décolleté gown.

"My dear Misses Mallory," he effused while

slobbering over their reluctantly offered hands. "How good to have you out of mourning and among us once again. Though some might question the quickness of that transition, I am delighted." He went on to spout offensive rhetoric until Kate was ready to scream her annoyance. Manners demanded she stand quiet and smile upon receiving such court from their host, yet as soon as the opportunity presented itself, she made excuses for herself and her sister and hurried them away.

"What a dreadful little man," Anne declared too soon for her words to escape him. He watched them in their lustrous plumage flitting from guest to guest and a cold smile curved his lips. Soon that opinion of him would change. Soon.

The moment Anne was sighted, the flock of beaux who'd been paying homage to Sylvie fled her side to cluster about the beauty. Their claims of devotion and despair over her long absence brought a fragile blush of color to her cheeks, unlike the mottled hue that stained her rival's. Content to see her sister laughing in the midst much attention, Kate was able to seek a quiet spot in hopes of spending the remaining hours unnoticed by the crush of revelers. It was not to be. Ned Blayne spied her and was quick to tow over several gentlemen and their disapproving wives to introduce them to the breeder of the Pacers that had consistently beaten theirs. She relaxed into the discussion of horses and began to think the elder Mr. Blayne had forgotten about finances until, upon taking his leave, he leaned confidentially close and murmured for her to come up to the house some day the following week. That put a dismal stamp upon the rest of her evening. With head throbbing, she sought out her sister.

Anne took one look at Kate's haggard features and relieved her of the task of begging they depart. Cool hands took up her damp ones. "Dear Katie, what is it?" she insisted in a low aside.

"A beastly headache 'tis all."

"You look so pale. I'll get my wrap at once and we'll be for home."

Though thankfulness sagged her shoulders, Kate made a faint protest that Anne quickly overrode.

"Oh, what nonsense is this about spoiling my evening. I'm all talked out and my feet hurt too much to think of dancing. Come. We'll go now."

Sylvie Blayne had overheard her and made a show of objecting. "Oh, dear Anne, you cannot be leaving so soon. Why, the evening's just begun and as there's not much chance that you'll ever know another like it, you should take full advantage."

Anne met her clever slur coolly. "I shall not mourn the loss of an invitation to your home."

The girl gave a malicious chuckle. "You mistake me. I'm speaking not of *our* home but any home. When my father forecloses upon your farm next week, no door will open to you." She tittered. "Except perhaps the back door."

Anne was very still. She could feel the pinch of Kate's fingers upon her arm. The cruelty of the jealous girl's joke went beyond excusable. "I find no humor in your foolish taunts, Sylvie."

"And you shall find even less in your approaching

circumstance. To think all of the proud Mallory girls up for indenture to pay their debts. I think I'll insist Papa buy your papers. 'Twould be amusing to teach you your place."

"Anne, get our cloaks," Kate interceded coldly. "I shall say good night to your hosts." When her sister turned inquiring eyes upon her, begging for an explanation, she gave a slight push. "Go on now."

They went their individual ways leaving the smug Sylvie to her vicious enjoyment. Kate planned to speak to Mistress Blayne but 'twas Ezra who waylaid her search.

"Ah, Kate, in such a hurry. It puts such a becoming flush in your . . . cheeks." His gaze lifted meaningfully from her neckline.

"Please step aside, sir. I am looking for your mother to beg our excuses."

"Oh, but you cannot go yet. I have the most interesting piece of news for you." He fairly puffed with childish glee and Kate had no patience for his games.

"It will have to wait—"

"No." That sharp command in tandem with the sudden crush of his flabby fingers about her arm drew her up short. Her cutting gaze for once failed to intimidate him. "This information is too, too prime to keep to myself. I thought you might like to hear it as it concerns the captain who piloted you to the Islands this spring."

Kate stood still, taken off guard and too surprised to hide her alertness. The casual tone she tried to adopt was faulty. "Captain Rogan? What of him?"

"Ah yes, the Rogue. 'Tis what I believe they called him. He's been arrested for smuggling untaxed goods."

Kate's insides shivered, yet she replied with a knowlegeable calm. "Surely 'twill be an inconvenience to him only. No colonial jury ever convicts on a smuggling case."

Ezra smiled as if he enjoyed baiting her with tidbits to tease her into a starved frenzy. "That might be true but 'tis more likely he'll be tried by the Vice-Admiralty court. Be sure they'll have no sympathies nor allow him to make no claim for damages. The poor fellow. Did you know him well?"

But Kate paid him no further attention. Her thoughts were bound in a tight concentration with only one focus: She had to get to Brady.

The trip across the Bay was bathed in brilliant moonlight. Spray misted in their wake, a glittery trail soon to be absorbed by the still, dark waters that erased all sign of their passing. Kate stood upon the deck, shivering in her tightly wrapped cloak, not against the dampness but against the crawl of dread that spread icily within her. The night was beautiful, one she might have appreciated had she been standing in the circle of Brady's arms aboard the *Elizabeth* instead of upon the deck of a stranger's skiff bound for Newport. The harvest moon hung low in the sky, larger and redder than the moon of any other season. It was a beacon guiding her toward the confrontation of her fears.

The hours between her departure from the Blaynes' and her boarding of one of their guest's boats blurred with haste. She'd rushed Anne home, giving scant reasons for her anxiety, and the younger girl, bless her, didn't press for them. Kate paused at the farm only long enough to gather a few things from her room, then instructed a sleepy Timmy to see her to the coast. The Bay shone like a black mirror and a faint breeze bore them too slowly for Kate's purpose into the harbor opposite where, at last, they docked. Calling her thanks, she leapt to the dock and rushed along it, giving little thought to where she would go. Benjamin's coin weighed heavily in her bag and her conscience troubled her not at all with the thought of using it to gain Brady's freedom. If it could be bought. Terror carried her thinking into dark, forbidding places: prison, the gallows. She forced trembling legs to support her desperate race. Did they hang smugglers? She didn't know and her ignorance was a torture. There had to be a way to free him. There was nothing she wouldn't do to that end, nothing she valued enough not to offer.

She burst into the customs house, breathless and wild with distress, only to be told by one puzzled official that Brady Rogan was not in their custody. That they might have already shipped him away gave her the strength of madness as she shook the poor man and shrieked to know what had become of him. Her behavior drew a gathering, curious over her rantings as well as appreciative of her dangerous beauty. Finally, one man stepped forward to state if it was the Rogue she sought, she should look to the

White Horse. In a swirl of red cloak, she was gone.

The mug of beer he was lifting halted halfway to his lips as Brady stared into eyes of mesmerizing emerald. As if he feared the image was borne of all his damp, restless dreams, he blinked but the vision remained. Slowly, his drink returned to the table lest it be spilled by the sudden tremor that affected his hands and, indeed, his very soul. God, she was spellbinding, lovelier than any lonely memory, more enticing than any remembered passion.

The ache of empty nights and anguished cravings beset him until the need to have her beneath him nearly had him forgetting place or circumstance. Had she stood within his imprudent grasp, he would have ravished her there without thought to propriety. The want to taste her honeyed lips, to draw on the nectar of her budded breasts, to feel the encouraging wrap of silken thighs about him caught him in a fever of urgency to bed her without delay, to drag her if need be to the nearest accommodations to let loose his engorged desires. It was not the pent-up lust for any woman, but a keening, obsessive demand for this one alone. And the singular violence of it was frightening.

Kate hesitated and that pause gave him time to suppress his blind impatience in lieu of the situation at hand. She stood pale and stiff, as if in shock, and he knew with a damning certainty that she'd come because she'd heard of her loss. That all his pressing expectations should come to a shuddering halt seemed too much to endure and the agony of it assailed him. How could he think of taking her with unbridled delight when the news he bore would destroy her want for his touch? She knew enough already to hold herself away from him and the distance seemed to foretell of a grim and unpromising future. All because of a failed promise.

"I thought you'd been arrested," she said with a strangely stilted voice.

The men seated at the table all looked up and Tobias, the one seated next to Brady, let out a loud, contemptuous laugh. "We made fools of them, we did. Without the goods, 'twas no cause for a warrant and they had to let us go." A quick glance from Brady stilled the man's tongue before he rattled on without thought. He went back to his mug contritely.

Kate's emotionless gaze went between the men at the table, then settled on their captain. "Then you are free?"

He nodded. Reluctantly, he said, "Kate, we must talk," but she seemed too dazed to hear him, probably with the irony that he should fly while she sank. He left his men and his mug forgotten to go to her side. She backed away, yet let him take hold of her elbow. All the while her huge, bright eyes never wavered from him. Don't let her fight me now, he prayed as he gave a slight, impelling tug. Docile, she followed, still afflicted with that odd stiffness bespeaking her distress. He led her straight to his room. What they had to say was not talk befitting an alleyway or public street, yet it was a far cry from what he had planned for his first night back in her company.

Those sentimental longings had no place in the seriousness of the moment and he mourned their loss. No, this wasn't at all what he'd planned.

The voyage had been miserable from beginning to end. The instant he'd kissed the sleeping figure beside him and slipped from the room and from Newport itself, nothing had gone well. The trip had been plagued with bad luck, bad weather, bad tempers, and a spectacularly bad ending. But none of those things were what made it such a personal hell for him. From the moment he'd lifted his head from the golden one upon his pillow, he'd missed her. He'd yearned for Kate Mallory the way a drunkard did his drink and, deprived, he suffered mightily. It wasn't the use of her splendid body he craved. Though the mere thought of it had him standing strong and anxious, 'twas the way she held to him during their intimacy, surrounding him, engulfing him with the warmth of her affection, bringing him a radiant sense of peace and of contentment. It was the way she completed him in thought, in strength, in passion and even in vulnerability. She confused him, true, but it was a marvelous bewilderment.

Over and again beneath the endless spread of stars, he recalled the bold, businesslike way she'd applied to be his mistress. He'd been propositioned before but never with such candor, never to his delight. She'd laid out the terms as if negotiating a contract, bargaining with him in the same way she had initiated their partnership. How amused he'd been. How aroused. The complexity of his response was fearsome, the connotations, staggering. Then

377

she'd asked if he wanted her. His world had crumbled. Want her? He was mad for her, for her fiery independence, for her wanton loving, for her startling beauty, for the entirety that made her so unique. She had called him beloved, had spoken it low and sweetly, and though he'd been too numbed to all but pain at the time, that gentle endearment played in a continuous chant, soothing, enticing him with possibilities he'd had no time to explore. And after having her that last time and having to leave her, he'd felt bereft, as if a vital part of him had been torn away. And even the assurances she'd given hadn't been enough to stave off the fear that she might not be waiting when he returned, that once he'd delivered her profits, she'd no longer have a need of him. The longing, the anxiety, had mulled and brewed and steeped into a potent drug of emotion. Perhaps that was what had made him careless, for never before had he fallen so easily into the grasp of the customs' patrol. He had only himself to blame for failing her, for having to bring her desolation instead of desire.

She walked with an uncustomary quiet beside him. The light touch she'd allow him upon her arm was a sore temptation, chafing him with an unsatisfactory tease of the pleasures that ran rampant in his memory. The hungering needs of his body refused to be checked by his sober turn of thoughts. This was not the reunion he'd desired nor could he expect the conclusion to meet with his presumptive dreams. He'd never been one to apply force as a means to tend his passions but he was perilously close to considering it should she withdraw from him if he'd the opportunity to embrace her. Once encouraged by the press of her, he feared his dangerous desperation would overrule her want to yield. And so, he kept his distance as not to be provoked.

As they climbed the steep stairs that led to his lodgings, his starved attentions were hypnotized by the sway of her concealing cloak as it moved with the seductive swing of rounded hips. The thought of those same gentle hips rocking in time to the persuasion of his own loosed a growling demand from an appetite long suppressed. An unsteady hand fit to the curve of her spine under the pretext of support and he took the step too hurriedly, crowding her with his impatient body, and frustrated needs flared to new heights. She appeared not to notice the devastating effects of that brief grazing. He sucked in a tortured breath and tried not to shepherd her too vigorously to his door.

The room glowed with a mellow light dispersed from a low-banked fire which burned just hot enough to cut the evening chill. Brady needed no external flame to see him heated. He already felt a feverish flush consume him. His hands trembled as he held an ember to lamp wick, but try as he would, he could not get it to catch. Kate leaned in front of him, relieving him of the thin stick and holding it steady until it rewarded with a flicker and spark. As she turned up the light, he shut his eyes and swayed, intoxicated by the scent of her, reeling with her closeness. Thankfully, she stepped away and her guarded scrutiny held his raging needs in check. The question in her uplifted gaze brought him back to the unpleasantness before them.

"Kate, I'm sorry," he began. His words were hoarse. His emotions quivered and stretched taut. The knowledge of her pending disappointment and accusation was crippling. She said nothing, those large, luminous eyes beginning to glimmer with the consequence of his inadequate apology. He continued wretchedly, watching her for signs of disgust, of betrayal. "It was unplanned. It's never happened before. Even now, I'm not certain how it did. We're usually so cautious." Except for this time, when he was so beset by the mystical lure of a pair of green eyes, he could scarce think straight. And disaster had struck.

"I was at a party when I heard," she said, and her soft voice played like melancholy music to wring his soul. "I came as quickly as I could. I was so afraid I would be too late."

"It couldn't be helped, Kate. There was no other way."

Her brow furrowed as she strove to understand him. "What do you mean?"

"There was no time. We had to dump the cargo. Had we been caught with it, all would have been lost: my ship, the freedom of my men, and myself. I know 'tis small consolation to you now and merely empty words, but had I the choice, I would have taken the risk. I could not ask my men to do the same. I tried to warn you that this could happen, that there were no guarantees." Did that sound too peevish, as if he was trying to shift the blame? He wasn't. He meant to bear the full brunt of it, for he had given his word to her, he had accepted her trust, and the choice had been his and his alone. She looked at him so oddly as he stumbled on. "There'll be other runs, Kate, and profits to be made. I promise I'll recover your losses. I will . . ." The wetness that streaked her face undid him. His words faltered and failed. Anguish clogged his throat. He could only plead, "Forgive me for failing you, Kate. Please."

With a soft cry, she flew into his arms. Her frantic words tumbled out, muffled by his coat front as she clung to him. "I don't care about the cargo. Dear God, Brady, I was so afraid for you. I didn't come to bemoan the loss of profits. I came for you."

Chapter Twenty-Two

"For me," he echoed. He felt as though he'd been struck by a four-pounder. The shock gave way to disbelief then elation as the importance of those two words revealed themselves. Of all the things she valued, 'twas him she held the highest. He had lost a fortune to her through his stupidity and it was his safety she wept over. Never in his life had he been so honored. Humility made a hot congestion in his chest and tenderness swelled to release it. In a dazed aside, he realized his cheeks were damp and that he shook as badly as the precious figure in his arms. Slowly, he dried his face in the soft tangle of her hair then simply held her, for that closeness was more expressive than any words.

Kate had quieted in the security of his embrace, though her grip did not lessen. "Your man said they had to release you. Is that true?" At his nod, she breathed, "Thank the Lord."

Her relief worked savagely upon his conscience.

Gruffly, he said, "Kate, did you understand what I told you? It's all lost. Your investment, your profit, all of it lost."

"But I still have you" was her sighing response and, suddenly, he was angry. He held her back and scowled fiercely. "Are you daft? Kate, I said I lost you all your coin. There's nothing left," he nearly shouted, and to his amazement, she smiled, a small, tight smile.

"I may be daft but I'm not deaf. You needn't yell at me. I heard and I understood. 'Twas a gamble I took willingly. You cannot hold yourself at fault. I knew there was a risk and a mighty chance I'd lose it all. It was important to me but it wasn't everything. I'll recover." That lie was said with convincing aplomb. He almost believed her. Then she delivered the completing stroke that felled him. "Brady, I love you."

She was looking up at him with a quizzical expression and finally he realized she was waiting for his response. He kissed her and, lost to the devastation of that long-sought union, he failed to register her vague disappointment. Then her arms were about his neck and she pressed close. That was all it took. His need was agony. The pounding of blood that filled his loins surged up to beat an urgent tempo in his head, and thought was impossible. Control was gone.

Three steps carried him to the bed with Kate suspended in his arms. The moment her feet touched the floor, he had her cloak thrown open and her garments yanked up to her waist. She half sat, half toppled to the counterpane, and his weight atop her took her down to her back. There was no time for finesse or courtly preparation. The instant his manhood sprang free of his breeches, he buried himself within her. Distantly, he heard her cry out and the thought that he might have hurt her in his impatience was drowned by the sensations of her so snug and hot about him. Wildly he plunged into her exquisite body, feeling her sheath him with welcoming fire and ice. It took seconds to rush him to the brink and over to burst into shuddering spasms of release. The violence of it left him trembling and replete.

For long minutes, even longer than the act itself had taken, Brady was overwhelmed by weakness. Finally, the brush of her hand through his damp hair roused a response. With his passion's demand met, he was awash with shame over the manner in which he'd taken her, carelessly, thoughtlessly on the edge of the bed like an unimportant vessel meant to slake his lusts.

"I can't believe that happened," he confessed with a lowly moan. He was afraid to look at her lest he see disgust. "Forgive me, Kate. It wasn't my intent to jump upon you like an unskilled boy."

Her lips creased his brow. "Believe me, that wasn't how it felt."

That throaty reply was steeped in satisfaction. When he reared back, he found her smiling, her features soft and aglow. It was a warm, womanly look that would have stirred a saint to decadent thoughts. And Brady Rogan was no saint. He grinned, his want to apologize forgotten.

"Well, now that we've exchanged hasty hellos, shall we get on with more polite conversation?" His black brow arched wickedly and Kate smoldered beneath him.

"I can think of nothing I'd like better."

He lifted off her, seeing her as if for the first time with awareness. "You look beautiful," he attested as he helped her to her feet and smoothed her gown only to begin unfastening it. His fingers lingered over the sleek fabric, stroking along her waist, grazing the fit across her breasts until they tingled in response. "Did you wear this as a last wish to a condemned man?" He pushed it clear of her shoulders and let his lips wander there in tantalizing sweeps.

"As I said, I heard you'd been arrested while at a party. I took no time to change." Her head fell back and her breasts arced in offering.

"Umm. I'm grateful for your haste. I shouldn't have wanted to miss the sight of you garbed in such splendor. And now that I've enjoyed it, I anticipate enjoying you without it."

The gown fell heavily, and Brady turned her to address the lacings of her brocade corset. When it, too, fell away, his hands assumed the molding support it had given her bosom. Kate sighed, letting her head rest back against him while his thumbs brought her nipples into eager peaks.

"I've missed you," he breathed into her ear. "I've dreamed of you. I've wanted you until the thought had me near madness. What have you done to me, wench? I starve in your absence and gorge when I have you."

Kate moved against his hands, rubbing her breasts within his roughened palms until the friction began a trembling in her legs. Her stomach tightened as his caress slid lower to meet with the cage of her panniers and full petticoats. The straps were freed and the linen encouraged to yield. The dangerous inconsistency of strength within her limbs began again as the heel of his hand pressed to the junction of her thighs and moved in small rotations. Her breath quickened and her hips circled impatiently to seek what he would give her, encouraging, urging, arching to meet his questing fingers until she was nearly as wild as he had been. She moaned his name then cried it aloud. His other arm tightened about her middle, steadying her on legs that buckled and shook, crushing her to him so he could enjoy the tremors of delight that raced through her slender body. His labored breathing vied with her uneven pants. And then he simply held her, letting her melt against his solid frame in a languorous liquefaction. An odd feeling that was both powerful and fragile commanded him. *Brady, I love you.* He trembled. Tenderness and desire created a potent complement of emotions.

Languidly, Kate revolved in his embrace. She looked up at him, offering her entire world in that unsheltered gaze. He was hesitant, too cautious to plunge without care into such uncharted seas. Tentative fingertips traced a heated cheek and drew along a determined jaw. Her lips parted and he could not resist the charm of that frank invitation. He dipped down to accept it and lingered to delve and discover anew the pleasures of her giving mouth. Her arms encircled his neck again, but this time so her fingers could unbuckle his stock and tempt the warm expanse of his throat it left bare. The furious pulse she inspired was proof of his excitement and inflamed her own. The buttons to his shirt gave one by one. By the time they came together upon the bed, a magnificent sheen of passion was shared and aided to the sensual thrill of flesh on flesh.

This time, it was not so much an unrestrained coupling as it was a total possession. Brady claimed her and she reveled in the conquering strength of him. Domination was gained by determined degrees and held with infinite respect. He mastered her quivering breasts with the greedy pull of his mouth and tamed her writhing thighs with his enslaving touch. And when she opened herself to receive him, there was a sweet victory in her resigning cry, as if to surrender was not a loss at all. His first commanding thrusts deepened and evened into long compelling strokes, coaxing her with each advance and retreat to respond with like intensity. Friction and tension built as they reached for their individual fulfillment and mutual satisfaction. The binding was perfect, completing, a complement like flint on steel and just as volatile. Feeling her climax imminent in the severe trembling beneath him, Brady drove himself harder, faster until it was accomplished. Her convulsive pleasure engulfed him, bringing on a mighty spill as he shared the consuming triumph of their union. That throbbing sense of attainment lingered and muted into a deep, contented lethargy and for a time, still joined, they dozed and luxuriated in the comfort of each other.

When finally Brady shifted to one side, he kept her close, their bodies measuring flush and arms and legs entwined so there was no sense of separation. And though his physical needs had been well attended, he had no desire to forgo the enjoyment of his companion. His loneliness and desolation were too vivid to relinquish even a moment to sleep until he'd assured himself that she was indeed beside him and would remain there until he awoke. He cuddled her like an adoring child and stroked her with the appreciation due a woman, all the while indulging himself in the sensations she afforded. Her skin was so smooth, soft like the gown she'd worn. He charted every curve, every crevice of her body until they were mapped upon his memory. He nuzzled her neck and hair, breathing in the summery woman scent that was hers alone until dizzy with it. Her responses were so natural, so in tune to his wants and needs and unspoken dreams, willing to sacrifice her precious independence to please him in the passionate bed they made together. And he was pleased —by her enticing performance as a sexual partner, by the indomitable spirit that challenged him without fear, by the tender emotion she'd claimed this night as she came into his arms. What more could he want? What more, indeed.

His thoughts had become as obsessed as his desires by the high-mettled Kate Mallory. Both had hungered for her in her absence yet, appeased, still knew the same craving. There seemed no way to purge her from his system, not with abstinence, not with overindulgence. She'd become a constant in his very act of being. He hadn't questioned their relationship, too satisfied to ask for more and too male not to take what was offered. Now those questions pressed with seemingly insurmountable consequence and he could avoid them no longer. He couldn't take this remarkable woman for granted lest he lose her. It had been tiny barbs of emotion pricking at his pride that had prompted his thinking. A child he could not claim. Another man bestowing his legal name. The fear that he would be replaced or forgotten lest he made himself invaluable. Secretly, darkly, he'd been glad to abandon the cargo that would see her free of her need for him, though such black thoughts made him sorely ashamed. They'd been prompted by insecurity, by the uncertainty of how he fit into her thoughts and heart. And now that she'd made that plain, instead of seizing his good fortune, he held back, too afraid to expose his vulnerability.

He'd loved before, deeply, compulsively, only to know rejection, and he'd reminded himself of that folly by refusing to release it. Keeping Elizabeth dependent upon him had eased that crushing failure but had proved a persistent torment. The knowledge that she was in his care was enough to content him and he didn't chafe for more. With Kate, he could never seem to have enough. It wasn't enough to know where she was and that she was well, he had to see for himself. It wasn't enough to set her aside in comfort under his protection. He demanded to be an integral, aggressive, intimate force in her life. He didn't understand that need to be assertive, especially when she was so capable, so self-sufficient that she didn't require his guidance or interference, as she'd told him pointedly in the past. It nettled him, that strength she had, yet it made him proud as well and he loved her for it. He loved her . . . Good God, he was in love with the woman!

Brady's sudden gasp startled Kate to full awareness. She leaned away so she could see his features, etched so darkly handsome in the flickering lamplight. His eyes were wide blue seas, their usual eddies now as smooth as glass. The way he stared at her roused feelings of alarm.

"Brady, what is it?" she asked, more confused because he was smiling with such endearing silliness. He shook his head as if to clear away a gathering fog but gave no answer. Instead, he pulled her close into an almost painful squeeze.

"I'm glad you're here is all," he murmured. That was said low, with hidden laughter and husky passion, and she was warmed by it. "Are you sure you're not angry with me for losing your profits?"

She sighed and soberly replied, "'Twas no fault of yours. I should have been content with what I had."

"And are you content with what you have now?" The double edge of that question made her frown.

"I am resigned to accept that which I cannot change."

That practical, biting retort was typical. He grinned with delight. "Such a brave, noble woman you are, my Kate. Yet you must admit you push awfully hard to change things to your liking."

Her chuckle brushed warm upon his collarbone. "'Tis determination, or one might say less kindly, stubbornness."

"I would say 'tis admirable." He shifted so that she was pillowed upon his chest. His hand was intrigued by the spread of her hair upon it. "And what be your plans now?"

She was quiet then and he puffed with pleasure thinking she meant to make another declaration of her feelings for him. Instead, her response was disturbing. "I must return home to tend matters there. And I've some promises to keep of my own."

He was provoked by that mysterious claim and prompted, "Promises to whom?"

"Your brother."

Kate felt the movement of his hand still and his breathing with it. She knew if she didn't pursue it, matters would only become more difficult. Better to bring it all into the open now when the mood lay so tender between them. Better she should pick the time, for she knew the subject of Providence would eventually arise. Now, while he was still enthralled with the heavy luxury of their spent passions, she could control the topic and perhaps his reactions. At least she prayed she could. To lose him now . . . oh, God, to lose him now.

"How did things fare with Benjamin?" He broached it cautiously, almost with reluctance, and she didn't know whether to be encouraged. Or mayhap he didn't want to betray his eagerness.

Briefly, Kate relayed what had occurred since he'd

left on the *Elizabeth*. She kept her recounting painfully accurate though the want to omit some aspects and emphasize others proved a mighty temptation. Her innate honesty held her to the truth until she came to the papers. The words would not come, try as she would to force them, until she had to skip ahead in her telling lest he grew suspicious of the pause. She concluded by briefly stating she'd spent the night on Benefit Street, then awaited his response.

He'd been listening carefully and had not once interrupted, though she had felt him draw several breaths as if he would. The caressing thread of his fingers through her hair had become a nearly hurtful twisting as the absent gesture reflected his agitation.

"You have the coin with you?" he asked at last. His words were purposefully level, even detached if she could believe that. How distressed he must be to struggle so hard not to display it before her. Was he aware, then, of how difficult it all had been for her? He had to know she was not an uninvolved party in the triangle of his past, that what he would choose to do now would affect her perhaps irreparably. Yet he gave no such indication, no assurances she was desperate to hear.

"Yes, I have it."

"'Tis a tidy sum?"

"A fortune, I would say. Enough to keep Elizabeth and her son most comfortably." That last was added with a hint of subtle meaning and he tensed to show it was not lost on him. She waited for him to expound on that tension, to react with jealousy, bitterness, even anger. Instead, he was surprisingly calm.

"Odd that he should be so stricken by conscience after all these years. As if his coin could make up for anything, either time or neglect." He sighed and then asked, "Was that all?"

"Yes," Kate told him quickly before the magnitude of the lie could assail her. She was thankful for the poor light and for the fact that she didn't have to meet his eyes so she could hide her guilt the way she did the truth, in darkness, in shame.

"I shall leave for Providence in the morning to make arrangements. Then I'll see you home from there."

Kate squeezed her eyes shut as if to close out the unwanted knowledge. How quick he meant to be shed of her. How eager he was to race to the house on Benefit Street to tend his "family." Did he fear the wealth of coin would replace him in Elizabeth's eyes. She knew better. Elizabeth Rogan wanted, nay, needed a man to tend her affairs, to give her the feel of security that no amount of money could ever provide. She would cling to Brady for his guidance and protection and so that she would not have to cope alone. Well, what about her? What about Kate Mallory? She needed him, too. Yet, he viewed her as capable and strong, whereas Elizabeth was fragile and in need of nurturing. She wasn't all that strong. And she didn't want to be alone either. Yet, if he had to make a choice, Kate knew with a cold certainty that Brady's obligation to the woman in Providence would outweigh his feelings for her. Lust was a fleeting commodity, well served by many. He'd have no trouble finding a slew of mistresses should she prove too difficult or demanding. Or would he be interested in even one? If he knew the final secret she held, would he seek the basic comforts she offered? Or would he race to find them where they'd always been denied.

"So quiet," he mused. The tease of his fingers became a lingering stroke along her shoulders and down the ridge of her back, stopping just shy of the cleft of her buttocks before making the return. She shivered, as he intended her to, with that slow, suggestive slide over her skin. She fought it and what it would mean if she let it continue.

"Just tired."

Brady responded to that confession with a slight shift of his body so that they weren't quite so entangled, so that she wasn't quite so available. "Yes, it has been a night of unexpected happenings."

There it was again, that deep, satisfied smugness as if he was bursting with some private amusement he wasn't quite ready to share. She didn't feel like chuckling or being the source of his entertainment. Crossly, seemingly by accident, she rolled away, glancing a hard blow to his ribs with her elbow as she curled onto her side. She heard his grunt of surprise and was savagely pleased by his discomfort. She could feel his eyes upon her, could sense his puzzlement but was in no mood to explain things he should have understood if he cared a whit about her.

Brady regarded the slender back that presented such a stiff barrier to the swelling heat he'd begun to feel stirring yet again. He frowned and contemplated the curve of her waist, the luxurious wave of golden hair that spread across both their arms, the measured rise and fall of her breathing. The rumble of interest would just have to go untended for now. She was tired. He was tired. She would be there in the morning. It wasn't as though a long separation faced them. He wouldn't starve for the want of her loving in the few short hours it would take for them to regain their strength. And he didn't want to wear his welcome raw on their first night together. He smiled and slipped an arm over the dip of her waist, drawing her gently back so they fit neatly one against the other. That closeness created a warmth of permanence that would placate him until morning, when he planned to rise very early. It was amazing how clear things had become. In the morning, he would make impassioned love to Kate and then he would see to matters of his future. He closed his eyes, content with that plan.

It was a plan with many flaws. When he awoke, the sun was already high. When he reached out beside him, he discovered Kate was gone. And then his fingertips brushed across a packet of folded papers upon the pillow where his love's head should have been resting. He sat up and began to read.

Chapter Twenty-Three

It was the right thing to do, Kate told herself firmly. She was a realist, not a dreamer, and the longer she allowed herself to live on dreams, the crueler the awakening would be. Better this way than to linger in hurt and shame, but still there was no quick way to sever the pain that dwelt in her heart, no way to discourage the sense of loss that numbed her hours and made the nights such an agony to endure.

While her gaze followed the passage of one of their new foals as it experimented with the inborn grace of its stride, Kate brooded as was her wont over the last week. At one time, the sight of that stocky colt would have filled her with cheer, the symbol of a future nearing her grasp. Now it seemed as distant a dream as all the others, a dream she hadn't been able to make come true. A moment of bitterness was quickly crushed. It wouldn't do to bemoan circumstance. Nothing would change if she gave way to the wails of unfairness that swelled in her breast. What she had to do was plan, to think of the best way to survive the disaster about to befall her family, not writhe in her own personal grief. If she threw herself into solving the one, perhaps the other would lessen. How she wished she could believe that.

It had already been a week. The fragile hope that Brady would come for her dimmed with each of those days until she had to accept the fact that what she feared was now truth. When she'd left the papers of divorcement, she'd given Brady his dreams at the cost of her own. It was ironic that even in his act of charity, Benjamin Rogan had managed to taint all with his spiteful sense of vengeance. He'd granted Elizabeth her freedom but in doing so had forced her and his brother to again be the pawns of his wry humor. Divorce was not a simple or casual matter in the Colonies. Adultery was one of the few reasons a court would consider dissolving a marriage and even then, the magistrates ruled the guilty party might not remarry. Though he knew it not to be true, Benjamin had petitioned by citing his wife's unfaithfulness with his brother Brady. And what court would deny the obvious facts that Elizabeth was being kept by her supposed lover. No matter that it was the only way to set her free of him, the means were unspeakably harsh. Elizabeth's reputation would be irreparably stained should she stay in her little house on Benefit Street in the shadow of sin her husband had cast over her. Her only happiness would be in leaving Rhode Island to settle in another colony where she and Brady could be wed in anonymity. It was what he'd always wanted—Elizabeth for his wife, Jamie to claim as his son. Kate wanted to be happy for him but her heart was not so generous. However, she wasn't resentful. He'd never lied to her about the importance of his ties to the past. She was the one who'd thought she could sever them. She'd been wrong.

She hadn't been wrong in leaving him the way she had, she knew. She wouldn't have to suffer his waning interest, or worse, his casual disregard as he turned to his life's love for the physical rewards long denied him. What use would he have for a lover when he'd obtained his love? And even if he didn't choose to give her up right away, could she bear the shame of being with a wedded man? Kate recalled those feelings of horror and humiliation when she'd thought that to be true and the compelling need she'd had to tell herself to ignore them to be with him. No, better to remove the temptation of Brady Rogan from her life lest she fall into unpardonable guilt. Besides, he would be leaving soon and she could not follow, not with her responsibilities here. All he could offer her was brief gratification, a future of misery and constant hurt. Better to forget him. If only she could. If only she could.

"Miss Kate?"

She turned to see Timmy jogging through the amber meadow grasses and waved. By the time he drew abreast, he was breathing in rapid hitches that made his words difficult to follow.

"Miss Kate, there be a man at the house to see you." The sudden catapulting of her heart into her throat became a painful wedge of disappointment to be swallowed. "Master Blayne's boy it be. He sent me to fetch you back."

"Did he, indeed." Ezra's boldness braced her

spirits. How dare he make demands upon her people. How dare he make demands upon her. She thanked the boy and sent him ahead while she walked more slowly, deliberately keeping to a leisured pace. She wouldn't come running for the likes of Ezra Blayne. And she was in no hurry to discover what he wanted.

Sarah greeted her on the porch, wringing her hands in obvious distress. "He be in the parlor, Miss Kate," she said, looking most grateful for her return, then scampering quickly toward the kitchen. Kate smoothed her gown and took a second to tuck any loose strands into her confining cap before entering the receiving room.

Ezra didn't rise. That in itself was enough to warn her, for he'd always taken great pains to display his courtly manners. Instead, he was brushing at his sleeve with irritation, pausing only to growl, "That foolish maid of yours spilled cordial all over me. 'Twere she in my service I'd have her beaten and shown the road. This velvet costs more than she could bring in indenture. Clumsy wench."

Kate paused within the doorway, her senses all alerted to this new, belligerent Ezra Blayne, his amiably unctuous manner apparently a thing of the past. His colorless eyes rose to rest upon her almost distastefully. That, too, was unusual. She almost preferred his blatant leering. "Don't just stand there. Come in. I've come to speak to you about some important matters and I will not be kept a moment longer awaiting your pleasure. Sit."

Kate paled in fury. To be ordered about in one's own home like a lowly servant, why she wouldn't allow such pompous behavior. She was about to snap a curt reply when he fixed her with a cold stare. A shiver passed through her unlike any she'd ever experienced. Warily, she came to do as bidden, feeling the wisdom of keeping her temper in check until she'd heard him out. To have fear inspired by such an unlikely figure was disconcerting, but she felt the threat of him and knew it couldn't be ignored. She assumed a remote chair and regarded him emotionlessly. One never let an animal sense fear. "Pray go ahead. I am listening."

Ezra gauged her with a cautious eye, then leaned back in his chair, pleased to have intimidated her so neatly. He folded his hands over the impressive pull of satin straining to contain his ample girth and smiled. "I've not come on my father's behalf, not yet. I needn't remind you that your mortgage date has passed and with it, your claim to this property. My father has every intention of foreclosing within the week."

Kate sat stiffly. This was not unexpected, yet hearing it brought it brutally home. Ned Blayne knew nothing of charity. He'd given her a stay of the inevitable because she'd amused him and because she'd made it worth his while to wait. Now there was no reason to. His amiable pretense was at an end and so, she feared, was their comfortable existence.

"Have you the means to pay?"

She winced at the crack of reality in those words and sought to forestall it. "When my fiancé returns—"

"Enough." Ezra's pudgy fist met with his thigh to create a jiggly reverberation. She might have laughed at that comical attempt at authority had it not been for his next words. "No more of this game. You and I both know there is no Earl of Bradington. There is just a lowly smuggler from Newport whom you bribed with your favors to play the part. I admire your resourcefulness, my dear but I cannot condone your playing this community for fools any longer."

Kate's pallor continued, but her rigid posture never trembled. She met his gaze steadily as if her ruse was not the last attempt of desperation to prevent her fate. Vaguely, she wondered how he'd discovered the truth, but then, it was of no matter. He knew and that was enough. And if he knew about Brady, he must also know the fate of her investments. The chill she felt seeped with cold certainty to encase her heart and her hopes. He had trapped her well and it would do no good to writhe upon her chair or plead for mercy. She would accept the consequence unflinchingly.

"Nothing to say, Miss Mallory?" he taunted. "You are usually brimming with wit. Not so clever anymore, are you? I am the one who's been clever. I've seen to your fall from haughtiness to humility. You thought me a fool, didn't you? Well, this fool has seen you stripped of every penny and beholden to me for your existence."

"You informed the customs officials." That was said flatly, with a grim certainty, and his grin confirmed it.

"I hope I didn't cause your lover any inconvenience," he sneered. "Was your race to Newport on his behalf or due to the fate of your fortune?"

She regarded him with a cold contempt.

Ezra sighed. "What does it matter. Both are lost to you now. And what have you left, pray tell? Shall we explore your future, dear Kate?" He waited and when she wouldn't oblige him with a sign of interest or despair, he continued rather curtly. "You are penniless, a parasite upon this community, having no means with which to repay debts you knowingly incurred. Your farm belongs to my father and everything upon it. You haven't so much as a peel, press, or platter to claim as your own. The very clothes upon your back are borrowed from this point. I can guarantee the townspeople are not going to be forgiving of your circumstance when they discover the trick you played upon them. The council will demand immediate restitution of debt, and as you have no possessions, the only thing you have of worth to sell is your service."

He watched as pride starched her back and hardened her stare. He'd anticipated that from her and was prepared to see it deflated most cruelly. "Oh, I've no doubt you'd meet that fate without a murmur, but 'tis not you alone who will suffer it. You've four younger sisters with no means to support them. I'm afraid they shall have to assume papers, as well. With luck, you shall be united in oh, say three to four years. Providing you can even find one another at the end of that time."

Kate's chin quivered and she clenched her teeth to firm it. Her nails dug deep into her palm to distract her from the incredible thickness of despair that collected in her chest. She wouldn't weep before Ezra Blayne. She wouldn't give him that satisfaction. Her agile mind spun wildly behind her steady stare as she sought some avenue by which she could escape the horror he proposed. In her desperation she considered for a moment snatching the matchlock which rested ornamentally above the mantel and putting a quick end to her nemesis. She realized that would be a temporary solution, but the satisfaction of it was provoking. She couldn't run with her sisters to evade their debt, for they had no means to reestablish themselves elsewhere. As Ezra claimed, they had nothing, they *were* nothing in the eyes of the community. She saw no way to climb from the bottomless well of futility. Until he smiled and she saw a hint of salvation. But at what cost?

"However . . . ?" she provided with a lift of one arched brow. He grinned at her astuteness. Such a quick wench.

"Yes, indeed, *however.*" Now, his look had warmed and began the familiar trek along the jut of her bosom. She held very still, allowing it by her lack of resistance. He noted that acquiescence with satisfaction. "I see no need to force such dire straits upon your family." That was a soft, vile purr and her skin crawled to hear it. "I see no reason they cannot continue to live here or even better. The debts could be paid and your name cleared of any slur of intent."

"Providing . . . ?" she encouraged coldly. She didn't like games and he was enjoying this one immensely.

"Dear Kate, I've never made any secret of my fondness for you. That affection still endures despite your actions of late. I am willing to set aside those deeds as wrought of desperation. You are a woman, after all, and living in a man's world must have exacted a terrible toll upon you." If he noticed the fearsome flash of her eyes, he paid no mind to it as his speech gathered momentum. "You were willing to accept a fiancé to extract you from difficulties before. Why not again."

Kate went rigid. Her words were frosty. "That was, as you pointed out, a pretense."

"But it needn't be. Dear Kate, I am willing to take you as my wife, to free you of familial debt, to save your sisters from indenture. All I ask is that you be wife to me. Is that so much?"

All? So much? A near hysterical laughter trembled upon her lips but she refused to loose it. She couldn't afford to offend him. She had to think clearly, concisely, without the rule of personal emotion.

Ezra was watching her like an expectant predator. She gave so little away as she sat there stiff and pale, her only color twin bright spots in her cheeks and the brilliance of her green eyes. His persuasive threat continued. "The banns could be posted at Thursday lecture. We'll explain away the loss of your previous betrothal by saying your fiancé had a sudden financial reversal and found he could no longer support a wife. Not such a lie." His laugh was gurgly, repulsive. "My family will provide your trousseau and appropriate wear for your sisters. Agree and you can bargain for the rest. I am of a mind to be generous. If I am forced to wait, that may change."

"You don't have to wait," Kate interrupted and he looked to her with a fat, smug smile, a disgusting crawly creature wanting the swift bottom of a shoe. "I can give you your answer now."

* * *

The kitchen was unnaturally quiet as Sarah and Roberta took away the removes. For Kate, the evening had been one of bittersweet reflection. The meal had been excellent, from leg of pork and turnips that were fork-tender to mince pies with no trace of scorch to the flaky crusts. Sarah worked the pothooks and trammels of the fireplace with ease and served the trenchers without hesitation. She had the makings of a fine house servant. Kate was gratified to know she would easily find work if need be. That was one success she could claim. Fitch was clucking at the younger girls, reciting the catechism of etiquette she'd been trained on when she was a child. The "don'ts" still replayed in her mind in times of stress. "Never sit at table till asked, ask for nothing—tarry till it be offered, speak not, bite not bread but break it, take salt with a clean knife, hold not thy knife upright but sloping, look not earnestly at any other that is eating, leave the table when moderately satisfied, say not 'I have heard it before,' never endeavor to help him if he tell it not right, snigger not, never question the truth of it." Good training for a wife, she thought ruefully, especially one expected to sit at a fancy table. The simplicity of her own pleased her. It always had and she'd never yearned for better. This night was so typical of others before it. She would hold each second in her heart after all had changed and things were simple no more.

"I would speak to you all for a moment before you go to your studies."

The girls looked expectantly to her, having sensed something brewing without having to see it boil.

Kate had spoken little since her return from Newport and that hurried journey had never been explained. They assumed she would tell them if they'd a need to know and now, perhaps, was that time.

Kate looked to each of her sisters in turn, cherishing their sameness and their individuality. Nothing in her life was more precious than those dear faces, so full of trust, so warmed with confidence. She spoke quickly before thought had a chance to foul her words. "I would ask you all to wear your very best to lecture day. 'Tis the day my banns will be posted."

Anne and Sarah exchanged knowing looks lost on the younger girls, then beamed at Kate. Why did she look so unhappily determined when they well knew her heart's desire?

"Oh, Katie," Anne began joyously. "I know you shall be so wonderfully matched. He is—"

Kate was quick to interrupt with a calm, "I know Ezra is not the type of man 'tis easy to grow fond of, but I do believe in time I shall—"

"Ezra?" Anne nearly shrieked his name. "Ezra Blayne? Surely you don't mean—"

"We decided upon our betrothal just today. We will be wed as soon as 'tis proper. I realize there will be no formal engagement, but the dowry and contract will be agreed upon tomorrow and signed. 'Twill be a simple civil ceremony, for you know I am not one for pomp. Ezra assured that we would have a fancy affair afterward, with bride-cake, good wine, Burgundy and Canary, even oranges and pears. 'Twill be quite the occasion and a chance to display the others of us soon to be available." She made her words light, even cheerful, while her stomach contracted with the same horror she could see on Anne's face.

"Kate, why?" the younger girl demanded. She spoke for the others who were still in varying stages of shock and disbelief.

Kate responded curtly. This was not the way she wished to approach her sisters with news of marriage. She'd pictured such a time as one of glad tears and much embracing, with her own cheeks blushed bright and warm with anticipation of the future to come. This felt more like the planning of a wake. It didn't seem real to her, not like she was arranging her own fate. And that made her frustrated and her helplessness made her angry.

"Why does one marry? I am very nearly on the shelf and you all know what a match it is to tie into the Blaynes. We'll want for nothing."

"But Ezra Blayne! Kate, how could you? I don't care how wealthy he is, the man is abominable. You loathe him. How could you condone such a match? I do not believe it is because you have a sudden fear of spinsterhood."

"My reasons are my own," she snapped, then seeing her sister's hurt, she softened her tone. How could she understand? And she couldn't tell her the truth of it. "Anne, marriages are made for worse reasons. You are still too young to understand obligation." She nearly choked on that term but managed to go on smoothly. "Though we women today are given considerable liberty in the choice of our life's mate, 'tis still common for a contract to be made for business rather than pleasure. I will not lie to you. I've no love for him, but I have a respect for what I can achieve as his wife. You will never have to alter another gown from the attic. There will be dance masters and French lessons. The farm will receive the care it needs with ample servants to staff it."

Anne was too quick to be bamboozled by her bright spun dross. "You speak of our benefits, of the farm's benefits, but what of you? What of Captain Rogan? He's the one you love."

Kate's features were stiff, as unyielding as her voice. "This has naught to do with love but of life. Were you not a child you would realize that." The sharp cut brought a wince and Kate hated the necessary harshness she spoke but couldn't risk exposing her true feelings. The mention of Brady's name had thrown her hard and it was a struggle to regain her balance. "I am content with my choice and I beg that you be also."

Anne rose to her feet, trembling with upset. "Content to see you cast your life away upon misery? Never. And I don't understand. I will never understand." With a sob, she fled the room. After an awkward moment, Fitch shuffled after her. A terrible ache had begun in Kate's temples as she felt the puzzlement and distress in the eyes of the other girls. Shortly, she said, "Go to your rooms now. See to your duties." They scrambled to do as told rather than incur the wrath of this cold stranger. Alone, or so she thought, Kate sagged in her chair. A brief movement from the hearth diverted her brooding stare.

"And what have you to say?" she snapped at Sarah. For once the girl didn't look away but met her glare directly, as an equal.

"'Tis not my place to hold an opinion, Miss Mallory, but if it was, I would say if you marry that man you'll be more a servant than I ever was. That's what I'd say if asked." She turned back to the kettle.

Kate stared at her unbowed back for a long minute, then wearily stood and made her way to her room, to the bed she'd made and now must try to find rest upon. What did they know about choice or hard facts? Reality had always been sheltered away from them to be carried by her capable shoulders. She had always taken care of them and now that must be her first consideration. What did it matter with whom she spent the rest of her days? It wouldn't be the one she'd chosen. If she was to be wed not for love, then it would be for the best bargain she could make, and that arrangement, she knew, was with Ezra Blayne. She would have to make sure the contract placed ownership of the farm in her family's hands. The Blaynes had proven they were not to be trusted. In time they would understand why she'd made this choice, but for now, she felt very alone in her decision. There was only one person she could think of who would empathize with what she'd done. Brady knew all about obligation, about sacrifice, yet, in the end, he'd gotten what he'd wanted. Not so with her, so she would get all else that she could.

As she began to undress, Kate's hand touched the warm gold of the locket she wore next to her skin. She held it for a moment then slipped it off. She didn't look at the etched words. She didn't need to see them to know how she'd been misled by what she wanted to read into them. Slowly, she opened her clothes press and made a small coil of the golden chain and laid the locket upon it. Both her father and Brady were lost to her. She had only herself.

She closed the door, wishing the past was so easy to shut out. She wouldn't look back. She would look ahead but only with tunneled vision. Why should she moan over the life she would lead. It would be one of luxury, of indolence. She would rise at nine, breakfast until ten, read until noon, dress for dinner at two, then make or receive visits or go about the shops until tea. Then there would be supper and the close of the day at eleven. She would have servants to attend her, to perform the tasks that now filled her days. She would be pampered and protected, even to the point of wearing long-armed gloves, complexion masks of velvet, and bonnets to ward off every ray of the sun that might harm her skin and let others mistake her for less than a lady of quality. Her hours would be filled with the trivial rather than worry . . . and how, she wondered, was she ever going to endure them.

Then she thought of the dear faces turned to her for guidance and the sacrifice seemed small. 'Twas indeed a tiny price, her empty future for the security of her sisters'. Kate was able to rest then, confirmed in the belief that she'd done the right thing for all.

Chapter Twenty-Four

Alone in the anteroom of the magistrate's office, Kate checked her appearance yet another time. The face that regarded her with a stoic beauty was that of a stranger. The mirror showed what everyone else saw—a lovely woman readying to be a bride—but that wasn't what Kate beheld, for there was no reality to her reflection. All was a vague dream that carried her body through the gestures while her mind and heart were detached and observing with a mild curiosity.

She looked every inch the bride. Ezra's gift of her gown was an incredible extravagance, not so much to prove his devotion but to encase her in befitting splendor, like a jewel at his side. The gown was of white crepe, trained and trimmed with white ribbons. Its showy petticoat was displayed where the skirt was drawn up in festoons capped in wreaths of flowers. Sleeves of white crepe were drawn over silk with bands of wispy lace near shoulder, at elbow and wrist. A matching wreath of flowers was artfully woven through her braids of gold A heavy ring adorned her finger as evidence of plighted faith. Only her neck lay bare of ornamentation, as barren as the heart of the woman within.

Kate turned away and considered what had happened since the contract had been signed. The Blaynes had invaded their quiet existence, dominating their every minute in a rush of preparation for this day. Of Ezra, she'd actually seen very little, which was uncommonly wise of him. He had even forsworn the bundling night after the contract was signed, perhaps fearing the clothed cuddle in bed with his bride-to-be would frighten her from the altar. In his stead came the promised trousseau, the wealth of which had stunned them. There were fourteen yards of Pompadore satin, a silk petticoat and negligee of brocaded lutestring, twelve dozen gloves, seven yards of printed cotton blue ground, flowered tissue in a sixteen-yard length costing at least nine guineas, a white hat and cloak that Sylvie claimed the newest fashion, and a pair of buckles made of French paste stones next in luster to diamonds. Solemnly, Anne had offered to see the lengths made into suitable gowns. It was the only time the two had spoken since she'd fled the kitchen. In silent defiance, Anne had worn her plainest gown on lecture day and had shunned the offer of new garb for the ceremony, claiming her crimson brocade would serve her. Her belligerent stand was wounding, but Kate understood it. Concern and fear prompted her petulance and, as they were well placed, Kate couldn't fault her for it.

In what might be her last moment of solitude, Kate congratulated herself with a removed calm on how well she'd seen to her responsibilities. Their debt was dissolved, her family elevated in standing to comfortable gentry. There would be coin and resources to see the farm free of the years of past neglect. Nathan Mallory would be proud. She smiled wistfully. She'd always imaged him at her side to give her into the care of her husband.

A chorus of voices outside her door told of the arrival of her sisters, but it was Anne alone who entered. The stiffness lingered between them as Kate was given a fresh nosegay of flowers, then Anne's reserve gave way to desperation. "Oh, Katie, please. You cannot mean to go through with this travesty."

Kate held up a hand as if to still the advance of her pleas. "I'll hear none of it, Anne. 'Tis my wedding day. Pray behave accordingly even if you do not approve of my choice."

"'Tis no wedding day. 'Tis an auction and you've sold yourself cheap."

Kate stared at her, too stunned to respond to the vehemence of her attack. Anne continued, her fervor mounting as her words went unchecked.

"How dare you do this. How dare you condemn all of us to suffer your unhappiness well knowing we're the cause. Don't think me too simple or *young* not to have linked this disgusting alliance with Sylvie Blayne's threats. Is that how he got you to agree? Worse the abomination. I always thought you so strong, and you taught us with your example. 'Tis ashamed you make me. You chose the easiest, safest road without giving us a chance to show our strength. Did you think we'd hold our comforts above your contentment? You insult us all. I would as soon be hand maiden to Sylvie Blayne with my pride intact then coddled at some ladies' seminary knowing the price paid to see me there.

"If you want to toss your life away on the likes of Ezra Blayne, I'll not stop you, but do it because of your want to take the smooth road not because we feared to follow the rougher one. We'll not be your excuse and we'll not bear the guilt of your choice. And know you now that when *I* marry, 'twill be for love, come with it what will. There, that 'tis what I came to tell you. I'll be going home now. I'll not linger to view your sacrifice. 'Tis wasted in my eyes just as your life will be wasted."

Anne paused in her speech-making to draw a fortifying breath and to await a response from the still figure opposite. Kate didn't move. She seemed frozen, a pretty fashion doll in her bartered finery. All her arguments had bounced off that immobile facade. With a soft cry of resignation, Anne saw to her promise and left the room and the building to climb with eyes blurred by tears into their wagon. Sadly, she shook her head at the other three who waited there and motioned to Cosgrove to begin the journey home.

The soft closing of the door opened another within Kate that she'd been struggling against for days. With the tiniest crack, it burst wide and all the emotions she'd pushed behind it sprang free to overwhelm her. She trembled from the onslaught, seeking a chair to support herself when her knees refused to oblige. She touched the pristine fabric of her gown and, for the first time, its meaning sank deep. Her wedding day. In but a few minutes she would be surrendering herself to a life she abhorred, to a man she loathed. And from what Anne had just told her, it would be for naught. Had she been so single-minded and self-seeking in her want to escape her pain over the loss of Brady that she'd convinced herself that what she was about to do was for the best for all? Had the wound to her heart killed her spirit? Granted, she might never know another love as soaring and perfect as that she'd held for the blue-eyed Rogue, but did that give her cause to forfeit all right to happiness of any measure? *No* came the forceful cry from deep within her soul.

She stood and began to pace, not caring that the agitated movements might wrinkle her gown beyond repair. She had to think with mind *and* heart. All her life, she'd been so quick to sacrifice her needs for those of others. She'd been proud of her strength when, in fact, that desperate want to please was an appalling weakness. Her pride made her shoulder all the worries, all the pain, rather than give others the chance to aid her and thereby share in the credit. Was that how narrow she'd become, how pathetic her need for approval. She'd let herself be responsible for the failings of her father rather than helping to build his strength. She'd taken disastrous risks with family funds without consulting those affected by the outcome. She'd run from the possibility of rejection rather than face Brady when he woke, telling herself it was his will when, in fact, she had no idea of his thoughts. Her impulsiveness and pride led her blindly, alone, when in the company of loved ones she might have gone with clear sight. Was it too late to begin to see clearly? The door opened and she feared it was.

"How lovely you are." The thickly said compliment was accompanied by the rake of an impassioned gaze. Ezra closed the door and continued his avid assessment, unable to believe that in a few hours, all he saw would be his to do with as he would. That stare halted at her magnificent bosom before gaining the face of his bride-to-be. He hesitated. He could claim no understanding of her moods but this seemed the lack of one. "All is ready."

Dawning awareness widened the eyes that beheld Ezra Blayne. What a caricature he was of the man she'd envisioned as her husband. In his straining satin suit of clothes with ornamental sword dangling impotently at his side, he was laughable, not dignified. This was the man pledged to be her husband? This was the authority she'd be bound to for the rest of her natural life? This was the figure that would lie beside her in bed each night? Horror clogged her throat as the full scope of what it would mean to be wed to him unfolded. She'd kept her thoughts relegated to the impersonal side of wedlock as she'd made her decision. Now the other aspects of that union were disturbingly clear to her. She would be expected to yield herself to her husband's will, to reveal her body to him and to allow him liberties unselfishly. The thought of Ezra's feverish eyes

418

devouring her naked form sickened her. The idea of his fleshy hands upon her quickened nausea. The realization that he would demand all that she'd happily given to another struck hard and Kate reeled. To endure his slobbering passions, his kisses, his caresses, would pollute the cherished memories she held. To compare the excitement of Brady Rogan's loving with what she would discover in her marriage bed spelled out the repellent impossibility of this union. No one could demand that kind of sacrifice of her. She would go to debtors' prison before she allowed those soft hands to claim her intimately.

"No."

"I beg your pardon?" he asked with owlish surprise.

"I am sorry. I cannot go through with this. I do not love you. I do not wish to be your wife." That said, Kate felt a crushing weight lift off her chest and she was able to pull her first full breath of freedom in days.

Ezra's florid face flamed dangerously as he stared in incomprehension. "What do affections and silly whims have to do with what brings us here? This is an arrangement of business. Papers have been signed. Coin has been tendered in your name. Cease this vaporish display and let's get on with it."

"My point exactly. What have feelings and dreams to do with this. Nothing. And that 'tis not the grounds on which I wish to make a marriage." Her strength was returning with every word, her determination increasing with each breath. She felt exhilarated, in control, and it was wonderful to be so alive again. The Blaynes could strip her of all else but never could they wrest her independent spirit. It was just as Anne said. How wise her younger sister had become and how foolish she'd been not to take her counsel.

Seeing she was serious, Ezra squeaked in protest. "You cannot refuse me now. 'Tis too late for maidenish ideals. I'll not allow you to break from your contract."

"Have me arrested then, for that is preferable to the prison you would see me in. I allowed you to bully and bribe me into thinking this was in my best interest. I was wrong. 'Tis in no one's interest, even yours. You'd not want to be saddled with a reluctant wife and I'd prove no eager partner."

"How could you refuse?" He was astounded. Not once but twice did this stupid wench fail to see the blessing he offered. Anger began to surge. Never did it occur to him to think himself the reason for her rejection. "'Tis that pirate, isn't it? You have some ludicrous notion that he will offer for you."

"He has nothing to do with it," Kate refuted quietly. That was only partially true. Had Brady not shown her the glorious heights emotion could reach perhaps she would not be so easily discouraged by the inability of others to do the same. Perhaps it was an impossible ideal to cling to, but she was determined to take no less. And if she never found it with another, she'd at least have memories of something more splendid than most women ever experienced. Of that she was sure.

Ezra was nearly foaming with outrage. "You

cannot do this!'' he shrieked. "I'll ruin you!''

"You already tried and failed. I survived your worst. What more can you do?''

His frenzied thoughts flew beyond the disappointment of knowing her as his bride to the consequence of losing her. He panicked and grew desperate. "You'll not make a laughingstock of me. I'll have no barefoot farmer sneering at my offer of a better life. Who do you think you are to spurn me?''

"Nathan Mallory's daughter, and that has always been enough for me,'' she concluded with pride. Seeing his distress, Kate softened toward the difficulty of his position, actually feeling sorry for his plight. She put a hand to his arm beseechingly. "Ezra, you'll be glad of this someday. We'd not suit. All would see in a moment that I am not the proper wife for a man of your station.'' She played upon his vanity, hoping to gain some leverage there. "I'd be an embarrassment.''

"And what is this? What do you call coming to the altar only to cry off in some silly lather of nerves. No, Kate. You'll see that I am right in my choice. You'll make a splendid bride, the toast of Briar Haven.'' He warmed to that image, forgetting her reluctance in his own enthusiasm. "Mama and Sylvie can school you in the graces. One look at your comely face and who would notice a flaw in etiquette. No, Kate, I'll not allow you to make this mistake. 'Tis in your best and that of your family to step with me before the magistrate. Come, now. Let's delay no longer.''

Kate sputtered. How could the man be so dense? How much clearer did she have to make it? "I will not

421

wed you." How much plainer could it be?

"If this be a ploy to gain more coin, I am not amused, but I am willing to negotiate. What will it take for you to step through that door with me?"

"Gunpoint," she said flatly.

Ezra frowned, for a moment completely at a loss. Then his pale eyes acquired a speculative spark and she grew wary, fearing she had unwittingly coaxed a noxious bloom into full flower. With a dramatic flair, Ezra jerked his short sword free and brandished it with a menacing smile. "Very well," he said grimly. "'Twas your choice. Let's not keep the magistrate waiting."

Kate gave a slight laugh and chided, "Ezra, put that away before you harm yourself." Then her amusement fled as steel touched to her breast.

"You will not mock me, madam. You have made sport of me for the last time. The man who awaits us has been paid enough coin not to care if you be willing when the words are said. There is no one from your family to bear witness and by the time you see them again, you will have learned the folly of your ways. A week or so on bread and milk should curb your impetuous nature."

Kate was still. Ezra did not frighten her. It was his threats and his ability to see them out. The Blaynes held incredible power within the community, enough to buy a judge, to purchase witnesses, to pay a doctor to say she was mad thus allowing them to keep her imprisoned in their home. They could keep her from her family almost indefinitely. That knowledge was terrifying, that realization of her own helpless situation. More than ever, she knew she must not fall prey to that noxious family.

She leaned forward until the tip pierced her gown and a tiny speck of crimson showed. Passionately, she told him, "I would rather fall upon your blade than be a victim to your will."

A tense silence stretched between them, Kate fiercely determined and Ezra reevaluating his position. He was frustrated in the extreme by this female who bested him at every turn and he was bound to curb her to his lead. Once she'd had time to experience the luxury of his world and was desirous of his skilled attentions, she would surrender this unbecoming hostility and act the proper wife. He couldn't very well run her through, but with enough coin in the bargain the judge might not care if she was conscious at the ceremony. Once at Briar Haven, she would be broken to her lot and later would thank him for it. A sharp rap on the head should do it. Nothing too vigorous as to addle her or careless that it might mar her perfect features. A slight tap and she would be his.

"Enough of this, Kate," he said reasonably as he lowered his sword. Covertly, he weighed the ornate hilt in his hand. It should do nicely. "I had no notion that you felt so strong about the matter. You know, of course, that I would never wish you harm. Come. Let us put aside our grievances and be friends." He extended one hand to her in an amiable gesture, and in her relief to believe the ugliness at an end, placed hers within it. Immediately, she knew of her mistake.

Ezra's grip tightened about her hand, twisting and

turning so that she was bent at an angle in order to save her shoulder from a severe wrenching. Shocked that he would actually do her violence made her slow to react and he took advantage of her daze. Trapping her against his heaving chest with the curl of one arm, he lifted the other to deal the conclusive blow. Seeing the movement, Kate realized her peril and screamed. Her eyes squeezed shut, awaiting the impact she couldn't avoid and, in that second, she saw the end to all her dreams at his despicable hands. Then, abruptly, she was freed.

Kate spilled to the floor in a crumple of expensive crepe and binding hoops. Fear-inspired dizziness robbed her of thought for an instant, yet when her vision cleared, she had reason to doubt it. From her awkward position, she could only stare and thrill in the rapturous panic that swelled within her breast. As if fulfilling another promise to see her safe, Brady Rogan had Ezra's corpulent figure suspended in air by a tightening hand about his throat. She was so surprised, so overwhelmed, she hadn't the strength to encourage or protest the impending violence. Quite easily, as if his burden had been a lad instead of a bloated toad of a man, Brady flexed his arm and, with a hard thrust, Ezra was airborne, landing with a stunning thump upon the chaise set against the far wall.

Then Brady was bending down before her, more splendid than even her most exquisite fantasy and his warm, large hands settled upon her upper arms. She began to tremble, from the aftershock of terror, from the devastation of seeing him again.

"Are you all right?"

The sound of his husky voice, all roughened with concern and tenderness, made all real to her. With a soft cry, she cast her arms about his neck to cling to his sturdy strength, to breathe in the scent of sea and man from the heated hollow of his throat. "Oh, Brady" was all she could manage and that brief moan quavered with disbelief and deliverance. Slowly, he lifted her to her feet, still very much wrapped about him.

"How dare you!" Ezra squealed as he picked himself up and tried to assemble his tattered pride. "I'll have you arrested. I'll see you in irons!"

Brady spared him a cutting glance. "'Twas not I who was abusing a helpless woman." He looked down at the crown of gold and his tone softened into a deadly purr. "Would you like me to slay him for his insolence?"

"Yes," she cried, still in the grip of her fear. Then, as Ezra's eyes bulged with apprehension, she remedied, "No, no, of course not. Just see me home. Please, Brady, take me home."

Seeing all his careful plans dissolve with the appearance of this unsavory hero, Ezra drew himself up and commanded with what he hoped would be authoritative strength, "You'll go nowhere with the likes of him. Take her from this room, sir, and I'll have the law upon you for absconding with my bride."

"Bride?" Brady held Kate away, his piercing blue gaze searching hers intently to find the truth of that unwelcome news. She shook her head and she could feel his relief in the ebb of tension within his powerful hands. His glance slanted to the puffing aristocrat. "You forget, sir, I hold a prior claim to the lady's hand. Perhaps I should sue you for breaching my contract."

"Nonsense," he responded in indignation to that leisured drawl. "'Twas all a lie. You were no more her intended than you are a lord."

"Oh, but I am."

Both Ezra and Kate stared at him.

"I am Charles Rogan, Fifth Earl of Bradington. My title stretches back farther than your limited imagination and my family's wealth makes you a miserable pauper in comparison. Think well before you take me on, for I will crush you, you insignificant whelp. Challenge me and you will know what power can do in ruthless hands. And know this, I will show you no mercy."

Ezra swallowed. All his braggart's confidence fled him before this cold-eyed, dangerous man who mocked him with his cruel promise. Then the arrogance that served him and his family swelled to give him brash, if false, importance. "This is not England, sir. Your title is nothing here in the Colonies and counts for little compared to the one you hold as pirate and thief. My family owns this county, just as it owns the Mallorys. She has been bought and paid for as my bride and I mean to collect upon that debt. You have no right to interfere there lest you show me written proof that your claim cancels mine."

"I cannot," Brady admitted, and Kate looked to

him in desperation. Surely he didn't mean to give her over calmly because Ezra cited legal precedence. Then his gaze caught hers and silently conveyed a message that she was not to despair. Trust me, that look said, and she did, completely. Seeing her faith, he smiled faintly before turning back to his challenger. Then that smile became a smug sneer.

"You are right. I have no cause to object to what you do today, no matter how reprehensible I think your methods, no matter how loathsome I find you as an individual. I have no stake in this affair. As you said, I am more rogue than lord and my ties to England would carry less far than the stranglehold you have on these poor villagers. Therefore, I seek your pardon for intruding where I'd no claim."

Ezra beamed and blustered with self-assurance. Kate stood quiet, her eyes on Brady rather than the preening buffoon who thought he'd won the point. She studied the lean, savagely handsome planes of his face, delighting in the sight and heartened by the gleam in his gaze that bespoke of a second volley about to be fired point-blank. She was a bit puzzled that he made no aggressive move to protect and hold her. He hadn't responded with an embrace when she'd thrown herself upon him. Even now, he was aloof, guarded before her anxious stare. Why had he come if not to claim her for himself?

"Were there no other way," Brady continued smoothly, "I would cheerfully use your own puny blade to run you through rather than to allow this sham to proceed. In fact, that was my thinking when I received Miss Anne's message."

Kate felt as though she'd been handed a direct thrust with that casual claim. He was here because Anne implored him. He had come to do a service, nothing more. A cold more desolate than she'd endured even when faced with the prospect of Ezra's treachery hardened about her heart. Again the fool. Courageously, she fought the tears of disappointment pricking behind her eyes, a mere annoyance compared to the stabbing of hurt that pierced her hopes. At least he was freeing her. For that, she should be grateful. After all, it wasn't his fault that she'd leapt eagerly to all the wrong conclusions.

"I hadn't meant for things to go this far. Had I not been unexpectedly delayed, I would have arrived in time to spare Miss Mallory this humiliation at your hands, would have seen to her debt, and to you, personally." That last was said with a rumble of intent and Ezra's Adam's apple bobbed nervously up and down beneath the fleshy folds of his throat. He was not mollified by the smile upon the darkly handsome face, for it was a baring of teeth, not a sign of amiability.

Brady went on coolly, flicking a mysterious glance in Kate's direction before saying, "Forgive the last-minute heroics. 'Tis not my want to prey on the dramatic, but I couldn't help myself under the circumstances. No, there is no need for me to intercede. I yield to one more worthy."

With that grand pronouncement, he made a sweeping gesture toward the door, drawing his audience's eyes to that opening portal. And in the style of the melodramatic stage, with scene set and cue given, Nathan Mallory stepped in.

Kate stood motionless. Her sudden blanch of color should have warned Brady to act quicker, but he never would have thought that the strong, indomitable Kate Mallory would choose this time as her first ever to swoon dead away.

Chapter Twenty-Five

It wasn't until she was at home, in front of her own hearth, basked in the love of her family, that Kate grasped all that had happened. When her eyes had flickered open to that small room where she had waited to become a bride, bringing her from the dark void of her faint, her father's beloved features filled her field of vision. It wasn't until she lifted a trembling hand to fit against his cheek that she knew it wasn't some cruel hoax. It was Nathan Mallory. He was alive and he was home.

In those first long minutes when she'd hugged to him, weeping in her joy, nothing else had penetrated that happy daze. His arms were firm about her. His well-worn coat smelled of his pipe. The gruff tones he used to comfort her were the same she'd heard all her growing years. She felt a child again, as if the weight of responsibility was gone from her weary shoulders, and never had she been so glad to surrender anything. Then, when a weak sort of strength returned, she straightened from his embrace to look about the anteroom. She had been stretched out upon the chaise and it was upon its edge that her father perched. They were alone. When she asked after Brady, she was told he'd gone to put things to right with the Blaynes. Disappointment mingled with her gladness and she suppressed it by seeking another hug. And when she felt able, the two of them, father and daughter, went home.

Now, from her chair on one side of the parlor's great fireplace, Kate watched as her sisters clustered about her father on the other. Even Fitch and Sarah were clucking around him, anxious to see to his comfort and hear of his adventures. They had listened in awed silence as he told of the sinking of the *Prosper* and how he'd managed to cling to life on a makeshift raft of broken timbers while the sea raged about him. As the storm quieted, a ship appeared and his cries for help aided. Both he and another survivor, the *Prosper*'s sailingmaster, were taken aboard a brig bound for the Gold Coast. Weak and ill from what he'd endured he never thought to protest the journey that would take him to the coast of Africa instead of directly home. He had no way of knowing that all would believe him dead and no means to tell them otherwise. He'd had to ride out the sweeping circle of trade until returned to the harbor in Newport where the ship and two refugees were met by Brady Rogan, who'd heard survivors of his perished craft would be aboard. From there, he'd been spirited quickly to Kingstown to intercede in what might have been a tragedy.

Kate was taken by an odd melancholy. Her father's return found her replaced as the family's provider and caretaker and she felt bereft of purpose. After long months of struggle to retain their home and maintain a livelihood, his return with his Indies gold settled their affairs instantly. It wasn't fair of her to believe he made light of all she'd done, for he'd praised her efforts endlessly over their meal. However, now that matters were out of her hands, they seemed empty, restless, and she didn't understand her depressed mood. All she could have wished for had come true. Her father was home and had put right their debts. She was no longer responsible for their future. No matter that she'd wished that were true on oft occasions, she missed the feeling of usefulness it gave her. She'd been demoted from head of household to one of Nathan Mallory's daughters and, though she hated to think it so, she resented it.

"Now that we've some coin to starch our backs, I've a new plan to see us well plumped in the pocket," Mallory was saying.

"I see no fault in plans we've already made." Kate didn't realize how sharply she spoke until all looked askance. A hot flush crept up into her cheeks and she wished she'd remained silent.

Her father was unperturbed. "Why, Katie, 'tis nothing wrong with them. They be fine plans and we'll keep to them. I'm speaking of something altogether different. But then, you'll see when my new partner gets here. Now don't be pulling such a long face with me, miss. 'Tis not one of your father's flights of fancy, I assure you."

She blushed that he would so read her thoughts and stayed silent as, inwardly, she fumed. How quick he jumped from the kettle into the fire. She would have thought that after what he'd been through, he'd be content to relax upon his laurels at least over the winter months. But no, another scheme, another risk, another opportunity ripe for ruin, no doubt involving some scurrilous adventurer who'd never be seen again once their money was in hand. Was there no end to them, these hasty plots concocted of an impractical mind?

So her father wouldn't read her discontent, Kate rose and moved aimlessly toward the window. It had already begun to darken though the hour was yet early, a sign of fall's waning strength. She felt a like fading within herself, as purpose and ambition drained away. She no longer need fear a forced marriage to Ezra Blayne, but what else was there to fill her future? Keeping house for her father and struggling to save him from his follies? Her attention was caught briefly by the sight of a cloaked figure dismounting in the yard, pausing to speak to Cosgrove before surrendering the reins.

"Your partner is here," she called over her shoulder as dispassionate eyes held to the yet shadow-clad man who approached the house. If this trickster thought to steal away funds from the Mallory household to invest in some nonsense, he hadn't reckoned on Nathan's daughter. Thusly fortified, she went to the door to hold it open in dubious welcome.

"Good evening, sir," she said, hoping her tone would convey her mettle.

"Hello, Kate."

He strode in while she clung to the door handle in an odd sort of paralysis of mind and body. Brady. Brady was her father's new partner?

"Father's in the parlor," she managed to force past lips frozen in shock and, with a nod to her, he walked that way, handing his cloak to Sarah in the process. The young maid dipped him a pretty curtsy and was even bold enough to venture a smile. Then she looked to Kate and said pertly, "Do you mean to let all the warmth out into the night, Miss Kate?"

Duly chastened, Kate closed the door and moved woodenly into the room where Brady had already made himself at home on the chair she'd occupied with Bertrice ensconced upon his knee. She held back from the warmth of the fire and the gathering to linger by the hall, as if an outsider to the closeness she observed. Brady and her father spoke easily as though friends of long acquaintance, and after the amenities were done, Mallory looked to her with a smile. "The captain and I are forming a shipbuilding company in Providence. You should be well pleased, as I hear the idea was yours."

"Something about an honest trade for my dotage, I believe." Brady grinned to remind her of the reference. She didn't need to be reminded. Every word exchanged between them was locked away within her heart. Her answering smile was stiff.

"That way," Nathan went on enthusiastically, "our horses can be cargoed free to the Islands. So you see, my cautious miss, we'll profit doubly. With the captain here to pilot the vessels, 'twill all be kept in the family."

Kate died inside. In the family. What she wouldn't give for those words to be true? But they were just casually tossed sentiments, representing business, nothing more. How was she going to endure Brady Rogan popping in and out of her life with indifferent frequency? How would she pretend a polite interest in hearing how well his life progressed while hers stagnated in lonely isolation? The thought of empty years ahead was cruel enough without the added insult of being tormented by what she couldn't have. After listening for several minutes to the plans they made together, speaking between themselves and oblivious to her opinion, Kate could maintain her composure not another moment. Tears of upset and unrealized longings were too close to the surface with Brady beneath her roof. Perhaps in time she could learn to barricade her heart against it, but now she had no defenses. Then, as Brady and her father lifted glasses in a toast that excluded her, quietly she slipped from the room and out into the night.

It was yet warm for the concluding months of the year and the stars with their showy winter constellations were just beginning to flicker against the deepening curtain of darkness that drew intimately about their farm. Kate breathed deep of the heavy, bruised scent of autumn, and for a time, lost herself in that somber fragrance until another intruded to send an alarming thrill through her. She didn't need to turn. She could feel him in every tingling sense until she all but quivered from his intoxicating nearness. She fought those excited signals that

436

pulsed new and vital blood to every pore. It wouldn't do for her to react this way every time he approached her, with anticipation, with unquenchable desire, for those quickened hopes were empty and only served to deepen her frustrations. Yet she couldn't control the sensations that had taken her unaware. She could only suffer them as best she could until he was gone.

"You're quiet tonight," he observed with a hush as rich and deep as the fast-engulfing eve. His long fingers brushed along her arm and she did tremble then, helplessly, clear to the core with the want that meaningless caress inspired. "Are you cold? I can go in for your cloak."

"No. I'm fine." The strength of her reply was surprising, as the weakness overtaking her was all inclusive. "I just came out to enjoy the serenity of the night. I've found little peace of late."

"Am I disturbing it now?"

What a question. She frowned over the subtleties of it but refused to partake in his gentle banter. "No."

Kate could imagine his smile as his hands began a sensuous stroke up and down from elbow to shoulder. He was standing close behind her. With just a slight shift of her position, she would be molded back against the solid planes of his body and the thought of that sturdy support both enticed and angered her. Why was he playing such an unkind game with her emotions, well knowing how vulnerable she'd be toward him? Instead of leaning back, she stepped purposefully forward and unconsciously rubbed her sleeves where his hands had strayed, warm and provoking.

"I had no chance to speak to you after our meeting this morning. I thought you'd appreciate some time to recover from the loss of a fiancé and the gain of a father."

"Thank you." Her words were vinegary, her manner just as tart. She wouldn't look at him, fearing he would read too much in her face even in this muted light.

"There is much I would speak of now."

Kate's eyes squeezed shut in torment, then opened again to stare at the sky. "There is no need, Captain. As I said, no regrets, no apologies."

Brady was silent for a moment, then said, "I had no intention of expressing either."

She whirled to confront him with all her congested hurt and fury. Green eyes gleamed like a fiery heaven-scorching comet leaving a trace of bitter feelings to trail behind. "What is it you would speak of then? 'Twould seem your business is with my father now. I cannot imagine what needs be said between us, but speak it and be on your way."

He gave a maddening smile that nettled her fiercely and drawled, "I'm in no hurry."

"Oh? I would think you had much to do. I know how difficult it is to move from pillar to post. I've done it all my life."

"What *are* you talking about, Kate?" he asked mildly. His fingertip drew along her jaw and she jerked away from the searing contact.

"I had thought you'd be settled into another colony by now seeing as how your wait finally paid the mark. I'm surprised that you'd consider my

438

troubles with marriage foremost in your mind these days. I hope the imposition to play hero didn't inconvenience you."

Brady was still smiling as if amused by her anguish. "No inconvenience. I would have come as soon as things were arranged in Providence but I got word that two survivors of the *Prosper* were coming in and I couldn't leave until I discovered who they were. I couldn't bring you false hope."

Sarcasm dripped venom from her reply. "How decent of you."

A dark brow arced. "By God, you are the worst-tempered woman I've ever known."

The insult made Kate blanch, then flush hot. "Well, there's no need for you to suffer me further." She began to spin away when his hands caught her none too gently and forced her not only back to face him but tightly up against his chest. She was too startled to struggle, too aroused to object.

"Oh, Kate, I plan to suffer you daily."

She met his kiss with a mewling of protest which served to encourage his unforgivable aggression until she couldn't breathe. Oxygen-starved and passion-starved factions warred within her urging rebel and yielded with like fervor. Then he settled the conflict and let her stand away, yet still retained her in the circle of his embrace. She gasped noisily for air and coherency. Finally, her palm cracked against his cheek. Instead of releasing her, he chuckled as if beset with the tantrum of an endearing child.

She seethed. "I won't be your mistress," she spat at him, but his mocking grin was unaffected by her claim. "I'll adulter myself with no man."

"But I thought the idea of mistress was one you held fondly." His embrace closed to encase her arms and their want to do him harm. "No? Well, no matter. I've no need of a mistress."

Kate went abruptly still in his grip, the fight squelched by that casual admission. The fire in her gaze was extinguished by a welling dampness as she stared up at him, her tattered heart displayed artlessly in those great, shimmering eyes. His tone gentled, humor absent, leaving it as luxurious as raw silk. "I've another partnership in mind for us."

Her fractured breathing halted. Speech failed her. She didn't dare guess at his words lest she prove mistaken yet again, and she could take no further disappointments. Kate waited for him to continue, trying to temper the thunder of her heart with caution, but its frantic beats were too strong, too sure of what she would hear.

"I only realized it that night," he was saying, each word sweet poetry to her ears. "I was foolish enough to keep it to myself in plans of making a grand announcement when we awoke a little more, shall we say, revitalized." Kate blushed at the reference and that warming heat spread throughout her body as she hung upon his words. "Then I woke and found you gone and never had the chance to tell you. Why did you leave me, Kate? Did you have so little trust that I would come to realize how much I love you?"

"You—?"

"I love you. When you said those words to me, I was struck by the rightness of them. Forgive me for

440

being so lax in telling you."

Still, Kate kept her joy in check. There was one more obstacle to meet and she broached it almost timidly. "Elizabeth?"

His large hands slid up her back and cupped her golden head between them, holding her tightly, possessively. "The moment I saw those papers and knew that I could have her, I realized that she was not the one I wanted to wed. I already knew how different the love I felt for you was, but until that instant I didn't comprehend that I'd never loved at all until I met you. I think we've both let obligation and duty rule our lives for long enough, don't you? Elizabeth and Jamie are well provided for. I don't mean to break from them entirely. They are family after all and it would be most cruel for me to desert them now that they've lost all else." Vaguely, Kate nodded her agreement. "And now that your father is home, you're not tied to your family's future and can consider one of your own, can't you?" Again, the nod. He hugged her tight, and this time she lingered against the firm bastion of his chest without reserve, letting the throb of his heart move her own.

"And now, seeing as how we're both so suddenly independent, what say you throw in with me, if you can tolerate being linked to such a dishonorable renegade as myself. What a partnership we can have between us."

"Brady, we will fight at every turn," she warned softly as she reveled in the feel of him. "We agree on nothing, you know."

"Umm, true enough. But think of the spice that

will give things. I'd rather a turbulent home and lusty bed than would both be docile.''

Kate leaned back to behold his features, loving them and him. ''And I promise you both.''

''A promise I'll see you keep.'' Lids began to lower over brilliant blue eyes as he anticipated the taste of her lips. Then he leaned forward to compare fiction with fact, but she turned away, saying rather hurriedly, ''I have to tell my father.''

''He knows.''

Kate frowned. ''How could he know when I've just agreed?''

''As you've always so uncharitably pointed out, I am arrogant and overconfident. I told him on the trip across the Bay that I was coming to claim you as my bride. He thought it a splendid idea, especially with the possible profits of having a business partner and smuggler in one for a son-in-law was explained to him.''

Her smile was rueful. ''Yes, I can well believe him easily swayed. Are you truly as wealthy as you boasted to Ezra?''

''I shouldn't say lest you be tempted for only the gain of coin, but yes, 'tis true. I'm embarrassingly well off and stand to inherit more upon the death of my father. Knowing my past as you do, you understand why I've preferred to leave that fortune in England and make my own here.'' His gaze probed hers, anxious to find her agreeable. He'd cut his ties to his family long ago and would keep them severed unless she insisted otherwise. He didn't think she would and she didn't fail him.

"I would not wish to be the wife of an earl in any course," she said glibly.

"'Twould be a marquis. Think on it, Kate. 'Tis much to give up."

"Yet you have."

"I have strong reasons. Those don't apply to you or our children. I'll not have you resent me for depriving our heirs of wealth and title." He was testing her, provoking her to think of what it would mean to accept his inheritance and he silently prayed she would not be tempted. She'd known such a life of struggle and poverty, he wouldn't blame her if she wanted it all to safeguard her future and he wouldn't argue if that was her wish. He waited, expectant gaze intent upon her own.

"Those things mean little compared to love, and that is what I would give my family. If we're to start a partnership between us, I say we rely upon our own resources. Does that comport with you, Captain Rogue?"

"Aye, Miss Mallory. It does." His gaze began the familiar smoldering she equated with mounting of passions. Hers returned the heat. However, aware of where they stood and the impossibilities of what they considered, she suggested, albeit with reluctance, "Perhaps we should go inside to inform the others *officially* of our plans."

Brady's hands moved restlessly over her shoulders and back, dipping low to tease her buttocks before remaining harmlessly upon her waist. Not so harmless was the seducing wake of his caress that had her impatient for further attractions. He grinned knowingly in the face of her agitation. "I've another plan, if you're agreeable."

That sultry hint of promise had her eager to hear more. "If what you're suggesting is improper, Captain Rogan, I am indeed interested."

Brady chuckled at her wanton display of passion and his glance canted off toward the fields. His words were thoughtful. "I seem to recall a very comfortable piece of ground not such a far walk away. We could watch the stars and discuss our partnership." He saw her anxious gaze turn to the house and said softly, "Let them see to themselves tonight, Kate. 'Tis time they got used to doing without you, don't you think?"

Kate looked from the windows warmed by the glow inside to the heat that flamed low in Brady Rogan's eyes and the decision was a simple one to make.

"Shall we walk a ways, Captain?"

"Lead on, Miss Mallory."

Dana Ransom loves to hear from her readers. You can write her c/o Zebra Books, 475 Park Avenue South, New York, NY 10016.

SURRENDER YOUR HEART
TO CONSTANCE O'BANYON!

MOONTIDE EMBRACE   (2949, $4.50)
When Liberty Boudreaux's sister framed Judah Slaughter for
murder, the notorious privateer swore revenge. But when he ab-
ducted the unsuspecting Liberty from a New Orleans masquerade
ball, the brazen pirate had no idea he'd kidnapped the wrong
Boudreaux—unaware who it really was writhing beneath him,
first in protest, then in ecstasy.

GOLDEN PARADISE   (2007, $3.95)
Beautiful Valentina Barrett knew she could never trust wealthy
Marquis Vincente as a husband. But in the guise of "Jordanna",
a veiled dancer at San Francisco's notorious Crystal Palace, Valentina couldn't resist making the handsome Marquis her lover!

SAVAGE SUMMER   (1922, $3.95)
When Morgan Prescott saw Sky Dancer standing out on a balcony, his first thought was to climb up and carry the sultry vixen
to his bed. But even as her violet eyes flashed defiance, repulsing
his every advance, Morgan knew that nothing would stop him
from branding the high-spirited beauty as his own!

SEPTEMBER MOON   (3012, $4.50)
Petite Cameron Madrid would never consent to allow arrogant
Hunter Kingston to share her ranch's water supply. But the handsome landowner had decided to get his way through Cameron's
weakness for romance—winning her with searing kisses and slow
caresses, until she willingly gave in to anything Hunter wanted.

SAVAGE SPRING   (3008, $4.50)
Being pursued for a murder she did not commit, Alexandria dis-
guised herself as a boy, convincing handsome Taggert James to
help her escape to Philadelphia. But even with danger dogging
their every step, the young woman could not ignore the raging desire that her virile Indian protector ignited in her blood!

*Available wherever paperbacks are sold, or order direct from the
Publisher. Send cover price plus 50¢ per copy for mailing and
handling to Zebra Books, Dept. 2881, 475 Park Avenue South,
New York, N.Y. 10016. Residents of New York, New Jersey and
Pennsylvania must include sales tax. DO NOT SEND CASH.*